Ber

Richard Taylor

Berlin Connection

Berlin Connection

by

Richard Taylor

Published by

Richard Taylor and WordTaylor Productions

Text copyright © 2012 Richard Taylor

ISBN-13: 978-1475018288

ISBN-10: 1475018282

Cover photograph from personal collection of father-in-law from beginning of the Cold War. Author photograph from author's collection at the end of the Cold War.

WordTaylors Productions

Atlanta, Georgia

Dedicated

To the "little people … "

Who chip away at dividing walls …

and those who sacrificed for freedom.

Table of Contents

Berlin Connection

Part I
Berlin Divided
1961

1

Night Train

The duty train from Frankfurt, West Germany shuttled troops and their families through Soviet-occupied East Germany into the very heart of western-occupied Berlin. The train always left on time but when it arrived depended on Soviet and East German border guards.

On this night, passengers swayed with the rocking coach, mesmerized by a metronome of iron wheels on rails. Nothing in the drizzling darkness beyond the coach disturbed passengers from their hidden introspections. They seemed to be literally holding their breaths and their silence only sharpened the rolling needle piercing enemy territory.

For Captain Victor Werner this ride was a recounting, a journey back in time. Each kilometer took him from his recent past to a more distant one he had only heard about, rushing toward a future he was unable to imagine. He knew his parents had escaped Berlin before Hitler could conscript his father as a scientist in his war machine. That story replayed itself in his mind as he rode along the rails. Vic had left Berlin in diapers; he returned in a U.S. Army uniform.

Vic didn't expect problems with the Soviets on the train ride, but he did expect problems—that was his job. Officially, he was to be a liaison officer to the Group of Soviet Forces in Germany but he would aggressively observe and report their activities to his American headquarters in West Berlin. This information would be forwarded to Heidelberg and Washington as first indicators of trouble. The Huebner-Mallinin Agreement gave both sides' the right to legally spy on the other but Vic knew the Soviets would disrupt him and make his job as difficult as possible. He fingered his official credentials but found no assurance there—he would need to rely on his wits if he got into trouble.

As the train rocked back and forth a feeling of *heimat* swept over him, a sense of belonging to that particular time and place. Even the dark countryside seemed familiar. He had recently been to Berlin on temporary duty but this was different, this time he would stay. His birthplace was still occupied by an enemy his father hated as much as he loved the old city. He could hear his father talking about the wide avenue *Unter den Linden*, the lush *Tiergarten*, the tall *Brandenburg Tor,* and the playhouse *Berliner Ensemble*; he had visited them all through his father's detailed recounting. He also remembered his father's fierce outbursts at Hitler and Stalin, East Germans and Soviets.

Vic had studied the East German political system and culture, their army and police while learning Russian in Bad Tölz. He had probed the Soviet mindset, listening to radio transmissions and matched faces with speech patterns. He already had his official Soviet identity card as a member of the liaison group and was anxious for his first mission.

That June of 1961 West Germany was fast rebuilding from the devastation of World War II but the East had hardly begun. The West was rapidly industrializing but the East lay poverty-stricken and desolate, littered with the skeletons of bombed and looted factories and enormous heaps of rubble. Fiery German passions had been lost somewhere in that debris and it showed in their vacant eyes and hardened faces. Vic could have been one of those had his family not escaped in time.

The train slowed for an unscheduled stop at a military checkpoint. Vic knew international agreements giving the United States access to Berlin through certain corridors did not allow stopping the duty train. Nevertheless, the train stopped and an East German soldier climbed aboard and marched between the rows of soldiers and their families.

"Present your papers for inspection!" he barked in heavily accented English.

Vic thumbed through his documents. He was technically protected from East German harassment, they all were. That premise was being tested.

The cabin door banged open as an East German major stormed inside. The enlisted soldier braced in the doorway with his assault rifle conspicuously across his chest. It was all show—no one would ever consider running into the East German countryside beneath manned machinegun towers. The major strolled through car, nodding at each set of flag orders. He stopped before Vic.

"*Das papier*—your papers!"

Instead of presenting orders or American ID, Vic purposely displayed his Soviet military identification card with his picture and thumbprint.

The major snatched it. "*Was ist das?* What is this?" He skeptically compared the handsome, blond haired, blue eyed Aryan in the photo with the man before him.

Vic glared back. "That's mine. I'm with the Soviet Forces in this stinking country and you have no right to stop this train!" He reached for his card.

The guard lunged with his rifle, jamming the AK-47 rifle barrel into Vic's chest. The other passengers shrank back in their seats.

Vic protested loudly. "Put that weapon down!"

The guard leaned hard into it, pinning Vic against the seat.

The major smirked and started for the exit with Vic's card in hand.

The guard glowered over him and slid his rifle barrel over the polished brass U.S. insignia pinned to Vic's tunic, scratching it.

Vic called to the major in German. "Bring back my card!"

"Go to hell!" He replied in English for all the passengers to hear.

Vic uncorked his right arm—violently—slamming the rifle barrel upwards. *BamBamBam!* Three bullets hammered through the overhead. Flash from the powder burned Vic's face. Women screamed. Babies cried. Soldiers froze.

Vic grabbed the hot barrel with both hands and jammed it backwards into the face of the stunned soldier, knocking him off his feet. Then he snatched the rifle away and butt stroked the guard, crushing his nose.

The East German major charged back, this time followed by two Soviet officers, one a colonel. All had automatic pistols drawn, pointed at him. The disarmed soldier on the floor held his bleeding nose with both hands. Vic dropped the rifle beside him.

Passengers held their breath, waiting for Vic to be dragged outside and arrested or shot. He ignored the fuming German major and addressed only the Soviet colonel in clear Russian.

"I have as much right here as you do, Colonel."

The Soviet officer holstered his pistol and took the identification card from the East German major, compared the picture with the face, and made a note of the name. Then he spoke to his cohorts: "Leave the train. I'll handle this."

They left quickly, followed by the guard dragging his rifle and pinching his broken nose. Blood dripped over his shirt and onto the carpets.

The Soviet officer spoke calmly in Russian, testing. "I could haul you in for a full investigation," he said. "Perhaps I should."

"You could comrade," replied Vic in his practiced Russian, "but your Commanding General expects me to report tomorrow." Vic glanced at the identity card pinned to the officer's tunic. "I can tell him Colonel Gorski handled an unpleasant situation professionally, or that the crazy East Germans are running this asylum. It's your choice."

Gorski blinked, but a smile ticked the edges of his lips. "I can see you'll be a pain in the ass, Captain Werner." He handed Vic the identification card, bowing slightly.

11

Gorski found the exit but stopped and turned to address the other passengers. "I hope each of you," he said in articulate English, "has a pleasant stay in the Soviet city of Berlin."

Vic straightened his uniform and pocketed his identification card. No one uttered a word until the train bumped forward. As it passed the checkpoint and the huddle of East Germans and Soviets, a sergeant in the rear of the cabin slowly clapped. Others joined him and the cabin buzzed with nervous relief.

Vic stared out into darkness until all was quiet again, wondering if he would survive his return to Berlin after all.

2
Berlin

Vic had lost his peaceful state, his *heimat*. He'd have to explain his actions to his new chief in Berlin, Colonel John Powell. Headquarters for the United States-Soviet Military Liaison Mission was situated in Potsdam, an East German suburb southwest of Berlin. A long steel bridge connected east and west across the Havel River. Potsdam was the official and ceremonial headquarters reflecting the aristocracy of former rulers and elite generations of Prussians. Vic would not work from there but at the protected nerve center in West Berlin where top secret intelligence reports were processed. He had met Colonel Powell before, less an interview than a sizing up.

Vic stopped at the security desk and presented his identity card and orders to the same sergeant who had been there the week before.

"Welcome back to Berlin, Captain," said the non-commissioned officer. "The colonel is expecting you. He wants you in his office, right away."

"Thank you, sergeant." *He knows already. Everybody knows.*

Vic ducked into a latrine at the end of the hall and checked his uniform in the mirror. He'd tried to polish out the scratches on the U.S. insignia, but they were still visible—signs of his own German arrogance. He had managed a haircut and shined his shoes before leaving Frankfurt but his blue eyes were red-rimmed from a sleepless night. He smoothed back a short lock of blond hair, straightened his shoulders, and raised his chin a notch. It was time to face the music.

"Captain Werner reporting for duty, sir!" He snapped to attention before a large mahogany desk and held his salute for acknowledgement. The colonel slumped behind the desk continued reading a single sheet of paper without looking up. It lay flat on his desk as if he didn't want to touch it. As he bent over it, the silver eagles seemed to fly off his shoulders.

Finally he did look up. "Stand at ease, Captain," he said, without returning the salute.

Vic held firm at rigid attention, blade of his right hand over his right eye in a frozen salute, unflinching.

Powell studied him another few seconds before touching a crooked finger to his right eye. Vic dropped his salute and snapped to parade rest. Powell held him in eye lock

13

for another minute. "Oh, hell!" he said. "Take a seat." He nodded toward an uncomfortable-looking straight chair.

Vic sat and saw Powell wagging his head disapprovingly. "I have plenty of cowboys in this outfit already, Captain, but this is the worst infraction in over a year and you haven't even started to work yet."

"Excuse me, sir?" Vic said. "What infraction? I didn't do anything wrong."

"Well, this report on my desk...."

"I can't believe that son-of-a-bitch would make a complaint. He was in violation, not me. I was only enforcing the rules."

Powell's eyes narrowed to slits. "Did I say the Ruskies complained?" he asked sarcastically. "You made an assumption, Captain. Assumptions start wars around here. I want only facts based on hard evidence. No assumptions. You can fuck up a lot of things, you can even get killed and I won't give a shit, but if you assume something and you're wrong ... that's war!"

Vic looked puzzled. "Then, what report is that, sir?"

"This report?" he snapped. "You want to know what this fucking report is?" He waved the white paper like a surrender flag. "This is a message from the Commander-in-Chief of the whole United States Army in fucking Europe. He wants me to explain how three bullet holes got in the roof of his train. That's what it is."

Vic sighed. "I'll pay for it," he said.

Powell suppressed a smile. "No you won't, Captain. I decide who pays for what around here. Like you said, you didn't do anything wrong. Get your ass ready to roll in two days. You're going to pay me back with some good intelligence work. Sign in with S-1; get your gear from S-4, your briefing from S-2 and your orders from S-3. Get over to Potsdam and find your driver; he'll be your best friend in this place—not me. And if you think you're going to be chasing skirts around Berlin, you're dead wrong. Now get going."

14

3

Potsdam

Vic went to work fast and spent most of his days speeding around back roads in a fast car. He had just run another reconnaissance mission in the Soviet occupied zone of East Germany and was returning to Potsdam when he spotted Colonel Powell's sedan parked at the official mission headquarters. He sent his driver to re-fuel the oversized gas tank while he looked for Powell. Villa Sigismund, a palatial estate in Potsdam, was miraculously unscathed by heavy bombing during the war. The grounds were occupied by the United States as the official headquarters for the U.S. Military Liaison Mission to the Group of Soviet Forces in Germany, an American island in East Germany. Powell usually worked at his principal headquarters in West Berlin but official meetings with the Soviets sometimes required him to be here instead.

Powell paced across the creaking floors, agitated by Soviet complaints. He buried his right fist into his left palm. "Shit! The piss-ants can just go to hell."

Soviet tirades about his team's aggressive driving came in every month, mostly because he had better drivers and cars. They regularly out-maneuvered Soviet attempts to obstruct them. "Horse shit!" But, he would discuss it with his team and write a more polite official response.

The mission of the United States Military Liaison Mission (U.S.M.L.M.), the acronym commonly pronounced "Smell 'um," was transparency between deployed Soviet and American military forces. Members of the team were assigned to the Soviet Group of Forces in Germany as liaison officers. Decision-makers in Heidelberg depended on them to report Soviet movements and discern their intentions. They were legal military spies, but Soviet commanders hated having them running free in their territory, especially when they were hiding something. Fourteen American officers and their drivers scouted East Germany in supercharged 1957 Chevrolet Malibu's. Soviets and East Germans tried to avoid their prying eyes, chased them away, or obstruct them in anyway possible. Sometimes *Stasi* secret police agents joined the chases in faster BMWs or Mercedes sedans.

These so-called "reconnaissance tours" were the chief means of putting eyes on the enemy in the field. A tour included an officer and driver roaming without communications or weapons, prying into training, assembly areas, communications sites, and headquarters. They often bent rules or broke international laws to do their job. If caught, they were slammed into detention until they either bluffed their way out or were expelled as *persona non-gratis*. NATO forces protected the inter-German border and trained for the big battle while these teams tried to provide early warning. These were among the most daring and reckless of all the cold warriors.

Colonel Powell sensed something was brewing. He wanted to know what it was and hoped his teams could tell him. He was afraid East Germans might close the border; they were getting desperate. Cornered animals always attack.

The door to the villa creaked as Vic entered, dusted his boots, and hung his field cap on a hook next to the only other hat there. He called out, "Any one here?"

The indigenous staff had been released for the weekend but some drivers were in their quarters on the top floor, music booming like a bad hangover in the quiet community.

"Werner!" Powell yelled back. "Come in here."

"Be right there Colonel." Vic had caught the colonel's attention with his in-depth mission reports. The incident on the train was old news now. "I need to hit the head first."

"Bring glasses." Powell claimed to hate drinking alone but that never stopped him. He could hold his own with any Russian at any bar in Germany and had left several under the table with the empties.

Vic sauntered in with two crystal shot glasses. He moved a chair with one knee and set the glasses in the center of the desk. They had practiced this drill before.

Powell pulled out the bottom desk drawer and found a bottle of Jack Daniels Tennessee sour mash, which he inspected. Satisfied the liquid still reached the grease pencil line he made when he last closed it and it hadn't been watered down, he removed the small strip of tape from the cap, double insurance. He unscrewed the cap with one hand and poured three fingers of bourbon into each glass.

Vic raised his glass to eye level and waited for the inevitable toast.

"To Georgie Patton, a real soldier!"

"To Patton," repeated Vic. They drank it down.

Powell studied Vic; his bravado reflected his mirror image from years earlier. "Captain, what's going on out there in never-never land?"

Vic had been recruited because of his German origins. His parents had landed with their only son at Ellis Island just before the big war. They fled Hitler's Germany but he clung to his German heritage. Vic's father spoke English at work but at home they used only their native German. The German language was as natural as his right hand. He had studied Russian in Monterrey and Bad Tölz; Russian was as his left hand. And Vic had something the Germans called *fingerspitzgefühl*, a sensory perception in the finger tips to detect what the Soviets were scheming, an instinct for seeing the Soviets through German eyes.

"Everything is pretty normal, Colonel. Refugees are still coming in droves."

"What do you hear on the street?"

"*Ossies* are frustrated by food shortages, hell, shortages of everything. They can't find what they want in the east, and they can't afford it in the west. *Wessies* are sympathetic, but if *Ossies* keep coming they'll break the bank—too many mouths to feed, not enough jobs."

"Yeah, well, what are the Ruskies doing?" Without waiting for an answer he said, "Want another drink—I'm having one." He filled his glass and pushed the bottle to Vic.

Vic poured a quarter full but only sipped this one. "Good question, sir. I know what you're getting at—I feel it, too. I don't know exactly what it is, but something's about to blow, something big."

Powell grinned. Vic saw a story was coming and waited for it. "Something big, eh?" said Powell. "Listen to what happened to me. This might explain something. I have to send an eyes-only telex to Heidelberg for General Clark."

Powell swished the strong whisky through his teeth like mouthwash before he swallowed. "I had a shitty little meeting with the Soviets here this morning about your driving, but later I was summoned from the tennis court. That was sixteen-thirty hours this afternoon. I was instructed to go visit old Ivan in person." General Ivan Yakulovsky was Commander-in-Chief of the Group of Soviet Forces in Germany. Powell was the senior American military liaison officer to the Soviet four-star general's staff.

"When I reached his headquarters, after changing clothes, the British and French mission chiefs were there already. We knew something was up but I expected the usual browbeating about the peace treaty Khrushchev keeps yakking about, you know. But nope … that wasn't it."

Powell refreshed his Jack Daniels. "When we walked in, old Ivan was there all right. He was standing right next to another Ivan—*Marshal Ivan Koniev!*"

Vic jumped at the name, eyes wide. "Koniev? You're shitting me! That sucker left the Warsaw Pact and disappeared, retired, or something." He filled his glass, his hand shaking this time. Koniev had led Soviet forces to link up with Americans in Berlin in the waning days of World War II.

"Oh, he was there all right. Listen to what he said." Powell lowered his voice imitating Koniev, and with a Russian accent said, "'Gentlemen, my name is Koniev. You may have heard of me!'"

"No shit! He really said that?"

"Yeah, then he announced he was the new Commander-in-Chief and that we're now accredited to him. Yakulovsky will stay as his deputy. That old coot didn't mutter a single word."

"Is this for real?"

"No shit, it's real. Koniev served champagne and asked if we had any questions. The Brit and I just said congratulations, stuff like that, but Frenchie really stepped in a pile of shit. He said 'he couldn't comment until he had guidance from Paris.' Know what Koniev said about that?"

"What?"

"He said, and this was in Russian, he said 'stop that diplomatic bullshit! We're all soldiers here.' Can you believe that? Coolest cucumber I ever saw."

"What does it mean; the mighty conqueror of Dresden, Prague and Berlin taking over East Germany again?"

"Well, that's our job, to find out. Are you staying around this weekend?"

Vic shrugged. "Nowhere else to go."

"Be vigilant, Vic. And it's imperative that you notify me immediately if you get wind of anything, you hear?"

"Yes sir, I will," he said. "Damn right." Vic stood up and ran his fingers through his blond hair. "Koniev! No shit?" He left shaking his head. "Now, that's something. Koniev is back. That can only mean one thing!"

4
Soviet Armor

Colonel Powell had told Vic, "Find out what the hell is going on!" Airman Reitz turned the ignition switch and the overcharged Chevy's engine rocked. Vic rode shotgun, in the right seat with a map spread out over his lap, as they cruised out of Potsdam into the countryside. The mission began early, long before the sun cleared the damp fog from lumpy potato fields.

The 1957 Chevrolet was militarized for special operations. The model was four years old but this one was still new, showing 128 miles on the odometer. Olive drab paint muted its appearance and all chrome had been removed or painted over; it was equipped with an overpowered racing engine and the suspension was jacked up so the undercarriage could pass over rutted tank trails. An oversized gas tank extended its range. They carried no radios or weapons. If they discovered Soviet tanks massing to attack, they could only race back to headquarters to report it.

When they left Potsdam a *Stasi* Wartburg followed, but the diesel powered city car could not match the Chevy on highways, much less over rough terrain. Reitz was an experienced stockcar driver from Alabama and was unequaled among East German or Soviet drivers. He drove instinctively; driving was both art and science, his only weapon.

The intelligence officer had briefed Vic that the Soviet Tenth Guards tank division was in a training area rehearsing for something; he intended to find out what. Ahead he saw rising dust and diesel fumes and was surprised to see them returning to their barracks. The rumble of tanks could be heard ten kilometers away, but these were much closer. An armored column rounded a bend in the road spewing black fumes and kicking up a dust storm, coming straight at them.

"Head for the trees!" Vic shouted over the din, indicating a woody spot at an intersection. He clenched his teeth through the near catastrophe.

Reitz spun the Chevy off road, braking in a cloud of dust in a clump of scrubby bushes.

"I'll count 'em," said Vic. "You get some pictures."

Reitz idled the engine while he screwed a telephoto lens on the large black Nikon. He glanced into his side mirror. "Shit! Here comes trouble," he said.

Vic turned to see a squad of Russian infantry double-timing toward them. They carried assault rifles at port arms with banana clips inserted, live ammunition loaded. The squad split into two files and surrounded the car.

Vic cranked the window down, and the muzzle of an AK-47 was shoved under his nose. "Do not move or I'll shoot!" the squad leader shouted in Russian. "Stop the engine."

"We have every right to be here," Vic insisted. He held his Soviet identification card behind the glass, intending not to have it snatched away again.

"Fine. That's exactly what you'll do—stay right here. If you move, I'll shoot." Vic glanced at Reitz, who killed the engine.

Two soldiers tossed heavy wool blankets over the car windows, obstructing their view in every direction. "Roll your window down," said Vic. "I can count the damned tanks by sound."

"Maybe we can breath, too," said Reitz. "I wonder if they'd shoot us for that."

They listened to a tank regiment barreling past on the dirt road. Their treads slung heavy sheets of dust that settled over the car. The voices of their guards became more indistinct, indicating they had backed out of the dust storm for shelter in the trees.

Reitz fidgeted nervously in his seat. "I have to piss, sir. I'm cracking my door so I can lean out." He twisted around in his seat so not to spoil the new-car smell. In a minute, he said, "They weren't close enough for me to piss on their boots, sir. I wonder if they lost interest in us."

"So, what are you thinking, Reitz?"

"I'll switch on the windshield wipers," he said. "Maybe it'll move the blanket enough to see out. If we're clear, we could make a run for it—follow those tanks."

Vic thought a split second. "Go ahead."

The wipers strained under the weight of the dusty blankets until one moved. It wasn't much, but enough for Reitz to catch a glimpse. "No one in front," he said. "Hang on!" Reitz turned the key and pressed the accelerator together. The Chevy thundered, tires spun against gravel, and it leaped ahead throwing rocks behind.

The Soviet squad leader reacted just as fast. "Halt!" he yelled. "I'll shoot!"

They couldn't hear him over the noise, but had no intention of stopping anyway.

He fired. Three shots split the air; the fourth struck the trunk lid. Blankets sailed over the top in the gathering wind. The Chevy bounced violently over boulders and through a ditch until it landed hard in the tank ruts, smack in the middle of the moving armored column. Reitz squeezed the thin-skinned Chevy between two behemoth tanks moving at forty kilometers an hour. The one in front kicked dust and blew black smoke obscuring their visibility; the tank behind closed perilously threatening to smash them between. Reitz clung to the one in front until they reached a crossroads. He swung the steering wheel hard, turning from one danger into another.

A Soviet jeep, a GAZ-69, swooped behind them and smacked their rear bumper with his front. The Soviet officer in the passenger seat jabbed his pistol into the air and fired it once, an obvious signal to halt.

"Outrun that son-of-a-bitch!" Vic shouted. "Head for Potsdam." He looked back to see if they were about to be shot at again but the officer was holding himself in the bouncing jeep with both hands.

Reitz's eyes were riveted on the road as the speedometer climbed to ninety kilometers-per-hour. "Did you see that sign?" he asked. "We just passed it."

"What sign?"

"Bridge out!" Reitz muttered through clenched teeth.

Vic glanced back at the GAZ, then at the map spread in his lap. "Stream ahead," he said. "Can we ford it?"

"We'll soon find out." Reitz stomped the pedal to the floor and the Chevy lurched into overdrive. The GAZ fell further behind.

"Shit!" Vic braced both hands against the dash. An open chasm gaped over the hood, emptiness where the bridge should be. Too late—they sailed off the end of the broken bridge. The Chevy's hood pointed up first, then down, doing eighty.

They were airborne until the front wheels struck the broken roadbed on the other side. The front bumper plowed dirt. Impact absorbed all the compression of the front shocks and they felt the road through the seats. Vic's legs felt numb—he was numb all over.

The undercarriage had slammed against the leading edge of the open bridge embankment. Front wheels found solid ground; rear wheels spun in mid-air. Momentum carried them forward, scraping off the muffler as the car slid ahead, sparks flying. Rear tires gained traction and the Chevy jerked up, lurched onto the paved road then stopped, engine still running. Reitz sat frozen, squeezing the wheel and listening to the exhaust's un-muffled roar.

"Don't yell at me while I'm driving, sir," Reitz said. He wiped the palm of his hand over his brow. "It makes me nervous."

Vic flicked a drop of sweat from his nose with a shaking fingertip and looked back at the chasm. The Soviet GAZ sat immobile on the far edge, turned sideways, two long parallel lines of burnt rubber trailing behind. The officer stepped out and looked across to them on the other side. He holstered his pistol, snapped to attention, and saluted.

Vic got out of the Chevy and returned the military courtesy while Reitz crawled on his hands and knees checking the undercarriage.

"Can it make it?" Vic asked.

"Motor pool will have to rebuild this baby. Frame's bent." They limped toward Potsdam, hot muffler dragging behind in a trail of sparks until it finally fell off.

Finally, Vic asked, "What'll you do after this, Reitz?"

"After this?" He glanced at Vic. "Hell, I'm never leaving here, sir. This shit is what I'm all about."

They didn't speak again until they reached the outskirts of Berlin. "Drop me at my apartment before you take the car in. I'll take some cigarettes from the back." They kept a box of cigarettes and Hershey bars in the trunk to pry information from the locals. It worked well among the deprived. A bullet hole had passed through the box.

Vic was the only bachelor officer on the team. His status gave him motive and opportunity to wander about streets while the others were home with their families. He changed into civilian clothes at his apartment near *Grunnewald Parc* and walked alone, offering a cigarette here, a pack there, catching fragments of conversation, the tempo of life in the city. Finally, he took a taxi to mission headquarters where such bits of information were combined with his tour report and processed into intelligence.

Vic heard Colonel Powell talking on the phone when he opened the door.

"No sir!" He shouted, overcoming a typically poor connection. "I don't have anything specific, but I know something's cooking, ready to boil. And this Koniev thing means something. He's not here on vacation."

Vic stood in the doorway listening until Powell dropped the receiver and waved him in. "My tennis game has gone to hell, and forget about golf." He reached into the familiar bottom drawer and plunked the half-empty bottle of Jack Daniels on his desk. "I've got to make another supply run, too. Damned Russians drive me to drink." He poured booze into his coffee cup and offered Vic a clean one.

"That was General Clark on the phone," he said. "He wanted to hear firsthand about this Koniev thing. How'd you spend your day?"

Vic sipped the bourbon from his mug. "Tenth Guards came back from training early. They went to their barracks at Krampnitz in a big hurry. Something's happening, but I don't know what."

"I heard there was more to it," Powell said. "Tell me all of it."

"We drove out to the training area, Reitz and I," Vic began. "The damned *Stasi* followed us but they couldn't keep up. We stopped at an intersection to count tanks, and a Russian patrol threatened to shoot us. They threw blankets over the car so we couldn't see. Reitz broke out but an officer in a GAZ followed us. Reitz lost him by jumping over a gulch. Scared the shit out of me; had to go change my pants. The Chevy will have to be fixed again."

"I'm going to start charging you for these repairs," he threatened. "Shit, you couldn't afford it on your pay. That all of it?"

"Trucks all over town," said Vic. "Unusual for a Saturday."

"Soviets are complaining about our driving again," said Powell. "Mostly you and Reitz." He watched for a reaction but saw none. "Were those military trucks you saw in town?"

"Some, but mostly construction-type equipment" he said. "They were all over. Are they building something new around here?"

"Maybe, don't know. What were they hauling?"

"Concrete blocks, wire, posts, construction stuff. Some bull dozers and cranes." The Soviets had appropriated most of the heavy construction and factory equipment from Germany after the war, removing it to Russia to boost their own economy. "Looks like they're returning some stolen merchandise. Now, that's something different."

"Hum. I'll check on it Monday."

"Oh, another thing," he said as an afterthought. "I walked through town coming here. I overheard a couple of *politzei* talking about a big exercise. They didn't say when, maybe it was supposed to be secret or something. When they saw me, they clammed up."

"Well, they do have that refugee problem. They might crack down on them."

"That's all I have, boss. Not much, but I've got a feeling..."

"Hell, I can't call the four-star and tell him 'Werner has a feeling.' Get me something!"

"Right, but my feeling is that whatever it is, it's going to happen before we figure out what it is."

23

5

East Berlin

That night, across town in East Berlin, theater patrons filed from the *Berliner Ensemble*, some heading for the light rail station on *Friedrichstrasse*, others for nearby cafés and *kellers*. Most had come over from West Berlin. The theater was in the Soviet-occupied zone—Americans, British, and French administered the other three. In one café, patrons discussed the play they had just seen.

Someone asked about the unheralded actress who stood in unexpectedly as the leading lady in the musical. "Who was she?"

"Braun. Ilse Braun. She wasn't listed in the program."

"She was superb," said another. "I've never heard of her before but she should be the lead. She was better than the real star."

Inside her dressing room, Ilse Braun scrubbed heavy makeup from her face. Her hair was pasted down, still damp from the heavy wig that quashed her natural black curls. She dried her face and ran fingers through the tangles, fluffed them with a brush, slipped a dress over her head, tucked stray curls under a black beret and checked the results in a mirror. After a swipe of red lipstick, she pinched her cheeks for color and headed to find Kurt.

It had been quite a night. Kurt Meyer was her manager, coach, and best friend—her only friend. As far as the production was concerned he was the carpenter who built the sets—to Ilse he was more.

The lead actress had reported with laryngitis only an hour before the show. The director considered canceling, but Kurt intervened. "Let Ilse go on. She knows the lines and the songs. She can do this."

"She's never rehearsed. I've never heard her sing. I can't take that chance."

"I'll guarantee her performance," Kurt insisted. "It'll be the best decision you ever made. Look, you would just have to refund all the money. Besides this is closing night, you have nothing to lose. Just do it."

Ilse was helping with stage props for the first act when Kurt told her she would be standing in. "Go dress for the lead. You're going on," he said.

"No—I'm not ready!"

He dragged her off stage and into the dressing room. She was trembling but, with no time to waste, she focused.
When the curtain rose a little later her knees were shaking, her heart pounding. But as she started singing she was no longer the Jewish orphan in the former Nazi capital, she was the star.

"*Wunderbar!*" the director exclaimed when it was over, blowing her a kiss.

"Congratulations! I have a perfect part for you in the next play."

"*Danke*," she said. "Have you seen Kurt?" Kurt Meyer, the set manager for the theater, had a tendency to get things organized then disappear. Isle backed him up when he did but this time he had thrown her to the paying patrons before he vanished. She needed to see him now, to share her unanticipated success, her breakout, her joy at overcoming her fears.

"Not since the show began," he said. "Are you coming to the cast party in the *theaterkeller*? Please come. Everyone wants to celebrate with you."

"Yes, I'll come. Thank you," she said looking around. "But I need to find Kurt first. If you see him, tell him I'm looking for him."

"He'll be at the party," said the director. "Come on." He took her hand and led her away.

But Kurt was not there and that upset Ilse. It had been the best moment of her life and Kurt had made it possible. Then he vanished again.

I don't know if I'll kiss him ... or kill him.

6

Hanover, West Germany

To casual passers on the street, a woman appeared to be sitting by herself on the lush park grass. The afternoon sun was warm over *Maschpark* between the Wietze River and the tram station. The park offered easy access to both city and suburbs yet was serene on a weekday afternoon. She was not alone.

Hilda Brunner coursed her slender fingers through Kurt Meyer's blond locks. His head rested in her lap, and he was stretched out with his shirt thrown open to the warm rays. The day was made for relaxing, and her skirt was hiked well up her thighs in the warming sun. The quiet day and familiar company soothed; the week had been cloudy and worrisome throughout Germany.

Kurt appeared to be sleeping with his eyes closed, arms outstretched and legs parted. Hilda stirred beneath him, bringing him back to Hanover from his vague memories of the first act of Ilse's performance the evening before in East Berlin. A half-empty bottle of Riesling stood nearby with the cork protruding next to a broken loaf of French bread and a jar of *Weichkaese* cheese. The grassy hillside park was nearly deserted on a Friday afternoon, but by Saturday morning it would be overrun with children playing while their anxious parents chased them. He would return to Berlin long before then.

"I miss the children," she mumbled to herself.

He stirred. "What'd you say, Hilda?"

"Nothing. Go back to sleep. I was just talking to myself."

He persisted. "Children? You mentioned children."

"I miss having them around ... here in the park. I miss their happy sounds."

"I missed hearing your voice. I missed the rest of you, too."

"Can we have children, Kurt ... I mean someday?"

"Of course, someday, but not right now. We have things to finish first."

"I know that, but I just want to imagine it," she said, casually running her palms over his chest. She gently scratched his nipple with her fingernail.

He twitched. "Um, that felt good."

She did it again. "That?"

He rolled on his side. "You'll have to stop. I'm already having a problem."

She chuckled. "Do you remember the night of the Freedom Council meeting in Berlin … to plan the organization?" she asked.

"Of course. That was when we started working together for a united Germany."

"I'm not talking about politics, silly." She slapped him playfully. "I mean the tram ride after the meeting."

"Ah! I may know that one," he teased. "Tell me about it."

Her cheeks flushed, suddenly pink. "I'm sure you remember well enough."

"Let me see.... If I remember correctly, I was riding the tram and it was late in the evening, after the meeting ended." His eyes were open, twinkling. "I was sitting next to a sexy *fraulein* and I sneaked one arm around her neck. She didn't slap me so I placed my other hand on her thigh. I slowly moved up her leg, over her hips to her belly. Just before I reached her breast she grabbed my hand and stopped me. That's all I remember."

"People were watching you! And you know that wasn't all. You took my hand and pulled me off the tram at the next stop. We went into a park and you made love to me, standing up with our clothes on."

"Yes, I do recall that now. Then we went to a nearby café and had coffee and cake and talked until very late. That's when we decided we would work together. And here we are."

She laughed. "I never found them."

"What?"

"I never found my panties."

"Ha! The park attendant took them home to his wife."

She scooped some soft cheese on her finger and held it near his mouth. He took her finger between his lips and sucked hard. She slowly pulled her finger out. "Kurt?"

"Yes?"

"I love you."

"I love you, too. I'm sorry we had to meet here instead of Bonn. I need to get back to Berlin right away."

"I understand. But I still want us to go to Knokke-Heist together. I love the sea coast. You promised."

"And we will. We'll take a week at a *Pensione.* Sailing, sunning, swimming ... and other things...."

"The North Sea is so romantic in the summer."

"How did you get away today?" he asked. "Won't they miss you at the chancellor's office?"

"No. Almost everyone is gone now, on holiday, like we should be. Besides, I'm only a typist—completely expendable."

"You're indispensable to me. I can't live without you."

He saw her life story etched in her sad eyes, and he knew it well: Her family split by the war, her mother fleeing with her to England before Hitler's invasions. Her father staying behind to hold onto a small potato farm but forced into Hitler's army, ordered to fight on the western front ... her mother dying during the German bombing of London and after the war her father's refusal to leave the farm near Kurt's birthplace in Halle. Her broken father lived there still, clinging to a fading hope that his property would someday be returned. Yes, he knew her story well—his was the other side of the coin.

He hated leaving her. He first spoke to her at that meeting with others wanting to push East and West toward reunification. He noticed her right away, but she was aloof and he was cautious until their eyes met. From that moment, he knew he never wanted to lose her.

That weekend meeting in Berlin, begun with a passionate affair, had progressed. Patriotic zeal brought them together but now kept them separated.

"What are you thinking about?" she asked. "You look so somber."

He studied the serious lines around her gray eyes which betrayed her own thoughts—she was afraid it would never happen. Occasional meetings in odd places, and some weekends together were just not enough. She needed more, and before it was too late. She wanted children and Kurt knew it. "My clock is ticking," she had warned him. She would be too old for childbirth in a few years and they hadn't even talked about setting a date. He hadn't really proposed anyway—it was just assumed, like a war without a declaration, a peace without a treaty. He kept putting it off—his mission got in the way. It was her mission, too! They were both trapped by it, their futures suspended. The war had never ended for them.

"I'm thinking you should go back to London and marry an English squire," he answered her question, speaking to those desolate eyes. "This is too dangerous for you. You need more than a roving entrepreneur who goes in and out of your life, with no promises for a future."

"Entrepreneur?" she laughed. "Is that what you are? You could be shot for what you do ... me, too, for that matter. And you have promised ... in a way."

"No more of this talk, not here. We must be careful."

"Kurt, I don't want an English squire," she said with the English accent she had acquired growing up in London. "I want you—all of you. Come back to the *gasthaus* with me. I need some time alone with you now."

He twisted quickly to his knees, immediately alarmed. "You didn't leave it in your room, did you?" His finger touched his left eyebrow and rubbed while his eyes swept over the grass.

"I'm not a beginner."

"Then where is it?" He stood. "Where?"

She blushed and smoothed her dress. "In my underwear—which I'm still wearing this time."

First they kissed in her room at the *Gasthaus* Edelweiss, hands caressing the curves of each other's body. He held her tightly against him and she pressed forward, pushing her hips against his. He pushed her back to arms' length. Her breathing came rapidly, breasts rising as she stood very still while he unbuttoned her dress. She shrugged her shoulders and it fell to the floor at her feet. His arms circled her while his lips found hers. His fingers unfastened her bra while she fumbled with his stubborn buttons. He hooked his thumbs into her cotton underpants and slid them over gently rounded hips. As he leaned down he fell to his knees, his face lingered at the smell of her and his tongue explored, tasted. She quivered under his touch.

They fell across the high bed, bodies moving together under the slow-whopping ceiling fan, in synchronized rhythm. Only that moment was real; everything else was washed away. He didn't even glance at the folded papers on the floor until they lay exhausted and intertwined.

Later, while she slept, he finished the Reisling and gathered three thin carbon copies from the floor next to her lingerie. He unfolded them quietly and read.

On the top margins of each, the words <u>TOP SECRET</u> had been typed in capital letters and underlined. She had been audacious enough to make unauthorized copies while she typed. Kurt envisioned her smuggling the carbon paper in and out of the chancellery. Reproduction of documents was *verboten*—strictly forbidden. Had she been caught, she could be tried for treason.

As a typist in the chancellor's classified typing pool, she had access only to papers that crossed her desk. For security purposes the administrative work was segmented and compartmentalized; no clerks could go into the safes to simply pull files. But she recognized important data when she saw it and delayed typing those documents until alone, during lunch or after hours. He visualized her hiding them in her underwear to get past security and the thought of the papers hidden there excited him yet again. He sniffed the paper and caught a scent of her. Hilda was indeed a remarkable woman—his lover and a fearless partisan.

Kurt examined each page carefully. The first was an abbreviated executive summary of NATO war plans prepared for the West German Chancellor to use at a meeting with his defense minister. The second and third contained troop lists for NATO's Northern and Central Army Groups along with the numbers and yields of British and American nuclear weapons dedicated to each sector. The nuclear weapons were strictly under American and British control but procedures to release them to NATO were summarized in footnotes.

He was certain East German intelligence already had the troop information; he had seen it before himself. But, the nuclear information was new. He wondered how Abel would react when he passed this to him. He could see his deep-set, dark eyes scanning the papers, a crooked grin cracking open his skull-shaped head, nervously thumping his cane on the floor. He despised Abel and only met with the devil as a necessary evil.

Bed springs creaked beneath her and he glanced in her direction. She opened her eyes to him as he sat in the fading light beside the window. "You're handsome, Kurt."

"*Danke*. And you're beautiful, my lovely." And she truly was, naked and with all her beauty exposed. She was unabashed and certainly had no reason to be ashamed of her body.

"Why do you do that?" she asked.

"What?"

"Rub your eyebrow that way. You do it when you're bothered by something. Why?"

"I wasn't aware of it," he said as he dropped his left hand onto the paper in his lap.

"I guess it's an old habit. But that's a long story."

"Tell me."

"I haven't much time. I must leave right away."

She swung her legs off the bed and slipped a housecoat over her bare shoulders. "We never know how much time we actually have. We have to take it when we find it. Tell me now. I really want to know that about you."

"It's a long story," he said again, "but if you must.... You know already that I was a U-boat navigator in the war. We were in shallow water near the English Channel to ambush shipping. We were detected and hit with a depth charge. I knocked my head hard on the bulkhead, right there," He rubbed his left eyebrow with his finger. "It split my eyebrow and knocked me unconscious. I came to when I was being shoved out a hatch as the boat sank. American sailors fished me out of the water and pulled me aboard a tanker, a prisoner of war."

Hilda moved the papers and lifted his hand to sit in his lap. "The Americans saved your life?" She kissed his eyebrow.

"Yes, after we had just sunk one of their ships. They rescued some of us along with their own sailors."

"I'm glad, but continue. I didn't know this before."

"In the hospital bay, a medic stitched my eyebrow together. Here." He touched his eyebrow again. "He said I was lucky to be alive and in American hands. I was surprised by that and thought about it all day in the brig with the other prisoners. That night another of our U-boats torpedoed the tanker that had rescued us. The same medic came to the brig where we were locked up and opened the door. He told us the ship was sinking and we'd have to save ourselves. I was amazed that he came to release us—why not let us drown? As the others rushed past, I asked him why he had risked his life to free German submariners. Do you know what he told me?"

"Certainly not."

"He said someday I would return the favor." Kurt rubbed his brow once more. "I remember that and sometimes wonder how I could possibly do it."

She pulled the sash of her robe around her narrow waist and left the room for the common bathroom down the hall, locking the door and slipping the large key in her pocket as she left. Kurt stared at the closed door long after she had gone.

He carefully re-folded the papers along the same creases and slipped them into the bottom of his boot, beneath the sole liner. He was still tying the laces when she returned, unlocking the door and again relocking it behind her. No intrusions.

31

"Are they worth anything?" she asked.

"I think so ... especially the nuclear information."

"How do you feel about handing over the American nuclear secrets to East Germans? You know the Soviets will get it."

"I try not to think about it. I believe it is for the common good."

"Are you going now?" she asked. She sat before the mirror and began brushing her hair with long, slow strokes.

"I must. The train leaves in an hour."

The mirror was a simple *gasthaus* version, expendable furniture almost ready for replacement, but the frame bordered her like a canvas stretcher, a priceless painting in a cheap frame. She followed his eyes in the mirror over her shoulder.

"When will you come back to me?"

"Soon, but I don't know exactly, perhaps next week. Next time, I'll go to your flat in Bonn and stay longer. I'm sorry our time together has been so short. Get whatever information you can, but don't take any chances. Please, Hilda—no unnecessary risks."

She stopped brushing and he studied her in the mirror, looking back at him. She had that look, wanting to say something but not able to get it out.

"What is it?" he prodded. "What are you holding back? Just say it."

She broke off one of the flowers from the arrangement in a vase on the vanity. She smelled it, finding strength in the aroma.

"Will you be able see my father this time?" She rubbed a palm nervously along her thigh.

"Yes." He saw her back arch in the straight chair as she slowly turned to face him. "I'll give him some money," he said. "Is that what you want?"

"Thank you."

"You should come with me at least once. I can get you over and back. You should do it for yourself, Hilda, if not for him."

"How is he?"

"He's getting older, and feeble," he said. "He seems to be giving up hope of ever reclaiming his farm. You need to see him before he dies. You'd never forgive yourself."

"Does he ask about me, ever?" Droplets swelled in the corners of her eyes.

He refused to look away, locking his burning eyes on hers, insistent. "He doesn't remember you, Hilda. I'm sorry."

"Me too." She lowered her gaze to her hands clasped tightly in her lap. A single tear fell onto her wrist. They watched it roll off, leaving a wiggly wet track on her arm. It splattered on the floor and spread into a wider circle. The tiny drop swelled into an ocean. Then another one fell.

Streams of tears passed over her cheeks unheeded. His chest tightened and he forgot to breathe. He felt helpless before her pain, old beyond his years. For a moment he imagined he was her father. He wanted to take her into his arms and stay the night, tell her everything would be all right, although he knew it wasn't true. Kiss the little girl's hurt and make it go away. He had to stop feeling other people's pain, especially fellow Germans torn asunder by the war's aftermath. The woman he loved shouldn't have to suffer still. But he was compelled to do what he did.

That was that.

He stood abruptly, swung his backpack over one shoulder and moved to the door. He stopped there, returned to her and kissed the top of her head. Then he left.

7
Schöneberg, West Berlin

Iron wheels of the *Deutsches Bundesbahn* clacked over rail junctions from Hanover to Berlin. Sounds and smells of the lonely night passage lulled most passengers into romantic diversions, but the steady beat, like a ticking clock, calculated kilometers between Kurt and Hilda. Returning to Berlin had become progressively more difficult after each visit. Before Hilda entered his life, this had been simple but she had tinted his perspective.

If it weren't for my family … and Ilse ... I'd take Hilda and disappear.

He couldn't carry her picture with him—didn't want it found on him if caught. He didn't need one anyway—close his eyes and she was there. He valued his family, as did Hilda, but her reluctance to visit her father was beyond understanding. Family represented one's history, the essence of life, the bond between troubled past and uncertain future. He must visit his father and sister, knowing every trip spelled danger for all of them. First, he would necessarily make up with Ilse for disappearing during her first stage appearance—he had left her to deal with her fears alone. Ilse—rising star of the new universe.

She was like another sister, not a real one like Ingrid, not family, but more than friendship—something enduring that neither quite understood. Hilda barely tolerated Kurt's relationship with the beautiful younger woman and then only because of their joint undertaking and shared hopes of an idyllic future together. Kurt's relationship with Hilda was necessarily secret, except to his family and Ilse. But the sinews with Ilse were almost indefinable—he could never explain it to Hilda's satisfaction. With Hilda, it was love—pure and simple. With Ilse, theirs was a friendship that surpassed generations, sexes, cultures, politics and religions. So vague, it was never discussed.

Kurt arrived in West Berlin in the midst of a hot, sticky afternoon. He pressed one of several buttons at the weathered entrance of a somber, three-storied apartment building in Schöneberg, a haven for Berlin's artists and intelligentsia. The key to Ilse's front door was in his pocket but he seldom used it—ensuring she was alone before walking in unannounced. He knew she would eventually find someone but she was taking so long! She was beautiful, irresistible to most men but she inexplicably shut them all out. She needed a man in her life, one besides him. But no one had pierced her invisible, impenetrable wall—not even Kurt.

He stayed there while he was in West Berlin, the basis of Hilda's jealousy. He rented the apartment in her name on the west side, near the *Berliner Ensemble* in the east.

Kurt didn't want any address registered in his name. Ilse thought that strange, but was happy to live in the one-bedroom apartment as her income from singing and acting was sparse. She trusted him completely but he usually slept on a cot in her basement storeroom—sometimes she insisted he sleep on her sofa for reasons not discussed. He assumed she was afraid of the dark.

"Yes?" Her refined voice sounded tinny through the old pre-war speaker.

"It's me. Can I come up?"

"Kurt!" The unlock buzzer sounded immediately and he vaulted the stairs, two at a time. At the top, he found the door opened wide. Ilse waited, her arms outstretched for a smothering embrace. "Kurt! I missed you so!" She pecked his cheeks three times, then his lips. Hers were moist—the kiss packed more than he expected.

She pushed away. "Where were you? Damn it, Kurt! You pushed me on stage and disappeared. Where did you go?"

"I had to see Hilda."

"So suddenly? I wanted you there—you were part of that."

"I'm sorry," he said. "I didn't want to distract you. You needed to focus on your lines, not what I was doing. I know you did well."

"Well? … I was the star! I won a leading role in the next production, thanks to you—you bastard!" She studied him. "What's wrong?"

"Nothing," he said. "I'm glad to be back here."

His eyes swept over her—stylish black skirt falling just below her knee, white silk blouse unbuttoned at the top, single pearl strand. Her heels were kicked off near the door and she stood in her nylons.

"And all dressed up. Going somewhere?"

"Just came from an audition," she said. "I tried out as vocalist in the music bar at the Hilton."

As her unpaid manager, he was surprised his apprehensive protégé took the initiative. "Congratulations!" he said. He recognized her talents but she usually hung back, now seemed to have found a measure of self-confidence. Ilse was a solitary person for a performing artist, lost in a secretive world, but she came alive on stage. Elsewhere, she was sometimes unstable—an invisible line blurring her fantasies and reality.

"How'd it go?" he asked.

"Very well … I think. Perhaps another girl is sleeping with the manager." Her dark brown eyes flickered. "But, *Herr* Eichmann's heart couldn't handle that much excitement. Show business *is* bitchy, isn't it?"

She studied him; saw he wasn't fully engaged in her fun moment. "I know your job is worse. I don't know how you can work as a carpenter all day, at the theater every night, and then go to Hilda on the weekends. You look exhausted." She took his calloused hands in her soft ones and rubbed his palms.

"I'm fine," he said. "A little tired, that's all."

"Something's bothering you, Kurt. You can't hide anything from me," she said. "Did you fight with Hilda?"

"It was a tiring trip, that's all." His pack slipped from his shoulder and hit the floor with a thud. "Hilda's depressed again. She's pushing me to.... She won't visit her father, but she always worries about him. She feels guilty about leaving him, not going back, afraid she doesn't know him and he doesn't know her, everything—as if she could do anything about it. She's still a victim of the damned war."

"Victim …?" She considered then pressed. "Look, her only problem is that you haven't married her yet. As soon as you do that ... when will you?"

He ran his fingers through his hair. "I don't know. Maybe soon, but I really don't want to talk about that now. Do you have anything to eat?"

"Men!" she said. "You only think about food." She stepped into her small kitchenette and he followed. She opened the icebox. "Looks like only apples, cheese, and wine. I'd like to go out for dinner anyway, if you're up for it."

She handed him a bottle of sauterne and a corkscrew. He knew what to do with it while she rinsed and sliced the apples and cheese into wedges. She arranged dishes and a sugar bowl on the small table like a stage set. He popped the cork and poured two large glasses half-full.

"*Prost.*" She raised her glass.

Kurt touched his glass to hers. "Your career!"

Ilse sipped her wine, and spoke over the rim of the glass. "You haven't even noticed." She barely nodded in the direction of her sitting room, adjoining the dining-kitchen area.

Kurt followed her with his eyes, scanning the sparsely furnished apartment. He brushed over the same familiar furniture until his eyes settled on a movie marquee poster, framed and hung above the fireplace, seeming a bit out of place. She confirmed with a smile and he moved closer to the bizarre artwork.

The poster was from Marlene Dietrich's first movie, *Der Blaue Engel*, filmed in Berlin. "Nice," he said. Then he noticed the inscription in English. *To Ilse, with my best wishes—Marlene.* "It's signed. How is that possible?"

"She signed it for me." Ilse beamed. "Our theatre group was invited to a private party after filming *Judgment at Nuremberg.* You were invited too, but you were gone as usual. I found the poster in the museum shop and she signed it for me. I was so nervous I could hardly ask her."

"You like her, don't you?"

"I adore what she's done—she's my idol. Dietrich is the best! I visit her birthplace every year on her birthday. I'll take you sometime. It's a short walk from here to Leberstrasse. It's beautiful there at Christmas time."

"You don't have anything else to do at Christmas, do you?" He teased.

"Damn you!"

Ilse, a German Jew, was a surviving victim of Hitler's purge—her parents snatched from Berlin and interned at Dachau, she with them as a small child. Ilse was only five when she was taken from her mother's arms to play with the camp warden's daughter. This had saved her life but she never recovered from it—her parents and part of herself lost in that sinister place.

She had been too young to comprehend all that was happening then, but sensed it was terrible. Doom, gloom, and desperation occupied the dismal camp, even penetrating the warden's warm cottage. She never forgot those last words of her mother, whispered in her ear as the cattle car screeched to a halt. "Ilse, dear," her mother held her close, whispering. "I want you to do whatever you must. This is your mother speaking, Ilse—do anything to live, even if you don't like it. You must live for all of us. Please trust me. Promise me that!"

The promise made no sense then, but her mother's words imprinted her on a primal level. She promised to survive and this promise guided her through her ordeal, but she was never freed of it. While she sang, danced, and pretended to be someone else in the camp, she escaped reality. She made herself so important to the warden's family that they kept her until the camp was finally liberated by George Patton's troops.

Ilse never saw her parents again but she never forgot her mother's burning eyes, or her admonishment—Survive! She bore that burden as atonement for living.

Kurt's voice came from far away. "You don't look like Dietrich." The sound veiled at first, then again. "I said, 'you don't look like Dietrich!' Where were you just now?"

She realized she was in her apartment in Schöneberg, not that other place. Dark hair curled above her forehead and she nervously twisted one curl around a finger—a child with captivating brown eyes, not the tall, svelte, sensuous actress like Dietrich.

Kurt had once told her, "You're like a prowling tiger—stalking your prey." She liked having that kind of control, that much power in reserve, but never used it. She did move with feline gracefulness, a purpose with every move and completely controlled—beautiful yet dangerous.

Kurt didn't understand her absentee spells, just worked around them. Before he realized her mind wandered, he would stop talking, but that was awkward. Realizing these occasional mental journeys, he repeated himself until she caught up—a small accommodation for a friend.

"You look better than Dietrich." He finished the thought, testing whether she was finally with him again.

"Watch out," she said, signaling she was ready. "You have Hilda, and if you hurt her, I'll track you down and claw your heart out." She showed her nails.

"You couldn't hurt a mouse," he laughed.

"When will you bring Hilda back to Berlin?" she asked. "She can stay with me. No, you can both stay here and I'll stay with a friend. I'll fill the room with all her favorite flowers."

"But ....?" Kurt puzzled. "... You don't have a friend, unless ...."

Her face showed how much his implication hurt. "No, but I will." She insisted, pouted. "Maybe I've just been looking in the wrong places. You can help me find someone tonight."

"Fat chance," he said. "But, fair warning—he'll have to meet with my approval."

"Of course," she said. "Kurt, you're the only family I have left...."

Kurt saw she had drifted again. He sensed the place was a dark one, and she had been there more often in recent weeks. He hoped she wouldn't cry this time. He didn't want another woman weeping over her lost father. Not tonight.

8

Ku'damm

Berlin's main aorta of *Kurfürstendamm* pulsed through the heart of West Berlin, pumping life through the heart of the city. The party district was giddy until early morning. Like the *Champs-Elysees* in Paris, or Bourbon Street in New Orleans, the promenade was ideal for studying characters.

Ilse held Kurt's hand as they strolled along Ku'damm. "This will be good for us," she had told him. "I promise. You've been depressed about Hilda and I need something. God only knows what I need." Humidity oozed from the air after a late afternoon shower. They skirted small puddles between the cobblestones as they walked.

"I know very well what you need," Kurt said.

"Don't get into that," she warned. "When I find him, we'll both know."

She wore a light print dress and her heels elevated her to his height. She insisted he bring his suit jacket to wear with his gray slacks. She had even trimmed his hair in her apartment before they left. "It'll cool off later. Besides, you look great in that jacket. Why don't you ever wear it?"

He slung it over his shoulder. "Too warm."

"Don't forget," she said. "Tonight we're American tourists. We'll work on our dialect. We both need practice."

She slipped into a different role as effortlessly as she changed shoes. "I live in the round," as she had previously explained her excursions. "I blend with my environment and it becomes real. I can be anyone I want, and you could too."

Now she told him, "You really should be an actor, Kurt. You're too good to be a stagehand."

"*Ich bin glücklich*," he said in German. "I'm happy with my life as it is."

"Whatever did you say?" she mocked. "I only understand English. Just for tonight, Kurt—do it for me, please. We're American tourists."

They took a table on the sidewalk before a small café and sat amidst the stream of foot traffic, the ebb and flow of passers-by. People swirled around them like water circling two stones in a stream. She studied them as they passed—their moves, speech and personalities. Kurt defended the table, daring anyone to get too close. He watched her studying people as if this were a floorshow. He wondered about her past, her flights of fantasy she openly discussed … and

39

secrets she locked away. He remembered the top-secret papers in his shoe, and the other secrets of his life he wouldn't confide to her.

Venturing out with Ilse the actress was always an experience. She used every sweep of her hand, turn of her neck, every move for a purpose. She seemed completely under control, everything she did to create an impression. She sat on the edge of her chair at the bistro; but she might have been on stage at the *Berliner Ensemble*. Actually, she didn't really need Kurt's coaching, just his encouragement. But she desperately needed something more and Kurt knew it was more than he had to offer.

She realized he was watching her and lifted her wine glass, touched it with her lips seductively. He looked away. Hilda was already suspicious of this remarkable actress and it was easy to see why. Her casual way said nothing else mattered; he knew it did. She lived as if her real life meant nothing, but he knew something was due her—what?

Since Kurt had introduced her to the theater and agreed to coach her, she learned quickly, actually taught him—it came to her as natural as breathing—costumes, setting scenes, lighting, props, mastering a line and delivering. She never stopped working on perfection, insisted he change his appearance and mannerisms to help her rehearse on the sidewalks in impromptu situations—improvising.

He sometimes wondered if she was rehearsing for the stage, or for life. Ilse had opened new worlds to him, like fine wine, art museums, even the damned moving pictures. He'd never wasted time on triviality before Ilse, yet she reveled in movies, came alive in them, and memorized the scripts.

As set director at the theater, he used his carpentry skills to construct props and sets. But she graced his sets and gave them meaning. She taught him makeup and disguises which he used in ways she never imagined. He used them so well his *Stasi* handler had code-named him the Chameleon.

A waiter approached, inquiring about menu selections. Kurt started to lead but Ilse interrupted in English before he spoke in German.

"We'll have *Wienerscnitzel*," she said with a southern American drawl—then silenced them both with her smile.

The waiter shrugged and walked away, scribbling a note in his pad.

"Where did you learn that accent?" Kurt whispered.

"At the movies, of course."

"It's so easy for you. How do you do it?"

"You know how," she said; "practice, practice, practice! Why don't you give up carpentry and act? It's more fun than working."

Kurt disapproved of the meal but complemented the chef anyway. He intentionally tipped too little as an American tourist would. The waiter snarled as they walked away.

"You're really getting into this," she said, patting his arm.

They ambled along Ku'Damm, window-shopping. On "American night," she watched for Americans to draw into conversations. "It's the only way to master it," she told him. "Try it. What do you have to lose?"

She touched his arm and stopped walking, whispered, "See the man talking with the others at the bus stop, the one in the blue shirt? He's an American pretending to be German—that's odd! Let's go over and see if he talks to us."

"Are you crazy?"

"Yes! Come on, it's fun. We'll play this by ear."

Ilse edged closer to the man, stalking him until within striking distance. She brashly touched his arm.

"Pardon me, please," she said. "Do you speak English?"

9

At First Sight

Vic Werner turned to face the prettiest woman he had seen all night, perhaps ever. He regained his bearing and replied in a Texas twang. "Yes Ma'am—how may I help you?" His eyes danced over her dress then slashed at Kurt, cutting him out of the picture.

"We seem to be lost," she said. "I was hoping you could help. We're looking for the Brandenburg Gate. Do you know how to get there?"

"Sure thing," he said. "You could take the next bus ... or ... I could even show you myself."

"Oh, that's so nice," she said. "But we don't want to cause you any inconvenience."

"No problem, really; I'm just killing time anyway."

"Are you a soldier?"

"Well ... yes. How'd you know?"

"You're so athletic and clean cut. You have that military posture, so straight and everything. You project! Has anyone ever told you that before?"

"Not like that," he said. "Uh ... I'm Captain Vic Werner, at your service. And, where are you from?" He extended his hand.

She offered hers palm down at first, but corrected and grasped his hand firmly in both hers and pumped. "I'm Jane Jones from Biloxi, Mississippi. This is my friend Jack. We're sight-seeing."

Kurt offered his hand, forcing a smile. "Glad to meet you Vic. I'm Jack Smith." He tried to duplicate Ilse's dialect, not quite right.

"You have an accent, Jack," said Vic. "German."

"My father was German, Schmidt—changed it to Smith when he got to Mississippi."

"That's interesting," said Vic. "Are you ready to head for Brandenburg now?"

"Oh!" she said. "My feet are killing me in these heels. We've already walked so far. Could we just sit with one of those German beers? We can go to that old gate another time."

"Sure thing," said Vic. "Are you going on to the gate alone, Jack?" It was plain what he hoped the answer would be.

"No. I'll just stay here, too." Kurt said. *Where is she taking this charade?*

Ilse and Vic talked continuously for an hour in a noisy *bierstube*. Her natural relaxed rhythm enchanted Vic. Meanwhile, Kurt frowned over a Pilsner. He wanted her to find a serious German businessman, not an American soldier. Kurt looked around the *bierstube*, wary, checking to see who might spot him.

Ilse talked about Mississippi with a familiarity that surprised Kurt and captivated Vic. To Kurt, Mississippi was more foreign than Moscow. Vic clung to her every word and memorized her every move. For Ilse, this encounter had begun as an English lesson but had progressed to something else.

Finally, Kurt yawned and checked his watch. He'd had enough. "Midnight!"

"He has jetlag," she said. "I suppose we must go."

"How long will you be in Berlin?" Vic asked, laying a hand on hers.

Kurt interrupted, "Nice to meet you, Vic." He took her other hand and led her away.

Kurt clinched her hand as they left, lest she turn back. She did look back over her shoulder and saw Vic was still standing there with his hands deep in his pockets, watching them go. She smiled and waved her free hand.

They walked on a few steps before she chastised him. "Why'd you do that, damn it? That was mean!"

"I don't need an American friend right now; that's all."

"Well, you were supposed to help me meet someone tonight. That's what friends are for. You promised."

"I'm sorry. I thought you were just teasing with him."

"I was, at first, but I ... I think I really like him," she said. "Vic ... Vic Werner. I wonder if it's short for Victor? That's German."

For Kurt, it had become too complicated for games. The papers in his shoe pressed against his sole. "Forgive me?"

"Of course I *forgive* you." She squeezed his hand. "I always do. You're all I have, but I'm still upset." They walked in silence for another block.

"Kurt ...?"

"...What?"

"Do you think there's something wrong with me?"

"Don't be ridiculous, Ilse. You'll find a handsome German. You're much too beautiful not to have a man in your life."

"How was my acting tonight? I want a review."

"No one's better than you," he said. "You're a natural. I've never known anyone who could invent a story on the spot the way you do. You could write screenplays."

"Really?"

"Absolutely."

"I'm on my way, you know?" she said. "I'm just as good as Dietrich. I only need the right opportunity. I know I'll get it somehow."

"I believe you will," he said. "You can do anything you set your mind to. Hey, I heard the American producer Billy Wilder is in town with James Cagney to make a comedy."

"Really?"

"Yeah, they're staying at the Kempinski. If you go over there, you might meet Cagney and get his autograph."

"I don't care about him, but Billy Wilder might be a good contact. He used to date Dietrich, you know?"

"No, I didn't know that."

They walked on in silence. Kurt was waiting for her to formulate her plans to ambush the producer but he sensed she wasn't even thinking about that, but something entirely different.

"Kurt?"

"Yes?"

She continued another long block before getting it out. He didn't push because by now he knew what was coming. When she finally spoke again, she whispered. "Would you sleep on my sofa tonight?"

"Bad dreams?"

"I don't want to talk about it. But would you?"

"Of course."

Vic wandered aimlessly up and down Ku'damm for an hour after she left. He had lost interest in the Russians. He walked fast then slow, and then finally stopped back at the *bierstube* where they had talked. *I think I need another* *drink.* The same table they had used was open, so he took it and ordered a nightcap. *Maybe then I can forget her.*

The waiter who had served them before approached his table. "Where's the *fraulein*?" he asked. "Did the German take her home?"

"Germans?"

"Of course," he said. "They're both German. You didn't know? They fooled even me at first. But I put it all together. Were you deceived by their silly game?"

Vic sucked in a deep breath and let it out through his teeth. "Not really," he said. "I knew it was too good to be true. Women like that don't just walk into my life."

Next Day

From the bedroom of Ilse's flat, a light slipped under the door. "Hurry!" She called to Kurt, who stepped from the bathroom with a towel around his waist. "We'll miss the beginning." She had insisted on a matinee at the Aladdin Theatre in the Soviet zone of East Berlin, still playing *Under Paris Skies* for the sixth and final week. She had seen it five times already and had memorized all the lines, but she wanted to see it just once more before it closed.

"Can't we just stay in tonight?" he pleaded. "We were out late last night and I have important business early tomorrow."

"Oh, Kurt!" she said. "You know I want to go. You don't have to pretend anything tonight, just be yourself."

"Thanks for that anyway."

"But hurry ..." The phone interrupted and she grabbed it. "Hello?"

Kurt watched her listening and smiling while he buttoned a clean shirt and stuffed it into his trousers. "*Vielen Dank.* Thank you. Thank you very much. I'll certainly be there." She hung up.

"Good news?"

"I got it!" She threw her arms up in the air. "I have the job at the Hilton." She flew across the room and hugged him. When she stood back, she said, "It's on a trial basis, though. I sing on Monday night and if the customer response is good enough, I'll get a contract."

"Wonderful." He said. "I'm very proud of you."

"Can't you stay just one more night?"

"Hum! ... I can't miss your second début," he said. "I'll stay and vote for you."

"It's not an election, silly. Customer response is measured by the bar tabs."

"That's what I meant."

They walked slowly in the heat to the movie theater. "I thought you were in a hurry," he said.

"Not any more," she shrugged. "I have other things to think about now."

They missed the beginning of the movie, but she hardly watched; her mind elsewhere. They left early as she was anxious to go somewhere and talk. They had dinner at the West Berlin Hilton, where Romano Tessoni's strings entertained on the roof terrace. She would sing in that very hotel on Monday evening and she was excited, wanted a preview.

Her happiness contrasted sharply with the scene in nearby Marienfeld. Hundreds of church and civic volunteers struggled to feed and care for two thousand new eastern refugees who swamped the facilities. The numbers had grown so fast and so large the U.S. Army had finally supplied C-rations to feed them all.

10

The Old Man

An old man hobbled from his small flat on *Kantstrasse* in the factory district of East Berlin. He lowered his head and refused to look at an East German policeman even when he spoke to him. It was late, or early, and he was in a hurry, but his gait was slow and pained. He grimaced each time his wooden leg met the pavement. Despite his difficulty, he hurried along on uneven cobblestones.

Karl Heinz Meyer knew he was late because the bell of the Dom chimed twelve times in the distance, signaling midnight. He was late again but the caretaker of the ancient church could walk no faster. The Priest's morning prayers began at five a.m., first worshipers by seven. He needed to dust the sanctuary, clean the floors, light hallway candles—his movements steady but always slower than others. His work kept the bomb-damaged church running and the old man was fortunate to have work at all in the depressed side of the city.

Dark and irregular pavement makes his walk more difficult. Hinges of his false knee sang haunting notes from years past, pain of each step a call for vengeance.

A Russian soldier had shot him in the leg at Stalingrad. A German medic applied a tourniquet to stop the bleeding but his leg was frostbitten in the snow. Unable to walk, he was left to die and captured by the Russians. A Russian field surgeon sawed off his leg with a hacksaw—no anesthesia—sending him into shock. He finished the war in a *gulag* in Siberia but the cold never left his bones.

Furrows of his brow deepened at the sight of a Soviet soldier talking with another East German policeman. "My people sold out to those butchers," he muttered under his breath, then spit in the gutter. "Vermin!"

He trudged along with his gray head down to watch his footing when the roar of heavy cleated tires bore down from behind. He stepped aside, tripped, but caught his balance against a building. Two military trucks plied past at reckless speeds. *Politzei* sat on rear benches of the first truck, rifles between their legs. The second truck was overloaded with concrete slabs, heavily weighted and leaning to one side, nearly losing its load. "What's the rush?" He hurled the allegation at them, not a question, his voice lost in the roar of more trucks peeling off in several directions.

He trudged a few more halting steps but stopped at the clamor of angry words spewing near Stetlin Station, a juncture of the *U-bahn* underground and *S-bahn* streetcars, a vital transportation hub where transit rails crossed from East to West.

Bam, bam. Two shots. "Russians!" He spit again and changed directions from the church to the trouble. God's work could wait.

The voices grew louder and more contentious as he neared. A man in a factory uniform rushed from the station, jogging towards him.

When he was close, the old man called out, "What is it?"

"They stopped the streetcars. Made us get off." He kept running, breathing heavily.

"Who?"

"Polizei!"

"Why?"

"Don't know. My wife works over there. I was to meet her."

"Where are you going now?"

"Find another way," the man shouted over his shoulder as he kept running.

The old man heard loudspeakers. He rounded a corner—blinded by spotlights and a line of policemen extending across the street. An army squad dragged barriers from trucks and strung barbed wire, blocking the street. Another squad pried up sections of streetcar tracks with long crowbars.

A man in the gathering crowd shook his fist. "Swine!"

"You can't do this," shouted another. The policemen and soldiers ignored them, continuing their disruptive work.

The crowd became rowdy and moved to a white line painted on the pavement delineating the Soviet occupation zone. The line, previously an administrative marker, now became something more sinister as police closed ranks to prevent crossing it. Several people darted around the barricade on one side. A police sergeant fired three warning shots.

"Halt!"

The throng panicked and scrambled for cover. A hearty few made last desperate sprints over the painted line and stood defiantly on the other side.

A college student with prior military service picked up one of the spent cartridges and examined the crinkled end. "They're using blanks!" he shouted. He held the cartridge high. "They're only blanks."

With that news, the pack surged. Policemen grabbed several and shoved them to the ground, but they resisted handcuffs. The mob gained the advantage of numbers and nearly overpowered the police. Just in time, a platoon of East German soldiers armed with assault rifles, double-timed to reinforce the police and soldiers armed only with shovels and crowbars. The old man spotted another platoon of Soviet troops concealed between dark buildings, eager to escalate with greater violence.

In the fracas aimed to stop crossovers, a police lieutenant was knocked backwards and fell against the old man. His hinged wooden leg buckled at the knee, and both sprawled together on the hard pavement. The young officer sprang to his feet snarling.

"Load live ammunition!"

The mob quickly quieted, the only sound heavy magazines snapped into *Kalashnikovs*. The old man felt about for his cane stand. He quickly found it—and something else.

The old man scooped up the officer's 9mm Lugar and concealed it under his belt, covering it with his shirt. The harmless old man leaned on his cane, stood, and limped away. The crowd had grown quieter and began to scatter. He mingled with others drifting away and chattering.

"What do they think they're doing?"

"They know exactly what they're doing—the bastards."

"They're locking us up, that's what. We've just been slammed in prison."

Chilling memories clawed at Karl Meyer in the warm August pre-dawn. He revisited frozen plains on the outskirts of Stalingrad strewn with frozen bodies in grotesque poses. His missing leg ached and he felt the Russian saw against bone. He had wanted to die then but he kept a promise to his beloved Inga to come home. "Inga!" Her name rasped in his dry throat.

He reached under his shirt and touched her framed picture. Then he wrapped his fingers around the automatic pistol. That was real and it was his. "I'll kill them!" He veered for the Soviet soldiers, but only stabbed them with hatred in his eyes.

He hobbled past, stumbling to his obligation with the old church. He owed the church everything he had for the little he had left.

11

Jack Hammers

The Heildeberger Krug served last call for East and West Berlin on Saturday nights. The *bierstube* stood conveniently in the American zone where it intersected with the Soviet zone at the crossing of Heidelberger and Elsenstrasse. East Germans could cross the painted line, grab a drink with their friends in the west and catch the last train back home in the east.

Vic Werner leaned on the bar and sipped a lukewarm beer. He chatted in German with anyone at the bar, listening for valuable information to solve the riddle posed by Colonel Powell—what are the Soviets up to? Strangers became friends the moment they walked into a Berlin *bierstube*. A middle-aged man entered and shouldered his way through. He wore a white shirt with sleeves rolled above his elbows and his tie hung loosely around his neck.

"Bartender, *eine grosse bier, bitte*!" He ordered a large draft to end what appeared to have been a hard day.

"Getting started late?" Vic asked in German.

"*Ja*, I was on a project in Rostock and just got through. Something's happening."

"What?"

"Troops are forming in Marx-Engels Platz and thirty Soviet T-34 tanks are parked on Wilhelmstrasse."

"*Nein!*"

"*Ja!* It took hours to get through the congestion. Trucks with troops and construction material are all over the roads."

"Excuse me." Vic headed for the door. "I have to go."

"Don't rush off," the stranger called. "You'll miss all the excitement!"

Vic opened the door to see fifteen brown-uniformed border policemen unrolling concertina wire in front of them. A restless crowd had already assembled. He needed to report this to Colonel Powell, but he couldn't tear himself away from the unfolding spectacle.

After a moment he looked for a taxi, but an earthquake stopped him—jackhammers ripping up pavement. A cargo truck backed up, concrete posts extending from the tailgate. Vic stood mesmerized until his drinking companion from the bar met him on the sidewalk. The German raised his large beer stein and shouted over the noise. "Just wait till the Americans come, you bastards. They'll kick your asses out of here!"

Vic had seen enough and ran to where his imported Mustang was parked then raced to Potsdam. Airman Reitz already had the Chevy running after its miraculous restoration by American and local-contract mechanics. Reitz waited behind the wheel for the passenger he knew would come. Vic jumped in and told Reitz to circle the periphery of the city so he could brief Powell at home at 16 Spechtstrasse in West Berlin.

What they found in Potsdam was even more alarming. Tenth Guards' tanks surrounded the outskirts of West Berlin with turrets pointed at the city, live ammunition visible on exterior racks. Berlin had been ruptured through the center and completely surrounded.

"Goddamn, sir!" said Reitz. "World War III just started, and we're right in the middle of it."

"Might be," said Vic. "But we're stuck here for now."

They sat stranded while convoys of tanks, troops, and supplies saturated Highway 10 into Berlin. Then they waited while cleaning crews cleared mud from the highway behind the tanks. When the highway was finally opened, they raced back to the Potsdam headquarters and Vic phoned Colonel Powell. He knew already—he was watching the show from his bedroom window.

12
Locked up in East Berlin

Earlier that fateful day, the leading spymaster in Europe had been at work in his headquarters in East Berlin. He rustled the pages of one newspaper after another and frowned at headlines bearing only bad news. *Refugees pour into Marienfeld!* The newspapers were from Western European capitals, forbidden fruit in the East.

Mischa Fox had long avoided having his picture appear in any newspaper, but more importantly he had kept it from Western intelligence dossiers. He was known as "the man with no face." Fox was the master of intrusive intelligence and effectively countered most Western intelligence collections—virtually unknown yet his presence loomed over Europe.

Fox was director of intelligence for East Germany's Ministry of State Security—the *Staatssicherheitsdienst,* commonly known as *Stasi.* He was also a major general in the Soviet Army. Fox's boss was Erich Meilke, who hadn't been seen all week. Fox suspected he was involved in a secret mission and the spymaster didn't like not knowing; that made him more irritable than usual.

"Newspapers are raw intelligence," he said frequently, defending his access to them. He poured over the *International Herald Tribune, Bild-Zeitung, Die Welt, The Times of London,* and *Le Monde.* They only confirmed what he already knew. Refugees poured from East Germany and the Soviet sector of Berlin in alarming numbers. He also knew why—better economic opportunities. In one day, nearly two thousand new refugees arrived at the Marienfeld refugee center, two hundred more than the previous day—new records. Fox's eyes fell to the chart below one article. The numbers of refugees skyrocketed straight up. East Germany's leaders were already anxious but this was a call to action.

Fox knew the worst of it was that the smartest, youngest, and best workers were leaving. In another chart on his desk he compared the birth rate to departures. While birth rates were up, population growth was headed down. Both figures must be reversed, and not by manipulating statistics. Fox knew this better than anyone. Survival of East Germany was at stake.

Fox was a complex man—clean-cut, slim, and athletic. His job provided the perfect cover for his many peccadilloes with women of every nationality, drawn to him for many reasons. His innate magnetism attracted people to his side, but he remained an enigma. His Jewish father had fled Hitler's Germany for Russia just before the outbreak of war and those facts alone predetermined Fox's directions. Yet his dual heritage complicated his struggles with his own consciousness.

He was surprisingly young for his position. A Major General in the Soviet Army at thirty-eight, had led the East German intelligence directorate for eight years already. His organization ran a network of three thousand clandestine agents outside East Germany in addition to those inside. He strived every day to increase the number.

Fox knew precisely how the refugee exodus threatened their future and that had to be stopped. However, unrestricted access to the West yielded a lucrative flow of intelligence as his agents crossed back and forth freely with refugees. Forty thousand *grenzgangers,* or cross-border workers, lived in East Berlin and worked in the west.

Major Heinrich Ebert, Fox's executive officer, interrupted his reading. "*Herr* General, you are scheduled to have lunch with the department heads tomorrow. Will you still meet them?"

"*Ja, natürlich.*" Fox dropped the newspapers and picked up a stack of official documents he had read overnight. "Ebert, I'm bothered by these agent reports. I've found nothing from Abel Herreck for the past two weeks. Have you heard from him?"

"Yes, *Herr* Fox. Abel reported that Chameleon has gone to Hanover for something. They'll meet next week and he'll report to you when he has some news."

"*Ah, Gut.*" He breathed in deeply and let it out slowly, looking askance at Ebert. "Have you read the newspapers today, Major?"

"*Ja.* The *Telegraf.*" East Berlin's local paper was dominated by communist propaganda.

"You should read these." He thumped the stack on the corner of his desk. "A good intelligence officer must always consider his enemy's point of view. How else can you understand them?"

"Those are filled with lies, General. I don't like them."

"Don't be naïve! They are not all lies and we use propaganda even better than they do. I ran the disinformation program before this—you know that. Besides, our job is to discern truth from lies and half-truths. I trust you don't believe everything you read in the *Telegraf?*

"Not everything."

"Are you following the disputes between Khrushchev and Kennedy?"

Ebert drew erect under Fox's examination. "I'm aware of their mutual dislike, General."

53

"Study the subtleties, Ebert. If you understand the trouble between those men, you'll understand the plight of the world. The tension is strained between them—a rubber band that could break—one irrational move could lead to war and ... and if there's war, Berlin is in the middle of it."

"I'll be more attentive, sir."

Fox sighed, doubtful, and reached for his suit jacket. "I'm leaving early tonight—taking Emmi to dinner and the opera. It's *La Boheme*. Do you know that one?"

"That's Italian, isn't it? Will they sing in German?"

"*Mein Gott!* I hope not, Ebert." He pushed his arms through his jacket sleeves while Ebert held the shoulders. "But, the best music in this one is at the very beginning. After that, I'll take a long intermission."

He reached for a second pack of Marlboros and caught Ebert's disapproving sneer. He held the American cigarettes long enough to thump one out against the heel of his hand before dropping one pack into his shirt pocket and another in his coat. The loose cigarette dangled from his lower lip and it danced there as he spoke.

"Have my car brought around, Ebert."

Fox adjusted his tie, patted his suit jacket over the leather holster and the special chrome-plated H&K 9mm automatic under his arm. The pistol was a gift upon his departure from Moscow years before, a treasured war souvenir. Hat in hand he trudged to the car where his driver waited with the engine running in the covered underground entrance. A sign on the front of the building announced it publicly as The Institute for Economic Scientific Research.

An enjoyable evening with Emmi was long overdue. He had been pressed for time recently as a crisis atmosphere enveloped the city and brought with it overtime and weekends of questions with immediate deadlines. He had chastised his superiors: "You just don't understand the hard work of intelligence gathering," he lectured them. "Important information doesn't just fall into our laps. I don't find answers in a crystal ball. I have to hire people to steal it or buy it!"

His father, Friedrich Fox, had been a notable German author before the war, and like his father, he appreciated Germany's rich culture—music, art, drama, sports, and nature. Fox the Jew had escaped Hitler's Germany with his family, seeking asylum from the purges in Mother Russia. His father eventually rejected Judaism completely, rejected all organized religion, but in its place he embraced Communism with a fervor.

Mischa was educated in the finest schools in Moscow and it was there he met his wife.

Emmi was also a German-Russian. She had used her language skills in the psychological warfare group during the war, and was wounded using her bullhorn on the western front persuading Germans to surrender. Fox had always loved Emmi, but that was irrelevant to his philandering. He trained his agents to use sex as a cold war weapon and set the example. He considered it his duty.

The car pulled away and Fox angled his hat lower, blocking his profile from any prying eyes or camera lenses. He followed the blurred panorama of the city as it slid past his window. His car turned from *Normanenstrasse* toward his apartment in northern Berlin and he watched the movement of people--walking, riding bicycles, streetcars, and a few old automobiles heading in the opposite direction.

His driver braked for a trolley in their path while passengers boarded. The clanging bell hurried them off and on like cattle. While they waited, Fox watched a line of restless women queued at an open market for a dwindling supply of groceries. He rolled his window down for fresh air and heard the ranting of one of the shabby women.

"They put Sputnik into space but we can't even find a green vegetable in the summer. That's socialism for you!" She shook her balled fist at his luxurious limousine.

That was not what he wanted to hear yet he knew it was true. He rolled the window up again, mumbling. "Socialism could work, old woman. We just need better leaders."

His driver turned. "Pardon, *Herr* Fox," he asked. "Did you speak to me?"

"*Entsculdingsen sie*—Never mind. I'm only talking to myself. Keep driving."

13

Wake up Call

Mischa Fox thoroughly enjoyed his night out at the opera and having dinner with Emmi in an exclusive restaurant. He had neglected his family too much. Back in their small apartment he paid the sitter and tucked their daughter, Andrea, into bed before slipping between the sheets with Emmi. He pressed against her bare skin. They hadn't made love in months and when they connected he wondered why not. He knew he was solely responsible that they had become so remote, their relationship so ordinary after such steamy passion ignited during the war. He wondered if they could ever reclaim such intensity.

He fell asleep at one a.m. only to be awakened by the strident ringing of the telephone bell on his bed stand. He reached groggily for the receiver, fumbled it on the table and knocked it with a clatter to the floor before he finally recovered it.

"Hel...um...." He cleared his throat. "Hello."

"Why didn't you warn me?" The voice that fired at him from the other end of the line took a cruel shot in his direction.

"Who is this?" Fox demanded.

"It's Abel. Why didn't you warn me to expect this?"

Fox cleared mental cobwebs—had he missed something? "I'm sorry, I dropped the phone. Please start from the beginning."

"Do you know what is happening right under your nose?"

"Yes ... no. What?"

"They shut all the crossings. How could you not know?"

"Impossible!"

"I'm standing at Brandenburg Gate at this moment. It's closed I tell you—closed like an iron fist. Listen." Abel held the phone outside the phone booth. Sounds of jackhammers, angry shouts, and occasional shots could be heard clearly over the receiver. Fox detected similar noises from his open window.

"*Mein Gott!* This can't be."

"Turn on your radio, General. East Berlin stations—they're still playing music in the west. They don't even know what just happened—or can't believe it."

Fox dropped the receiver into the cradle. Now wide-awake, saw Emmi up as well, covering her exposure with a housecoat.

She switched on a bedside light. "What is it?"

"They've shut all the crossings. The city is sealed." He pulled his trousers on. "Make tea, Emmi. I have to call someone." She left the room, searching for the sleeve of her robe.

"...and turn the radio on," he called as she disappeared.

Emmi rattled dishes in the kitchen and lit the gas stove. The impassioned voice of a German radio announcer spieled a didactic recitation, instructing people to remain inside. Fox lifted the phone and dialed a number.

Elrich Meilke's wife answered on the first ring.

"Where is he?" Fox asked.

"He's out ... overseeing the operation."

"I need to talk to him. Where can I find him?"

"He'll be out all night, but he can be reached at headquarters."

"Thank you." Fox depressed the cradle button to redial but his phone rang before he could get a dial tone.

"Fox!" He shouted, annoyed.

"Mischa, this is Nikoli--I need your assessment." Soviet Major General Nikoli Rubski was frequently in touch with Fox by phone on orders of Khrushchev. He was Fox's contact in the Russian KGB and a direct link to Khrushchev himself. The call was from Moscow.

"How can I possibly give you an assessment? I wasn't even informed until this very minute."

"Sorry. Security was extremely tight. But I must know how the west will respond."

"My agents are cut off. I don't even know where they are. I can't reach them."

"I don't want second-hand reports or a formal appraisal. I need to know how Kennedy will react—your opinion."

"How the hell should I know what that crazy man will do?" Fox was shouting by the end of the sentence.

"Calm down, Mischa. No one knows the Americans better than you. I need your estimate, your best guess ... right now, this very minute. I must call him back in two minutes."

"Him?"

"Yes. You know who."

Fox contemplated the question in silence. After a minute passed, Rubski asked. "Fox, are you still there? Khrushchev wants your opinion. He listens to you. What shall I tell him?"

"Tell him the West won't do anything." His voice was calm and deliberate.

"They'll do absolutely nothing but sit on their fat asses like the fools they are and watch you build your damned wall. Just like I'm doing—like big dumb sheep."

14

After a Movie

After the movie, Ilse avoided sleeping as long as possible by keeping Kurt talking. But when he fell asleep on the sofa as she described the script for the new play to open at *Berliner Ensemble*, she gave up. She found her bedroom and stretched out on her bed with her eyes opened. She knew when she closed her eyes she was vulnerable to her nightmare. She had almost drifted off when voices outside her open window brought her back. She listened quietly until she caught disturbing bits of conversation. Urgency in their tone compelled her to awaken Kurt.

He was hazy when he sat up, squinting his eyes against the table light. "What is it?" he mumbled. "Did you have another...?"

"There's trouble. Come to my window." He followed her in his under-shorts and she gathered her nightgown tighter.

He caught some comments about the police, the border, and something about wire, so he shouted down to the people milling about. "What happened?"

They all looked up. "They closed the crossings," one shouted up.

"*Grepos*--the border police?"

"Yes, and the military."

He pulled back and walked to the living room to find his trousers. She switched on the overhead light.

"What does it mean?"

"They said something about the border being closed. I'm going to take a look."

"Don't go tonight," she pleaded. "Just wait here with me. It's temporary; it'll all be over in the morning."

"I must see for myself."

"There'll be trouble!" She scrunched her shoulders and crossed her arms. "Kurt ... I thought I heard shots."

"I won't get involved. I'm already a day late for a meeting over there and I need to see my father, and Hilda's father. I must know the situation tonight, or leave right away."

"When will you come back?"

"An hour or two—go back to sleep."

"I can't sleep—you know that. I'm going with you."

"No. Just wait here. Make coffee. I'll tell you about it when I return. We'll have a good laugh."

"Hell no! This is stuff for movies. I'm not staying here." She raced for her clothes and in her haste removed her nightgown in front of him. He looked away.

Kurt knew resisting her was pointless. "This is against my wishes, but come on ... hurry!"

She wiggled into slacks and buttoned a blouse, stuffed her feet into boots without bothering with socks and pulled on a New York Yankees baseball cap. She flashed a Texas-sized smile. "Let's ride, cowboy."

They walked briskly at first but as the commotion near Brandenburg Gate grew louder they started to jog. A stream of taxis raced away, each filled with people who had planned to ride trains or streetcars but were stranded. At Brandenburg Gate, brown-uniformed policemen unrolled barbed wire while jackhammers split the pavement. They mingled with the restless crowd.

A woman nearby broke and ran to the wire, read a paper tag hanging from the coils. She snatched it off, looked closer then she waved it over her head. "The communist bastards are using English wire. They bought wire from England to imprison us. What good is NATO?"

People shouted back and forth across the barbed wire, relaying urgent messages to friends and family on opposite sides. One man leaped from a second floor window of his apartment all the way over the wire. He collapsed when he struck the sidewalk, but got up in time to catch a woman following him. They hugged hurriedly and rushed into obscurity, taking nothing but the clothes they wore.

The mob grew increasingly disgruntled and fights erupted on both sides of the wire. Filthy insults were directed at police. When emotions were about to explode, a truck hauling a water pump appeared east of the barrier. Firemen rapidly uncoiled long, heavy hoses to disperse the unruly crowds. Before the water was switched on, Kurt grabbed Ilse's hand and pulled her away.

"No." She yanked her hand free. "I don't want to miss this. Let's watch."

"No! We're going now!" He was unyielding, remembering the documents stuffed in the bottom of his boot. "This shouldn't happen, not this way. This is all wrong; we'll defeat this monster ... just not tonight."

60

15

Warnings Missed

Colonel Powell secretly admired the brazenness of the Soviets but was furious about their success—mad at himself for not anticipating it. He was fuming in his office when Vic walked in early. "Goddamned Russians," Powell grumbled. He slapped a bulging file of telexes on his desktop. "Never trust them."

"Colonel, what's does this mean?" Vic dragged a chair in front of Powell's massive 19th century desk, looking for the senior officer's take.

"The Easties are solving their refugee problem and the Ruskies are using them to piss on us."

"Us? You, mean the United States?"

"Damn right! Khrushchev is sticking it up Kennedy's ass again—just like he did at that Vienna summit."

"Hum." Vic overfilled a mug of coffee and spilled some. He plopped a *European Stars and Stripes* over the spill to soak it up. "Want some more coffee, Colonel?"

"Try to keep it in the cup, would you?" Powell pushed his cup over and the message file out of the spreading path of spilled coffee. "Worse—we had plenty of warnings and missed them."

"Yeah?"

"Shit, we knew something was up, we even talked about it. They broadcasted it and we ignored it."

"Broadcast...?"

"Koniev's the muscleman—he came here to intimidate us! I knew he spelled trouble and so did you. But the clearest signs were the refugees. They had to stop them. I knew that, you knew it—hell, everyone knew it. Their economy was in the crapper—they had to survive. Kill or be killed. Then ... then there were Ulbricht's trips to Moscow, secret meetings with his buddy Khrushchev. Hell, everybody knew about those, too. Ulbricht wouldn't go to the john without checking with Khrushchev. That told us everything we needed to know, right there."

Powell sipped his coffee but burned his lip. "Damn it!" He wiped the dribble from his chin with the back of his hand.

He continued, "Finally, Ulbricht let the cat out of the bag at that press conference last June when he said 'no one was considering building a wall.' Hell, nobody even asked about a damned wall, he just threw it out there like a rotten fish and nobody noticed how bad it smelled. It stunk then and it stinks now. We're idiots for not stopping this before it got this far."

"What can we do, Colonel?"

"Keep tracking the Soviet army ... we have to know if they're hankering to fight. And, we have to ensure our occupation rights aren't violated. We have equal status with the damned Soviets and we can't give an inch on that. We owe nothing to the fucking East Germans. So we'll keep pretending the Soviets are our friends while they plan to wipe us out. Fuck them and the East Germans. Fuck them all!"

"They'll test us."

"I know that, damn it! They already are."

Powell raised his voice, shaking coffee from his cup. "We have to be tougher than them. If we aren't, they'll drive their tanks over us like rabbits—road-kill on the autobahn to Normandy!"

16

Fox, Abel, and the Chameleon

Fox paced the floor at *Stasi* Headquarters, a habit that had worn tracks into Persian carpets overlaying hardwood floors. A Marlboro dangled from his lips. All day he had interviewed his spy-managers about difficulties getting around the new barriers. He would present his findings to his boss, Minister of State Security Erich Meilke, although he knew it would change nothing—the damage was done. They must find ways to work operations around it. He blew smoke rings and watched them float away, then swiped to erase his game when the door opened.

Major Ebert announced, "Abel Herreck is here, *Herr* Fox."

"Show him in."

Fox moved to meet him and offered a hand to the gaunt apparition coming through his doorway. "Abel. How are you?"

Abel ignored Fox's extended hand and limped inside leaning on a well-burnished cane with a golden eagle's head as a grip.

"I don't like this," Abel began, his voice raspy. The sound came from the skeletal face—a man like the living dead. "It complicates matters."

"I agree, of course." Fox lit another Marlboro and offered one to Able, who reached for it. Seeing the brand, he disapproved and shook one of his own from a crumpled pack.

"I'm assessing this. I must know where our agents are now and when we last heard from them. I also want to hear your plans to operate under new sanctions. I'll brief Meilke tomorrow."

"All right," Abel grumbled.

Fox led him to a conference table covered by a map of Germany, east and west. "The names of your main agents, where they are, and how you contact them." He pushed a pad of paper and a pen toward the older man.

Abel laid his cane over the table and wrote Top Secret at the top of the paper, then listed the name of each agent, explaining the details of each one. "...And then there is a new one, Hilda Brunner." He scrawled her name on the last page under the heading of Bonn, just beneath the name of Hans Globke.

Wolf drew a circle around Hilda's name. "I don't know this one," he said. "Tell me about her."

"She's a clerk in the Chancellor's office."

"Does she work with Hans?"

"No. Neither is aware of the other. She is not on our payroll but I am only aware of her through other sources."

"Tell me about this Hilda Brunner."

"She's an attractive single woman living in Bonn. She's about thirty or so and well positioned to see classified material in the Chancellery. Sometimes she finds something interesting and sends copies."

"How?"

"Her boyfriend is the courier, another independent agent I use when he cooperates."

"He's not one of ours either?" asked Fox.

"No, not on our regular payroll." said Abel. "But he's an East German and has provided useful information, sometimes from Frau Brunner."

"Why haven't you recruited him?"

"I've tried," said Abel. "He wants his independence. He accepts only projects that suit him, his high-flouting morality. And Hilda Brunner works only with him. He won't complete a written application, neither one will."

"Is he hiding something?"

"Yes," said Able. "But no one can hide much. I know his background."

"Are these two involved ... romantically?"

"Yes, of course. They came together several months ago," he said. "They're lovers and they will only work together. He speaks of German unity and she is of the same mind. Their motives are idealistic and totally unrealistic, but I could not refuse their offer to help."

"Who is the man?"

"His name is Kurt Meyer. He's originally from Halle but he has no known address. He visits his father in East Berlin. He has another girl friend in West Berlin—a double life. He's a freelancer, pays no taxes on either side, has no public records. He works at the Berliner Ensemble, the theater."

"He's an artist then, like my father?"

"He's a stage hand, a carpenter. He builds sets with a hammer and nails, paints and decorates them, something like that. He's more a craftsman than an artist."

"Continue."

"He poses as a carpenter going into the west, a *grenzganger,* a weekly crosser."

"So, Kurt Meyer is a carpenter like the Jew of Nazareth," said Fox, "yet a spy. And his job gives him freedom to travel at will. He has no address, hangs around with artists but is a blue-collar worker, has a lover in Bonn he refuses to be separated from yet he has another in West Berlin. This man is strange. Why do you trust him?"

"He's different from most, sometimes reckless yet extremely cautious at the same time," said Abel. "He served in the Navy during the war, a navigator on one of our U-boats. He has a sterling war record but refused to join the party. He was captured by the Americans and escaped. I don't like him … but I trust his information."

"Where is he?"

"I lost track of him on Sunday. He went to Hilda Brunner and I expected to meet him last night. He didn't show. He must have been cut off by...."

Fox interrupted. "Do you know what he has?"

"Documents from Bonn, I imagine," said Abel. "But I don't know the contents."

"I assume he has official papers to get through the checkpoint?"

"No," said Abel, the creases in his face deepening. "He only had *grenzganger* papers. He refused anything more. He rejected special documents, but he'll need them now."

Fox stubbed out his cigarette and lit another. "The west is very enticing," he said through the smoke. "Why would he return at all?"

Abel glared at the pack of Marlboros on the table. "He'll come. I know his type. He's an idealist and a capitalist and a fool. He talks about high principles while stealing secrets. His kind believes the righteous will inherit the earth, religion is more than myth, and everything will have a happy ending. He ascribes to all that drivel. I met many like him during the war. But the reason I know he'll come is that his family is here. That is his biggest weakness."

"Ah, family," said Fox, rubbing his hands together. "That's good. I believe you're more cynical than ever Abel."

"Cynical? *Herr* General, I'm merely a realist."

"Are we paying him for this work?" asked Fox, "or does he do it on high principle?"

"Oh, yes, we pay," said Abel. "We pay handsomely, our highest commission for each delivery. He may be a fool, but he's still a capitalist."

"*Ost* Marks or rubles?"

"Neither," he said. "I told you he's confounding. He demands *Deutsch* Marks. Insists he needs them for his contacts in the west and I suppose that's right because he pays Brunner out of his own cut. He controls her efforts and pays her as well, so in a way we are getting two for the price of one."

"Cash?"

"No. A Swiss bank account."

"Shit!" exclaimed Fox. "You'll never see him again."

"I hope you're wrong, *Herr* Fox. He knows too much—names, places, what information we have. If he doesn't come back, I'll have to send someone...."

"Never mind that!" Fox cut him off. He crushed out the cigarette in an overflowing ashtray. "I have a specialist for such business if it becomes necessary. Give him a few more days. If he doesn't turn up this week, I'll send a professional to clean up the mess."

17

"I'll Kill Them"

The old man, Karl Meyer, balanced on a rocky chair near the only window of his first floor apartment in the East Berlin factory district. Darkness blanketed the city but no lights were on inside his *Kantstrasse* apartment, the only illumination coming from dim streetlamps that cast eerie shadows around the room.

He tuned his small radio between classical music on East German stations or American-based RIAS news reports, preferring that to the standard propaganda. He kept the volume low, one ear near the speaker and an eye on the street. If anyone approached, he switched the radio off.

He still seethed over what he had witnessed from the window an hour before. Factory workers in the sweatshop across the street had walked off the job, protesting long hours, low pay, and unreasonable production goals. Police met them on the sidewalk with clubs and beat them back inside, all but one. They finally hauled the leader away in an ambulance—no urgency in response, no sirens, no lights, and the medics tossed his body inside without a gurney.

Karl had seen plenty of dead men in the war, and this was war. They hosed the blood from the sidewalk, erasing the evidence.

He saw his daughter walking briskly along the same sidewalk and waved to her from the window. She stepped around the dark stain, seemed to see something in it. He noticed how she walked with resolve, just like her mother. He remembered his wife Inga saying, "I know where I'm going so don't get in my way." Ingrid walked the same way.

The small kitchenette contained one sink, which served for shaving, food preparation, and washing dishes or clothes. A kerosene burner perched on the countertop, water already warming for Ingrid to use. His detached wooden leg leaned against the wall, so he balanced on a homemade crutch and hopped to the door, unlatched it with his free hand and waited for her spark light into the dreary room.

Most tenants in the building worked in the factory across the street and shared a common bathroom at the end of the hall, their families crowded into single rooms. His Spartan furnishings included a Murphy bed that pulled down from the wall and a small table handmade by Kurt from scraps he had uncovered in the ruins.

His radio rested on the table near a vase of dead flowers and a single picture frame—no other pictures in the room. The table was unsteady so a match cover was wedged beneath the shorter leg. Kurt had promised to cap it. Two sturdy handmade chairs, also from scraps, flanked the table and an oil heater waited patiently for winter.

The Dom's Priests arranged the state-owned apartment, rent slipped to the proper official by revenue from monastery wine. He also received a small stipend for food from the same source. He was too proud to accept money from Ingrid or Kurt. He leaned against the door jam on one leg, waiting for her.

"Hello, father." She kissed his stubbly cheek as she slipped past him. "Why don't you wear your leg?" She switched on an overhead light.

"Hurts," he groused. "Damn Russian contraption tortures me every day of my life."

"You keep it too dark in here." She took the wilted flowers from her last visit out of the vase and replaced them with a freshly-cut bouquet. She moved the picture of her mother to make room for the fresh flowers then scooped up the fallen leaves and petals in one hand before adding water to the vase.

Karl watched her scurry about doing wifely chores—Inga would do this if she were alive. Her hands were in constant motion, not rushed but no effort wasted until she had finished. He studied the photograph—how much alike they were.

A shrill whistle broke his spell. "Water's boiling," he said. "Would you make tea?"

"Of course," she said. "And I brought some pork. I'll put it on the burner. You aren't eating well. Are you having any vegetables?"

"There's no decent food in this God-forsaken city."

"Well, I brought some from the commissary. They have plenty there." She dropped a sweet potato on the counter and cut it in quarters. Ingrid worked as a file clerk on avenue *Unter den Linden*—the wide street under the linden trees. She controlled documents, keeping a record of every file leaving the file room and verifying signatures when they were returned. It was a good job that paid well and gave her access to better groceries than the average East Berliner, access to many things.

She hung once-used tea bags in mismatched cups and poured steaming water over them, then dropped small strips of pork into a sizzling frying pan, lowered the flame and crossed the room with their teacups. She tested the table for steadiness, nudging it with her thigh, before setting the cups down. Karl bent to adjust the match cover under the shorter leg.

"Kurt will fix it." He sipped his tea, looking at her familiar face. "Why did they do it?"

"Close the city?"

"*Ja.*" He said. "Why did the filthy Russians do that?" his voice rising in anger.

"Shh!" She closed the window and drew the curtains over them despite the heat. "Ulbricht did it," she whispered. "He had his own reasons."

"He couldn't do anything without Khrushchev's approval." He spit in his hand after saying the name.

"It was the refugees, mostly ... and he wants to force the Americans out. Both, I think. But he didn't consult me about it, Papa."

"But, what about the families?" he lamented. "This splits families on both sides."

"They don't care about families," she said. "They never have."

He sipped his tea while she starred at him.

"Papa, have you heard from Kurt?"

"No."

She nodded west. "Is he still over there?"

"Yes. He's overdue."

"Well, he can come whenever he wants. He's a *grenzganger,* " she said. "He can come back, but then he can never leave again."

"He had an assignment," he said. "He won't just walk though like nothing happened, not now."

"Oh, my God!" Her hand covered her mouth. "He has something with him?"

"Yes. I think so. He went to see Hilda."

"Are they expecting him?"

"Yes."

"Then he must come. They'll find him. They can be very ... you know ... convincing."

"I know. And these are our own people," he said, slowly shaking his head. "But, he'll know what to do." He sounded resolute, but then he blinked.

"Everything is different now, more dangerous," she said. She wrung her hands in her lap out of his sight, but he noticed and looked away. "What if we have another war?"

"We're in one, child," he said. "It never ended, not even after Germany was ruined and trampled. We're doormats for the Russians. When the shooting begins I'll kill some of them."

His last words were more a growl than a statement. She stifled a laugh. "Ha! What will you do, Papa? Beat them with your cane?"

His clinched teeth were not laughing. "They killed my Inga—your mother." His tone was chilling. "They took my leg." He reached into his pocket and pulled out the Lugar and dropped it on the table between them.

"No!" Her hands covered her mouth again, eyes wide. "Where did you get that? What have you done?"

"Someone lost it. I found it."

"Get rid of it! If they catch you...."

"I'm an old cripple, Ingrid. I can't do much but I can do something, like you and Kurt. I want the bastards out of my life. I'll kill them."

18

Dietrich Redux

During the day Kurt had hiked twenty kilometers along the barbed wire fence, guarded on the east and scorned in the west, searching vainly for a crease to slip through. He even met some who had dashed over during the confusion of the initial moments, but security was tightened with each passing hour. By night it would be nearly impossible to cross without unacceptable risk of being detected, shot, or captured.

Watchtowers, spotlights and heavy weapons sprouted at intervals and some streets were split along the centerline. Windows along those streets were filled with bricks and mortar. Strips of land were declared "no man's land" and were manned with bunkers, machineguns, and dogs. Kurt grew more discouraged with each step.

Daylight faded and shadows crossed his path back to Ilse's apartment. He wished a bath would wash away his frustrations along with his sweat—no such luck. He had promised to hear Ilse sing at the Hilton and he couldn't let her down again. He was already past due with Abel so another night couldn't matter.

Kurt was late for Ilse's singing debut. When he entered the crowded bar she was already on stage. He had thought he knew her but he was unprepared for what he saw in the spotlight. She swayed sensuously behind the microphone, singing *Falling in Love Again.* Most of the men in the bar appeared to have fallen in love, too. She was ever beautiful but the man's tie, fedora, and shorts made her alluring, erotic, and a little dangerous. She *was* Marlene Dietrich.

You could hear a pin drop—even the bartender stopped washing glasses and watched. When her song ended, the vacuum of silence exploded with applause. Kurt clapped with his hands high so she could see him, and he blew her a kiss. She smiled and mouthed, "Thank you."

For those few moments the small crowd had escaped the ugly travesty of the wall, returning to 1930. Her songs had released them from their newly imposed bondage and they yearned for better times.

Kurt slipped onto an empty stool and watched her in the mirror over the bar as she began her final number. *Lili Marlene* had been Hitler's favorite and he wondered why she chose that one. They loved it, though many had lost family because of Hitler. Kurt ordered a lager and wondered how much longer he had to live and if he would ever see Hilda again.

The show ended and she threw kisses around before vanishing backstage. She washed the makeup, changed into slacks and a silk blouse, and draped a light sweater around her shoulders.

Kurt, still pondering his impasse, was unaware of her presence until she whispered, "Buy a girl a drink?" Others nearby were still talking about her, but failed to recognize her after her makeover.

He bumped her chin softly with a knuckle and signaled the bartender, who brought a glass of wine. Kurt reached for his wallet but the bartender held up his hand. "Her drinks are on the house."

"Looks like you have a job," said Kurt. "Your premiere was a smash."

"You realize it's only a mirage, don't you? That was just a glimpse of something somewhere else in time."

"Yeah, I guess," he said, "a look back into the past."

"No," she said, "the future. I must get to Hollywood somehow. How can I?"

"You're already a star," he said. "Just keep doing what you do so well."

"Well...." She mulled over her wine and asked, "Did you find what you were looking for?"

He frowned. "No. I don't know what to do."

"Come on." She took his hand and pulled him from his stool. "I want you to meet someone."

He swallowed the last of his beer and followed her around the bar, through the kitchen, and to the housekeeping area and a door marked: Hotel Staff Only. Behind that door uniformed employees washed and ironed the hotel's linen and stored them on shelves for later use.

Ilse waved to one young maid who smiled back. She stood on a box behind an ironing board almost as tall as she was. She looked tired, but brightened for Ilse.

Kurt pulled open a heavy delivery door and they followed him out onto the loading dock. He shook a pack of unfiltered Camels and offered them one. Ilse ignored it, smoking was hard on her voice, but the child maid accepted.

He offered her a light but instead she slipped the cigarette into her skirt pocket to barter later.

Ilse made the introductions. "Ursula, this is my good friend Kurt. This is my new friend, Ursula."

He flipped his lighter, lit up and nodded to her.

"Ursula has worked here for a year," Ilse said. "She lived in the Soviet zone until today."

He inhaled deeply. "Today—you crossed today?" he asked, the importance of the diminutive girl increasing.

She nodded. "I crawled most of the way," she said, "through a vegetable garden. *Herr* Eichmann gave me a room here until I find a place to live. They were happy for me ... getting away and all."

Kurt considered that. "Could you show me where you got through?"

"Yes," she said. "I get off in an hour."

"I'll meet you here then," he said, "in an hour."

"We'll meet you," Ilse corrected.

19

Barbed Wire

Kurt and Ilse were waiting at the Hilton's loading dock when Ursula punched off. The young girl carried an easy confidence when they started out but as they approached the barbed wire she hung back. Ilse took her trembling hand.

"All's fine, Ursula," she whispered. "You're safe with us." She placed an arm about her shoulders. "We're friends, aren't we?"

Ursula barely nodded.

"Don't you trust me?" Ilse asked again.

"Yes. I trust you."

Kurt walked several steps ahead but slowed then stopped near the place Ursula had described. A clock gonged in the dark, signaling the first hour after midnight, one full day spent under the shadow of the menacing fence. Street lamps and lights in free German homes caused the barbed wire to glisten on their side—only darkness stretched beyond. However spotlights threatened to illuminate targets on command anywhere along the fence line. Armed guards with shoot-to-kill orders tramped alongside the sharp wire or stood guard from watchtowers at formerly free crossing points. A hungry German Sheppard barked somewhere in the night.

Kurt led them into the shadows of an arbor. When they caught up, he spoke to Ursula. "Tell me exactly how you did it. Don't leave out any details, please."

Ilse squeezed her hand.

"*Ja wohl,*" she answered. "I came through the wire right over there." She pointed in that direction. Kurt squinted and could see a slight bulge at the bottom of the wire.

"*Erschreckte*—I was scared to death." She shuttered. "I thought I would die there."

He softened his voice. "Don't be afraid," he said. "Start at the very beginning and tell me what you did, in order, every single detail, please."

"*Ja.* I'll try. My mother and I were walking after dinner. It was nearly dark but there was some light left. I was hoping to find a way to get back here, to my job. I had been looking for somewhere to cross all day. I wanted mother to come but she wouldn't leave her home and all her things. I didn't want to lose my job. There are no good ones over there, only the factories and they beat the workers.

Mother stayed with her past, praying for something better, but I ran for my future with all my strength."

Ilse hugged her and as she looked up, a tear trickled from her eye.

Kurt prodded her again. "How did you decide where to start?"

"I was lucky. I saw the vegetable gardens and intended to steal a cabbage for my mother. We found it unguarded. Mother said she would guard the vegetables, not the stupid fence. We laughed about that."

"Go ahead," he urged. Ilse gave him a "Be Patient" look and tapped his shin with her toe.

Ursula crossed her arms and shivered.

"Poor dear!" Ilse slipped off her sweater and wrapped it around young girl, buttoning it at her throat.

Ursula blinked back her tears and continued. "Mother waited on the street while I looked for cabbage—that was my story if I was caught. I didn't think they would shoot me for stealing a cabbage—beat me up maybe. But I still didn't see any guards so I lay flat on the ground and crawled. At the first fence the barbs cut me when I crawled under but I was more careful after that. I was really scared—shook so hard I couldn't move for awhile. I knew mother would wait for me a long time. I wondered what she thought; when she would know I wasn't coming back. We never said goodbye." She smeared her tears with her fingers.

Ilse handed Ursula a silk handkerchief from Paris, monogrammed with her initials—I.B.

"I knew I would never see her again." She choked up, sobbed a bit but worked it out. "That was when I started crying hard. I almost stopped breathing."

"Go ahead," Kurt prodded impatiently.

Ursula took a deep breath and continued. "I crawled over plowed dirt and fell into a deep ditch; it was over my head. Then I smelled cigarettes and I wanted to run home, but I peeped over and saw the smoke coming from a bunker. They had guns but no one was even looking where I was. The soldiers were laughing and talking, telling awful stories about doing things to women. I covered my ears and crawled away. Then I just ran to the second fence and tore my clothes because I hurried. But when I got under it, I was right there." She pointed to the same spot as before.

"I jumped up and ran as fast as I could to these lights. I prayed they wouldn't shoot me in the back. People ran out of these houses to meet me. They were shouting I'd made it. They kissed me and hugged me and I was so happy I cried even more. I had nothing and my clothes were torn. A nice man gave me his streetcar token and some change. I went to the Hilton and *Herr* Eichmann was happy for me and gave me this uniform and a room in the hotel." She took a deep breath. "I'm so worried about my mother."

Ilse brushed a tear from her own cheek. She and Ursula hugged, both missing their mothers.

Kurt intruded. "When did you do all this?"

"Last night. Just before I met *Fraulein* Braun." She pulled up her sleeve, baring the Mercurochrome-covered cuts on her forearms.

"And you came out right there ... under that sign?" *You are approaching the Soviet Sector of the DDR. Beware!*

"Yes."

"Thank you." He handed her a fifty Deutsch Mark note.

"Thank you, sir. Is that all you need to know?"

"Yes," he said. "Welcome to the Federal Republic." Ursula started unbuttoning Ilse's sweater.

"No," she said. "You keep it, and the handkerchief, too."

Kurt studied the wire from afar while they said goodbye. Ursula started away, retracing alone the path they had taken together. At the end of the block, she stopped and looked back.

Ilse called out to her, "I have some work for you at my apartment next week—cleaning. I'll pay you very well. We'll talk Monday when I sing."

They waved and the girl disappeared around the corner.

Kurt asked, "Will you be all right?"

"What do you mean?"

"Will you be all right here alone? I must go now."

"Oh!" She stood on tiptoe and pecked his lips. "You've done so much for me, Kurt. I want to do something for you."

"Dedicate a song to me," he said. "You're successful and that's enough. And you found Ursula for me. You do more for me, Ilse, than you'll ever know."

"I want to meet your family, Kurt," she said. "I don't have anyone, only you."

"I'll work something out," he said. "But, I must get started now. This may take all night."

"Why don't you just use your *grenzganger* papers, like you always have?"

The secret papers in his boot pressed against his sole. "I just can't, Ilse. You ask too many questions."

76

"Are you in trouble, Kurt?" she asked. "I can help if you are."

"You have a great career ahead of you. Don't forget to rehearse."

"You're my coach. I need you to help me. And Hilda needs you more. What if you can't get back out? What then?"

"Go home, Ilse. I'll see you Monday night."

"But, what if...."

"I'm going." He pushed her away. "I'll be fine. When I get back, you can help select a ring for Hilda."

"Kurt...."

"What?"

"Never mind. Just be careful. Please?"

He embraced her suddenly as a West German police patrol passed them on the sidewalk, paying no attention to the apparent lovers. When they were gone, he quickly crossed the street without looking back. He fell to the ground beneath the ominous warning sign, and rolled under it and out of sight.

He carried nothing to slow him down, only his clothes and the three carbon copies in his boot. Still, the barbed wire snagged the back of his shirt and it ripped.

Then he heard another sound and froze. Leather shoes slapped the pavement, running toward him. He rolled several times and crawled away toward the ditch Ursula had mentioned. He heard cloth rip once, then again.

"*Scheisse*! My blouse." He knew the voice too well.

He crawled back to the wire on his hands and knees. He whispered, "Ilse! What are you doing?"

"Coming with you," she whispered, and pulled against the wire until she pulled free. "I tore my best blouse."

"Go back," he said, "before it's too late."

"It's already too late."

"Damn it—this is crazy!"

"I want to meet your family. Maybe I can help you; did you ever think of that?" Her whispers were too loud. "And, I want to do something exciting—like you."

"Shhh!" They froze. Germans were talking nearby. They held quiet and steady as guards were changed twenty meters away in the guard post Ursula had mentioned. He guessed the old guards had been sleeping but the fresh ones would be more alert.

They listened as goose steps marched away. A sergeant called cadence—*"Eins, zwei, drei, vier. Eins, zwei...."*

The replacements talked about soccer and girls until they quieted after an hour. He slid closer. "We'll wait another hour," he whispered.

"But I'm cold."

He remembered how she had given away her sweater and wrapped his arms around her. They shivered together against the damp earth, waiting for the guards to lose interest in nobodies in no-man's land.

20

East meets West

"Ilse!" Kurt shook her.

"Huh?"

"Get ready," he said. "They're snoring."

"I'm freezing."

"Follow me, and keep quiet."

He crawled on his stomach and she followed. Moving was tedious but they took no chances on alerting the guards. After an hour of inching along they crossed a plowed field and dropped into the ditch Ursula had described. It was deep enough to stand erect, deep enough to stop a tank.

They massaged their arms and balanced on unsteady legs until circulation returned. "We'll climb over the top and go under the last fence," he whispered. "Then we'll find the garden. Are you ready?"

"I'm filthy," she said, "but I'm ready."

"We must hurry! It'll be daylight soon."

Kurt locked his fingers into a stirrup. She stepped into it with one foot and he boosted her up and out of the trench. She lay flat at the edge and reached over to help him up. He took her crooked elbow and kicked the toes of his boots into the dirt, climbing up. He reached one hand over the top and was quickly beside her.

Breathing heavily he wiggled on toward the second fence and she followed without commentary. He pushed the bottom strand up and she slid under.

"Damn!" she stopped half way.

"Go." He pushed her.

"Damn it all. Now I tore my slacks ... and my blouse. Double-damn!"

"You'll have holes in your head if you stay here. Move!"

She tore through and raised the wire enough for him to get under with a few snags. He jumped to his feet and grabbed her hand, pulling her forward. They plodded through the softly plowed dirt into the square patches of vegetable gardens Ursula had mentioned.

Kurt dropped among the rows. Ilse fell beside him.

"Rest," he said, breathing hard.

"Where ... are we ... going?" she huffed.

"It's a little late to ask, don't you think?"

"I trusted you," she said. "I always do."

"You're too trusting," he said. "This isn't make-believe. This is real—a war."

She punched him in the chest, hard, with a balled fist. "I know about war, Kurt!" she hissed. "Don't tell *me* about war!"

He considered that a moment but then considered their next move. She edged away, rustling in the garden.

Day was breaking. "Be still," he whispered. "Listen. We'll run across that street and around the corner," he pointed, "over there. Then we'll just walk down the street like we belong here. If the police see us, we run like hell. But if they shoot, we stop. Okay?"

"Shoot?"

He took her hand and they stood and ran across the street, turned the corner, and then slowed to a walk. They raced straight ahead for one block, around another corner, and slowed to a walk. He draped an arm over her shoulders; she circled one about his waist. They looked like all night lovers, just catching their breath.

"Do you know where we are?" she asked.

"We're going to my sister's flat. I know this neighborhood."

She looked disapprovingly at the surroundings. They walked on for several more blocks. Then it happened.

"Halt!"

That command was startling enough—followed by a round chambered. Hob-nailed boots came fast, at least two pair.

She looked for a signal from him, her eyes wide.

"Run!" he said, "into that alley." He shoved to get her started. "Hide," he hissed as she ran into a dead end.

Kurt raised his arms slowly into the air, looking away from her. But he shouted, "Don't go, *Fraulein*. I haven't paid you yet."

Then he grunted as the muzzle of a Kalashnikov rammed hard into his kidneys. He bowed his back away from the sharp pain.

A sandpapered voice demanded, "Papers!" The mention of papers sent a chill up his spine.

"What's the problem?" he asked.

"Violating curfew! Where are your papers?"

Kurt pulled his *grenzganger* work-permit from his hip pocket. He held it out to the policeman in front of him.

"Work permits are revoked. *Grenzgangers* are not authorized any more. I'll keep these. Where have you been?"

"I've been in the park ... with a woman."

"She almost tore your clothes off, a wildcat that one. Where is she?"

"She was afraid and ran away. You saw her run."

"You're under arrest."

"Don't do that ... please," he stammered, thinking fast—improvise! He considered what Ilse would do in this situation. Then said, "I'm ... I'm to go away tomorrow ... to be ... to be a monk."

"A monk?" The policemen laughed. "Ha. You were just with a woman."

"I'm not one yet," he said. "But I needed a last night with a woman. To get it out of my system, you know, just to make sure. Something to remember."

"Ha!" They laughed together. "You won't last a week without your girlfriend. What's her name and address? I'll keep her company while you're away."

"She's not my girlfriend ... she's a whore. I don't know her name."

"Ha! That's hilarious!" This time Kurt laughed with them. "A monk with a whore ... ridiculous!"

"I'm sorry about the curfew, officer ... this was my last night ... you know how it is."

"You're either guilty of something or a complete fool," said the policeman. "But that's the best line I've ever heard. Go on home, but you'll never last as a cleric."

Kurt scurried away before they changed their minds. When he turned the corner, they were laughing about finding a whorehouse when they went off duty, lamenting that the western whores were now off limits.

When it was clear, he ran back to where he had last seen her.

"Ilse?"

She raised her head from a heap of uncollected garbage.

"Are you all right?" he asked.

"Damn you!" She spit.

"I didn't invite you."

Her face was smudged even more than before. She surfaced holding her nose. "Did you just call me a whore?"

"Forget it. Let's go."

They reached Ingrid's apartment at six a.m. as the few working street lamps flickered out. A faint kitchen light glowed from a first-floor apartment. He tapped on the door.

"Who is it?" The voice was muffled behind the door.

"Kurt."

The lock clicked and the door opened wide. "*Mein Gott!* What happened to you?"

He brushed past her. Ilse followed.

"And who is this?" she asked, frowning.

Kurt started to answer, but Ilse interrupted. "I'm Ilse Braun!" She held out a grimy hand, which Ingrid ignored and returned to the kitchen.

Ilse followed her. "I brought something," she said. "Fresh from the garden." Carrots, beans, and onions spilled from her torn blouse onto a counter top.

Ingrid looked them over and slowly shook her head. "You may stay here but I must go to work." To Kurt, she said, "Your clothes are in the closet where you left them." She looked at Ilse. "Perhaps something of mine will fit her, after she cleans up." She slung her purse over her shoulder and left, locking the door behind.

When it closed, Ilse said, "Well ... your sister seems nice, I guess. Where does she work?"

"The Soviet embassy."

Ilse blinked. "Are you insane?"

21

"So this is a Real Family"

When the other tenants on the floor left for work, Kurt and Ilse took turns using the common bath. Ingrid's State job made possible an apartment with a private toilet and sink, but no shower or tub. Ilse used it first and by the time Kurt finished she was asleep on Ingrid's single bed.

Kurt rested on the sofa for an hour, considering the Top Secret documents and passing them to Abel. He rose and went into the bedroom where Ilse was sleeping, dressed quietly, and scribbled a note to her. He folded it and placed it conspicuously on the bedside table. He shut the front door quietly and locked it from the outside with his key. He followed a circuitous route to a lamppost on *Taubenstrasse* where he found the two chalk marks that signaled Abel still waited. He headed in another direction to the old church, formulating a plan.

Kurt by-passed war rubble, entered an alley, and approached a side door of the ancient church—exterior walls pockmarked as collateral damage from World War II bombing runs targeting Hitler's nerve center. Rusty hinges creaked but the heavy door opened to a small vestibule. Another passageway, barely detectable in the dim light of a single candle ensconced in a wall crevice, emptied into a narrow stone stairway with well-worn steps. The temperature fell as he descended and the air was musty. At the bottom the staircase opened on an expansive cellar filled with tall racks of unlabelled wine. In one corner a gigantic oak keg stood empty, formerly a cask for aging beer that now merely gathered dust.

The stone floor shook beneath his feet and he stood still, waiting, as the vibrations increased. Bottles rattled on the shelves until the disturbance faded away. The underground train annoyed the ancient foundation and disturbed the ghosts of centuries buried there. The noise, so deafening in the basement, was inaudible in the sanctuary above two meters of solid masonry. When it passed he continued to the opposite side of the cellar.

The temperature rose again as he left the moldy wine room for drier air near the furnace. He passed through a heavy door in a rock wall where a coal burner warmed the sanctuary in winter, only heating water in the summer. The caretaker's office was between the furnace and wine rooms, one wall warm and the other cool. Karl Meyer worked there most days, keeping separate records of the wine stock, one for the tax inspector and one for the priest, and maintenance records for the outdated boiler. He also cleaned the entire church weekly. A folding cot, where he slept in winter to keep an eye on the cranky furnace, leaned against the wall—no good reason to go home to an empty room anyway.

Kurt pushed the solid oak door; it swung open and he glanced at the ledgers along one wall, empty wine crates against the other. Karl Meyer was hunched behind a small desk nearer the cool wall, figuring in an open ledger.

"*Guten Morgan.*"

The old man looked up. "Kurt!" He grinned and waved his only son inside.

Kurt dragged an empty wine crate beside his father's desk. "Are you all right?" He studied the old man's furrowed face. "Have you been eating?" he said, meaning *have you been drinking?*

"Don't bother about me," he said. "Did you see what they did? That *scheissmaur*—that shit wall?" He examined his son. "Ingrid was worried about you."

"I saw her this morning. I some had trouble coming back."

"Bastards!" Karl slammed his fist on the rickety desktop.

Kurt nodded. "I'm meeting Abel tonight."

"You'll work after this?" His voice cracked. "How can you?"

"I must, a little longer. I'll change the terms."

"Make them give you official papers, Kurt."

"I don't want their papers. I'd lose my freedom. They could control me then."

"Meeting him is dangerous. He'll arrest you."

"That's why I need your help."

"Me? What can I do like this?" He rapped his knuckles against his wooden leg. "Kick him with this?"

"Just watch my back."

"*Ja.* I can do that," he said. "What time and where?"

"The meeting is at ten tonight," said Kurt. "Come to dinner at Ingrid's. Someone wants to meet you." Kurt stood to leave. "Come when you're finished here."

"About seven then."

Kurt moved to leave but stopped at the door. "One more thing," he said. "I need to get back over. If you have any ideas ... never mind." He closed the door and left.

Karl stared at the empty doorway long after Kurt had gone. Then he returned to his notes.

Kurt returned to Ingrid's flat in the afternoon and found Ilse at the small kitchen table sipping hot tea.

"Could I have some of that?" he asked.

She poured boiling water over two second-hand teabags and passed the cup to him. She silently pushed a sugar dish and spoon across the table.

"Did you get some rest?"

"Where have you been?" Her tone was icy. "I don't like being left here alone. I need to shop for new clothes. Ingrid's don't fit; they don't suit me. They're old."

"Shop?" he laughed. "There's nothing to buy here. And I was on business, just like my note said. Didn't you read it?"

"I saw it," she said. "It was vague. What business? Were you making a scene with another actress? What? Were you cheating on Hilda? Where were you, damn it?"

"This is my real home. I went to see the old man. He's coming for dinner tonight ... at seven."

"Your father?"

"Yes."

"Why do you call your father 'the old man?'"

"He is an old man, for Christ's sake."

"The pantry is bare," she said. "Second-hand tea bags? Good that I found some vegetables on the way. What will we eat? Does Ingrid know he's coming?"

"Ingrid brings meat from the commissary" he said. "I'll get bread and cheese from the market."

"We'll need wine, Kurt. I want some now."

"The old man brings wine from the church. It isn't the quality you're accustomed to, but don't complain."

"Communion wine?"

"Well...."

She looked at him as if she were seeing him for the first time. "Kurt?"

"What?"

"You were right ... I shouldn't have come. It was a terrible mistake and I'm sorry."

"It's all right. I wanted you to meet Ingrid and the old man, anyway."

"But, I must go back—right away."

"I'm working on it but it might take a few days. Besides I have to meet someone tonight. It's important."

"Kurt?"

"Huh?"

"Why do you live this way? You could do so much more with your life, but you just go back and forth like you can't decide where you belong. That's not like you—never understood why you do this."

"Ilse, believe me," he said. "The less you know about all this, the better for you."

"Kurt?"

"What, Ilse?"

"Are you a spy? I mean ... don't be mad with me ... I mean the way you live makes no sense, unless you are. Are you?"

"Ilse...."

"Which side are you on, Kurt?"

"Ilse...."

"It doesn't matter, but I want to understand."

"Germany," he said. "I'm on Germany's side."

"East or West Germany?"

"Just Germany. I don't accept east and west." He had long known this conversation would be necessary, but avoided it as long as possible. It was dangerous for both of them for her to know, but now it was out. "You're right, Ilse," he said. "You really shouldn't have come. But now you're here, so ... well ... you've put yourself into the middle of something I wanted to protect you from. We have business tonight, so you'll know anyway, but please understand my entire family is at risk."

"You're the only family I have, Kurt," she said. "Your family is mine, no matter who or what. Even if they don't like me, I want them to accept me."

He saw something in her face that troubled him.

"The Nazis...." she started but changed tact. "You're not one of them, are you?"

"Hell no!" The very question provoked him. "The old man will help me in a meeting with my contact. I'll deliver a document from Hilda. It may get complicated."

"Oh no!" Her hands pressed her cheeks. "Hilda, too? How could you, Kurt? Oh, my God!"

"All but you. I tried to keep you out of it."

"Ingrid?"

"Yes," he said. "She gathers information from the Soviets. That's why she was suspicious of you. She must be careful. The Russians would shoot her."

"Information going to the west?" Dizzy, her hands shook. "Kurt, you're working for both sides? That's insane!"

"Yes," he said. "My country is on both sides of that damnable fence."

"A double spy," she said. "And your father knows this?"

"My father hates the Russians. They killed my mother and he would gladly die to avenge that."

"You've been my best friend—only friend—for two years, Kurt," she got up and tried to walk around but the apartment was too small. She stood in the center of the room and glared, hands on hips. "I feel betrayed. Why didn't you tell me this?"

"It was too complicated."

"It's not that complicated. You have a dangerous job and I could help."

"I don't want your help," he said. "I want you to use all your energy on your career. I only need from you a place to stay in West Berlin."

"That's *all* you want from me? You bastard! I have so much more to give you. What am I to you? Your *hausfrau*? Your *whore*?"

"I don't want you involved!" He clenched his fists above the table.

"You no longer have a choice," she said. "You're my lifeline. You can't shake me off like that."

"Your lifeline? Ilse...."

She snapped her fingers. "This is how you can afford my rent on your carpenter's wages? You're just buying a place to stay. I really am your whore!"

"You're all wrong, Ilse. Don't do this, please."

She moved to the window and opened the curtains. After several minutes of staring onto the street, she said, "This will never work, Kurt. You must choose one side or the other; you can't work for both. You must choose."

"I have," he said. "I chose Germany, a single country without troops wiping their boots all over us."

"If that's your decision, then I'll help you. You can't exclude me, we're family aren't we? You said we were."

The door banged open and they jumped as if they had been shot. Ingrid had kicked it with her foot, arms laden with groceries from the Soviet commissary. Kurt jumped to help her and Ilse rushed to the bedroom to make the bed.

"Thanks for letting us rest here," he said as he gathered some of the parcels.

Ingrid busied herself putting away the groceries. She glanced sideways at him. "You look a little cleaner, at least. Have you two been fighting?"

"Fighting? No."

"Kurt?"

"I know what you're thinking, Ingrid. Please. I've had all the advice I need today."

"It's too dangerous, Kurt. And, you'll have to stay with father, or at the church, or get your own place. They make random checks on us, especially the Germans. And bringing her...." She stopped when she saw Ilse at her bedroom door, leaning on one shoulder, wearing Kurt's clean cotton shirt hanging over her torn slacks.

"I'm sorry we met this way, Ingrid," said Ilse. "Kurt didn't want me to come—I'm here against his will. Your brother is my best friend, my only one. I need a big brother—and a sister, too."

Ingrid softened at her words. "I worry about him, and father, and Hilda. I worry about all of us. That's all I do—I just worry about everything. And now I can worry about you, too."

"The old man is coming over for dinner at seven," said Kurt.

"I guessed as much," she said. "Why else would I bring all this food?"

"Ilse wants to meet the old man," said Kurt. "He's going with me to see Abel tonight."

By seven p.m., vegetables were steaming and pork broiling, filling Ingrid's apartment with delectable aromas. The small table was set for four and the women talked while they worked together. Kurt returned from Emil's bakery with fresh bread and a small block of cheese. A soft rap at the door interrupted them and Ingrid went to it. "Who is it?" she said, her face near the door.

"Me," the old man grunted.

She swung it open, kissed his grizzly cheek and pushed him toward her only cushioned chair. He dropped onto it, laying his cane beside his wooden foot. He glanced at Ilse then away.

She walked to where he sat, dragging a straight chair along side. "I'm Ilse Braun, *Herr* Meyer. I'm the daughter you didn't know you had."

"Did you come from over there?" He sized her up.

"Yes."

"You're a fool then. Everyone with brains is going the other way."

"But you're here," she said. "I wanted to meet all of you, and I want to help Kurt."

"Please don't help him get killed, *Fraulein*." He handed over four bottles of wine from the bag still hanging over his shoulder. "Perhaps you could help by opening one of these."

They ate a simple meal of carrot and onion soup from Ilse's foray in the garden, pork knuckle with Sauerkraut and noodles from the Soviet commissary, dark bread and cheese from Kurt's sojourn, and Karl's fruity monastery wine. The wine loosened their conversation. They spoke about the wall—*das Undoing*—and East Berlin and the *Berliner Ensemble*, which led to her stage career. They were all interested in that and her stories of how she helped Kurt decorate sets, things he never talked about, and especially his role in getting her first part. She entertained them with a monologue from her favorite scene, one that slipped into a song. That led to applause, a toast, and more wine. Within the span of two hours she remembered what a family was, the first time since she was five. Her eyes moistened as she saw their faces, looking back at her.

At nine o'clock, the old man nudged Kurt. "She knows?" They had business to discuss.

"Yes."

"What do you want me to do?" he asked.

"I meet Abel at ten," he said. "Normally, I just give him what I have and leave, but things have changed so I want you to lookout for trouble."

"I'm going, too," said Ilse.

"No!" Kurt shook his head emphatically, "absolutely not! You're not included in this."

A sudden chill replaced the warming mood. Ingrid brought a pot of freshly brewed coffee and arranged cups and saucers. "If you're out late you'll want to be awake."

Karl asked, "Where's the meeting?"

"Café Gazebo, a booth in back."

"That's in plain sight," said Karl.

"That's the safest place."

"Kurt, I don't have eyes in back of my head and I'm slow. You'll need someone else. I can watch the door while she watches your back." He nodded toward Ilse. "Let the girl come. Ingrid can't for obvious reasons."

Kurt massaged his temples, throbbing under a tension headache. "Let me think."

Ilse left for Ingrid's bedroom, leaving them with the strong coffee. They sipped quietly and watched the hand of the clock creep to 9:30. The door to the bedroom opened and standing there was a young man in work boots, a lineman's helmet, and blue coveralls—scratching his crotch. He needed a shave.

"Who...?" Ingrid stammered.

Kurt smiled at the way Ilse had surprised them.

"Okay..." he said. "Both of you leave now, before me," he nodded to Ilse and his father. "Take a booth near the front door. If you spot trouble, make a small disturbance so I can get out, but don't do anything to get arrested, just spill your beer or something." He placed his hand on her shoulder. "If there's trouble, disappear fast. Come back here as soon as you can but don't be followed, Ilse; you don't have papers." Nodding to his father, he said, "You'll have to cover for her too, since you can't run anyway."

Karl found his cane and stood with Ilse.

"Leave now and take the streetcar." Kurt emptied his pockets of change. "Here's something for fares and drinks at the cafe. We don't have much time. I'll leave after you and walk. If you see me outside, pretend you don't."

"Let's go," Karl said, taking her hand.

"I'm ready," she said in a deep voice.

Ingrid smiled and Ilse smiled back. *So this a real family?*

22

Bonn

Hilda loved Kurt's hands on her, all over her. She was in a hot sweat with waves washing over her, wet, knees open, "Now, Kurt, inside me. Make a baby in me." Her thighs closed tightly around ... not him, but her hand and her dream. Her memory of it was so real. Finished, she pulled her gown down and sat up, wrapping her housecoat around herself; face flushed, she headed for the shower. She was embarrassed like a schoolgirl, but her needs were strong. Enough of this, she must go to work. "Maybe I'll find something good for him today; make him proud of me, make him want me more."

Hilda had returned to the Chancellery typing pool in Bonn after meeting with Kurt in Hanover, only to find her desk and electric typewriter waiting and her basket overflowing with new typing assignments. Her healthy glow masked the loneliness deep inside. Colleagues were curious about her weekend and assumed she had spent it with a man but none of them knew about him. She never mentioned him in Bonn—"discretion," he always warned her. She smiled and allowed them to believe whatever they chose, yearning for the time when she could spend every night with him and make real babies together.

She noticed a distinguished gentleman loitering near the typing pool door—out of place there. She knew he was from the uppity offices near the Chancellor's suite. Sometimes she delivered completed typing there but never lingered in the restricted zone. She had seen him there once and remembered him—obviously someone important. He went into Anna Jacoby's office, her supervisor, where they talked. Hilda couldn't overhear them, didn't even try, but she was curious that he seemed less interested in the attractive widow than the typing pool. His eyes darted about sweeping the bay filled with busy workers, then back to Anna, then another sweep.

Hilda dismissed her curiosity, assumed he was waiting for some work to be completed and it might be in her basket. Still, she thought it curious that she had never seen him in the basement before and he was staying a long time. Her typewriter clacked away with amazing speed as she entered the data before her into tables as requested by the author.

Other than the forgotten stranger, the morning passed as usual and she lost herself in her routine, until a particularly interesting document landed before her. She didn't understand all the detailed technical data, but recognized a new weapon under development in the United States, a long-range nuclear missile. This one capable of delivering multiple warheads—she had never heard of one like that. This was an information sheet for the Chancellor, informing him for the first time. She had a scoop, as they said in the Brenda Star comics. *This is complicated data. If I only had a camera!*

Hilda studied the paper as she painstakingly typed, double-checking each page, carefully reading and re-reading, committing to memory as many details as possible. She didn't dare try to slip in a carbon. When she finished typing, she proofed it once more before pinning a Top Secret cover sheet and dropping it into her out-bound box. She scooped up her purse, slipped a narrow stenography pad and pen inside, and rushed for the ladies room, avoiding any distractions along the way.

The bathroom was empty, so she was alone. She selected a corner stall and closed the door, latched it and sat on the lid with the pen and steno pad on her lap. She transcribed as many of the details as she could recall, read it over several times, adding information and filling in blanks each time. When she was satisfied she had reconstructed the information as well as possible from memory, she ripped the papers from the pad leaving telltale scraps of paper in the coils. She folded them flat, lifted her skirt and slid them inside her underwear. She patted her dress, examined herself in the mirror and opened the door to leave.

"Oh!"

The man blocked her exit. He stood there with his hands on his hips like a Prussian guard. The image of the man loitering in the stenographic pool flashed back until they merged. He had been there while she worked, typing that very document now tucked against her private place. He had been watching her!

His hand on her chest shoved her backwards into the lavatory. He pressed her against the full-length mirror. It was hard to breathe. He latched the door with his free hand.

She felt dizzy—no air to aching lungs. "What...what do you want?" she gasped.

He pressed one hand over her mouth, stifling the scream rising in her throat. With the other hand he dumped the contents of her purse into the basin and ruffled through the papers in her steno pad. Tiny shards of paper from the pad dropped on the floor. She pried at his wrist with her fingers but was unable to remove his hand from her mouth. She separated his fingers just enough suck in some air.

He shoved his free hand into her blouse, then her bra. He ran his hand over her skin, her breast, behind her back. She pulled against the one covering her mouth and clawed at the one inside her dress. A button popped off and rolled across the floor, making a wide circle before toppling into a small puddle near a toilet. Finally, he removed his hand from her blouse but not her mouth.

Her eyes stretched wider and she struggled to breathe through the tiny space under her nose. He shoved her head hard against the mirror. She nearly fainted when he lifted her skirt, his fingers finding the elastic band at the top of her panties—snaked inside. Her knees wobbled, strength waned. She could fight no more—stopped struggling and closed her eyes. Her knees bent and she nearly fell. He touched her stomach, pubic hair—a place only Kurt was allowed. She trembled—wanted to throw up. He snatched his hand out, the papers firmly in his grasp. She wanted to die.

Hans Globke held them between his face and hers. "I thought so." He released her mouth and she gasped for air.

"What will ... what will ... you do?" Caught in an act of treason, espionage—life in prison in the Federal Republic.

He ignored her desperation and quickly reviewed her handwritten notes. He nodded his head confirming his suspicions. He leaned close, his face an inch from hers. His breath smelled like peppermint. Giddy! She couldn't believe she had noticed that and almost laughed—this was impossible—could not be happening.

"I've been watching you," he said. His voice firm—not as callous as his actions. "You were blatantly obvious."

"But ... but, what will you do?" Tears glistened on her cheeks, now sallow, color lost to fear.

He ignored her concerns and unashamedly studied her face, her figure, and her fears. When he spoke again he was calm with a hint of compassion. "Compose yourself first, then return to the typing pool and complete your work for today." He shook the papers in her face. "No more of this." He slipped her notes into his coat pocket.

"What will you ... will you do?" Her voice cracked.

"I'm taking these to my office for safekeeping. I'll notify you of my intentions by the end of the day. I must warn you not to leave the building until you hear from me. I'll have you arrested if you try."

She still labored for air, struggled to stay on her feet when he released the hand that held her up. He unlatched the door and said, "Say nothing of this." He opened it and said over his shoulder, "Good day, *Frau* Brunner." He checked her again, running his finger around his lips, a signal of something. Then he closed the door behind him.

She saw in the mirror her smeared lipstick. Moments before—a lifetime before—she was pressed against that glass, struggling to breathe. The pale image that starred back at her now was that of a stranger, someone condemned to wait for the executioner's call. Her makeup was ruined and she used tissue and the contents of her purse to restore her face. She ran the tube around her lips, recalling his signal. Then she rushed to the toilet and threw up. She used a fingernail to lift the small button from the water, rinsed it, and dropped it into her pocket to repair later.

Back at her desk, Hilda's fingers trembled so she couldn't type and her face was ashen through the makeup. Anna, her supervisor, approached her straight away. Hilda reckoned she was about to be fired, or worse—arrested. She thought of Kurt and their dreams destroyed by her stupid mistake.

"Hilda, are you all right?" Anna asked.

"I think so."

"You don't look so well. What's wrong?"

"Sick. I was sick ... I don't know what...."

"Go home, Hilda. We can manage without you today."

"No!" she said. "I want to stay, please. I'll be fine. I prefer to keep working."

"I think you should go."

"I'll stay. *Please?* I took something for my discomfort. I'll be fine in a few minutes."

"Are you having a hard period?"

"Yes. That's it."

"Okay, but don't be so stoic. If you feel ill, just tell me you want to go. It's all right. Really, it is."

She worked on, afraid to do otherwise. The clock had ticked to 4:45 and she had watched every single minute pass. Her shift would end in fifteen minutes and she still hadn't heard from the man—Hans—about his decision. Acid dripped into her stomach, burning the lining until she bent over in an ulcerous ache. She straightened when she saw Anna's concerned look.

At five o'clock sharp, she was slowly clearing her desk when a well-dressed woman from the second floor entered the bay. "*Frau* Brunner?"

"Yes?"

She handed Hilda a sealed envelope with a curt smile and vanished as suddenly as she appeared. Hilda stuffed it into her purse unopened and returned to the restroom where he had confronted her. She ripped it open and read an address and a time—seven p.m. Shaken, she stuffed it into her purse and walked to her nearby flat. She recognized the address—also close but in a more affluent neighborhood. She assumed it was *Herr* Globke's residence. At least she would have time for a drink before she met the persecutor.

23

Hans Globke

Hilda left her apartment for the short walk to meet Hans Globke, unsteady but somewhat fortified by two glasses of sherry. *I wish I could talk to Kurt; he'd know what to do.* She reached a larger, more imposing apartment building, but walked past it. She was too early. The address was more elegant and the uniformed security guard at the front desk guaranteed exclusiveness. At precisely seven p.m. she stepped inside, displaying more confidence than she felt as her heels tapped across the marble tiles. She reported to the uniformed officer. "*Frau* Brunner to see *Herr* Globke; he's expecting me."

The guard thumbed through a visitors log then motioned to the lift. "Penthouse Suite—*Herr* Globke will meet you at the fifth floor and escort you from there." He lifted the house phone before the lift arrived.

The elevator rose to fifth floor and she was alone under a camera's blinking eye. A moment later, Globke opened a door in the center of the hallway and beckoned her to follow, no welcoming words. He led her up one flight of carpeted stairs, unlocked the only door on the floor, and led her inside his penthouse.

The ambiance of the room unfurled in waves. The living room alone was more spacious than her entire apartment. A wood fire crackled in the fireplace despite the warm evening, and polished hardwood floors were adorned with Chinese silk carpets. Exquisite antiques were posted like timeless sentries along every wall beneath ceilings at least fourteen feet high, the tallest she had ever seen outside a museum. Most spectacular of all lay beyond opened double French doors overreaching a dimly lit balcony. Lights along the near bank of the Rhine pointed the direction for the river to wind its way between castled bluffs.

Hilda knew some lived in opulence, but when this man barged into the ladies room she didn't think he was one of those. She guarded her gaping mouth and just stood alone in the center of the large room, unsure what to do next.

"Thank you for coming, *Frau* Brunner."

She hesitated. "I ... I wasn't aware it was optional. I considered running, but I presumed it would be pointless."

"Why so?"

"You caught me and you have the evidence. Is this blackmail? If so, you're out of luck; I haven't much money."

"I only want the truth, *Frau* Brunner ... Oh, I apologize." He appeared to morph into another person. "You must think I'm an ogre. Please, have a seat near the fire. The air from the mountains becomes chilly in the evenings and I enjoy the open doors. If you get cold, I'll close them. Can I offer you a glass of wine? I'm having some."

"I had sherry ... but ... yes," she said. She needed another. "Please."

Globke poured and entered with two crystal glasses half filled with expensive French Bordeaux.

"This will relax you." He offered her the glass, which she gratefully accepted. She sipped and it did help her nerves.

"You've surprised me again, *Herr* Globke."

"I suppose the first time was in the ladies powder room?"

"Yes," she said, "that you didn't arrest me then."

"I apologize for being so rough."

"And now you serve French wine to Germans. Isn't there a law against that?"

"There are many laws, some more serious than others."

"What do you mean?"

"I want to know why you chose to break one, what were you planning, who do you work for. That would be an excellent beginning."

"I don't think I should tell you anything; you could use it against me."

"You have no choice, really. As you pointed out earlier, I have the evidence. I could still have you arrested tonight."

She thought about it and sipped again, buying a moment, calling on more reserves. "I don't know where to begin, really. It's complicated."

"Just start talking and let's see where it leads us."

"Well ... I'm originally from East Germany," she began. "My father is still there. My mother took me to London before the war...."

"I know the biographical data already, *Frau* Brunner. If it's all correct you may skip over that part."

"But it goes to motivation..."

"Motivation?" he said, more interested. "That's what I want to know about. Is it money?"

96

Berlin Connection

"No. I'm paid but it goes to support my father. I don't touch it—don't want that kind of money for myself."

"Ah, a lover then?"

"That's a very personal question. I won't discuss my personal affairs with a stranger—not even you."

"Then I'll accept that as a yes."

"Frankly, I don't care how you accept it."

"Is he a Russian?"

"Never!"

"Who, then?."

"Another German."

"An East German?"

"Just a German. We want to see Germany reunified. I don't want to be punished for the sins of Nazi's any more and I want to see my father and visit my home. I want the Russians to go away, the Americans too, all of them, but especially the Russians."

"Ah, *Frau* Brunner, was that so difficult?" Globke refilled their wine glasses and strolled to the terrace, blending with the panorama. "The Rhine is so beautiful here." He faced her again and raised his glass. "You may be surprised, but there are others who feel the same as you."

"Are you one?"

He edged a couple of steps nearer. "Yes, I am. That could be considered treason, you know, betraying the alliance's secrets to the other side. But, *Frau* Brunner ... may I call you Hilda?"

She nodded, waiting for his next surprise.

"Hilda, there are those who feel the same way on each side. Some are enlightened but others will sell out at any price, so we must be very careful with whom we work. And we must screen what we hand over—we don't want NATO defeated to be replaced by more Soviets. We only want the troops out of Germany. Avoiding another war on German soil is the only aim."

"That's what Kurt says. Will we work together?"

"Not officially," he said. "We aren't even supposed to know about one another, but I suspected you and investigated on my own. I knew if I could discern what you were doing, someone else could. I didn't want you caught, you see."

"So ... you won't turn me in?"

"No. But now that I know about you I must *ensure* you are not caught, because you know about me."

"Will you return my papers?"

"No," he said. "I've already destroyed them. I have a photographic copy of the originals for you."

"A copy ... photographic?"

"You must stop what you were doing. I take no documents myself of course, since I work at a much higher level with concepts and ideas, not tactics and weapons systems. I need to ensure the information you send is not something to inadvertently weaken NATO and cause a war—we want to avoid one. Every few months I meet with a high official from East Germany to discuss broad strategy, not details. Even though, I don't trust him completely."

"I can't do that. I'm not a professional."

"I know, but I can ensure you have the most pertinent papers for your courier. There were some critical errors in your written version that could have created problems. I'll find documents for you and you can pick them up here. We must not ever meet at the office or in public. If you see me, pretend not to know me and I'll do the same. My secretary, who knows nothing of this, will be our go-between to deliver discrete messages when I have something for you—she may believe ours is a liaison of another sort. When is your next delivery?"

"I don't know—we don't work on a schedule. I get what I can, when I can, and he comes when he can. He doesn't want me to take any chances."

"Then he must love you for who you are, not what you can give him."

"I think so. But that fence has changed everything. I gave him something last week and now I don't even know if he's safe. He said he would come to Bonn soon. I have an emergency number in West Berlin, but I never call the east."

"Very good," he said. "When he comes, just leave a coded message for me with the guard downstairs. Just say 'Brandenburg' and I'll understand."

"Brandenburg? The Gate between East and West Berlin?"

"Exactly. Can I interest you in more wine, Hilda? Now that business is out of the way?"

24

Café Gazebo, East Berlin

Kurt entered the Café Gazebo just as a cuckoo sprang from the clock over the bar—ten o'clock sharp. The silly bird pranced next to a snarling boar's head—totally incongruent. Kurt found his seat, the place was nearly deserted.

Among the few customers, a crippled old man faced the entrance nursing a tall *dunkle* beer with a younger man in blue coveralls and a knit cap sipping a light pilsner. A lineman's helmet lay on the table. Kurt took his usual back booth for these meetings with Abel. He watched the entrance, avoiding eye contact with the others—amused by Ilse's disguise, concerned for her safety, and sorry she had gotten involved.

He ordered a lager and pulled his Russian sailor's cap low. The door opened and he glanced in that direction. Abel Herreck stepped through the doorway and spotted him. Abel grinned, displaying teeth darkened from coffee and tobacco between thin lips set in a skull-shaped head. He limped past the table where Karl and Ilse were seated, cane thumping with each step.

Before Abel had entered, Ilse had been talking casually with Karl, nervousness suppressed, completely in character for the scene. But as the breeze from the opened door drifted past, she fell silent—drained of color, terror-struck. Two opposing worlds collided.

As Abel hobbled past them with his gold handled cane, he noticed the old man's rustic walking stick, and glanced at him. His evil eyes swiped over Ilse as she sat petrified. He moved on with his cane tapping an uneven rhythm. When he reached Kurt, he swung his legs under the table and hung his cane from a hat hook at the end of the booth. The golden-eagle handle winked under flickering light from a kerosene lantern.

"Ah, Meyer," he began. "I worried you had taken residence in the west. I've come here every night this week looking for you."

"I had trouble as you might imagine."

"That's unfortunate."

"Unfortunate?" Kurt said, his voice rising. "Are you idiots? Why did they do it?"

"Calm down," said Abel. "I can arrange official documents to make it easier for you to get through."

"I don't want your damned documents."

"They will simplify matters. You've done good work and we want to show our appreciation. The director is interested in you."

"I'll bet he is," Kurt said.

"Yes, it's true," he said. "We were talking about you this week. Did you bring something for me?"

"Yes ... but it's coming with a higher price."

"Higher? We pay you top money already, and in Deutsch Marks no less. What more do you want?"

A commotion near the door alarmed Kurt, already primed for some signal of warning.

Ilse was on her feet, terror on her face. She ran for the ladies room, pressed her hand on the door, realized her near-fatal error and dashed into the men's room.

Kurt wet his dry lips. He listened painfully as she retched behind the paper-thin wall. He glanced toward his father but the old man sat stoically facing away. Kurt braced against rising panic, sipped his lager and concentrated on keeping calm—their lives depended on it.

"Youngster can't hold his beer," Abel chuckled. "What's the world coming to with Germans who can't drink? This generation isn't up to the task. We'll never defeat the Americans with this sorry lot."

Kurt pretended to ignore her, but she was close to blowing cover. If Abel suspected they were with him there would be more trouble than just a sick woman.

"Yeah," Kurt agreed. "I'll bet he's never been laid, either."

Abel nodded, smirked, and returned to business. "All right, what is it you want?"

"I'm giving you something new." Kurt brushed Abel's knee under the table with an envelope. He slipped it into his pocket in one motion.

"I want to talk to the top man," Kurt said. He glanced to the still-closed toilet door. "I want answers."

"I can explain all of it," Abel said.

"I don't want you to explain it!" said Kurt. "I want to hear it from the top, from the one who's so interested in me."

"Well ... when I give him these, I'll raise your concerns."

"Not good enough. I want to see you here tomorrow with details about a meeting ... or you'll never see me again."

"Don't be brash."

"Tomorrow night, same time, no signals. If you're not here, we're finished. And don't forget to make the bank deposit."

Kurt left Abel alone with repeated flushing from the men's toilet. He walked past Karl without looking back.

As he hastened back to Ingrid's flat, he tried to comprehend the terror in Ilse's face.

25

Living Nightmare

Ingrid busied herself while she waited—constant motion around the small apartment, washing dishes, changing sheets, dusting—anything but thinking. She was the worrier. She checked the time, boiled water for tea, and hung fresh teabags over four matching cups. She arranged the table setting, rearranged it, and fidgeted some more. She dashed to meet the first tap at her door.

It was Kurt. "You're upset! What happened?"

"A disaster!" he said. "Ilse got sick." He saw the teacups and asked, "Where's the Schnapps?"

Ingrid pulled a bottle from beneath the kitchen cabinet and set four shot glasses beside the cups. He didn't wait for the others, but poured one and drank it down. Then he refilled his empty glass and left it on the table while he went into the water closet. He came out after two minutes and rejoined her at the table. Another knock at the door startled them but she hurried to open it.

Ilse, still pale and shaken, rushed past her into the bedroom. The old man headed straight to the Schnapps and filled his own glass. He drank his down, poured another and left it on the table beside the one Kurt had left there.

"What happened?" Kurt asked.

Karl lifted his second glass, searching for words in the clear liquid. Not finding them, he swallowed it and asked for tea.

Ingrid poured steaming water over fresh tea bags.

"Why did she get sick?" Kurt tried again. "She looks awful. I've never seen her that bad."

Karl's eyes were cast down, to a place Kurt had never seen. He said, "I know that look."

"Did she say anything?"

"She didn't have to. I've seen it before. Poor girl."

"What?" Kurt asked. "What is it?"

"Is she Jewish?"

"Yes."

He nodded. "She'll tell you when she's ready ... perhaps."

Kurt stood and walked to Ingrid's bedroom, tapped gently on the door and called, "Ilse? Do you need anything?"

"No!" She answered between sobs. "Leave me alone ... please!"

He shrugged and returned to the table where his father and sister spoke only with their eyes. She refilled their glasses, then put the Schnapps bottle under an arm and took a cup of tea in her hand. She went to her bedroom, bumped the door open with her hip and disappeared inside, closing it with her foot. A moment later she went into the water closet and reappeared with a pill bottle and damp cloth.

"What next?" Karl asked Kurt.

"I demanded to meet his boss," he said. "He didn't like it but I didn't back down."

"That's not such a good idea," said Karl. "The director? He's ruthless! His name is Fox—that says everything."

"I'm meeting Abel tomorrow night for specifics on the meeting. If he refuses to meet with me, I'll quit."

"No one quits, Kurt. You know that." He drank his Schnapps, pushed the tea aside and went to the kitchen for the last bottle of wine. "You can't quit the *Stasi*. They'll kidnap you or kill you outright. If you do quit, leave Europe. Even then they'll look for you to kill you."

"No matter ... I have to quit sometime. I must consider Hilda ... we have a plan...."

"Where will you meet him?" Karl asked, emptying his teacup and refilling it with wine.

"Wherever...."

"No!" said Karl. "You must name the place. Make sure he comes alone and above all don't let him see your face."

"Where then?"

"At the church ... at night. I can help you there."

"Okay."

"And be careful about that ugly skeleton. Don't trust him—assume he's a Nazi."

"A Nazi? How is that possible?"

Ingrid returned with her tea cup, Schnapps bottle and pill bottle, all empty. "I think she'll sleep now. I'll use the sofa. You'll have to sleep on the floor, Kurt."

"Perfect."

"Give her some space—she needs time." Ingrid cast a hard look at Kurt. "How could you bring her here?"

"I didn't bring her! She just came, just like tonight. You took her side on that."

"I'm going now," said Karl, standing unsteady. "Do you want me to go with you tomorrow night?"

"No. This must be fast. I'll go alone."

26

Fox's Lair

Fox examined three Top Secret documents Abel delivered from Kurt. "These are good," he said. "The order of battle is old news but the nuclear weapons allocation to the Army Groups is fresh and timely. Now, we must learn their targets. Tell Meyer that, so he can tell the Bruner woman what to look for. But don't tell him Khrushchev wants this. I don't know his sentiments about the Soviets and I don't want him to know how important this is."

"Khrushchev?"

"Yes. This request came directly from Moscow—General Rubski."

"We must handle Meyer carefully."

"What do you mean?"

"He wants a meeting with you."

Fox lit a Marlboro and inhaled, nicotine lighting his eyes. "That can be arranged … in due time."

"Now—he insists on a meeting immediately. He wants details tomorrow night."

"Hum." Fox stood, stretched, and rambled around his wood-paneled office. He thought aloud as he paced and an ash fell on the carpet. He stepped on the spark, putting it out, leaving a small black scar. "He's demanding isn't he? Okay, then. I meet key operatives occasionally, so it's not so unusual. We could profit from this." He lit another cigarette and waved the match out before tossing it toward a trashcan, falling short. "Tell me about him."

"He's a headache," said Abel. "Egotistical, demanding—always trouble. I doubt he's worth all this."

"He shows me something," said Fox. "I like his spunk. He has the nerve to demand a meeting with me. He's smart enough to realize he has something we badly need. Perhaps, he anticipated our needs before we knew them—this information was quite timely," he said, shaking one of the three secret documents. "He has guile to cross the wire without our help." Fox sucked on his Marlboro. "I'm impressed!"

"What are you thinking, General?"

"You'll meet him as he asked. I'll have someone inside ... where is it? The Gazebo?"

"Yes, the Gazebo Café."

"I'll have someone there to discretely capture his picture and tail him. I want to know about this mysterious Chameleon, this Kurt Meyer."

"They must be well concealed. He's in no mood to be trifled with. He's angry about the fence, and by the way—he hates Russians."

"I'm also upset about the fence, as you well know, so I can sympathize. Meilke should have warned me." Fox moved Abel's cane to make room and sat beside him. "Have him come here for the meeting, better yet, bring him yourself in your car. We'll pose for photographs here and we can tape the conversation here. When finished, I'll have writing samples, fingerprints, voiceprints, everything I need to round out our dossier, and he won't even know it. We might need this."

"Okay, when?"

"Friday afternoon. We'll have a small, private ceremony. Formally introduce him. You praise his work to me. I'll present a memento before we have caviar and champagne—make him a hero, one of us. What do you think?"

"Such extravagance for a *grenzganger?*"

"Flattery is cheap. We need him on our regular payroll instead of freewheeling. I can use such a man—a chameleon. We might have to change colors quickly someday."

"I hope he'll agree to this. He can be quite contrary."

"Convince him, Abel." Fox snuffed out his cigarette in an ashtray. "I've read your war record—you can be very convincing."

27

Mayor Brandt, West Berlin

West Berlin Mayor Willy Brandt had been in crisis mode all week. He was especially annoyed by allies' ineffective responses to the partitioning of his city.

"Johnson?" he shouted at his secretary. "Why is Kennedy sending the second fiddle over here? Why doesn't he come himself? Khrushchev spit in his face and he sends the Vice President to answer the challenge?"

"I don't know why," Trudy replied, exasperated. "The Americans are a complete mystery to me."

"We'll just have to make the best of it, Trudy. Find out his itinerary." Brandt walked around his desk barking orders. "Of course, we'll have a ceremony when he arrives, make a pilgrimage to the fence then come here for speeches. I'll host a big party. We'll need plenty of media coverage. And find out if Bonn is involved in any of this."

"*Ja wohl, Herr Bergermeister.* Anything else before I go?"

"What does Johnson eat? Does he have any special diet restrictions? Perhaps he has ulcers?"

"He's from Texas; steak or barbeque, I suppose."

"He'll have to settle for German food for a few days. I'm not killing a cow for a substitute president. Or, maybe we can come up with some fried chicken. Awful—but if he likes it we can do that. Check with his staff. Music—what does he like?"

"Country and western, maybe?"

"Don't keep guessing, Trudy—find out!" Brandt shooed her out, then took her arm to stop her.

"Wait! I heard there was a sensational new singer at the Hilton who looks and sings like Marlene Dietrich, the perfect combination of German and American—a Berlin connection. Book her for Johnson's party."

"Yes, *Herr* Mayor. Anything else?"

"Don't you have enough to do already?"

28

Ingrid's Bedroom

In Ingrid's bedroom, ghosts haunted Ilse's drugged sleep, her worst episode ever. She tossed on sheets soaked in her perspiration, writhed under the spell of a demon visible only to her. Such horrors had appeared frequently at the orphanage in the years following the war but more recently her commitment to the stage and a family connection with Kurt had blocked most of them. Only a few slipped in to ruin her nights when she was unprepared and sometimes brief spells during the day. She had not experienced one so terrible for over three years; on this night sleep was a virtual theater of horrors....

...The air was frigid in the Dachau Concentration Camp in January of 1945, as two small girls played together in the relative safety of the warden's cottage.

The little girl with long, straight brushed blonde hair was not as pretty as her playmate with unruly dark curls. The blonde wore a dress her mother had specially made in a city tailor shop and she sat crossed-legged before the fireplace. The darker girl wore a crude gray smock, a Star of David sewn on front. They were both five years old, sang nursery rhymes and clapped their hands, the dark-haired girl leading and teaching the words to the blonde. China dolls lay scattered over the floor. An older woman, a maid also wearing a six-pointed star, kept an eye on them as she hustled about the room with a long feather duster, brushing powder from all the surfaces.

Frau Hoestler entered wearing a navy blue dress over high-topped, tightly laced house boots. Her hair was also blonde like the girl's, but pulled into a tight bun. She noticed an open window and slammed it shut.

"Keep the windows closed," she admonished the maid. "The soot is especially heavy today. Major Abel will stay here tonight and I want the house spotless."

Frau Hoestler towered over the little girls. "And what are you playing, Heide?"

The blonde answered, "Ilse is teaching me a new song, mother."

"Well, that's nice. Pick up your dolls and take them to your room. Make it sparkling clean. I'll be there to inspect in an hour. You'll both have your dinner in the kitchen tonight. Major Abel will join Captain Hoestler and me for dinner in the dining room, so don't make any noise and go to bed early."

"All right, mother. The major scares me anyway. I don't want to see him—he's a monster!"

"He's a German officer and a hero—wounded in battle. So mind your manners. Go along now."

The girls carried the dolls upstairs, tucking them into a painted doll bed. They cleaned the room, picked up all the toys, and after Frau Hoestler's inspection they went to the kitchen for their dinner. They heard grownups laughing in the dining room. Little Ilse tried not to listen but was unable to avoid hearing unpleasant words when the cook opened the door shuttling dishes. She covered her ears whenever the door was opened.

After dinner, Heide was escorted into the sitting room to say goodnight to her parents while the young Ilse waited in the kitchen. Afterward, the housemaid ushered both girls upstairs to bed. Heide climbed into a soft sleigh bed with fluffy pillows and a cheerfully colored downy comforter. Little Ilse slept on a canvas cot at the foot of the bed under wool blankets without sheets.

"Ilse, do you want one of my pillows?"

"No, thank you. They might punish you for giving it to me."

She heard Heide's breathing grow shallow as she drifted peacefully into a little girl's innocent dreams. She heard her own mother's whisper, "Do whatever you have to do, Ilse." Nightmares came before sleep. She was terrified to close her eyes; she hated the dark. She prayed for the grownups to keep talking downstairs because she knew that when the talking ended, her real nightmare began.

She heard footsteps and soft voices enter the master bedroom further down the hall. The door closed, muffling them. She listened for the uneven sounds of hob-nailed boots on the hardwood floors—clomp, tap-clomp, clomp, tap-clomp; but all was quiet. Then she heard the scuffs of the maid tiptoeing upstairs and terror stabbed at her heart with each footfall. The door opened and a thin beam of light sliced across the floor.

"Come." The maid took her hand, pulling her gently along.

She rose reluctantly out of bed, her mind racing. "It's time to be Olga now—Ugly Olga!"

The maid stopped at the door of the sitting room and gently shoved her in, alone with him. The major sat in a single chair before the fireplace, drinking dark liquid from a crystal glass. He turned his head slightly, showing a boney profile. "Who's there?" he asked over his shoulder.

"Olga," she answered softly.

"Well, come here little Olga." He swung his arm in an arc. "Come sit at my feet. I want to talk with you." He spoke for several minutes, questioning her about her day. Then he said, "Sing to me, little Olga. Sing me a nice song."

She sang a nursery rhyme she had taught Heide while he stroked her cheek with the gold handle of his polished cane. She sang several more lyrics as he caressed her shoulders and stomach with the cold metal symbol. If I keep singing, that's all he'll want. She tried to convince herself of that.

"Toss more coal on the fire, Olga," he instructed. He moved his chair closer to the fireside.

She did as he asked and stoked the fire. The flames grew higher but she kept her back to him, staring into the light, afraid to turn around.

"Here, Olga. Face this way." She slowly obeyed, finding him sitting down again, trousers around his feet. His hairy legs were hideous, his knee malformed and circled by an ugly red scar. "Take off your night gown. The fire keeps the room warm enough. You won't be cold. I want to see you."

She unbuttoned the front of the smock, letting it fall to her feet. She shivered and crossed her arms, standing naked before Major Heinrich Abel.

"Take this oil, Olga." He handed her a bottle of pine-scented lotion. "Pour some on your hands and rub my knee while you sing."

She did as she was told while he rubbed the bare skin of her neck, shoulders, and back with the shiny head of the cane. She kept her eyes fixed on his horrible knee and the angry scars, especially the empty space where the missing kneecap should have been.

She heard the cane fall to the floor with a clatter and he started doing something else, breathing heavily. She didn't know what it was and was afraid to look. She kept her eyes fixed on the horrible leg before her. She concentrated on her lullaby and thought about the baby dolls tucked into their safe beds near Heide.

"Look up, Olga. Do you see this?"

She trembled as she raised her eyes along his leg, above his knees. She shuttered at the sight of the thing, uglier even than the awful knee. He held it in his hand like his cane.

"Rub the oil here, Olga."

She numbed her mind, steeling her nerves for what lay ahead. She poured some of the lotion on her hands and reached out, touched it, eyes closed tight.

"Up and down, Olga. Rub it. Harder. Yes, that's it." She felt the thing throb, heard his breathing increase.

"Now kiss it." He grabbed her head from behind, pushing her mouth down on top if it. Then it exploded, into her mouth, eyes, hair, and face. He gasped. She spit it out.

"Go and get cleaned up now, Olga. Then go to bed. We'll have another talk when I come next month. You can sing for me again."

Grabbing her smock and underwear, she ran from the room as fast as she could. As soon as she reached the tiled kitchen floor, she lost her supper, retching bitterly. She lay shaking beside the ugly mess until the old maid picked her up and sat her in a large tin washtub. The maid poured warm water from the kettle into the cold water. She rubbed soap all over her and washed her hair, then wrapped a towel around her head. She shook quietly in the warm water while the maid cleaned her.

The old woman leaned close to her ear and whispered, "It's all right, Ilse. We do it only to live. God doesn't hold us responsible for when we have no control."

She looked up into the woman's kindly, sad face. "That wasn't Ilse! That was Olga!" she hissed. "I hate Olga! And I hate the major, too. I want to kill him! Will God forgive that?"

"I hate Olga!" she screamed. Her screams woke her. She sat straight up in bed, eyes wide but not seeing. Ingrid hugged her tightly, gently rubbing her back. Kurt stood in the doorway watching.

"Don't worry, Ilse. No one will hurt you here. You're safe. You had a nightmare. Here, take this." Ingrid placed several tablets on her tongue, handing her a glass of water. "Go back to sleep now. You'll feel better tomorrow. I'll leave a candle on the table for light."

Ingrid turned away, pushing Kurt out of the room and closed the door then she cracked it open very slightly. "Shhh!"

29

Claustrophobia

Ilse had sought refuge from her horror with sleeping pills and Schnapps. She had made it through one more night, but when she woke the pounding inside her head reminded her of everything she wanted to forget.

She was deep-down sick as she stumbled into the kitchen at ten a.m. after Ingrid had left for work. Kurt was at the table browsing through a week-old copy of the *Telegraf* and working on a fresh pot of coffee.

"*Guten Morgen,*" his greeting too cheerful under the circumstances. "Feeling better?"

"*Nichts.*" The word stuck to the top of her mouth. "I need something." She reached for his cup but coffee sloshed over her trembling hand. She steadied it with both and raised it carefully it to her lips while Kurt found another cup.

"Where's Ingrid?" Her voice was groggy and untamed hair kinked wildly out of control—still wearing coveralls from the night before.

"She left for work."

Ilse saw a blanket neatly folded on the sofa with a pillow on top. "Did she sleep there?"

"Yes."

"And you?"

"It doesn't matter," he said. "Look, we were fine."

"Oh, God! I've made such a mess."

"Ingrid was worried—we all were."

"She was kind. I wasn't so sure when...."

"Ingrid is always suspicious, but she likes you. She always wanted a sister instead of a brother."

"She loves you, Kurt. You're the leader in your family."

"Well...."

"What did he say ... your father ... about last night ... at the café?" She let steam from the cup rise over her face, swimming in the warmth.

"He didn't say much."

"He was ... gentle. He held my hand. I wanted ... I missed my father." She stifled a sob, shook.

Kurt considered. "He said something about 'the look.' That's what he called it, 'the look.' I didn't know what he meant. Something he saw and I missed. What did he mean, Ilse? What upset you?"

"I don't want to talk.... I just want to go home, Kurt. I want to leave."

"I've already explained, Ilse. You can't just check out of here. This is a police state. They'll shoot you if you try to leave. They shut the city to keep people in. Just relax—you'll be home for your performance."

"I want to go now."

"You can't. I have a meeting with Abel tonight and another with his boss. I'll take you back after that."

She stumbled into the kitchen and fumbled through cabinets. "Did you drink all the Schnapps?" Her bloodshot eyes flitted from shelf to shelf.

"You did. That's why your eyes are so red."

The cup slipped from her fingers and shattered in the sink. "Oh, *scheisse!*" She pounded her fist on the countertop.

"What's wrong with you?" he asked. "You've had bad nights, but I've never seen you this way. What's going on?"

"I told you—I don't want to talk...."

"You shouldn't have come. You can't handle this. I don't need this kind of help."

"I can handle it, damn it! You don't understand. You never did."

"Try me. Talk to me."

"I'm getting claustrophobia here." She touched one wall and then another. "I'm trapped."

"Just tough it out a few more days. I'm working on a way out."

She palmed away streaming tears. "Damn!"

"Ilse," He stepped toward her, his hands out. "Come here. I'm sorry."

"No!" She smacked her wet palms against his chest, elbows locked, and shoved hard with her weight behind it. He lost his balance and hit the wall, which stopped his fall. Stunned, he grabbed a chair for balance.

She raced past him and knocked his coffee cup off the table, leaving shattered china in a dark pool. By the time the door slammed, she was already down the hall and on the sidewalk.

Kurt circled the table after her, but she was away. Her thirty-step lead increased when she ran across the street. Tires screeched as she dodged traffic in the center of the block.

"Ilse!" he shouted to her back. "Stop! Ils..." He cut off his cry. Such a scene would attract police, or nosey neighbors who would inform them. The light changed and he hurried after her.

She had already disappeared, running blindly through an unfamiliar maze of streets, alleys, and shops. When he reached the spot he last saw her, she was gone without a trace, a fugitive from her past and present.

Ilse knew Kurt would come after her with good intentions, but she ran from bad memories she could not escape—could never stop running. She took a narrow lane and ducked into a small coffee shop, darted into the single restroom and slammed the deadbolt. She sat on the toilet lid sobbing into sheets of rough tissue, temples throbbing against the hangover.

A hard knock at the door startled her. "*Fraulein*, you can't stay in there. It's for customers only. Come out, please."

She combed fingers through her tangles and opened the door. A shabbily dressed matron with graying hair stood there. "My, my—just look at you," she said. "What's wrong, dear?"

"A fight with my ... my brother," she said. "I ran away and don't know where .... I'm lost. I can't go home."

"I'm Helga," the old woman said, looping an arm around her. "We aren't busy so have some coffee and a roll. Your brother will be worried. You can go home after you're eaten. He'll be happy to see you, I promise."

"I ... I can't go home.... I want to, but I can't."

The woman looked her over, messy hair, wrinkled coveralls, red eyes and tear-tracked traces of disguise makeup still smeared on her face. "Are you from over there?"

She nodded. "I'm in trouble."

"Who's helping you?"

"Only him."

The front door opened and a man in a dark suit walked in looking around. Helga stiffened. "*Stasi*," she whispered with a hand over her lips. "Do you have papers?"

"Noooo!"

"I'll stall him. Go back to the restroom and lock the door. Use the window. Then run, dear. Go now."

Ilse acted calm, but she had never been so frightened in her life. Running away had worsened her agony, now each step was in slow motion. Her hand touched the door-handle.

"*Fraulein. Halt!*"

 She ducked in, slammed the door shut and threw the bolt as before. She strained to open the small, high window—it wouldn't budge. She pushed harder, but nothing. Then she saw the latch still fastened. "Idiot!" She twisted the latch and shoved the window up again. It opened partway. She stepped on the rim of the toilet bowl and clawed for leverage over the high casement.

A crash against the door startled her. Her foot slipped into the toilet bowl. She pulled up again and managed to squeeze her shoulders through. Another crash ripped the deadbolt from the door facing.

"Halt!" The suited man seized her soaked ankle with both hands. She squirmed, but he held fast—twisted her ankle to hobble her.

She glanced back—uncorked a heel at his face.

He grunted, released one hand to hold his bleeding nose. She kicked again. He lost his grip.

She pumped both knees against the windowsill and found earth. She was out—running fast in one shoe. She kicked the other off and ran faster in bare feet. Cobblestones hurt—she ignored that.

She rounded the corner from the alley to a main street. A uniformed policeman waited to block her path. He reached for his pistol as the *Stasi* agent sprinted from the front of the shop, a bloody handkerchief pressed to his face. His command was muffled. "Stop her!"

She jinxed right into another narrow alley and tried several doors, all locked. Losing time, she sprinted away as heavy steps rounded the corner behind her.

She slipped making a sharp turn at an old churchyard littered with debris. She got up quickly and surged in an effort to break away. She reached top speed—hit something solid, hammered like a clothesline.

Her feet flew up in front, and she expected to land hard on her back.

But she didn't fall.

A strong arm caught her and she was swallowed up in darkness. She landed a few kicks with her bare feet, to no avail. She sucked air to scream, but a large hand clamped over her mouth. Her heart pounded and she struggled to breathe. Her eyes were wide but she could see nothing.

 She heard boots as two policemen run past. Her vision gradually found some images. An ugly, bearded, hooded figure loomed over her, holding her in a gentle vise. Even in her fright she was too exhausted to struggle—pointless anyway. She gave in to the inevitable.

"Do not scream," the shadow said. "You're safe here. I'll release you." He slowly relaxed his grip. "Be of good faith. You're in the Dom."

His words were mildly reassuring, his voice gentle. He removed his fingers from her mouth, freed her arms and allowed her feet to touch the cold stone floor. Still adjusting to the darkness, she made out his full robe and hood. She heard a familiar creaking sound approaching.

"Ilse?"

She ran to Karl Meyer—nearly knocked him down. Threw her arms around his neck and clung to him. Tears streamed onto his broad shoulder.

"Ilse, we must talk. Come with me, please." He unwrapped her arms and started towards his chamber, holding her hand as he had the night before.

She turned to thank the monk but he was gone.

She clung to the old man's hand and followed him through the corridors to his small office. She sat in his chair, still breathing hard, and he dragged a wine crate and sat next to her. Then he poured red wine into a water glass and handed it to her. She drank it all and he poured another.

"Kurt came after you ran away," he said. "He was worried. Why won't you tell him what happened to you?"

"You don't know what happened to me."

"Whatever it was, it happened to many of us. I know it was bad."

"It's too hard. I've never talked about it. That Nazi ruined me, the one from last night. Kurt works for him."

"How do you know he's the same one?"

"I know!"

"Ilse, many of us have been hurt. For you it was the Nazis. He looked to the battered wooden frame on his desk then back at her. "For my children and me it was the Russians. We must be strong before our enemies, face them with courage or all is lost. Kurt is in danger now and he must know the truth—his life depends on it—yours as well. We need allies in our battles."

"Could I tell you and you tell him for me. Would you?"

"No. You must do some things yourself—today."

"I can't."

"Sometimes we dwell in our misery so long we believe we can never be free. But we must act and accept the consequences. Go to him. I'll have the monk take you."

"Must I?" She stared at her bare feet.

He lifted her chin with his knuckle.

She looked into his brave and wise eyes. She wanted her father more than ever.

"Yes dear. You must do it."

30

"Never Forget"

Kurt prowled the confines of his sister's small flat like a caged animal. He had touched something forbidden in Ilse's mind and her reaction had spun out of control, putting her in danger. He caused it by taking her to the meeting with Abel—he was responsible.

The door opened and he turned.

She stood like a pale specter, disheveled and barefoot, hair tangled and curled wildly. Her eyes were bloodshot and cheeks streaked. She stepped in, closed the door, and faced him alone. She held up her hands, signaling him to stay away.

"We need to talk," she said, her voice husky.

"Where have you been? What happened to you? Where are your shoes?"

"Sit down," she said. "I must tell you something while I have the courage."

He pulled out a chair and sat with his arms crossed on the table, one finger nervously rubbed his eyebrow.

"This ... this is very hard for me." She walked to the window and looked out, turning her back and speaking into emptiness. "I don't know if I can, but I'll try...."

"Ilse...."

"Hush!" She raised the back of her hand. "Only listen. Don't interrupt."

"I had that dream last night ... worse than ... than for a long time. It's always the same. You knew I had them but we never discussed them. I couldn't." She glanced back at him, then away again. "But first I want to know about that man ... the one at the café. What do you know about him?"

"Abel? Not much. He's my contact. I see him when I have something to give him ... he sees that I am paid. I keep my distance, especially since I'm working for both sides. If they figured...."

"You called him Abel. What's his full name?"

"Abel Herreck."

Footsteps approached in the hallway. The muscles in her neck strained under tension, and she didn't breathe again until the steps continued to another apartment.

Kurt said, "A neighbor."

"I'm scared," she said. "I want to leave but I won't run again. I'll face this like you do. I realize now I must confront it."

She looked at him, brown eyes saddened. "This isn't just a bad movie, is it?" She closed her eyes.

"Did he remind you of someone?"

"He *is* my nightmare. He's the most evil man to ever.... He's responsible for the death of my mother and father. He destroyed my life and left me in hell. I know him. His name is Abel ... not Abel Herreck. His real name is Major Heinrich Abel of the Waffen SS."

"Surely, you're mistaken, Ilse. East Germans don't allow Nazi's in their government. The Russians hate them."

"I'm not mistaken. He's slept with me every night since I was five years old."

"How can you be sure it's him?"

"How can I be sure? His dark and evil eyes inhabit my soul. Every step he takes is a nail in my heart. I've forgotten my own father's voice, but I know his and I'll never forget it as long as I live. I know his scent, and ... and he still smells like ashes. He'll never be cleansed of the smell of burning Jews."

Kurt bristled at a side of her he had never seen— vulnerable yet dangerous. She could never hurt a mouse but had the countenance of virulent hatred. He kept still before this stranger he once thought he knew—saw a transformation beginning.

"I was at Dachau," she began. "I entertained the warden's daughter and he spared me the ovens for that. *That* man was a frequent visitor, a houseguest. He came to inspect," she shuttered, "the ovens ... and processing Jews into the camp—never out. When I saw him.... I had almost shut him out of my mind until last night. I smelled him, Kurt, I heard his walk, heard him speak—I'll never forgot that voice. I saw into his eyes, his despicable face. He didn't even know me—I was never anything to him."

"But that was a very long time ago, Ilse. You were only a child then. It could be a mistake."

"A mistake! What he did was a sin—no mistake. Even then he carried the same cane with the gold eagle. And I know his wounds. His scars are my scars, burned into my brain."

The venom of her words stunned Kurt. He saw the Ilse he once knew slipping away—one who once danced and sang replaced by someone set on vengeance. He remembered the strange voice shouting, "Olga!" Olga had returned for revenge.

He leaned forward to hear better her hoarse whispers. "His kneecap was shot away and his leg nearly severed. A jagged scar circled his knee and the hideous stitch marks were plain." She lifted the collar around her throat and wrapped her arms across her chest, trying to shut off a chill from inside.

She recited these lines as if memorized from a script. "When he came to the cottage, he sat before the fire after everyone had gone to bed. Olga would be summoned, a child to entertain that evil man alone, to sing to him. He made her kiss his cane, that shining eagle. When the others were asleep, he made her undress. Then he made her massage that hideous leg ... with oil on her hands, that stinking liniment. He invaded her then, he still invades her nights, and last night seized her mind again."

She was shaking as a leaf in a storm. "I always vomit when I think of him."

Kurt was transfixed, unmoving but feeling something rising inside. His lips formed but no sound came—only disguised fury.

Isle, now near collapse, said, "I don't think we should ... don't want to talk any more..."

"Ilse...." Her name caught as a bone hung in his throat. "Ilse, I need to know all. Now! We must settle this. I need to help you with this."

She fixed upon a small nail hole in the wall behind him, a place where a pretty landscape once hung but was now gone. "I've never admitted any of this before, not even to myself. I pretended it wasn't real, only a bad dream. I'm so ashamed of it. He made me do things to him ... with my hands ... my mouth." She sobbed, buried her head in her hands, and stood shaking before him, her fears exposed.

He slammed a fist on the table. Cups rattled and coffee spilled.

"Swine!" He will pay for this!"

She cringed from a rage in him she had never seen.

Then softly, he said "Ilse, I'll fix it. I'm so sorry. I'll fix it."

"You can't fix it!" She ran to Ingrid's bedroom and the door crashed shut. She locked him out.

Kurt buried a fist into his palm, over and over. He didn't know what to say but he knew he could fix it.

31

Enraged

Kurt ducked beneath a low overhang into the Dom's familiar old cellar. Ilse's story had seared him and he hastened to his father. He was enraged at Abel and disappointed in himself, saddened Ilse never before trusted him with the truth. Acting clearly served as a diversion from her past and he had enabled it, but Abel was solely responsible.

The old man was hunched over his desk, wooden leg unfastened and set aside. His empty pants leg dangled from the chair. He moved the crude prosthesis to make room for Kurt. A wine bottle half empty stood erect on his desk.

"I thought you might come," said Karl. "You look as if you've seen a ghost!"

"Don't you think it's a little early to start on the wine?" said Kurt.

"I had a visitor before you."

"She came here?"

"Yes."

Kurt hesitated, off balance. "So you believe I should meet Fox here?"

"Not here," said Karl. "Above. They'll try to get you to headquarters, but that's a trap. They'll know everything about you before you leave, if they even allow you to leave. Meet him in the confessional and talk through the shroud."

"I don't want to put you in danger again."

"Ha!" laughed Karl. "I'm always in danger. Don't worry about me."

"I'm sorry."

"Don't be."

"Have you heard of anyone getting across the border? I need to get her back as soon as possible."

"Perhaps." The old man rubbed the stubble on his chin. "I've heard some talk among friends. I'll set it up."

"As soon as possible."

"How is she?" Karl asked.

"Not good," he said. "Did she tell you?"

"No," said Karl.

"What did you say to her?"

"I told her to confront her ghosts—face her enemies," he said. "And I told her to talk to you."

"Abel was a Nazi, and he did things to her."

"I saw that much. I've seen it before with my Jewish friends."

"Is that what you meant by 'that look?'"

"Do you think she'll ever get past it?"

"I don't know." Kurt faced away. "I don't know if I can help her. I'm trapped in her nightmare now."

"Are you meeting the old Nazi tonight?"

He paused then said, "Yes."

"Be careful," said Karl. "Here." He slid the Lugar across the table.

"You might need this."

Kurt was not surprised his father had a gun. He had carried one similar on the U-boat, so it was familiar.

He picked it up and felt the balance, jacked a round into the chamber, and shoved it under his shirt and into his belt. He caught his father eye and left without a word.

32

Cemetery of the Jews

Abel arrived early for the meeting at the café. He confirmed Fox's photographers were unobtrusive, found their usual table, sat facing the door and waited. Ten o'clock arrived and passed and he endured the annoying cuckoo. Meyer was late. He reached for his hat and cane to leave, but stopped as a young boy entered the café and approached him.

"Why are you out so late, boy? Where are your parents?" The boy only looked up at him and his cane.

"Would you like to take a ride in my nice car?" asked Abel, grinning. "I'll give you some candy and take you home."

The boy stared at the gold handle of his cane.

"I'll let you hold it if you'll come with me to the car."

The boy looked away from the ugly face but extended a letter-sized envelope. Abel took it and the boy ran out, gone before the door slammed. He ripped it open and read: *Change of plans. Meet me in the Jewish cemetery in Wiessensee. Come alone.*

He shoved it into his pocket and waved away the agents with their concealed miniature cameras. He limped to his black sedan parked at the curb, mumbling as he walked.

The driver stopped the car at the main gate of the ancient cemetery, a desolate and run down graveyard, a forgotten universe. The largest Jewish cemetery in Europe covered 100 acres with 115,000 graves. Only 200 living Jews were left in East Berlin, too few to care for the graves any more.

He instructed his driver, "Wait here. This won't take long." He hobbled alone into the dead place, knowing many of these Jews had sacrificed for the Fatherland in World War I, only to have the guns turned on them. He also knew 3,000 had taken their own lives, sometimes as whole families, to avoid the hell of his ovens.

A stone arch marked the main entrance, an old beggar sitting in the weeds, leaning against one pillar. The vagabond rattled the coins in the bottom of a tin cup. "*Pfennings* for the homeless?"

"Go away," Abel admonished. "You can't stay here." He prodded the drifter with the tip of his cane. "Leave, or I'll call the police." He hobbled past him into the dark and brooding place.

But the beggar called after him, "The God of the Jews will see you in hell!" Abel turned but the vagrant had vanished, so he hobbled along the path, gravel crunching under foot. Dim street lights cast irregular, moving shadows across the tombstones as trees swayed gently in the wind gathering rainclouds. Occasional moving headlights on *Lotheringerstrasse* chased the shadows away, but they crept back after the cars passed. He muttered, "The bastard didn't say where to meet—too many dead Jews here."

"Some were friends," said a voice behind him, "but none friends of yours."

Abel recognized the voice and turned to face him.

"Don't stop!" Kurt said. "Keep walking."

They passed through rows of gray stones until Kurt asked, "Did you arrange the meeting?"

Abel turned and faced Kurt in his disguise. "What's your game, Meyer? I'm not impressed by your Chameleon act."

"The Scriptures tell us if you are kind to the smallest among us, you are kind to your savior ... or something like that."

"I have no time for religious drivel."

"Where's the meeting?"

"*Stasi* Headquarters. I'll take you on Friday afternoon."

"*Stasi* has a headquarters? I've never seen it."

"It's called the Directorate of Economic Research. You might as well know since you're going there on Friday."

"Who will I meet?"

"His name is Major General Mischa Fox, head of international intelligence. You're swimming in deep water, sailor. Watch out for sharks—they have sharp teeth."

"Perhaps I'll show mine."

"We'll see.... I'm leaving, now," he said. "This meeting is a waste of time. I have important things to do. I'll meet you Friday at the café and take you there. Three o'clock sharp—don't be late."

"We're not finished ... Major."

"Why do you call me that?"

"Sit down, Major Abel. Let's talk."

"We could have talked at the café. There's nowhere to sit here."

"Sit on that tombstone," said Kurt. "Get comfortable with it. It may cover someone you've forgotten."

"You're insane!" said Abel. "I'm leaving." Kurt blocked his retreat. Abel shoved. Kurt kicked his bad leg and he crumpled onto a tombstone. "*Scheisse!*"

Abel twisted the gold handle of his cane with one hand and unsheathed a thin, razor-edged knife blade. He swung a wide scathing arc.

Kurt fell back, avoiding the slicing blade. Abel pumped for another swing but stopped when he saw Kurt pointing the Lugar at his face. "Drop it."

Abel glared at him then dropped the cane and sharp blade on the ground.

Kurt picked it up and shoved the Lugar into his belt. He examined the handle in the dim light. It was exactly as Ilse had described it, but he had known that already.

"You don't know what you're doing." Abel pulled himself erect, his gimpy leg extended. "You're crazy, Meyer. You're throwing away your life."

"We'll see about that," he said. "What happened to your leg, Major? Why do you carry this cane?"

"Colonel!" shouted Abel. "I was a colonel. And, I was shot during the war. The Americans blew my kneecap away. I almost lost my leg."

"I know who you are, Major Heinrich Abel, Waffen SS and death camp supervisor."

"Liar! I was an officer fighting for my country."

"Push down your trousers."

"You are crazy!" Abel shouted. "Give me my cane, you fool! I'm leaving now."

"All right." Kurt sheathed the blade into the cane and twisted to lock it in place. He grasped the tip of the shaft and swung the handle hard. The heavy gold eagle cracked against Abel's knee and he howled.

"Drop your trousers, I said."

"You bastard! I'll stand you before a firing squad." He jabbed his hand under his jacket and pulled a Walther P38. "I'll kill you myself."

Kurt had anticipated and was already swinging the heavy end of the cane. This blow smacked the back of Abel's hand and the Walther spun into the grass. Abel groaned, cradling broken bones in his hand. Kurt swung once more and cracked him in the mouth, splintering teeth and splitting his tongue. Blood drained down his chin, over the front of his white shirt.

"You bastard," he sputtered. "Why?"

"I'll tell you why," said Kurt. He leaned in and whispered. "Remember Dachau? 1945? You burned Jews during the day and molested little girls at night. Have you forgotten the little child you...."

"No!" said Abel. "It's not true."

"She grew up and become a real person. Her name is Ilse. I want to hear you say her name, bastard. Say it!"

"No!"

"Damn you!" Kurt swung the eagle with unchained fury, caving in Abel's temple. He toppled onto lush grass over a grassy mound.

"Don't say it then," Kurt said. "Filthy swine!"

He unbuckled Abel's belt and yanked his trousers to his ankles. Scar tissue surrounding his deformed knee was visible in the pale light. Kurt withdrew the long blade again and held it above his head. Abel's eyes opened wider. He raised his hands in self-defense.

Haunting silence of the old Jewish cemetery was pierced by a primeval scream. Kurt drove the blade with all his weight, pushing it through Abel's right hand, through his chest. He leaned on it, burying it into the earth until it stuck into a coffin, pinning Abel to a dead Jew, the golden eagle centered on a widening red circle of blood.

There was no turning back; they would come after him now. He grabbed Abel's P38 and identity papers and disappeared into the tombs.

An old beggar mingled with street people on the sidewalks, merged with them, and disappeared into the night.

Abel's driver charged up the path, searching, calling and listening for his master's voice in the cemetery.

33

Something Lost

West Berlin's Mayor Willy Brandt had only one thing besides the wall on his mind—Vice President Lyndon Johnson's visit. Trudy, his secretary and right arm, was in the midst of his daily briefing on the details. "Have all these arrangements been finalized?"

"Yes, Mayor. Everything is fine ... with one possible difficulty."

"And that is?"

"That singer you wanted, the Dietrich imitator ... her name is Ilse Braun ... the Hilton said she worked there only once and they've been unable to contact her since. She's scheduled to sing again on Monday night. Perhaps she's on holiday?"

"Monday? That's the night I need her for Johnson."

"If she appears, you'll have her for your event. The Hilton is offering their Italian strings as a backup."

"I don't want Mussolini's violins. I want Marlene Dietrich, or whatever her name is. Get her here for Johnson!"

"I'll try, mayor."

Vic scouted city avenues most evenings, officially collecting intelligence, but mostly searching for something lost. Before the barricades he had sometimes ventured into the Soviet sector but that was now off limits. He was the best scout on the American team and he knew he would eventually find her, too.

Yet she never appeared—night after lonely night passed with no sign of her. He knew she was German, suspected she was a Berliner, and prayed she was not a *Stasi* agent. East German intelligence sometimes used beautiful women to penetrate Western defenses—especially effective against American males. He knew all that, but if she was a spy, she was a good one—more reason to find her.

He came up empty handed again so he returned to headquarters. A notice on the bulletin board advised officers to have their dress uniforms cleaned and pressed for the Vice President's impending visit. He read it and shoved his hands deeper into his pocket. His was already at the cleaners; he had to remember to pick it up.

127

Colonel Powell had golfed with his British counterpart during the afternoon and worked late to catch up on never-ending paperwork. Reading reports of Soviet electronic surveillance and comparing them to information from his tour officers, he tried to decide where to look next. Vic watched from the open doorway.

Powell saw him and waved him in. "What brings you back so early? Aren't you going out watching *frauleins*?" he asked. "Damn! I wish I was single again."

"I guess I'm losing interest," said Vic. "Are we doing anything special for the Vice President."

"Nothing special—just the mayor's party," he said. But it would be nice to know if the fucking Russians are planning an invasion. Heard anything?"

"Same old mumbo-jumbo," said Vic. The wall is being reinforced, they just keep adding to it. How much longer are we going to put up with this shit, Colonel? Can't we do something?"

"We are," he said. "Johnson is coming to look at it. Meanwhile, we'll just wait as long as necessary—it may be a long wait." He remembered something. "Oh, did you get your dress blues cleaned? Clear your busy social calendar for Monday night."

"I don't have a social life so all my nights are wide open. I can't seem to find her so the rest of my life is free."

"Such problems!" said Powell. "Some day you'll have a ring in your nose like the rest of us. The mayor's formal bash for Johnson is a command performance for us. Don't get any ideas about having fun—we're just decorations. Be there smiling, show off your dress uniform, stuff like that. We'll be dancing instead of doing the job we were sent here for."

"Free booze?"

"Naturally," said Powell. "Fried chicken, can you believe that? Music, too."

"Square dancing? My future looks pretty square."

"You know the mayor—he might have Turkish belly dancers," he said. "The mayor does like the women.... Hey! Maybe you should take some lessons from him. Just copy him and you'll have to fight them off."

"Well, I'm certainly doing something wrong."

34

Blood on his Hands

Kurt made his way toward Ingrid's flat following deserted side streets. He walked slowly in the beggar clothes to avoid attracting attention but sirens from the cemetery made his pulse race.

Ingrid watched nervously from her window and saw him approaching. She stood in the open door, waiting anxiously until he reached it. She pulled him inside and closed the door quickly, locking it. Karl and Ilse already sat silently at the table.

Ilse rose as he entered and stood aside, uncomfortable after their last conversation. She hadn't known where he'd gone until Ingrid told her about the meeting. She was frightened of whatever demon she had released. Now she could only wring her hands and watch, wanting an answer but afraid to ask for one, afraid to know the truth.

Karl asked, "What happened?"

Kurt wiped a grimy sleeve across his mouth. "Wine."

Ingrid moved, but Ilse intercepted. "I'll get it."

She hurried into the kitchen, uncorked the bottle easily as they settled at the family table. She brought four glasses with one hand and the bottle in the other. She filled each glass nearly to the top. She took the open seat beside Kurt and folded her hands in her lap.

Kurt reached for his glass, but Ilse took his hand and held it near her face. She turned his palm up and studied it then looked into his face.

He snatched his hand away and scraped his chair back, heading for the kitchen sink. He opened the tap and waited for trickling water to build some pressure. Ilse followed him and stood beside him. Together they looked into the sink at the blood on his hands.

She nudged him with her hip, plugged the drain, and added heated water from the teakettle. She took one of his hands in hers and rubbed soap over it, up to his elbow, then the other. He stared numbly away while she scrubbed his hands with a rough vegetable brush. Dark water filled the basin until she uncorked the drain. She pushed his hands under the stream, rinsed them again, and dried each finger.

When she released his hands, she looked behind his eyes, dropped the towel, and covered her mouth. The answer was all too plain. She rushed into Ingrid's bedroom but this time her eyes were dry.

Ingrid stood. "I'll go."

"What happened?" Karl asked again.

Kurt pulled the Lugar from his belt and pushed it across the table. "I didn't use it."

"Keep it," said Karl. "You'll need it now."

"I have one," he said. He raised his shirt, showing Abel's Walther P38.

"Did you do it?"

"Yes."

"Did anyone see you?"

"No, but there's no mystery. The only question will be why."

"What now?"

"He set up a meeting for Friday at Headquarters."

"Remember what I told you."

"I'll change his plan."

"How?"

35

Bad news Travels

Mischa Fox's day had been one of those dreadful ones when nothing seems to work out but he ended it on a low note with one of his many ladies of the night. It was well after midnight when he slipped through his apartment door. But his awful day wasn't finished. Emmi was waiting.

"Where have you been?" Her stern demeanor meant she knew the answer already.

"At work," he lied easily. "Why are you still awake, *Liebchen*?"

"Major Ebert called every hour," she said. "He was at work but you certainly were not."

"My work is not always in my office, Emmi," he said. "You know that. I had a rendezvous with an agent."

"Who was she?"

"I can't name the person. You know that."

"You lying bastard." She stamped her foot.

"Emmi ... Emmi...." He approached, arms outstretched.

She turned her back and brushed his hands away. "I smelled your whore's perfume the moment you walked into our home."

"Emmi, the agent was a woman."

"You pig!" She ran to their bedroom and slammed the door, locking it.

A small cough behind him confirmed his fear and he turned to face little Andrea, watching him from the doorway. She scurried to her bedroom and slammed her door as her mother had. He heard the deadbolts locked.

Then he noticed blankets and a pillow stacked neatly on the end of the sofa. "Shit!" He sat on the cushion and leaned to pull his shoes off. "At least she didn't change the locks." The phone rang.

He grabbed it. "Fox."

"*Herr* Fox, this is Ebert."

"Ebert! You got me into shit again. Why are you calling here at night?"

131

"I'm sorry General," he said. "I thought you'd want to know right away. Have you heard?"

"Heard what?"

"It's Abel. He's dead."

"Impossible!" Fox was up on his stocking feet. "Explain."

"Abel planned to meet Chameleon at the Café Gazebo."

"I'm aware of that."

"Chameleon didn't go to the café. So Abel dismissed the photo team and had his driver take him to the Jewish cemetery. His driver heard a scream and ran to investigate. He found Abel's body. There was a note in his pocket that said the plans had changed and they were to meet at the cemetery. Abel went alone."

"That's all?"

"His driver left him at the gate and waited in the car, as Abel instructed."

"Did the driver see anyone?"

"There was an old beggar there and hc had words with him. The beggar followed him into the cemetery."

"Chameleon."

"Yes, we believe so," said Ebert. "General, it was a horrible crime. Abel was beaten badly with his cane and then speared with it."

"Speared? With his cane?"

"It conceals a long knife," he said. "The man plunged it right through his heart." Fox imagined the ugly scene. "And, there's more...."

"Yes, what is it?"

"Uh ... His pants were down around his ankles."

"What?"

"His pants were pulled down."

"Disgusting!" said Fox. "Perverted!"

"Abel's papers and pistol are missing."

"*Scheisse!* Now what?"

36

The Package

Fox slammed his office door, lit his fifth cigarette in an hour, and after one drag, crushed it in an ashtray. He paced, following a path worn thin in the oriental carpet. When he was calmer he sat behind his desk, swiveled his chair toward the window, and watched shadows stretching out under a setting sun. He ignored the first rap at his door. Ebert, undaunted, knocked again and harder this time.

"Yes, Major!" He hadn't intended to shout, but the bottled-up pressure spewed over. "Come in." He said with pretended calm.

"*Herr* Fox, a package...."

Fox was still contemplating his string of bad days. "Ebert, my meeting with Meilke was dreadful. He doesn't understand or appreciate anything we do here. And, he rebuked me because Abel was killed—can you imagine? It wasn't my fault. Abel had a dangerous job, but he doesn't care about that. The man doesn't understand the sacrifices we make. He can go to hell for all I care!"

"*Herr* Fox," Ebert persisted. "A package was just delivered—a curious package." He held a manila envelope, already ripped opened at one end.

"You opened it?"

"As always," he said, "for security." He emptied the contents onto Fox's desk.

Fox touched the items before him. "Has anyone else seen these?" he asked.

"*Nein, Herr* Fox."

He lifted Abel's identification card and checked the ugly photograph laminated on front. "How was this delivered?"

"A street urchin brought it to the door guard. He said an old man paid him to deliver it here. The man gave him ten marks in advance. The boy had never seen the man before."

"I know him," said Fox. "The package is addressed to me by name only, no address." Fox dropped the identity card and picked up a folded note. "Have you read this?"

"Yes, my General."

Fox read aloud: *Change of Plans. Come alone to the Dom at nine tonight. I'll explain then. Chameleon.* He read it again and stuffed it into his pocket.

"Bring me the file on Chameleon."

"I've already pulled it, General," he said, handing Fox a personnel file. "There is very little in it."

"That's exactly why we need him on our payroll and in our personnel records. But Abel told me some things about him. His name is Kurt Meyer. Start a very quiet investigation, Ebert. I want to know everything about Meyer, but I don't want him to know he is being investigated."

"We've already begun," said Ebert, his chest swelling. I ordered it immediately after Abel was murdered. He was the obvious suspect, of course. Is there anything else, General?"

"Don't mention this note to anyone."

"You're not planning to meet him, are you?"

"Of course I am and I'm going alone," said Fox. "Don't even consider having anyone follow me."

"I strongly advise against it, General—in the strongest possible terms. The man is a psychopath. He has shown himself as a bloodthirsty vampire."

"Don't be fooled by the blood, Major. I told you to study nuances. Chameleon is not a madman. He may be reckless, he may be angry, but he is not insane. I want to know more about him."

"Yes, sir."

"But, there is one surprise," said Fox. "I can't believe I'm actually going to church again after all these years."

37

Atheist in Church

Fox's black sedan slowed to a stop at the front entrance of the sooty old church, still partially in ruins from heavy bombing of Berlin more than fifteen years before. He was precisely on time. He double-checked his wristwatch and swung his legs out of the car. He jogged up the front steps, wondering about the millions of footsteps that had worn curves in the stones. He wondered why they came to church and why he was really there, but he hurried on.

The streets were dark and the windows of the sanctuary hinted it was darker still inside. He pulled on the massive oak door, half expecting it to be locked, refusing his entrance. Instead, it swung easily on well-oiled hinges. He stepped into the narthex and let the door close behind, killing the faint light from outside. He tried to penetrate the darkness.

"Chameleon!"

A scratching sound startled him. A long matchstick ignited and when it touched a candlewick the light expanded with a flickering glow. A hooded figure stood near a dark passageway, beckoning him to follow. The monk cupped the candle while moving, face hidden.

"Where's Chameleon?" Fox showed impatience but followed. "Where are you taking me?" The silent monk entered a confessional chamber with Fox trailing. A second monk observed from a short bench, leaning against the wall with one stiff leg projecting from beneath the robe, his right hand concealed inside.

The guide monk stood aside, gesturing toward one of the confessional booths. Fox ducked inside and lowered the bench. "Are you there?" he asked through the veil.

"Mischa Fox?"

"Yes," he answered confidently. "Meyer, I presume?"

"Yes."

"Ingenious idea," Fox said. "I should have anticipated as much from the Chameleon. First a carpenter, then a beggar, now a priest, always a spy."

"Are you alone?"

"Well, my driver is waiting outside," said Fox. "No one else. Are you alone, Meyer?"

"Only these two monks and me. Are you armed?"

"Of course. Aren't you?"

"Yes."

"Well, now we've gotten the pleasantries out of the way, why did you kill my staff officer? I thought he was your friend."

"I was disappointed to learn you had Nazis on your staff. I wouldn't have helped you had I known."

"Abel, a Nazi? That can't be true."

"You have spies everywhere, Fox. Children spy on their parents in this corrupt city. You couldn't miss a Nazi right under your nose?"

"I did see a report alleging as much," admitted Fox. "But Abel denied it and I believed him. He was a valuable officer, after all."

"Either you're a poor judge of character, or it was more expedient to ignore the facts. I think you're better than that, or you wouldn't have met me here."

"How much do you know about me, Meyer?"

"Very little—the man with no face, no biography, no history, no office. I know almost nothing about you. No one does."

"Then I'll make a confession to you and your two monks eavesdropping on us," said Fox. "I'm half-Jewish. My father was a Jew. I fled with him to Russia to escape Hitler. I hate Nazis, Meyer. If I had proof about Abel, I would have killed him myself. But sometimes, even angels must work with devils. I'm not professing to be an angel but I do work with many devils, including you. This is an unpleasant topic to discuss in church. Do you think I'll go to hell?"

"Absolutely."

"So, tell me what you know about Abel. Why should I believe you?"

"His actual name was Major Heinrich Abel, Waffen SS and superintendent at Dachau. He killed thousands of Jews but he missed one. My source is an unimpeachable eyewitness. I confirmed the facts myself, facts even Abel could not refute. You'll have to trust me on that."

"I'll conduct my own investigation," said Fox, "but for now, let's assume you're right. Why did you want to meet here?"

"I want to know why you built that damned wall dividing my city, my country. I don't like it. You can't fence people in like sheep, put a whole country in prison."

"Meyer, I represent this government so I must be circumspect with my answers, but you'll also have to believe me. I've argued all week with my boss about this. I told him the same, though for other reasons. I opposed the wall because it impedes my access to the west and it makes our eventual consolidation more difficult."

"Eventual consolidation?" asked Kurt in surprise. "At least we agree on something."

"I suspect we agree on much more than you realize," said Fox. "Will you continue to work for me?"

"Only as long as I continue to trust you."

"I'll need to arrange a new manager for you and prepare official papers for you to cross freely."

"No!" said Kurt. "I don't want either."

"Impossible. You can't cross now without official papers. You'll not only endanger yourself, but the entire operation."

"I've done it before and I'll do it again."

"If our soldiers catch you, you'll be shot. I won't be able to save you, never mind if you're caught on the other side."

"That's my problem. I still don't trust you *that* much."

"I anticipated as much," said Fox. "But, this poses serious problems. How will we communicate?"

"Did you see the documents I gave Abel?"

"Yes. The nuclear information was quite useful."

"There is more where that came from. I'll get a message to you when I want to meet, the same as this time. But I don't want to see any more Nazis. If I do, it's over."

"Agreed," said Fox, clapping his hands. "Am I free to go now, *Herr* Chameleon?"

"Of course," said Kurt. "You didn't have to come at all—you know that."

"Alas! I wanted to meet you face to face," said Fox. "Not through some veil. Someday we shall meet." Fox opened the door of the confessional and saw the guide monk waiting for him near the passage. The candle lit the dark hallway and the hooded monk led him quietly to the front of the church.

Fox pulled on the door to leave, allowing slightly more light inside, a breeze fanning the candle's flame higher. He hesitated in the doorway then faced his guide, who looked away. "Two things," he said. "First, monks are no longer permitted in East Germany, they have been banned by official decree, so you are in violation of the law," he said. "Second, I suppose it doesn't matter, because unless I've lost my senses, I've just met the first female monk. What is the world coming to?" He left without looking back.

Karl and Kurt disrobed and used hooks behind the door to hang them out of the way. Neither spoke about what they had heard until Ilse arrived, thus assuring Fox was gone. When she arrived, Kurt put the question first to his father. "What's your assessment?"

"We're still alive," he said. "That's a good start. But I tell you, that man is very dangerous. He must have ice water in his veins."

Kurt turned to Ilse, also out of her robe by then. "Thank you for helping. You did well. How are you feeling?"

Her eyes were clear and focused and showed no signs of frayed nerves. "Don't worry so much about how I feel, Kurt!" Her words were sharp. "I'm not helpless!" She flung the cloak over a wine crate and faced them with hands on her hips. "I made several observations."

"What then?" Kurt asked.

Both men watched and listened closely to what she said, how she handled herself after the previous nights.

"First," she said, "he knows I'm a woman."

"How?" Kurt asked. "You didn't speak to him, did you?"

"No, I'm not stupid! He told me he had seen the first female monk. Frankly, I'm amazed that he could see that so easily. I'm pretty good and that robe concealed everything. I didn't utter a sound. I walked like a man, moved my hands like a man. He has excellent instincts."

"I told you he's dangerous," said Karl. "He has a killer instinct."

"He's more than I expected," agreed Kurt. "What else, Ilse?"

"He has tremendous self-confidence and courage just to come here at all, much less alone. He didn't have to and only a fool, or an extremely strong person, would have dared. He was fearless while he was here, not because he trusted us, either—he just wasn't afraid of us. I think he wanted us to trust him though. I was scared of him."

"I agree with that," said Kurt. "He handled himself well under pressure. I've seen well-trained submariners panic under less."

"Well..." Kurt prepared to move on.

"I'm not finished," she said. "I know more about him."

"What?" he asked. "He's not a Nazi, is he? At least I don't think he is."

"No," she said. "I think he was truthful about that but he deceived us about one thing."

"What?"

"His name. Did you ever listen to the radio in the days just after the war?"

"That's it!" Karl snapped his fingers. "You're right. His voice was familiar to me, too. I've heard it before."

"Michael Storm," she said. "He had a Russian propaganda program under the name of Michael Storm. I hated the program and disagreed with everything he said, but it was a fabulous name and he had such a marvelous voice."

"I can't believe you picked up on that," said Kurt.

"That's what I do," she said. "I'm an actress. I study speech, inflection, and tone. I could imitate him if I had to. I practiced his voice when I was growing up."

"I can't believe you pulled all that from one meeting!" said Kurt.

"And last," she said. "I'm encouraged that his father was Jewish. He would never lie about that."

"He has a sense of humor," Kurt said.

"Don't get too cozy with him," Karl cautioned, "either of you. He may have German and Jewish blood in his veins but he still has a Russian mind. I'm not yet convinced about his loyalties."

"You hate everything Russian, old man," he said.

Karl looked hard at his son. "I do. And well you should too."

The old man pressed his hands against the desktop and pushed himself to his feet. "But if you want to go west tonight, we must end our discussion. My friends are leaving at midnight and have saved two spaces for you. We must go now."

139

38

Sewer Rats

Emil's East Berlin Bakery was on the brink of closing for good. West Berliners with money had come daily to buy fresh rye and pumpernickel at premium prices from the Moroccan baker but the wall that kept him in now shut customers out. While line crossers had kept Emil in business, East Berliners just couldn't afford much fresh bread on socialist wages.

The bakery fronted away from the demarcation line but the border police had bricked over the backside including his loading ramp. Bags of grain and flour had to be dragged through the customer door, requiring more time and closing the shop to the few remaining customers. Prospects for Emil's business and his family's future had diminished, leading him to a difficult decision.

The bakery was dark when Emil and his wife were normally in the kitchen kneading dough.

Karl tapped twice at the door, paused then tapped twice more, then twice again. Emil swung it open and waved him in. Ilse and Kurt crossed the street from a dark doorway. The nervous baker checked both ways before closing and latching the door.

"Hold hands," he said, and led them single-file between racks of bread gone stale. He scuffed at a rat nibbling loaves, shunning the large slap-trap.

Emil opened a storeroom door, stooped and lifted a false floor and signaled them to follow him down creaky steps. Candlelight flickered deep inside the pit. Kurt saw Emil's wife, Safra, and others he recognized as frequent shoppers sitting on their small bags. Fresh dirt and stone filled the corners, leaving a small space for them to huddle in the center.

Hasan, their only son, crawled out of a tunnel just large enough to squeeze through. His clothes were soiled but his white teeth conveyed a broad smile. He brushed dirt from his clothing, creating small puffs. "Is everyone here?" he asked.

"Yes," said Emil. "Seven of us and you, Hasan. That's eight."

"Thank you, father. I can add." He smiled and bowed slightly from the waist.

Ilse whispered, "This reminds me of *Casablanca*." Kurt concentrated only on what lay ahead.

"This is the plan," said Hasan. "I've dug a tunnel under the street; it opens into the sewer. There, we'll turn left and crawl to a manhole cover. It's very dark in the tunnel, but a small beam of light comes through from the opening. We'll help each other out. It's safe enough but you'll get dirty and wet in the tunnel. Watch out for sewer rats. Tie your bags so you can drag them behind or push them ahead of you. Stay close. Are there any questions?" He looked around and added, "Prepare to go. We'll begin in ten minutes when I've finished my last meal in East Berlin." As he unwrapped some bread and sausage, he added, "Getting out will take us an hour...."

"Shh!" Emil silenced him. "Someone's knocking."

They held their breaths, listening for the sound they had missed. More knocks brought nervous looks and restless stirring.

"Were you expecting anyone else?" Hasan whispered.

"No," said Emil. "Everyone's here."

"Then we must leave immediately," said Hasan, tossing his sausage aside for the rats to find.

"Go," said Karl. "I'll investigate." He drew the Lugar from his belt and creaked slowly up the steps.

Hasan squeezed headfirst into the opening while Karl hobbled stiffly up the steps, his cane in one hand and the pistol in the other.

"I'll go with you," Kurt said to his father, fingers tightening around Abel's P-38. He whispered to Ilse, "You know the way out. If there is shooting get in the tunnel immediately. Don't wait for anything. Just go!"

She started to speak but he touched a fingertip to her lips and hurried to catch his father, already at the top of the stairs.

They groped through the darkness to the door. Two more rats had joined the first at the lower bread rack and sizeable chunks of the loaves were already gone. The rats glared at them defiantly, refusing to leave their gains.

Shutters were closed over the windows and Karl peeked through the keyhole in the door. "It's Ingrid."

"Ingrid?" said Kurt. "Open it."

Karl wriggled the key, and when it clicked he pulled her inside. "Were you seen?"

"No, I don't think so," she said calmly. "I brought this for Kurt." She handed him an envelope.

He slipped it into his back pocket. "Thank you," he said, hugging her. "But be careful," he said, "even more than before. This is the last one for us. I've decided."

"You must go," Karl told him and pushed him back. "You'll be left behind."

A brief light appeared from the cellar door—Ilse stood in it.

"Ingrid," she said crossing the floor.

Kurt took Ingrid's arm. "Come with us now," he said. "This is your best chance."

"I'll stay." She looked at her father. "My home is here."

Kurt looked at her, not agreeing but understanding—she would do her duty as she saw it.

Ilse had seen duty as a driving force in Kurt's life and she saw the same streak in his entire family.

Kurt shook his father's hand. "Be careful. I'll be back soon."

Ingrid looked at Ilse, but said to Kurt, "Keep her out of this. She's been through too much already."

Ilse hugged Ingrid and said, "Thank you for being my sister. I love you, Ingrid."

"My heart aches for you, Ilse. If you are truly my sister, you'll never come back here. Forget what happened to you and move on with your life. Promise me that."

"I can't promise," she said. "You're my family now. I love you all." They had lingered too long—Karl took Ingrid's hand and pulled her to the door.

Kurt pulled Ilse to the dark hole. They hurried down the creaking stairway into the pit. Hasan had already led the others away. Safra was already in the tunnel and Emil looked back at his small shop for the last time, shook his head sadly and crawled away from the only life he knew on hands and knees.

"Go," said Kurt.

Ilse knelt and crawled into the dark hole. Kurt blew out the candle and felt his way, following the scuffling ahead of him.

The tunnel soon became muddy from seeping water. When it connected with the sewer, ammonia from stale urine burned their noses. Kurt couldn't see Ilse ahead but he stayed close to her sounds. He tried not to think about the sinking U-boat as it slid under water.

Very near, a shriek brought him back to the present. He thought it was Ilse's cry at first, but then a rat scratched over the back of his hand, running toward her.

He waited for her inevitable scream. Instead, he heard a heavy rock thud into the mud. "Damn you to hell!"

When they emerged from the manhole an hour later all eight were wet, muddy, and smelled of sewage. They embraced one another in the deserted street, rejoicing in their freedom but fearful of any sound to draw attention.

A small cluster of people from a nearby tenement gathered with them, many still wearing pajamas or nightgowns. Several had brought wine or champagne to the impromptu street party. But the new arrivals were not much inclined to linger with strangers and they drifted away to find family or friends and to begin new lives from scratch.

"Let's go," She tugged on his arm; he needed no other encouragement.

39

Finally, Something Good

Mail overflowed from the slot in Ilse's stairwell and she gathered it before going up to her apartment. Kurt opened the front door with his key and she tossed her mail on the table.

"Kurt...?"

"Huh?"

"Never mind," she said. "I'm going to clean up. Heat some water for tea, please." She grabbed a fresh towel and a nightgown, unbuttoning and stepping out of the wet and filthy coveralls she had worn for four days.

When she returned from her bath Kurt was sitting at the kitchen table. His cup was empty, but he poured hot water over another tea bag for her.

"Go ahead," she said. "Clean up while I drink this and look over the mail."

He stood to go but she stopped him.

"Kurt..."

He waited for her to say whatever was in her troubled mind.

She blurted it out. "Do you want to sleep in my bed tonight?" They had never dared that before. "Only to sleep?"

"Could we do that?"

"No one would ever know," she said. "I want you close to me tonight. We could try it for one night."

"Does this mean you've forgiven me?"

"Forgiven you? Kurt...."

"Never mind—forget it."

"Thank you."

The first rays of sunlight peaked through the curtains as Kurt went into the bathroom to clean up. When he finished his bath, he was ready to sleep in a bed instead of on the floor. Ilse was still at the table, but her head rested on her folded arms and she was already asleep, tea untouched and mail unopened. He lifted her like a rag doll, and laid her on one side of the narrow bed and stretched

144

out on the other. She rolled over and threw an arm over his chest and a leg over his. She sighed but both were already asleep.

Four hours passed. Kurt didn't know how long the phone had been ringing before he finally heard it.

"Please...." she pushed him toward the disturbance without opening her eyes. He rose clumsily and stumbled toward the irritating noise. He hoped it would stop before he reached it, but it persisted.

"Hello?"

"*Frau* Braun! Where is Ilse Braun?" A man's irritated voice demanded above background office clamor.

"Who is this?"

"*Herr* Eichmann." When Kurt didn't respond, he added, "...manager of the Berlin Hilton. Is she there?"

"She's asleep."

"I must speak with her—right now!"

"It'll have to wait, *Herr*...whoever...." Kurt depressed the cradle severing the connection then laid the receiver on the table. He returned to bed for two more hours without allowing the telephone another chance.

At noon, Ilse made a farmer's omelet from goods Kurt found at the street market. She had brewed the coffee extra strong and they were both numb but on the road to recovery. While they ate, she thumbed through her mail, setting aside three envelopes with Hilton logos in the upper left corner. She opened the thickest and shook out a folded contract. She pushed it at Kurt. "I hate legal documents. You're my manager, be a dear and read it for me. I'll sign if you think it's fair."

Kurt glanced down at it but left it on the table, choosing coffee. "Later."

She pulled a check from the second envelope. "This must be for my one performance. It's so little!" She frowned. "This will never do. You must negotiate better terms."

She picked up the third, but the downstairs buzzer interrupted.

"Expecting anyone?" he asked. "It's noon."

She shrugged and went to the door, leaning into the tinny speaker. "Who is it?"

"*Herr* Eichmann," he said. "I must speak with you."

"One moment!" She turned, her eyes wide, and panicked. "Oh my God!"

145

"I forgot," said Kurt. "He called this morning while you were sleeping." He went to the phone and returned the receiver to the cradle.

She rushed to the bedroom. "Quick, straighten the room, Kurt."

He slugged his coffee and collected dishes, pans, and mail from the table. He looked for some place to stow them but there was none. He pushed everything else aside in the pantry and stashed it in a pile.

She ran from the bedroom half dressed, looked around quickly then pushed the buzzer to unlock the front door. "Fluff the pillows on the sofa," she said, brushing her hair and fumbling with her lipstick at the same time. She disappeared again as her visitor tapped softly at the door.

Kurt opened it to a short, chubby man with pink cheeks, breathing heavily from climbing three flights of stairs. "Come in *Herr* Eichmann," he gestured towards the sofa. "Ilse will be out in a moment. Coffee?"

"No, thank you," he wheezed. "Water, please."

Ilse sashayed in, her panic concealed. "*Herr* Eichmann, what an unexpected honor!" She sat near him on the love seat. Kurt handed him a glass of tap water then stood out of the way in the kitchenette, holding his coffee cup and saucer.

Eichmann croaked, "Where have you *been*, dear girl?" He drank the water without waiting for her answer. "I was completely unnerved by your sudden disappearance."

"I was out of town," she said. "I'm afraid I haven't signed the contract yet. My agent is reviewing it."

"Never mind—throw it away."

"Throw it away? Is anything wrong?"

"Everything *was* wrong until just now," he said. "But I've found you now, so all is well."

"*Herr* Eichmann...?"

"Haven't you even read the letter?"

"I was just about..."

"My goodness!" he said. "You don't even know." He straightened his back before delivering an important message, an emissary from the potentate. "You, my dear, are performing for the vice-president of the United States at the mayor's special request."

"What?" She looked at Kurt then back at Eichmann. "When?"

146

"Tomorrow night," he said. "Mayor Brandt is having a huge party at the Hilton for Vice President Johnson. He specifically requested you, my dear, as his headline entertainment. This is a feather in our caps."

Her brown eyes were wide. "Why ... why me?"

"Ilse, dear, where have you been? On another planet? Since your show last week the hotel has been swamped with people every night waiting for you to sing again, and the entertainment reporters are calling. They want interviews. They want entertainment. They want a story. They want you! Your unveiling knocked this city off its feet—you're the other biggest item in town. I've been searching for you non-stop every single day and night. The mayor insisted on you and only you but no one knew where you were. I was beside myself—no one says no to Willy Brandt!"

"I need to rehearse!"

"Of course you do. I've had a stage and soundman waiting all week, and the pianist is already practicing your numbers without you on the hope we'd find you in time. I'll send my car for you in two hours. This is *wunderbar!* Both our futures are in your hands, *Fraulein* Braun."

She was already on her feet but she jumped in the air. "Finally, my big break!"

She hugged Eichmann then swirled and turned her eyes to heaven. "Finally, something good has happened to me. Thank you, God!"

40

Falling in Love Again

While Ilse rehearsed at the Hilton, Kurt listened to radio coverage of Vice-President Johnson's arrival on RIAS while his father listened to the same station in East Berlin. The outpouring of support on both sides of the wall encouraged them both. Kurt was pleased when Johnson walked into the crowd, shaking hands and talking to common people though he knew he was a second team politician. He found little else to like about the tall Texan.

It was too late for Ilse to get an official invitation for Kurt to attend as her manager so she demanded a security pass for her bodyguard. "I just won't go without him." Marlene Dietrich was either loved or hated in Berlin so her imitator faced threats of being mobbed either by her fans or her enemies. "I insist my body guard be with me at all times." It worked.

Kurt wore a tuxedo supplied by Eichmann when he escorted her to her private dressing room. Once she was locked in securely, he used his security pass to check out the grand ballroom.

The hotel was decorated lavishly in the state colors of Germany and the United States with bunting and ribbons draped from the tall ceiling. The flags of joint Berlin custodians France and Great Britain were also displayed with those of Germany and the United States behind the head table, but an empty flagstaff made the absence of the Soviet flag conspicuous. Lyndon Johnson sat next to Mayor Brandt at the head table set with silver, crystal, and china.

Johnson, the consummate politician, would not stay in his seat. He worked the room, talking and backslapping anyone within reach.

The mayor circulated too, but concentrated only on attractive ladies. Although he was still campaigning for Chancellor, the race was already lost and he knew it. But he still enjoyed being mayor of Berlin, an international city at the center of world news.

Kurt hung in the shadows and made his assessments of both men.

When the orchestra burst into Wagner's *Emporer March, Bundeswehr* officers in dress uniforms waltzed into one side of the grand ballroom, while lovely ladies in dresses from a century earlier entered from the other side. They converged in the center, waltzing for the delighted guests. They continued dancing to Brahms's *Waltz No. 15* followed by Chopin's *Minute Waltz,* but none

148

by famous Russians. Brandt had reviewed the program beforehand and struck a red line through all of his personal favorites by Tchaikovsky.

When the waltzing dancers retired, the orchestra made a radical transition to square dances as cowboys and cowgirls hit the dance floor in honor of the Texan Vice President. The guests applauded with the equal gusto as for the traditional waltzes.

The early show ended and Brandt officially welcomed Johnson to Berlin by presenting him a peaked Alpine cap with a pheasant tail feather. In turn, Johnson thanked Brandt and gave him a ten-gallon cowboy hat. Brandt flashed a ten-dollar smile beneath his Stetson, but Johnson's grin vanished when he saw in a mirror how the Alpine hat accentuated his ears. He removed it quickly and passed it to an aide.

With formalities and the fried chicken dinner out of the way, the orchestra played dance numbers, alternating between classical, modern pops, and country and western.

Kurt waited for a prearranged signal to escort the star and when it came, he hurried to her dressing room. When he saw her makeover he was struck by her likeness to Dietrich—a natural beauty that surpassed the famous star. A sleek black gown, slit up one leg, had replaced her skimpy bar costume.

"I'm nervous," she confessed.

"You don't look nervous," he assured her.

"It's an act. I'm scared to death."

He reached out but she blocked him with her hands. "Don't mess my makeup. I spent hours getting it right."

"You'll be fine when you're on stage. This is your big break."

"But now it seems so ... never mind."

"What is it?"

"Later. Let's go now before I change my mind."

When they were backstage a pianist had replaced the orchestra and was warming up the grand piano. A few couples danced while others huddled in conversations. When the pianist saw she was ready, he nodded to the spotlight operator. The lights faded and he began his introductory number.

Fading lights sent guests scurrying to their seats for the main show. The buzzing ballroom fell silent as the spotlight framed her entrance on stage in the lengthy, form-fitting dress, exposing one long leg, a feather boa draped over her bare shoulders. She dangled a cigarette in a long holder and held a silver lighter in her fingertips.

Applause rattled the crystal chandeliers. Entertainment and gossip columnists had run competing stories about the mystery singer all week though none of them had seen her. Their pens came out as flashbulbs popped. This was their first exposure and she was set to give them something to write about.

She sat on the piano at the first lyrics of *Falling in Love Again*. Her lusty voice blended perfectly with sensuous chords from the piano and her jitters disappeared. Johnson was nailed to his seat but she forgot about him while she performed.

This was a dream—so sweet she wondered if she could live without it. This was the air she breathed. She was on stage and in her element—far better than real life.

Johnson leaned toward Willy Brandt: "How the hell did you get Dietrich out of Hollywood?"

The mayor smiled. "Marlene Dietrich is a Berliner after all. I thought you knew that."

She enchanted them with *I've Grown Accustomed to Your Face, Lili Marlene* and *Another Spring, Another Love*. All other women lost out with the mayor as he scribbled a note and handed it to his aide, whispering instructions.

She left the stage after the program, but a standing ovation brought her back for an encore. She told the pianist to play *I Can't Give You Anything But Love*.

After the final, final, number, she blew a last kiss and left, ignoring entreaties for just one more. "You have to hold something back," she reminded Kurt as he rushed her back to her dressing room. "How was I?"

"You were fabulous," he said. "You'll be famous after this." He was grinning. "You have fans up there," he pointed to the crowd still clapping above them. "Your time has come, Ilse. There's no turning back."

"I'm not so sure, Kurt ... I...."

A muscle man in a tuxedo blocked her dressing room door. The burly gentleman stood with feet apart, a distinct bulge under his left arm. He wore a small silver pin like Kurt's on his lapel, security identification, but Kurt stepped in front protectively and moved his hand inside his own tux jacket.

The man held both his hands up, palms out with an envelope in one. "I have a note from the Mayor. He asked me to wait for your reply, *Fraulein*."

"Wait here." Kurt opened the door for Ilse and blocked his access, locking the door from inside.

"I'm wearing gloves," she said. "Open it and read it to me, please."

"*Fraulein* Braun," he read aloud. "Your performance tonight was magnificent. Please join me in my office at ten on Tuesday for coffee. Willy Brandt."

"Oh! Accept for me."

"I'm going with you," Kurt said matter-of-factly. "I don't trust our mayor's intentions."

"Thank you," she said. "Tell his man *we* accept the mayor's kind invitation. I'll change; I feel like dancing. I haven't felt this way in ... maybe ever."

Kurt opened the door and spoke to the mayor's aide. "We accept. We'll both be there—tell him that."

He closed the door again and locked it.

41

High Spirits

Ilse was in high spirits as she slipped out of her costume in the dressing room suite. Kurt reopened the door to a line of porters bearing gifts—Champaign and caviar from the hotel, candy from the mayor, and flowers from her many other fans.

Kurt had bypassed the fried chicken and was hungry, so he helped himself to caviar and toast while she changed. She reappeared in a long red chiffon evening dress supplied by the Hilton.

"Beautiful!" She no longer resembled Dietrich, rather a rising star in a new universe.

Isle beamed. "Is this how it feels to be a celebrity?"

"Get used to it."

When they reached the ballroom the top officials had already departed but many of the guests partied late after the tensions of the past week. Ilse dragged Kurt onto the floor and rocked with new energy from an emotional high. A slow song began and she held on to him near the edge of the dance floor, apart from the crowd.

They turned slowly together until she saw a familiar face standing alone. She became lightheaded as the other man studied her, filming her in his mind. He didn't move until she smiled at him then winked.

She asked Kurt, "Remember the American officer we met last week?"

"Yes, why do you ask?"

"He's coming this way in a magnificent blue and gold uniform."

Kurt stopped dancing and turned to face Captain Vic Werner.

Vic said, "I do believe its Jack Smith. Do you mind if I dance with Miss Jane Jones from Biloxi?"

"Why, it's Captain Werner," Ilse said in her practiced southern drawl. She smiled to Kurt and was in Vic's arms so suddenly he nearly stumbled.

"I'd be delighted, sir." She took his hand and the lead with the most handsome man she had ever seen.

Vic held her close and she moved closer. "Did you just come to the party?" he asked. "I saw your friend earlier but I didn't see you anywhere."

"You didn't see me?" she teased, wondering if he actually hadn't recognized her on stage. "I've been here all along. I guess you just didn't notice me before."

"Not likely," he said. "I've been looking for you. I wondered what happened to you since the night we met."

"Well, whatever for, Captain Werner?" she said. "Am I under military surveillance?"

"I ... I just wanted to talk to you again, ask you some questions."

"An interrogation? I confess, Captain. I told you a little white lie before. I've never been to Mississippi. *Ich bien ein Berliner.*"

He said, "*Lügen Sie nicht.* I thought so. Why did you play that silly game?"

"I'm an actress, you see. I enjoy make-believe, and I'm preparing for Hollywood, so I practice everyday."

"So you want to be like ... her? Holy Cow!"

"Marlene Dietrich?"

"You're her!" He held her away and examined her again. "Damn! You're the singer!"

"Shh! That's our little secret."

"And I suppose he's...?"

"My fiancé? No, Vic," she laughed. "Kurt's my agent. He's my family and my best friend—everything that's important to me, except my fiancé. He's my mentor, security guard, and big brother rolled into one."

"I can't compete with that."

"You don't have to," she said, "but you'd better be nice to him."

The orchestra announced the last dance at one o'clock in the morning. "Could we go out for coffee?" he asked.

"That would be very nice, but not tonight I'm afraid. I have an early appointment with the mayor."

"Can I see you again? Just to talk?"

"I don't know ... if you only want to talk." Flirting confused them both—s he was especially confused about her feelings. "Maybe some other time. Give me your telephone number."

Vic pulled an official business card from his jacket pocket and offered it to her. "May I have yours?"

"I don't have a card. Besides, it would be indiscrete for a lady to be handing out her number," she said. "And, I don't have room in this dress for anything else."

"I noticed."

She left Vic and returned to Kurt. "I have a new friend."

"So I see," he said, "a friend who might like to see me gone for several reasons."

42

Ost Politik

Kurt and Ilse reached the Mayor's office promptly at ten a.m. Kurt planned to leave for the *Bahnhof* immediately afterwards to catch a train to Bonn at 12:03. He slung a small pack over one shoulder and dressed casually. Ilse wore her best navy blue suit, white blouse, and high heels.

Trudy, the mayor's executive secretary, met them and seated them in the outer office. "You can wait for the mayor here," she said. "I'm sorry, he's always behind schedule."

When they were seated, she apologized again. "I'm sorry he's late, Miss Braun. He's in a long staff meeting. I'd offer you coffee but the mayor wants to pour himself in his office."

"We don't mind waiting for the mayor," Ilse assured her.

"I heard you sing last night," said Trudy. "My niece is one of your biggest fans. Would you sign a photograph for her?"

"Of course." Ilse blushed, her first autograph. She fumbled the pen but Kurt caught it and handed it to her with a wink.

"How shall I sign it? What's your niece's name?"

"Sign it to Trudy, please." Then Trudy blushed. "Just like mine."

While Ilse was signing the marquee photo from the Hilton, Berlin's leading city officials streamed from the mayor's conference room, talking about Johnson's visit and the arrival of American troops along the Helmstedt autobahn. Willy Brandt stood in the doorway looking puzzled.

Ilse handed the photo back to Trudy and went straight to the mayor. "I'm Ilse Braun, Mayor Brandt. You were so thoughtful to invite us this morning. I know you're very busy."

"Ah, *Fraulein!* I can see it now. Without your costume and makeup, you do look different, but even lovelier." He held the back of her hand close to his lips and bowed.

"Thank you," she said. "And this is my manager, Kurt Meyer."

"*Herr* Meyer." The Mayor touched his brow, a casual salute. "Please come into my office. Trudy, would you bring the coffee?"

They followed him into his large suite, and he positioned them around an oval coffee table. Pictures of the mayor greeting numerous international personalities covered two walls. One caught Kurt's eye—the mayor and Johnson from the previous night, already framed, signed, and prominently hung. A photographer stood by, ready to record this visit as well.

"I document official visits in pictures," he explained. "I find with these visual reminders I seldom need written notes. Would you mind?"

"Of course not," she said, standing next to the mayor. Kurt stood well away from the camera's eye.

"*Herr* Meyer. Won't you join us?"

"No, thank you, Mayor. This is Ilse's visit."

"Very well." They smiled and waited for the flash and several backups. "I'll send a signed copy to the Hilton for you when they're developed, Miss Braun. And another for you to sign and return to me, please. I'll hang it next to Johnson."

The mayor sat beside her on the divan, Kurt across the table. He poured coffee into China cups from a sterling silver pot, holding a linen napkin beneath it to catch any drips. He nodded to Trudy and she uncovered an assortment of fresh pastries, deliciously decorated.

"*Fraulein*, your performance impressed Vice President Johnson very much. He even asked me how I got Marlene Dietrich out of Hollywood. Of course, I reminded him Dietrich was a Berliner before she was an American. I don't know if he ever figured out that you weren't her, but I certainly didn't tell him."

She laughed politely, finding the story amusing and remembering how wonderful she felt on stage.

"How's your coffee, *Fraulein* Braun? Sugar? Cream?"

"This is fine, thank you. And please call me Ilse, Mayor."

"Well Ilse, just call me Willy, until I'm Chancellor then you will have to call me Your Excellency."

Kurt asked, "And how is the election going, Mayor?"

"Ha! My slim chances vanished with this crisis. Blame the Russians, but I'm better known now from all the publicity. I don't have time to campaign but my supporters criticize me for being away from Berlin too much, my enemies for being here too much. The wall that traps our people in the east confines me. Berlin is the front line in this battle—a page in history being written and we're writing it, you see? I should drop out of the campaign but I won't. I've never quit before and I never will."

"What will you do about the wall?" Kurt asked.

"What will I do about the wall? That's the wrong question, sir. What will I do about *Germany*? What will *we* do about Germany?" His voice rose as he continued, "All I can do now is spew hot air, but that's a start. We've been hurt by this occupation—families separated, cities split, and farms divided, alienating people all across the land. Russians use Germans to prop up their failing economy and faltering political system."

He stirred his coffee to catch his breath then redirected the same question at Kurt. "So, do you have any good ideas, sir? What are your suggestions?"

Kurt had been surprised by the mayor's vigorous exposition and low-keyed his reply. "I certainly don't have the answers, Mayor. But, I know it's wrong to build walls and close down connections. We need more openings, not fewer."

"Of course, I wholeheartedly agree. That's my entire agenda in a nutshell. The question is how to achieve it?"

"We must approach it in all ways," said Kurt, "at every opportunity. Each side needs confidence about the other's military intentions as a start, to avoid an accidental war, a miscalculation. The suddenness of this latest move could have easily started an all-out war."

"But giving credit where it's due," said the mayor, "swiftness of action prevented that. They hit fast then hesitated to gage our reactions. When they saw none, they started building the wall. When NATO and all our illustrious leaders caught on to what they were doing, it was over. Germans are masters of *blitzgreig;* they beat us at our own game."

"We still need better information to avoid mistakes."

"Of course, that's why we have so many spies," said Brandt. "Berlin is filled with spies and lies. For all I know, you may be one, *Herr* Meyer."

That note pinged like sonar off a submarine. "I can assure you my only interest is Germany's future."

"The KGB and *Stasi* run circles around our intelligence services," Brandt continued, "penetrating all of our governments, even NATO. We rely on families and friends in the east for our best information, but it shows that even the Wall can't change the fact that Germans live on both sides."

Ilse grew uncomfortable with the thread of discussion, which hit too close to her recent trauma. Brandt leaned forward to press his point, but she touched his hand.

"Surely, there are other means," she said. "We need other communications too, cultural for instance—the arts, painting, music, stage, festivals, wine, and for goodness sake, beer. We can't ever accept having our German culture divided, can we?"

157

Brandt settled back, nodding. "Thank God for our common heritage. That will be our ultimate salvation. You have good ideas, both of you. Politics is communications, doing what's achievable and talking about what isn't until it becomes so. I'll give all this some thought. I'm refining my theory of *Ostpolitik*—reaching out to the East. When I'm Chancellor, and I will be eventually, you should join my staff, Miss Braun." He refilled half-empty cups and selected a frosted pastry. "Cultural attaché—how does that sound?"

"I'm not suited for politics," she said, glancing at Kurt. "But you're very kind to suggest it."

"So," he said. "Tell me about your singing career. You're certainly well suited for that."

"Actually, I'm an actress—singing is a form of acting to me. I enjoy music but it's only a route to the cinema."

"So, you'll follow Dietrich to the United States?"

"That remains to be seen, Mayor," she said. "But, it is a sweet dream of mine."

43

Pursuit of Happiness

While Kurt and Ilse confronted Abel the Nazi and Fox the spy master in East Berlin, Hilda's meeting with Hans left her disoriented. She called the emergency number at Ilse's apartment several times but the phone rang unanswered. She needed to tell Kurt what had happened and reaffirm their plans—pull him closer, solidify their future. Until Hans caught her, the game had been exciting, but now it had suddenly become dangerous. Kurt was the steady one, full of confidence and courage, the leader; she had been naïve before but now realized how precarious their situation. She was scared. She wanted out.

Yet Hans had protected her when she was vulnerable, and excited her in a different way. Her dreams had become vivid, intense—her heightened sexuality confused her. She was ashamed of those feelings—how she had trembled under Hans touch. She was desperate to reaffirm her future with Kurt.

But Hilda relaxed more at work and that was a blessing. Hans could channel more suitable material so she no longer had to smuggle documents out of the chancellery. Several intriguing documents crossed her desk but she let each one pass, confident Hans would fulfill his promise. Her doubts slowly ebbed and she settled into a new tempo. By the end of that day she had cleared her desktop to leave when Han's secretary came into the bay looking for her. She handed her a note and actually smiled before leaving. Hilda slipped it into her purse unread. When she reached her flat she dropped her purse on the table, poured a glass of wine and drank it quickly. Then she read: *I need to see you. I hope you can come this evening at eight.*

She breathed in a sigh of relief. "I was afraid I'd have nothing for Kurt."

A rap on the door startled her. She ran to open it and flung it wide. "Kurt! Thank God you're here." She fell into his arms and her lips devoured his.

He pushed her back far enough to clear the hallway and closed the door behind.

"I've missed you so much," she said between kisses. "I tried to call you but no one answered."

"I was stuck in East Berlin. It's been a bad week."

"Kurt, I have a meeting in an hour," she said breathlessly. "Are you staying tonight? Please?"

"Yes. We need to talk."

"We can talk later," she said. "I have other needs right now." She pulled him toward her bedroom, strewing clothes behind.

She dressed quickly and hurried along the river walk, already late for her meeting with Hans. She announced herself to the security guard who recognized her and smiled. Hilda went straight to the elevator while the guard phoned ahead. Hans met her in the hallway as before, but this time he smiled, took her hand and led her to his penthouse. Hilda noted the cozy wood fire and the view from the veranda was just as beautiful as she remembered.

He didn't speak until they were behind closed doors. She remembered the rules. "Thank you for coming, Hilda. Would you like a drink?" He turned on classical music.

"Yes, thank you."

He opened a fresh bottle of Chapelle Chambertin and she recognized the label as very expensive. She wondered why anyone could pay that much for wine. He sniffed the cork, tasted, half-filled two glasses and sat beside her on the sofa. "So how is work?" He smiled at her in a way that reawakened stirrings she thought had been satisfied.

"Fine, thank you. I'm more relaxed so my error-rate has improved, thanks to you." She sipped the burgundy and was surprised how pleasing it was. "This is quite good."

"Thank you. It's a special order. When will your courier come?"

"Actually, he arrived an hour ago. That's why I was late."

"He's at your flat now?"

"Yes. He had trouble crossing the border but we haven't really had an opportunity to talk."

"Is he staying the night?"

She considered the question and decided on honesty. "That's personal, but I suppose you should know. Yes, he is staying with me. I intend to marry him and have children. I'm very much in love with Kurt."

"I see."

Hans looked through the French doors, beyond the Rhine. "Wait here while I retrieve some documents. These are nuclear targets and Fox is expecting them, a special request." Hans swung a Dutch oil painting away from the wall, exposing a safe. He dialed until it swung open and removed one of several envelopes. He dropped it on a table by the door and returned to sit beside her.

160

"Tell me about your man, Hilda."

"He's my age—a little older. We met at a resistance meeting in Berlin," she said. "He's a patriot, handsome, strong, and brave. And, I adore him."

"Does he work for *Stasi*?"

"No. I mean yes, but only under special terms. He isn't a *Stasi* agent. But now with new security measures, I don't know what will happen. He's paid well enough and gives part of my share to my father; the rest goes into our savings."

"So you're in love with him?"

"Why is that important?"

"I've become.... I find you very attractive. I couldn't stop thinking about you after ... you know ... the incident."

"Oh!" She blushed and swallowed hard. "I've ... I've had dreams. But, we shouldn't be talking...."

"I want to see more of you, to be closer."

"Hans, I do appreciate your help, and your honesty about your feelings. I'm flattered, really, and if I weren't so much in love with Kurt, I'd certainly be interested in ... us. But, it would never work. I hope to plan our future with Kurt tonight."

"Well, I am disappointed, but if that ever changes...."

"If is a very big word, Hans. Let's change the subject, please."

"Change!" he said. "That's the main reason I wanted to see you tonight—big changes are in the offing!"

"Big changes?"

"I'm being posted to NATO Headquarters in Paris next week. It's a prestigious assignment and will open new doors to me."

"I see," she said, clearly disappointed. "So I'll be gathering snippets of information again."

"Snippets? That's so English," he said. "But not back to the old way," he said. "You see, I'm taking my assistant with me. Her fiancé lives in Paris and it's a reward to her for loyal service. They're to be married at Christmas and they'll be together Paris."

"How does that involve me?"

"Her position here in Bonn will be vacant and I've arranged for you to have it. You'll be working in the Chancellor's office and will have access to material in your own right. It will not be completely risk-free, but much safer than before."

"I see."

"Mine is a good job and a promotion," he said. "It'll be good for my career and good for the cause."

"And how will you ensure my selection for the job after you're gone? There are procedures for civil service."

"It's already arranged. Don't worry about it. You'll be paid considerably more, a promotion from clerical to professional standing. You could even afford a small apartment in this building. There is one available, not a penthouse, but it has a very nice view of the Rhine and a small balcony."

"Oh! That would be nice."

"Hilda, I'm glad we got to know one another. I hope we can stay in touch. I'll come to Bonn occasionally for meetings, perhaps we could have dinner."

"That would be wonderful. I'm very appreciative for how you've helped and protected me, Hans. But, I really must go." She stood and smoothed her dress. She felt dizzy, whether from the wine or her mixed feelings from the past two hours. "Kurt's waiting." She picked up the envelope and rolled it to fit in her purse.

"How long will he stay?"

"I don't know."

"Perhaps you can visit again before I leave for Paris?"

"I have these papers already. What would we do?"

"We could have dinner here. I do cook. We could get to know each other better. Perhaps I can help you decide about the apartment. We could celebrate our mutual success."

"Maybe." She smoothed her skirt again, remembering his hands on her, frightening yet thrilling. She wondered about different circumstances, felt her certainty melting like snow in sun. She blushed and left quickly without looking back.

Hilda closed the door to her apartment and leaned back against it. Kurt was waiting. She had rushed back to him but not before stopping at a street vender for fresh flowers and a bottle of wine. She quickly put the arrangement into water and fluffed them before setting the vase on a table.

Kurt sat on the sofa with several newspapers disassembled and spread before him, in the background the radio broadcast news and political commentary. She dialed the radio to popular music and pushed the papers aside, settling close to him. Her head nestled on his shoulder. "I can't get enough of you, do you know that?"

"Are you ready again so soon?"

"Yes, but let's wait until bed time. Can we talk now? There's so much to discuss."

"Why don't you start?"

"I just had a very interesting meeting with Hans...."

He held up a hand to stop her, closed his eyes against what he had to say. "Don't use names, Hilda. Better if I didn't even know his name. I hope you didn't say my name to this man."

Her cheek reddened as her hand covered her mouth.

"Damn, Hilda! This is serious. You must be discrete."

"I'm sorry." Her hands covered her eyes and her head bowed lower.

"Hilda, listen, our lives are at stake here. Please, be more careful. When I arrived I was angry when you opened the door without asking who was there, but I didn't want to start with a fight. So I didn't say anything then, but please, don't open the door to strangers."

"I'm, I'm..." Her eyes filled with tears.

"Don't be upset," he said softly. "I'm telling you this because I love you. If anything ever happened to you, Hilda.... I just don't want anything to happen to you."

She wiped her eyes. "Let me collect myself."

She went into the kitchen and patted her eyes with a dishtowel. She felt again like the little girl who had violated light discipline during the London bombings. Her mother had corrected her then in the same way.

She needed some more time. "I'll make some tea."

She stood by the teapot urging the water to boil. He asked her, "Can I see what you have while we're waiting?"

"Oh, yes ... I forgot." She opened her purse and handed him the envelope. He held her hand a moment as he accepted it but she turned back to the whistling kettle. He opened and studied the documents while she readied teacups and saucers on a tin tray with a tea advertisement on the bottom.

She delivered the tea and sat next to him again, chastened and forgiven.

"Have you seen these?" he asked. "They were sealed."

"No. Hans ... uh," she flushed again. "He just gave them to me tonight."

"These are photocopies."

"That's what I was trying to tell you." She described how Hans had cornered her at the Chancellery, but not about his intruding hands. Then she related their first meeting at his apartment when he finalized arrangements to work together.

"He simply handed you these papers? How do you know they aren't forgeries? They'll be furious if we pass phony information."

"They're real. I typed the originals and he gave me photocopies of the other information, from when I was caught. And another thing, he's being posted to Paris, NATO headquarters, and he arranged my placement into the political office as an executive assistant. Can you believe that? He works for the Chancellor here, and for a man named Fox. Have you heard of him?"

"Mischa Fox? I've met him—a dangerous man."

"He said I would have a salary increase and could afford to move into his building. It's much nicer, Kurt. Do you think it would be all right?"

"I thought we were saving for our future together?"

"We are, Kurt. But you're always gone and this little flat is depressing. The other one has a terrace and a beautiful view of the Rhine. Don't I deserve a little happiness now?"

"Yes, you do," he said. "Go ahead."

"Oh, Kurt! Thank you. I hoped you'd say it was all right. I love you so very much. And when you come here we can sit on the balcony at night with the lights along the river in the distance. It'll be wonderful."

"I'm happy when you're happy, Hilda. But I do worry about you. Please, be more careful." He rubbed his finger along his eyebrow as he said it.

"I promise," she said, looking into the lines of his face. "But something else is bothering you. Tell me about your trip. Did you see my father?"

"No, I didn't," he said. "I know I promised, but things got out of control with the wall. I'm sorry. I'll see him next time."

"It isn't that important anymore, Kurt. I hardly remember him. I wish it had been different, that I had known him better. Sometimes I feel guilty, like it's my entire fault, leaving him. I asked you to do something I should do myself."

"Sometimes we must do things we don't like, Hilda."

She considered what he said and watched him still rubbing the line of his eyebrow. "You seem depressed. What have you done, Kurt? What happened?"

"I killed a man."

She pulled his hand to her lips and kissed it. "You wouldn't have unless you had to. Who was he?"

"My *Stasi* handler."

"Oh God! Why?"

"He was a Nazi. He was at Dachau and he abused Ilse as a child. I killed him and then I met with Fox."

"Oh my God! Will he come after us?"

"I don't think so, not right away. But we must get out soon. We can only do so much."

"I want to stop now," she said. "I want to go away. I'll be too old for children soon. Do we have enough money saved?"

"We have plenty of money, enough to take new identities and start over. I've invested it but I can't keep track of it when I'm running all over Europe."

"Let's go now, tonight Kurt!"

"Not yet. I have some documents Ingrid gave me—important war plans. I must get them to the Americans—I owe them a debt. And I'll take these to Fox. Then we'll go. I've already told Ingrid to stop work and prepare to leave, too."

"What should I do?"

"Just keep doing your job," he said. "Go ahead and move to that new apartment as he suggested, start working in the new job. Act normal. But be prepared to disappear soon. Be ready in your mind, but don't pack or anything like that—give no indications you plan to leave. Especially don't tell Hans—he works for Fox. I'll return in the next few weeks, and we'll vanish overnight. Just be ready. We can't take much with us."

"Oh, Kurt, I can't wait. This is what I've dreamed of my whole life."

"We're just beginning, Hilda. We do deserve something for ourselves. We deserve some happiness."

44

Meanwhile

After their big meeting with Mayor Brandt, Ilse had walked with Kurt to the train station. They found a bench at trackside and discussed their meeting as they waited for the Bonn express.

"I thought he was open to new ideas," she said.

"An open mind?" said Kurt. "He's already decided about everything political."

"Politics—is that all you think about? There must be something more in life."

"Cultural exchanges won't win this war, Ilse," he said.

She frowned but let it slide as the train rumbled into the vast covered *haupbahnhof,* overrunning all conversation. "Give my love to Hilda," she mouthed the words and he nodded his understanding.

He swung his pack over one shoulder and stepped aboard, grabbing a seat near a window. They watched one another through the glass and each saw a wordless pantomime of images from the past week. Much that had passed between them remained unspoken. Shortage of time was a worthy excuse not to deal with it. The big clock on the platform ticked down to 12:03.

She waved from the dais as the train pulled away. Double-checking the clock she confirmed it was exactly on time, the train was punctual to the minute. As long as the trains ran on schedule there would always be hope for Germany. Neither the Americans nor the Russians would ever match that.

She lingered a few moments after the cars had disappeared in diesel fumes, undecided about her next move. A pretzel vender tempted her with a sample so she bought one, dipped it in brown mustard and wandered aimlessly in the station. She pulled Vic's business card from her purse, glanced at it but dropped it into her suit pocket.

She tossed the remains of the pretzel into a wastebasket and checked the card again for an answer. Not finding it there, she dropped it back into her pocket and walked from the station.

One block away she stopped, turned around and returned. She stood beside the phone, one finger twisting a curl over her ear.

"Sometimes, you have to just act," Karl had told her. Ilse stepped into the public phone booth, held the card to read his official number and dialed.

A sergeant answered. "Military Liaison Mission; this is Sergeant Burns. How may I help you?" He sounded Midwestern.

She answered in Mississippian. "Hello, is Captain Werner there?"

"No ma'am. He's out."

"When will he be back?"

"I can't say."

"How can I reach him?"

"You can't. We don't have commo with him when he's out in the field."

"I see."

"Do you want to leave a message?"

She pondered the question a moment too long.

"Ma'am?"

"Oh, yes, thank you. Tell him I'll wait for him tonight at the same place we had beer the night we met."

"The night you met, huh?"

"Yes. At seven this evening."

"At seven tonight at the place you met. And who shall I tell the captain is waiting for him?"

The phone line hummed while she considered that one.

"Ma'am? Who is this?"

"Hollywood. Just tell him it's Hollywood."

"Hollywood, eh? You a movie star?"

"Do you like the movies?"

"Yes, ma'am."

"Please, just give him the message."

"Yes ma'am. If he doesn't show up and you get lonely, just call back here and ask for Sergeant Burns. I get off at seven-thirty."

"I'll make a note of it, Sergeant."

Having found the courage to call, she was disappointed not to have reached him, and sorry she had left such a silly message. She felt like a secret agent arranging a clandestine rendezvous. She made one more call, to the Berlin Hilton.

"Ursula, could you come over this week? I have some work for you."

"Yes ma'am. When?"

167

"Just call me Ilse, please. And could you come at night? I like having someone to talk to at night."

"Yes ma'am."

"I'll call you back with the date."

She walked the streets alone, winding her way to her lonely apartment. She closed the curtains and stretched out on her bed to rest with the nightlight on. At six p.m. she gathered herself, changed into clean slacks and a new silk blouse to replace the one torn in the wire. She stuffed most of her hair inside a beret and walked along Ku'Damm until she reached the sidewalk café.

She was early, so she ordered a Pilsner knowing she could stretch one beer for a while. Every few minutes she checked her watch and rubbed her wrist under the wide watchband. She coached herself to act calm at least, so she sat on her hand to prevent it from twisting that loose strand of hair around her finger.

At seven-thirty, she pushed the half-finished beer aside and reached for her purse. Someone behind her said, "Hollywood?"

She looked to her right as Vic circled her table on her left. When they connected she met his crooked grin with a relieved smile. Blue eyes twinkled above his freckled nose. He wore jeans and a shirt unbuttoned at the top, loafers with no socks, his hair was still damp from a fast shower and he smelled like soap—the all-American boy.

"You came," she said, her voice quavering.

"Of course," he said. "I just got your message a few minutes ago. Sorry I'm late." He was very relaxed, James Dean cool.

"I was beginning to think it was a mistake. I was about to leave."

"Why would it be a mistake? Why the code? Hollywood?"

"Did you know it was me?" she asked.

"Who else could it be? So, what's the big secret?"

"I'm getting to be known in Berlin. I was just being careful." She took another sip of her beer, flat and warm by then.

"Mata Hara; I feel like I'm meeting a spy." He signaled a waitress for a beer. "Want a fresh one?" he asked her. She shook her head.

"So, where's your bodyguard? It seems he's always standing between us."

"Kurt went out of town but he'll be back tomorrow."

"I'm surprised you actually called."

"Why surprised? You asked if you could see me sometime, just to talk."

"Yeah, but I didn't think you really would; a big star and all. My love life really stinks, and when you wouldn't give me your number either time I thought you were giving me the brush off."

"We just have to ... I just want to be careful, that's all."

"We, huh; you mean you and him? You're like Siamese twins."

"This was a bad idea, Vic," she said. "I hardly know you, and you're already jealous. Maybe we should just call it off."

"Don't go! Please?" His eyes read sincerity, pleading with her to stay. "Please," he said it again with feeling. "I was teasing you. Let's talk, just talk, like I said. Really, that's all. It's harmless—you said you would."

"Okay, but only if you answer a few questions," she said.

"Okay. Shoot."

"Do you really follow the Soviet army around Germany or do you just chase German girls?"

"That pretty much sums up my whole life."

"Which one is it?"

"Both."

"So you have lots of girlfriends?"

"None--I just chase after you."

"But you can go into the Soviet zone whenever you want?"

"It's my job. They try to slow us down, especially if they're hiding something. There are some restricted areas we aren't supposed to go into, but we usually get in. We're pretty good at shaking them. Hide and seek is a game we play."

"How do you get away?"

"We have really fast cars." He flashed his James Dean smile again. "We have '57 Chevy's with superchargers and a racecar driver to handle the extra horsepower. Mercedes' and BMW's are pretty fast on the highways but we use tank trails mostly. Their roadsters are slung too low. We go where they can't."

"What do you look for?"

"Signs they plan to attack."

"Do you ever get caught?"

"It gets hairy sometimes. When we're clobbered, they question us, threaten us, and make a big deal of it."

"Can they send you to prison?"

"Maybe—but not likely ... not for long anyway. We're under a bi-lateral agreement, so we'd have to break the rules so bad we couldn't deny it. Usually we bluff our way out after a few hours, even if we have *technically* violated rules. If we get nailed red-handed, we would be declared *persona non grata* and sent home. End of career ... or if some guard gets trigger happy...."

"How do you get information?"

"We use what God gave us—eyes and ears. We snoop around caserns, training areas, follow them around, and go through their trash. We talk to people, civilians mostly, to find out what they've seen—soldiers won't talk. That's why it's important to understand both German and Russian. We do whatever it takes."

"Do the civilians talk to you?"

"Sure. But, they talk to the Russians, too. Tell them when they've seen us, but who cares, because we're already gone by then. They talk more if we have cigarettes and chocolate."

"Then I guess you are a spy, sort-of?"

"In a way, I guess—kind of a legal spy. There are fourteen of us with official passes, licensed to snoop. Attachés do the same, but this is unique. We're actually assigned to the Soviet forces."

"You're a very unusual man, Vic Werner."

"You're pretty unusual too, Ilse Braun. Let's talk about you. I know you're a singer, a damn good one. What else?"

"I'm an actress—an actress who also sings!"

"I told you about me; I want to hear about you," he said. "And don't leave anything out."

"I'm a girl," she said, "and a German, and an actress and a singer. There really just isn't much else."

"And Kurt, what does he do?"

"He's the set director at *Berliner Ensemble*; at least he was before the wall closed the east. He's my agent, but mostly he's a carpenter. He was a *grenzganger* before that program ended. Sometimes he sneaks back over to see his family."

"That's dangerous. They shot and killed a crosser yesterday."

"Do you think they'd shoot me?"

"Hell yes! But they'd rather capture you. If you're crossing illegally, don't do it. You could spend the rest of your life in an East German jail. This isn't a game, you know."

"Sometimes I don't know the difference between real and pretend. Being an actress confuses me about real life sometimes."

Vic, confused by that, changed the subject. "Do you want something to eat? I haven't had dinner yet."

"What are you hungry for?"

"I don't know, anything, if you'll join me."

"I know a great little Hungarian café nearby. Its quiet there and the goulash is *wunderbar*."

"Let's go."

She took his hand and led him into a side street, then along back streets for several blocks. She found the quaint little restaurant where an organ grinder's monkey danced near the door. Vic headed to a table near the front, but she pulled him to the back. "It's quieter."

The proprietor's wife was already wiping a table near the kitchen, out of hearing of the other patrons.

"Looks like you've been here before."

"They know me."

The goulash was everything she promised. They discussed American movies and chasing Russians, they even laughed and two hours flew past. The restaurant dimmed when the owner closed the shutters and his wife wrung a wet mop into a bucket of water.

"Looks like the curtain is coming down," she said.

They walked back to Ku'damm to say goodnight on the busy avenue where they met. Then, he kissed her.

It was sudden and gangly, but she went with it. She had kissed men before but never like that. She felt her pulse quicken and an unfamiliar stirring, an urgent need for something missed, a vessel to be filled up.

The sensation was new. Perhaps Kurt had fixed her problem.

"Will you give me your number now?" he asked.

"Yes." She fumbled in her purse for a pen and tore a scrap of paper—jotted her number and address on a flap torn from an envelope. She slipped it into his hand. "Call me." She turned toward her apartment, but he caught her wrist and brought her back to him.

"You can bet on it," he said. And he kissed her again.

She actually skipped on her way home, humming a new song she had heard on the radio earlier in the day. It resonated in her head with his image and she didn't want to lose either.

Vic stared blindly into the emptiness of busy Ku'damm long after she was out of sight.

45

Stand by Me

Ilse floated back to her apartment—feet dancing to the music in her head. Her date wasn't actually a date but it was fun. Her spirit soared. She wondered which was better, her practiced performance for Lyndon Johnson or her improvisation with Vic Werner. She was happier than she ever remembered—more than she believed possible. If she could hold onto that, the world would be good. She flung herself backwards across her bed and wished he were in her arms still. *We might actually....* She slammed the door on that thought.

In one week she had climbed from the depths of despair to the mountaintops and her head was in the clouds. All of it flashed before her—she had crossed the wall with Kurt on a great adventure and met his family, adopted his family as hers and loved each of them. She thought of Karl, the wise old man, and his call for courage. And Ingrid who understood her and accepted her troubles without question. She had been in danger several times and escaped. Exhilarating!

And she escaped East Berlin by crawling through a rat-infested sewer. She recalled her meeting with the mayor. She relived every detail of her performance at the Hilton, singing every song in her mind, a virtuoso performance. She smiled as she thought of Trudy pretending her niece wanted the autograph, her first one. She thought about Vic and the fun they had, laughing, and his kisses. Her head was spinning. She was just too happy to sleep so she got out of bed and poured a glass of wine—then it all started again.

The room was dark, except for the drifting silhouettes of trees swaying before streetlights. Curtains rustled like phantoms in the breeze beside a raised window. Sitting alone she became slowly aware of her solitude, her first night alone since that terrible night in the East. Loneliness crept up first, opening the door for her nightmare. She was defenseless and not even a burning candle kept Abel Herrick's ghost at bay.

She desperately needed Kurt. He had given her back her life, a start in her career, made his family hers. He had saved her time after time, slayed her dragon, killed the evil man, but the real monster wasn't vanquished. Before she even closed her eyes, Abel Herreck stood shaking his cane at her, accusing her for his death.

!!!! The shock was like a heart attack! She jerked straight up, her heart pounding against her chest. It was only the telephone! The jarring ring broke her spell. Her heart surged in fear—a klaxon for trouble. *Why would Kurt call so late?* She snatched it.

"Kurt, was ist los? What's wrong?" She listened to the hum of an open connection on the other end. "Kurt?"

"*Nichts.*" The voice was familiar, yet strange. "I'm sorry to call so late. It was a mistake to call at all."

"Vic?"

"Guilty. I'm sorry I woke you."

"Vic!" she shouted his name this time. "I'm *so* glad you called. I wasn't asleep. I was just worried about Kurt, out of town, so late ... I'm sorry, I'm rambling. Let's start all over...." After a moment, she said, "Hello?"

Another pause until he acknowledged her fresh start. "...Ilse—This is Vic. I couldn't sleep and I wondered if you were sleeping. I tried to wait till morning, but...."

"No, I wasn't sleeping either," she laughed. "Isn't that a coincidence?"

"I don't think it was a coincidence."

"You don't?"

"I thought we really connected tonight. And I hoped you felt that way, but maybe ... Kurt.... I was wrong."

"You're jealous!" she said. "If we're going to see each other you're just going to have to get over Kurt. He's the only family I have. He's the price of your admission."

"The price of admission? When can I see you again?"

"Can you come over for breakfast?"

"I can come over right now."

"No," she said. "I don't think so. Breakfast would be great.... Say that!"

"Breakfast would be great, Ilse."

"Say ... about eight?"

"I'll be there, about eight."

"Good. You have the address. I'll see you at eight. Good night."

"Ilse...?"

"Yes."

"Good night." Click.

She dashed into the bedroom and plundered her closet for the light blue dress, her favorite one. It was there, and clean. Relieved, she returned to her wine and snuggled with her pillow on the sofa, smiling as she replayed their last conversation in her mind, remembering every word and laughing out loud. Then she hurried into the kitchen and inventoried her pantry. She found eggs and coffee, but she would need to go out for fresh bread and butter as soon as the market opened at six-thirty. Then she could bathe, dress, and make breakfast, all before eight. She knew she would be exhausted when he arrived, but she didn't care. She wouldn't sleep at all that night anyway, wouldn't even try. Maybe she could just rest on the sofa for an hour....

..."**Damn that buzzer.**" The front door buzzer jazzed again, longer this time. *Kurt has a key. Why doesn't he just use it?* She sat up on the sofa and looked around, puzzled. Daylight streamed through the curtains. A single chime from the nearby town clock told her it was half-past, half-past what? Half past eight. She had fallen asleep. The buzzer rang once more, longer. She darted to the window and looked down.

Vic stood on the door stoop, looking up. He had a bag of groceries in his hand, and flowers. She saw his lips move, exaggerated but silent. "Open the door." She touched the buzzer. A moment later, he knocked on her front door. She opened it laughing.

"What's so funny?"

"I fell asleep."

"What's so funny about that?"

"You'd never believe how funny it is. Sleep! I'm a mess. I haven't even changed from last night."

"Why should you? You were perfect last night."

"You're sweet, but I'm going to clean up and change anyway. Do you think you could manage coffee?"

"Can I say good morning, first?"

"No," she said. "Not until I've brushed my teeth. Start coffee."

She disappeared and when she returned in her blue dress, the coffee, eggs, bread and jam were all on the table. He had arranged the flowers in water. "Good morning," she said.

"Good morning." Then he kissed her, a long one. After a few seconds, she pushed him back. "I'm starved, and aren't you the domestic one? Just look at this table."

"I wouldn't say domestic. More like a survival instinct."

"Let's spend the whole day together," she said. "We could go to the park, a museum, have lunch. You can even go to rehearsal with me."

He took a deep breath. "I'm afraid I have a mission. I'll have to leave right after breakfast."

"Damn."

"Yeah, double-damn. What was so funny when I got here?"

"Oh, I have trouble sleeping sometimes, like last night. After we talked, I just ... fell asleep."

"I'm that boring?"

"No!" she said. "It's not like that at all. I guess I was reassured."

"That's something anyway."

"It's not a bad thing, Vic. Believe me."

"What'll you do all day?"

"I'll meet Kurt at the train station when he returns from Bonn. And I have a rehearsal for a new show at the Hilton. Will you come to the show?"

"Sure. Let's start these dishes. I have to go find some Russians."

"You clear the table, while I fill the sink." She hummed the tune that had stuck in her head while she worked.

"That song you're humming sounds familiar. Dietrich?"

"No, not even close," she said. "Its American pop—*Stand By Me.* I'm doing it tonight if I can get it right at rehearsal. You are coming?"

"Of course. But that's a man's song isn't it?"

"Ben E. King. So what? Don't you think I can do it?"

"Well ... I suppose if anyone can, you can. But I have to go." He moved to kiss her but she offered her cheek."

"Didn't like breakfast?"

"You know I did. And I like you, too. Just go slow, okay? You might decide you don't like me so much when you get to know me better."

"You'll have to convince me of that. See you tonight." Vic started out the door, but stopped when he heard her singing *Stand by Me* in the kitchen.

He closed the door behind him, stood in the hallway leaning against it, listening to the only voice he wanted to hear for the rest of life.

46

"Die for a Promise"

Ilse rushed home after rehearsal and changed from her blue dress into a blouse and slacks and pushed her hair under the black beret. She walked quickly to the *Bahnhof,* intent on meeting Kurt's train. She thought about how he had casually told Fox about killing Abel yet he had never spoken of it to her, even after she washed the blood from his hands. It was something they might never discuss—Kurt was just that way. He thought nothing of putting his life in jeopardy—dismissed it as nothing, discounted her feelings about his actions. Well, this was important to her.

The train arrived at 3:49 p.m. on the dot. She stood in the shadows of the train tunnel and watched him step off the last car. He looked about casually, not for her, just checking around. He walked her way, not seeing her at first. Then, when he spotted her, a smile broke. She ran into his arms.

He braced for impact and laughed when they collided like a train wreck. "Why are you here? I thought you had rehearsal."

"I did. I practiced for an hour and it went really well. We broke so I could see you."

They strolled toward her apartment. "I have something to show you, Ilse," he said when they were inside. He opened his pack and removed a small box. "I want your opinion on this. I got it for Hilda."

"*Mein Gott*!" she shrieked. "That's the largest rock I've ever seen." She smothered him in a hug. "Have you asked her yet?"

"Not exactly, but we've talked about it. She wants to do it right away."

"Why don't you?"

"It's complicated."

"Everything is complicated with you, Kurt Meyer. Sometimes you think too much. Just do it."

"You sound like the old man. It's complicated. Before we get married, we'll have to disappear, take a new identity, and live somewhere else."

"You won't just leave me will you? I still need you, you know?"

"I'd let you know where we are when it's safe, but we'll have to vanish first. The old man was right about one thing—I can't just quit the *Stasi*. But I have some other business to finish anyway. I can't stop in the middle of this."

"Life as duty? Middle of what—you'll always be in the middle of something."

"I have some things for Fox. I must find a way back in once more. And I have something for the Americans, too."

She frowned. "It's gotten worse, Kurt. I had dinner with Vic last night and we had breakfast. He said they've shot people, and the wall is stronger with wire and guards, more concrete, lights, dogs, everything. Please don't go back."

"Dinner *and* breakfast?"

"We didn't sleep together," she said. "It isn't like that, not yet. But I really do like him. I want your approval. But you changed the subject—what I was saying is that the situation is more dangerous. Don't go!"

"I'll be careful. I need to scout around this afternoon. I'll stay at your place tonight … if he's not coming back. I must get Ingrid out and explain our intentions to the old man. And I need to take some money to Hilda's father—I promised her."

"You and your promises—you'd die for a promise, Kurt Meyer. Promise never to desert me."

"I never will."

"I'm so happy for you and Hilda, but I don't want to lose you either. I'll understand when you go, but don't forget me. Promise me that?"

"I do."

"I'd do anything for you, Kurt, anything! I promise you that."

"What's with all these promises?" He didn't expect an answer.

He asked, "What are you doing today?"

"I must finish rehearsals. I'm working on a new number I heard on the radio. Will you come tonight?"

"Sure."

"I invited Vic, too. I want you to talk to him. Please try to like him. He could help you."

"How? He'd have me arrested if he knew what I'm doing."

"He wouldn't do that, not if I tell him not to. He'll help. I just know it. Somehow he'll help you too, for me if for no other reason."

He looked hard at her. "You're both in love, aren't you?"

"Maybe—I don't know. I've never felt this way before. Is this it?"

"Yes, it is," he said. "And I'm happy for you."

"And guess what? After he called me on the telephone, and after talking to him, I fell asleep, can you believe that?"

"Now that's a good sign."

"I thought so, too," she said. It was all from meeting Vic, and, and, what you did for me over there, to that man, Kurt. Abel. I'll never forget what you did for me."

He took her shoulders and shook her, an angry shake that startled her.

"We'll never mention that again, Ilse. Never!"

Berlin Connection

Part II

Bridge to Freedom

1962

47

Security Breech

Mischa Fox's driver parked in the concealed garage at *Stasi* Headquarters as usual—nothing else was usual. Uniformed police had surrounded the international intelligence headquarters and sealed it tighter than ever. Sedans awash in flashing lights blocked every corner, armed guards at every door. Major Ebert waited—looking like a death in the family.

"What the hell is this, Major?"

"Big problems, *Herr* Fox," he told the undertaker. "I'll explain inside." Fox marched into his office with Ebert trailing silently, head bowed.

As soon as the door slammed, Fox swirled and demanded, "What is all this?"

Ebert spit out words that had been choking him. "Dieter Haus defected."

"What? Impossible!"

"Apparently he was a double. He took all his files as well as others—he's gone."

"Goddamn! Can we catch him?"

"We're sure he's already in western hands. He had an all-night head start."

"*Scheisse!* How much damage is done?"

"We'll need time to assess."

"Why are all these police here? This is a matter of internal security."

"Meilke sent them."

"Send them away! They're no help. They're sitting out there with their lights flashing, advertising our predicament like neon signs on a brothel. The west will be laughing at us. Get rid of them, now!"

"*Ja, Herr General.*"

Dieter Haus, the double agent, had been working in *Stasi* Headquarters with Abel. In the middle of the night, he opened his safe and removed all his files. But worse, he knew the combination to Abel's safe and took those files as well. He simply walked out the front door with a briefcase full of damaging state secrets, left his car at the airport and boarded a flight for Amsterdam into the open arms of western intelligence—NATO's biggest ever windfall of Warsaw Pact secrets.

NATO would need months to capitalize on the information but it would take years for Fox to recoup his losses. Actions to limit additional compromises began immediately. No one realized the magnitude of this latest disaster better than Fox—his favored spy boss killed by his best document currier. Further, this damage was humiliating for the head of security. Even the "man with no face" could be exposed.

His phone rattled, jarred him back to reality. "Fox!" he answered.

"This is Meilke. How bad is it?"

"Terrible. He took his files and Abel's, too."

"The old Nazi?"

"Yes, the damned Nazi." Fox had been severely chastised for keeping a Nazi on his rolls and he was still embarrassed by that—now it resurfaced, worsened.

"What are you doing about this?"

"We're warning our agents they may be compromised. I'll give you a further assessment in a few days."

"Will there be any more of these?"

"I don't know! You can't fence in intelligence operations like you did the city. Agents must be free to do their jobs. If some go astray … it just happens. That's the way this damned business works—so keep your pants on!"

"Watch your mouth, Fox!" Meilke slammed the phone down. Immediately, it rang again.

"Fox!" He shouted in answer, expecting Meilke again.

"Mischa, its Nikoli," said General Rubski—as in the same room, not the usual scratchy Moscow connection.

"Nikoli? Where are you?"

"Here in Berlin. Khrushchev sent me."

"Not because of this, I hope?"

"Because of what?"

"An agent defected last night. He took files. The damage is serious."

"That's too bad. I know you must deal with that but I need to see you about another matter."

"When?"

"Could you come to the Embassy later? I want you to read something important."

"All right. Late this afternoon?" he asked.

"Dinner afterwards," said Rubski.

"Fine."

"Give my best to Emmi and Andrea."

"I will. How's young Ivan since his mother passed away?"

"He's a hand full—sent him to boarding school. He needs discipline, an iron hand—too much like me. I'll see you later."

Fox unlocked his desk drawer and withdrew the maps he had prepared for briefing Meilke. Selecting the one for Dieter Haus and Abel Herreck, he unrolled it over his desk, placed a paperweight on one end to hold that side flat, holding the other end flat down with his hand. Not finding another paperweight, he withdrew his chrome-plated automatic and placed it on the end of the curling maps.

I'll have to stop these leaks—once and for all!

48

"Lock This Up"

Ingrid worried about her father coming to her apartment for dinner. The commissary was already closed and she had shopping to do if she could only catch a market open late, not likely.

She was anxious to leave work, but her instructions were to stay late for an important Soviet general who had just arrived from Moscow and needed access to a sealed Top Secret file. Her responsibility as file clerk could not be delegated therefore she simply had to wait it out.

At least her father had a key to let himself into her apartment.

Wire mesh doors rattled as the shaky elevator settled in the basement of the Soviet Embassy—men's voices approached her station.

The Russian was a very big one, not fat but burly, muscular and heavy-set—he was ugly, with a shaved head, bent nose, and a red burn scar creeping up his face above a collar so snug it tried to strangle his massive throat. A red star emphasized his importance—major general. Colorful ribbons crossed the broad chest of his tunic, contrasting sharply with his dark demeanor. He looked almost out of control. Ingrid thought of the phantom of the opera.

His companion was quite the opposite, handsome, stride poised and athletic—physically and emotionally under control. He was tall, blond, slim, and clearly German. However, his finely tailored civilian suit was cut from a fashion magazine—style and fabric chic western. He had enough confidence to wear such suits while contemporaries wore clothes recycled from pre-war bins. She found it remarkable that he smoked American Marlboros in the Soviet Embassy. She thought of Clark Gabel.

She caught some of their conversation as she made her assessments. The handsome one was saying, "...It's more difficult, but not impossible. This latest setback was bad enough, but we won't know the full extent until we see their reactions." He spoke in German but she missed the beginning of his sentence and had trouble giving it context.

The Russian examined her badge and said, "*Frau* Meyer, you have a special folder for me. Could I have it from the safe, please?" His German was a bit off.

"Your name, sir?"

"Rubski, Major General Nikoli Rubski." He showed his identity card. The phantom had a name that suited him.

"*Ja, Herr General,*" she said. "Would you sign the control sheet while I open the safe, please?"

Ingrid hurried to open it, listening more to them than concentrating on the numbers as she dialed the combination. She overshot the third one and had to start over from the beginning.

"Hurry, please," the ugly Russian called to her back. To the handsome German, he said, "How serious is the damage?" His German was broken but understandable.

The handsome one answered in Russian, effectively shutting her out of their conversation. She wanted to hear more, but realized she was listening. She no longer understood his words but realized his mastery of Russian which flowed with a natural easiness—better than the general's halting German. She wondered if she was wrong –perhaps he was a Russian after all.

Ingrid brought the file to Rubski, initialed beside his signature, and entered the time. She asked, "Will you take it upstairs, General?" She handed him scissors to cut the tape enclosing the diplomatic package.

"*Nyet,*" he answered in Russian. He checked her badge again. "*Nein, Frau* Meyer. General Fox will read it here. We'll return it in ten minutes. Then you can go."

So this was the famous Mischa Fox—his name suited him. She had thought he was civilian, but Rubski called him general. And he was cleared for the Russian classification of Top Secret. Kurt would be interested in those tidbits.

The men seemed friendly as they spread the thin file over a special reading table under a lamp and fell silent while Fox read. She opened her log and studied the names of Major General Nikoli Rubski and Major General Mischa Fox.

She attended mindless paperwork while eavesdropping for other fragments of information. She heard the names "Khrushchev" and "Kennedy" several times. At one point she looked up—both of them were watching her.

She buried her face in her papers until a shadow crossed her. She found the big Russian blocking the light with his bulk.

"Lock this up, *Frau* Meyer," he said, slapping the file on her desktop.

"*Ja, Herr General,*" she said over her shoulder. "Please sign the log again before you go, *Herr* General." She returned it to the safe while he watched her back.

When she locked the safe and turned, they were both gone. She checked that the log was signed a second time. She studied their names again, wringing her handkerchief in her hands and remembering her father waiting alone in her apartment.

Then she went back to the safe, reopened it, and removed the small file. It was typed in Russian, translated into German. She read all of it.

"*Mein Gott!*"

She closed the folder and returned it to storage, spun the lock and called for the security guard to clear her time card for the evening. Her hand trembled as she signed out.

49

Soviet Embassy

The posh dining room on the top floor of the Soviet Embassy overlooked the broad avenue *Unter den Linden*; in the distance the green cap of the Dom was faintly visible in the deserting twilight.

Rubski splashed vodka from a frosted bottle into two glasses, spilling some. He lifted his. "*Na zdorovye!*"

Fox touched his glass to Rubski's and they slugged their first of the night. Fox reached for the menu while Rubski reached for the bottle.

"You seem quite at home here in little Moscow," said Rubski. "Our culture, language, food; everything about you is Russian, except those Seville Row English clothes and those damned American cigarettes. You're a strange mix, comrade."

"True enough," agreed Fox, lighting another Marlboro. "Remember, I was a Berliner before I was a Russian, and now I'm an expert on the western mind."

"You're a Russian, Mischa—it behooves you to never forget it! You're a Russian citizen and a general in our army. That's why Khrushchev trusts you. Don't ever forget that very important fact."

"Yes, you're right, of course," he said. "In here," he tapped his temple with a finger, "I'm a Russian, but inside my chest beats the heart of a German."

A diplomat in a crumpled wool suit approached their table from across the room. "Good evening, Gentlemen." The Soviet ambassador hovered at the edge their space. "May I join you for a moment?"

"Certainly," said Rubski, standing. He clapped his beefy hands. "Waiter!" Other diners watched. "Bring a glass for the ambassador, please."

The waiter arrived promptly, still drying one with a white cloth. Rubksi filled all three glasses with vodka. "*Na zdorovye!*" They drained the artic-iced vodka. Rubski recharged the empty glasses immediately.

The ambassador spoke first to Rubski, "Welcome to Berlin, General. I want to make clear my complete support while you're here." He knocked his glass against Rubski's in a courteous salute, a thin expression of support aimed directly at Khrushchev's emissary nosing in his backyard.

"Thank you," said Rubski. They drank on that excuse. Fox watched as Rubski recharged the glasses once more, needing only a few drops to fill Fox's nearly full glass.

"I see you finally got General Fox here. You should come more often, Mischa."

"I was his instructor at the academy," said Rubski. "This is a reunion."

The ambassador asked Rubski, "How long will you stay in Berlin, General?" meaning *when will you get out of my hair?*

"I don't know—as long as it takes. I'm doing an analysis for Moscow."

"Moscow? For Khrushchev, don't you mean?"

"Of course—one and the same."

"Is General Fox assisting you?"

"He doesn't know it yet, but he will."

"Well, General," the ambassador turned to Fox. "I heard something about a defector this morning. I trust you'll keep your miscreant agents under control."

Fox was embarrassed and angry at the remand, but his reply restrained. "The winds of war blow in all directions, Ambassador," meaning *it could happen to you.*

"Indeed they do," he said, ending his ambassadorial visit and standing, although a bit wobbly already. "Gentlemen, please excuse me," he said. "I must complete my evening visitations. Enjoy your stay, Nikoli. Tell me if I can open any doors for you, that is, if General Fox hasn't already stolen the keys."

He walked unsteadily away, already hailing diners with a fresh bottle of Vodka at another table.

Fox asked, "Why are you really here Nikoli?"

"Several reasons. Khrushchev sent me to first check security here at the embassy, and then to work with Marshall Koniev on the timing for his big shocker—you've seen part of the strategic plan that I'll brief to the Ambassador. That plan and Koniev's plan are to work in concert. I must prepare an overall assessment of what might happen as a result of those two plans. Berlin is a weather vane—whatever direction the war wind blows, it blows first over Berlin. He wants an evaluation of the political situation, security, the economy, everything. He wants you to help me with that. Remember when I called you that night when the wall went up? He values your opinion about the west. Khrushchev wants to know how they'll respond to what we're about to do—before we do it. Their reaction to the wall gave some clues about their reaction to the plan you just read, and Koniev's plan."

"I'll help you, of course," said Fox. "Yours is a big job, but frankly I'm relieved that's all it is. When you appeared unexpectedly, I assumed you were here because of my security problems with reprobate agents. We had a serious lapse and the Ambassador's jest was not amusing. Stalin would have responded with the ultimate solution—my head."

"No, Mischa," said Rubski. "I didn't come here to kill you. We're old friends. I'd warn you first—you could put your pistol in your mouth and save me the unpleasantness. What are friends for?"

"Your humor escapes me."

"It wasn't a joke, Mischa," said Rubski. "And I'm surprised you thought the ambassador was making one. He was quite serious. But, to change the subject, what do you think of the plan?"

"Cuba?"

"Yes."

"Brilliant. When will the missiles be ready?"

"Soon ... in six months they should be ready to fire. Some convincing must be done with Castro. He's already angry about the Bay of Pigs fiasco so I think he'll go along. The missiles are being disassembled and hidden aboard freighters. When they arrive in Cuba they must be reconstructed, concealed, and calibrated. Soon we'll be ready to strike."

"Do you trust Castro?"

"No," said Rubski. "But we'll convince him with military equipment and a sugar tax. It's a good deal for him. We pay him to do what he wants to do anyway—crush the United States."

"He's still angry about the Bay of Pigs?"

"Of course," said Rubski. "The CIA botched it and they left a trail right back to Kennedy. They should have hired the KGB to do it for them," he chuckled. "We cover our tracks."

"What will Kennedy do now?"

"No one knows what he'll do, not even the CIA. Khrushchev believes you understand Kennedy's thinking better than anyone else after your correct assessment about the wall. The KGB said he would attack, but you said he would sit it out like a lamb. They were wrong; you were right. What do you think they'll do about Cuba?"

"Nikoli, my sources were cut off by that wall. My analysis is based on many sources over time."

"I need your personal assessment, Fox, Khrushchev needs it," said Rubski. "The stakes here are much higher. Koniev is here to organize the ground assault that follows our nuclear first strike from Cuba. We must anticipate how NATO will react when Washington is destroyed."

"I haven't seen the tactical ground plan yet but this is an interesting concept. I've only been looking for the strategic nuclear options so far."

"Each depends on the other. Think about it and give me your thoughts soon."

"I need more information but Haus' defection has compromised many of my best sources. The west is already conducting investigations, making arrests. Almost every day I lose another one."

"That's too bad."

"Worse—last week my best courier killed my best manager, Abel Herreck."

"The old Nazi?"

"That's the one," said Fox. "But you should know there's a leak in your house as well."

Rubski rubbed his hand over his shaved head and dropped another slug of Vodka. His red burn scar deepened while he waited for the unsavory rest of it.

"That woman in the basement of your embassy—*Frau* Meyer—she's the sister of the man who killed Abel."

"No!"

"Yes."

"I'll have her arrested tonight," he stammered, his red scar turning bright purple.

"Don't move on her yet," said Fox calmly. "Her brother is bringing better material than any of my other agents and he's one of the few still getting across. I expect him to deliver the nuclear information you requested. He's very important to us right now, with so many of my other sources exposed. We need him—Khrushchev specifically needs him. Besides, it was a good trade, the Nazi for Meyer."

"I see, but this is taking a big risk," said Rubski, uncomfortable while agreeing, looking for another way. "I still must do something about her immediately. She could cause us both to eat a bullet."

"I just can't lose Meyer, but you must also keep an eye his sister. If she's leaking critical information, we need to know that."

"I'll have to move her out of the basement," said Rubski. "I can't overlook the danger she poses there, but I'll keep her nearby to watch her better. Besides, German women make good bargaining chips with German men. I learned that valuable lesson when I was fighting these people in the Great Patriotic war."

"Fine—that's your decision."

"So much for her," said Rubski. "But you'd better watch her brother closely." He swilled his vodka and poured another. Fox's glass was still full from the second refilling.

"Berlin is a very interesting city, Fox. No wonder you like it here. Let's have another, just for old time sake." He signaled the waiter for another bottle.

50

Nuclear Strike

Ingrid fumbled with the top button of her thin sweater and drew it tighter against the falling temperature, but wind sliced through as she hurried home to rush dinner for her father. She considered the winter coat hanging uselessly in her closet. She would need to press it—winter was at the door.

She pushed her door open and found him sitting alone in the dark near the window. She switched on a light and dropped her small shopping bag on the countertop.

"I'm sorry, father." She struck a match to light the gas oven. "I'm sorry I'm so late. There were late visitors at work."

"Don't worry about me. I had some tea."

"I see you've opened the wine as well."

"Of course."

"*Sauerkraut* is already made. I'll warm it with some *bratwurst*. That will take only a few minutes."

After a moment of silence, "I'm worried about Kurt," he admitted. "I've heard they're shooting people crossing the barricades. They're even placing antipersonnel mines in no-man's land, the automatic-firing kind."

Ingrid hurried dinner along; her hand still trembling from invading northern winds, or apprehension. "Where is your heavy coat, father? Winter is here early."

"The Siberian Express," he declared, "just an early Christmas curse from Russia. I'll dig my coat out of the trunk, but I'll smell like mothballs tomorrow."

"But, you'll be warm," she said setting the table. "Air it out overnight. Come now, dinner is ready."

Karl filled two water glasses with wine while she filled their plates with cabbage and sausage. "Who were these important people?" he asked.

"A general from Moscow—Major General Nikoli Rubski," she said. "He brought Mischa Fox with him to read a file."

"Ah, Fox. We met Fox at the church last week. The Soviet bastard must be a big shot to bring the Fox out of his lair."

"He is," she said, "big and ugly. Did you know Fox is a Russian general?"

"A Russian general?" He digested that with the bittersweet *sauerkraut*. "No. I didn't know that, but I suspected his loyalties leaned toward Moscow. Why were they there?"

"Rubski showed Fox a very secret Russian war plan." Her eyes studied the contents of her plate but she wasn't eating any of it.

He watched her while he chewed his sausage. Finally he bit again, "Did you read it?" he mumbled through a mouth already filled.

"Yes." She gulped too much wine and choked, coughed, cleared her throat and swallowed another sip. Her hand still trembled. "I wish I hadn't read it."

He chewed silently, slower, watching her stir cabbage in tight circles, thinking how Ingrid would do that when stalled over asking for hard-to-get money. Finally he said, "Tell me about it."

"Father," she said, "you don't want to know."

"As you wish," he said and returned to his dinner.

He cleaned his plate with a crust of bread while she nibbled silently. He pushed his plate aside and finished his wine then reached for a second bottle.

She nodded for a refill and said, "I'll tell you if you really want me to." She moistened her lips. "I have to tell someone; it's gnawing at me."

He smiled. "Just like your mother. You can't keep anything from me." He wiped his mouth on a napkin and leaned forward, elbows on the table. "I've seen everything there is to see in my lifetime, girl. Nothing surprises me anymore."

She blurted it out before she changed her mind. "Khrushchev is planning a first-strike attack against the United States. He's already moving nuclear missiles to Cuba."

His expression was unchanged by the news, but he emptied his glass and turned it bottom up on the table. "Do you have any Schnapps?"

She went to the cabinet and returned with an unopened bottle. He snapped it open and drank from the bottle. She protested. "Wait! I'll get fresh glasses." When she brought two clean ones he baptized them while she cleared the table.

"What will you do with this knowledge?" he asked.

She shrugged. "Taking the paper is unthinkable. Besides, Kurt warned me to stop working."

"The Americans will never believe him if he tells them this without evidence."

"I know." She left the dishes as they were and sat down with him again. They looked into each other's faces, reflections of themselves.

"Fill my glass father, and don't forget your coat tomorrow."

51

Duty to Report

Kurt reached the Hilton before the show started and sat at the bend in the curved bar. "Just hold this seat for my manager whenever I sing," Ilse had told the bartender. It wasn't unusual to hold a seat but tonight was different; she was testing a new routine. Vic arrived shortly after Kurt and sat on the next stool.

Her new pops collection had been culled from top hits of the radio top forty. Ginger, the marquee announced, was from Haight-Ashbury of San Francisco and the sack dress, long wig, and beads transposed the hippy flower girl to Berlin; the smell of burning incense could be a mask for marijuana. Ilse wore a flower in her hair, stood before a photo of the Golden Gate Bridge and sang pops from Mary Wells, Joan Baez, Dee Clark, Pat Boone, and Clarence "Frogman" Henry. She saved her main selection, *Stand by Me,* for last.

The show electrified the audience—applause and bar receipts a good indication her contract would be expanded. One night would be reserved for Ginger, the other for Dietrich drawing two different swaths of Berlin's night life.

Herr Eichmann stood rubbing his hands together in the doorway. "We'll do anything within reason to keep you, including a percentage of bar sales," he told her. "Just don't disappear again."

After the show, she ducked backstage to change into street clothes.

Vic and Kurt had not spoken throughout her performance—tension evident as they measured each other. They sat sullenly side-by-side, tending personal thoughts, until she returned to call a truce.

She stepped between them and draped on arm over the shoulders of each.

"I'm hungry," she said. "Who's buying dinner?"

"I will," Vic volunteered, hoping it would be only the two of them. "Let's go to that Hungarian place again."

She took Kurt's hand and pulled him off his stool. "Come with us. Vic's treating."

The organ grinder and monkey were still entertaining at the café with the same lively tunes. This time, Vic knew where to sit. Ilse pushed the men into one side of the back booth together and she slid in facing them. "This way I can see both of you," she said, noting their surliness. "Try to get along ... please."

"Goulash again?" asked Vic.

"Don't be afraid of something new," she said. "I'll order. You'll like it, I promise." She chose a large platter of the mixed grill special and three large steins of lager. "I told Kurt you chase Russians," she said to Vic. "Is that all right?"

"Sure," he said. "It's an open secret."

"You said you aren't exactly a spy, but it sure sounds like it to me," she asked, trying to draw Kurt's interest.

"What I do is perfectly legal and the Soviets do the same to us. It's an agreement we made after World War II," he said, "…for transparency. But we've been over this already."

"What about the Russians?" Kurt asked. "What are they like … in your professional opinion?" She smiled as Kurt entered the opened door; she would compel them to get along by undaunted persistence.

"They're heavy handed," said Vic. "They kill mice with a sledgehammer."

"My father hates them," said Kurt. "He lost a leg at Stalingrad."

"Was he a Nazi?" Vic asked.

"Of course not. We detest them, too," Kurt said, checking Ilse. "He was forced into the Army. I joined the Navy to avoid the Eastern Front. He wants the Russians out of East Germany; so do I."

"The Russians want to have all of Germany," said Vic, "I expect you'd like us Americans out too."

"Sure," said Kurt. "But Americans are different."

"You said you were in the German navy?"

"U-boats."

"Sink any ships?"

"I'm a good navigator," he answered indirectly.

"Why'd you do it?"

"No choice. You Americans don't know what it's like to have no choices."

"There are always choices; sometimes there just aren't many good ones. I'm curious how you handled your situation."

"I satisfied my conscience but still did my duty. Once when I placed our boat on a shipping line, I positioned us perfectly and we sunk two American ships. As far as I know, all lives were lost." Kurt rubbed his eyebrow as he talked. "I realized then I could miscalculate slightly and position us out of effective range.

195

The captain eventually adjusted, but only after several targets had passed. We didn't sink so many then."

"I hope you don't expect my thanks for that."

"Hardly—you asked a question and I gave an answer."

"I like to keep my feet dry," said Vic. "I'll take my chances with tanks."

"Do you think the Russians will attack?" Kurt asked.

"Not likely. Not against our nuclear weapons. They won't risk it; it's called deterrence."

"How about their missiles aimed at Washington?"

"They have some big ones with long range but our targeting is more effective and more flexible. And if they attack Europe or the U.S., they know we'd go straight for Moscow—MAD—Mutual Assured Destruction. Plus, we have new technology on the drawing boards."

"Multiple warheads?"

"How'd...?" Vic paled.

"None of this is as secret as you believe," said Kurt. "Anything can be learned for a price. Do you think they'd hit Washington in a preemptive strike?"

"It's a long way from Moscow to Washington and our early warning line would pick it up in plenty of time." Vic frowned, took a defensive stance. "We really shouldn't be discussing any of this."

Ilse watched him closely, trapped in the booth—the backrest like an execution wall.

"Excuse me, I need to get out." Kurt moved and allowed Vic to slide over. He walked directly to the men's room.

Ilse whispered, "Don't push so hard, Kurt. You've upset him."

"I'm sorry," he said. "I didn't want to come at all—you started this."

"I just wanted you to talk, to like each other. If you can't get along, I have a serious problem—I need you both."

"I'm sorry." He stroked his eyebrow. "I had to test him. If I can't trust him with the document Ingrid gave me, I also have a serious problem." Vic returned and Ilse slid over, patted the seat indicating he should sit beside her.

"I was afraid you'd left," she said.

"Were you talking about me while I was gone?"

"Of course," she said and took his hand under the table.

"I'm sorry if I was out of bounds," said Kurt. "Can you tell me how you get in and out of East Germany?"

"That's not a problem. I don't have to sneak around. We just drive in and out. It's legal. I have a pass. They try to make it difficult but they can't deny us access. We don't officially recognize East Germany as a country—our business is strictly with the Soviets—the East Germans are just their tools."

"What do you do?"

"Keep an eye on their military—snoop, take pictures, listen, try to figure out what they're doing before they do it."

"What about their plans? How do you know what they plan to do—if they'll attack, where or when?"

"Professional assessments —based on what we see— educated guesses, really."

"But you can't get their actual plans, can you?"

"No, of course not."

"What if you could?"

Vic's eyes narrowed. Their verbal fencing had reached a sharp point. "What are you getting at?" he asked Kurt, but before he could answer he looked at Ilse. "What's really going on here? You didn't invite me here to eat, did you?"

The proprietor swooped in and dropped the sizzling mixed grill platter on the table. Steam rising from the hot plate seemed to release some overpressure. The oblong blue and white Dutch platter was filled with a mix of grilled lamb, beef, pork and a variety of sausages around the edges, a mountain of red cabbage in the center. The Hungarian's wife dispersed plates, utensils, and three fresh, frosty mugs.

Kurt started on the food and they followed, postponed breaching the communications barrier, a temporary cease-fire. But the unanswered question teetered with zesty aroma of spicy food.

After a while, Vic reopened their unfinished business, "I'm still waiting for an explanation, or should I just guess?"

He glanced at Ilse but she avoided eye contact, stirring her food with a knife and fork. Kurt kept chewing, his attention fastened on the table. Vic realized he had glimpsed a disturbing truth before the door was slammed in his face, but his quest for intelligence and professional pride were at stake. He tried again. "What do you do, Kurt? What's your job?"

Kurt swallowed, chased it with beer, and slowly wiped his mouth with a napkin. "You could say I'm a *geschäftsmann*—an entrepreneur."

"Now that's a real two-dollar word. What exactly does that mean?"

"I sell things."

"What do you sell?"

"Whatever is needed?"

"I thought you were a carpenter."

"I am that, too."

"So if I wanted a piece of furniture, you would build it and sell it to me?"

"Yes," said Kurt. "But I deal mostly in unusual articles, rarities, things almost impossible to obtain."

"So ... for example, if I needed something hard to get, I could place an order and you'd get it for me … for a price, of course?"

"Perhaps," said Kurt. "More often I find something of significance and look for an interested party to buy it."

"Well, let's use a hypothetical," said Vic. "What if I wanted some information, say something about the Soviets, could you get that?"

"Depends."

"On what?"

"Value," said Kurt. "Mine is a business of risk and return. It must be worth the risk, not only to the customer but to me as well. And the return must satisfy our aims."

"So this is all about money?"

"No," said Kurt. "I want what I do to be important. I'm not a mercenary. Money is only to protect my interests and ensure that my risk is worthwhile. My primary concern is Germany's future."

"Can you show me an example of your work?"

Kurt hesitated. They were back at thecrux, the invisible crevice dividing theoretical from hard reality. "Perhaps."

Vic noticed Ilse following his reactions. "Are you in on this, too?" he asked her. "Is this why you've been singing my song?"

She found his hand. "Listen, Vic." She swallowed. "I'm not using you. I would never do that to you. I want to help you, and I want to help Kurt, too. That's all, honestly."

"This isn't helping or using—this is abusing," he said. "I find these prospects disagreeable."

He pulled back his hand. "I'm a military officer doing the job I was sent here to do. I'm not CIA. This is way out of my league. I need to go." He stood to leave.

"What will you do?" She was suddenly alarmed. "Vic?"

"I'm obligated to report such approaches," he said. "But frankly, I don't know what I'll do."

She stood closer to him, but didn't touch him. She whispered, "Vic, I trusted you." Her appeal was a plea. "Don't ... please."

She reached for his hand, but he turned and walked out.

52

Hand off

Ilse feared she had permanently lost Vic upon his abrupt departure from the restaurant. She had innocently tried to find common ground between them but didn't anticipate such strong reactions. Naive interference might have cost her dearly, ending her budding affair with Vic and exposing Kurt to increased risk. Her nightly horrors became a daytime hell.

"Why don't you simply invite him over?" Kurt asked.

"I can't," she said. "He hates me now." Her eyes watered but she blinked hard, chasing the flood away, visible evidence of her failing. "Didn't you see the way he looked at me? He thinks I deceived him, and I did. I might have ruined his career, his whole life. He'll never want to see me again."

"Face it," he said. "You can't avoid this—just phone him and see what happens. We must know what he intends to do now."

She considered—it couldn't be that easy. Kurt became his father: "Face your fears," the old man had insisted at her lowest point. She lifted the phone, steadied her hands. Surprisingly, Vic accepted her call and she asked him flatly to come for dinner at the apartment.

"Okay," he said evenly. "I'll come."

"Thank you." Her temple throbbed, a hammer-on-anvil headache. "Have you mentioned last night?" she managed. She didn't want to deal with that one, but had to ask.

"Would I come if I had?" he snapped, a wounded animal pursued.

"I suppose not."

"You don't have to ply me with dinner," he said, his temperament a bit lighter. "I told the colonel I was working on a new angle."

She couldn't speak, just closed her eyes and thanked heavens.

Vic continued, "He just looked at me like he always does and poured another round," he said. "See you tonight."

She opened her eyes and cried in repentance, regret, and relief.

Vic buzzed the main door to her apartment building promptly at seven. Kurt pushed the release button upstairs, unlocking the street entrance and waited with the apartment door ajar. Vic trudged the steps with a bottle of tax-free single-malt scotch from the military exchange grasped in one hand.

"Come in," Kurt said dryly. "She'll be right out."

Vic stood the brown paper bag on the table near the door. "I thought we might want something stronger tonight." He hung his overcoat on a rack beside the door. "It's getting colder."

He browsed, wandered to the Dietrich poster which he hadn't noticed before. "She's certainly a Dietrich fan," he said to himself, but smelled her perfume and turned. She stood inches away in a black cocktail dress with a simple string of pearls, matching earrings, short hair brushed straight almost to her shoulders.

"Do you like it?" she asked, indicating the poster. "Dietrich represents my aspirations." She kissed his cheeks formally the traditional three times, then his cold lips once lightly. "She showed me the way, left bread crumbs for me to follow."

He said, "You look great."

Kurt pried at the scotch across the room.

"Let's have a drink before dinner," she suggested. "It's almost ready." She sat on the small love seat, near the center. The aroma from the oven wafted through the small apartment.

Kurt stayed out of the way, lighting a fire in the fireplace with black coal, leaving Vic alone in his quandary over where to sit. Vic glanced at the narrow space beside her on the love seat but moved instead to a lone chair.

"Sit here, Vic." She patted the cushion, lips pouted. "I promise not to bite."

He sat uneasily near the edge, inches away.

The fire caught and Kurt brought in three glasses with one hand and the bottle in the other. "Neat?" he asked.

Vic nodded and Kurt raised his glass.

Ilse toasted. "To friends. Germans and Americans."

Vic drank to that and said, "I'm German, you know. My parents went to America before the war but I was actually born here in Berlin."

"That's interesting," said Kurt, surprised and smiling.

Ilse remembered Kurt insisted she find a "good German man." She stood and Vic stood with her.

"I'll finish dinner if you'll excuse me?" she said. "And Vic, please don't stand for me. Make yourself at home here." She went to the kitchen and busied herself with dinner preparations, but remained attentive to their conversation.

"That explains your good German," said Kurt, resuming where they had left. "Most Americans only learn about ten survival words."

"My father demanded we speak German at home. We had to share something with the family every night, a little speech, which was critiqued for content and diction."

"Strong family values. We have family meetings, too."

"Isn't your family in East Berlin?"

"Yes. But when I do go there I have meals with my father and sister and we talk."

"Do you have papers?"

"Revoked."

"Have you been back since?"

"Yes."

"Going again?"

"Yes."

"How?"

"I don't know—more difficult now." They traveled a long road with a few steps—important understandings passed with sparse words.

Isle tinkled a miniature brass bell over the small table and they assembled around it without urging. Ilse served delicate medallions of roasted pork tenderloins, steaming English potatoes, and fresh *spargle* under candlelight.

Once dinner had begun, Vic looked to Kurt, "You mentioned your father and sister but not your mother."

"She died in the war. When my father returned from the Russian front and learned of her murder, he went crazy. Monks cared for him and my sister until he recovered. He's the maintenance man at the old Dom now."

"My father once spoke of the Dom, but I don't know much about it. And what does your sister do?"

"She has an administrative job but mostly looks after the old man. He likes having her close." Kurt caught Ilse's eye with a warning.

"How does he like you being over here in the west?"

Kurt laughed. "I don't count for much with him. I think he blames me for not being there to protect my mother when she was killed."

Ilse redirected the conversation. "Tell us about your family, Vic," she said. "I'm intrigued." She returned a warning look to Kurt not to interrupt.

"There's not much to tell," he said. "They fled Berlin for America before the war, lived in New York for a while then moved to Kansas. My father was an aircraft design engineer in Wichita until he moved to Houston to work on rockets."

"Hitler needed engineers," she said. "Why did they leave? Are they Jewish?"

"God no!" he said. "Protestant. My mother is a pacifist, opposed to all violence. They just didn't want to be part of any war, anytime, anywhere."

"But you went into the army?" she asked.

"It almost killed my mom," he said. "It was against everything she believed in, but she eventually got over it."

After dinner they adjourned to fireside with coffee and cheesecake from the bakery on the next block.

"Dinner was great," said Vic. "Thanks for inviting me back."

"Thank you, Vic, for coming. You surprised me with that wonderful breakfast before. Kurt never cooks."

"I want to know about your family," he said to her. "You keep dodging that."

"I'm an orphan, Vic. Both my parents are dead, killed in the war when I was quite young. There just isn't anything more to say."

"I'm sorry."

"I think I'll change into something more comfortable," she said. "Make yourselves at home." She disappeared into her bedroom but left the door cracked an inch to listen.

Kurt asked, "Have you thought about what I told you?"

"Actually you didn't tell me much—had to read between the lines. Your secret, whatever it is, is safe for now, but I do want to know why you do this. Money?"

"The money is good, but I do it for Germany, my hope for a reunified Germany."

"Yeah, right! The Nazis will take over again."

"There are still a few of those around," he admitted. "And a new breed almost as bad. When the old thinking is finally gone we'll be rid of all those ghosts and have our country back."

"The Soviets aren't convinced it will ever happen and frankly, neither are we."

"The Soviets want to suck the life out of Germany," said Kurt, "but eventually they'll have to leave. They can't survive as a flawed state and neither can East Germany—a country that builds walls to keep citizens is already failing. NATO will accept this when Germany acts like one country instead of two. The United States will support us, too."

"Perhaps," said Vic, "but not in our lifetime. Willy Brandt can do nothing. Kennedy is powerless. Khrushchev wants to bury us. What can anyone do?"

"We first must envision it. We must believe it is possible and do one thing every day to bring it about. There is hope for Brandt—he already sees it and talks openly about it. That's only the beginning but he's limited in what he can do publicly, except talk. When the chips are down, he'll come through. We'll make it happen."

"Well..." Vic said. "I think it's only a pipe dream."

"You're wrong. We can actually do more than Brandt or Kennedy simply because we're beneath the radar. We're not even perceived as a serious threat, just expendable pawns on the cold war chess board. Those in power can't even see what we're doing."

"You can't possibly believe that."

"I do believe it," said Kurt. "My life is built on this belief, as is my father's, my sister's and my fiancé's."

"And Ilse?"

"She got involved accidentally. She's not committed to this. She's naïve as you saw at the restaurant."

"I wish she wasn't in it at all. I haven't prayed in a long time but I prayed last night that it wasn't true. I feel like a complete fool."

"I wish she weren't involved either," Kurt said. "I tried to keep her out of it but she's very headstrong."

"Why did you tell me all this? This is dangerous information to share."

The moment of truth had arrived and Kurt made a leap of faith. "I have a top secret document and I don't know what to do with it. Will you take it? No strings attached."

"I don't want it," said Vic. "If I even see it, I'll have to explain it. If it becomes real, I have to treat it that way."

"You can't say no," Kurt pushed. "You must see this one. It's your duty—the future depends on what you do." Kurt drew a line in the sand, an inescapable challenge.

"Horse shit!" Vic exploded, pushed into a corner.

"I'm asking only for your trust," Kurt said. "I'll leave everything in your hands—follow your heart."

"Why should I do anything for you?"

"It isn't for me, Vic—this is for Germany *and* America. Consider Ilse, too. She *believes* in you. She *loves* you. She *hopes* you'll do the right thing."

He opened a desk drawer and removed the crumpled envelope with water stains Ingrid had given him at Emil's bakery. He held out it to Vic and after a moment's hesitation he accepted it. The Rubicon was crossed.

Kurt refilled his drink, turned his back on Vic and gazed outside the frosty window where snow was piling up.

Vic scanned the document quickly, looked to Kurt's back then the papers once more, reading carefully. "Do you know what this is?" he finally asked.

"Of course," Kurt said. "This is the Soviet outline of a ground attack on NATO, driving all the way through Germany, France and Belgium to the Atlantic and North Sea—the ultimate conclusion of World War II."

"Why should I believe this is authentic?"

"Disregard it at your own risk—and the death of us all."

Vic double-checked the concept plan and focused on the signature block—Koniev. It had to be current since he had just returned. Vic had seen his initials—this looked genuine and it was original, something the CIA could verify. "What should I do with it?"

"You'll know what to do."

"I can't pay you anything for this."

"I'm asking for nothing. I'm getting out of this business and this is something I promised an American sailor years ago."

Vic paced the confining apartment, legs wobbly, burdened by a load he didn't want to carry. He stopped before the crackling fire, the papers loosely in his hand. He watched the flames lick at them, unaware when Kurt went out.

He smelled her perfume only when she slipped her arms under his, encircled his chest with her hands and pressed to his back.

He turned in her arms and her lips were inches from his, her breath and perfume alluring. The loose sweater and bobby socks beckoned. They were alone with his dilemma.

She kissed him with warm and open lips. He pushed away, conflicted and resenting his predicament. "Why are you doing this to me?"

"Do you think I'm seducing you?"

205

"Yes." He waved the papers at her. "You're adding too much pressure."

"I didn't put you in this position, Vic," she whispered. "Life did. God gave you a German heart and the United States army sent you to Berlin. What brought us together on Ku'damm? Can you tell me that? You're an instrument of fate, Vic, just as I am. I didn't ask for this either, but we must do our duty now. Someday we'll be judged by how we do."

"How will you judge me?"

"That's not fair, Vic. Whatever you do, don't do it for me. Do it for yourself and your country."

She kissed his cheek and started back to her bedroom. She said, "Don't stay tonight, Vic. I don't want you to do anything for the wrong reasons." She quietly closed her bedroom door.

Vic held the damned thing in his hand, waved it over the flames again then retreated. He knew what he had to do, but he didn't like it.

He poured a bracer and tipped his glass toward the closed bedroom.

He slipped his overcoat on and dropped the envelope into his pocket, dowsed the lights and walked alone into the first snow of winter.

53

Face the Music

Vic sat on the edge of his bed unable to sleep, having given up someone he loved for something he didn't want. Ilse couldn't possibly love him if she used him this way. She was an actress, a pretender—he should be skeptical of anything she said. The cost of discovering the truth might be an act of treason.

He had neither the authority nor the training for what he was involved in—consorting with spies—even unwillingly but compelled by some inexplicable bond, an accident of birth, time, and place.

Kurt had risked his life to hand over a top secret plan from the enemy commander's camp and sought nothing in return. It was pointless to try to sleep with a Warsaw Pact attack plan under his pillow. He imagined being tortured with thumbscrews. He wrestled with his problem through the night until the dreaded daylight arrived—he must do his duty.

Powell arrived at his office early and Vic was waiting. As soon as the colonel saw him he knew he had a problem. "I thought you worked late last night!"

"I have to show you something." Vic waved the envelope but Powell ignored it and began his start-of-business routine. He hung his cap, scarf and overcoat on hooks, thumbed through waiting phone messages, pushed a pile of folders aside, and settled behind his desk.

Vic shoved the envelope across the desktop before he changed his mind—he squirmed before his confessor.

Powell still ignored it—an interminable delay. "Want some coffee?" he asked pleasantly.

"Maybe later ... after this."

Powell stalled, leaving to fill his cup in the kitchen. When he returned he busied himself rearranging pens on his desk. Vic wondered if he had only dreamed about the torture chamber.

Finally Powell shook the document from the crumpled brown envelope and let it fall to his desktop. Vic cringed as if it would explode. He saw Powell watching him instead of the paper. Vic took a chair uninvited and waited.

As Powell read his expression registered increasing alarm.

"Holy shit!" he said finally. "Do you know what this is?"

"Yes sir."

"Where the hell did you get it?"

"Someone gave it to me, an anonymous source."

"Anonymous my ass!" His face turned red. "Who, damn it?"

"A German...."

He read it again and aimed his sights at Vic. When he next spoke, he sounded as if he had grit in his throat. "Shut the door, Captain." He pointed as if Vic might be confused. "Lock it!"

He did as he was told. Vic felt he was already in prison—the screws turning.

Powell was calm. "Now, Vic. This is a very hot document. Whether it's even real or not is another question, but it is significant. You stuck it in my hands and expect me to do something with it. What? Give it to the CIA? Send it to The Pentagon? The Commander-in-Chief? Who? And you want me to just say we found it on the street? Some German handed it over? Is that what you expect?"

"I guess they wouldn't buy that."

"No shit! Would you?"

"I guess not."

"I don't think you realize it, son, but you just graduated from having one of the more dangerous jobs in the United States Army to *the* most dangerous ... hell, it isn't even a job. I don't know what it is. You're way over your head here."

"Yes sir."

"I know you're protecting someone, Vic," he said in a fatherly way, "but I can't help if I don't know who it is. Do you see my point, son?"

"He's a crosser," he offered. "He doesn't want to be identified. That would put him at risk. I'd lose my source. He might be killed."

"I could keep his identity secret—Top Secret, by God. All our agent's names are Top Secret."

"Shit, sir!" he said. "Look at what you're holding in your hand. That has Top Secret all over it, but you have it and you don't even know where it came from. Secrets get leaked all the time and people get killed."

"Give me something to work with, Vic. I need something tangible to hang onto here. I'm trying to help you with this, don't you see?"

"Okay, sir. He's a German national I met in a bar. A mutual friend introduced us, but I can't reveal either identity—like I said—to protect them. Is that enough?"

"No," said Powell. "But, it's a start. That'll buy you a day but not much more. You'll have the CIA tailing you by tomorrow, just so you'll know. Not to mention the *Stasi* and the KGB—they'll stick to you like flypaper, because there are leaks—just like you said. They'll miss this paper, you know."

He thumped it with his index finger. "Look right there—it's a numbered original—initialed, by God, by none other than Koniev! Your own government will treat you like a criminal just because you turned it in. I've been where you are and there's nothing more I can to do for you. You better cover your ass, son."

"What will you do?"

"The first thing is to lock this up in the tightest safe in Berlin. Then I'm going to doctor my coffee and think about the next step over a pack of camels. I won't get any rest until I get rid of it, I know that much."

"I know what you mean." Vic walked to the door to leave.

"Hey, Captain!" Powell stopped him.

"Yes sir?"

"Go get some sleep," he said. "You look like shit."

"Yes sir."

"And, Vic," he said, "One more thing."

"Sir?"

"Damn good job." A faint smile crinkled his lip before he got it straightened out.

"Let's work with it ... but be careful, son. People do get killed over shitty little things like war plans, even phony ones."

54

Dragnet

Hilda was bewildered. Hans had stirred feelings in her as she prepared to start a new life with Kurt. She knew she was vulnerable during Kurt's absences but she vowed to stay loyal despite her needs.

She moved mechanically, oblivious to her surroundings while reveling over their last night together. She wondered if her thoughts were revealed on her face—cheeks felt hot. They would soon leave this insanity behind and relax on the coast of Spain and have children—two or three. It wasn't too late for a normal life. Kurt was her everything—everything would be wonderful when he came—she hoped it was soon and forever.

Hans had already packed most of his belongings for Paris, but had selected several antiques from his collection to leave behind in her sparsely furnished apartment. She had rented it although she knew he would return to Bonn and try again to seduce her. He even purchased a larger bed for her bedroom and placed a love seat before the fireplace. He claimed it was just to store for him until he returned, but she knew otherwise—he hoped to get her into that bed. She hadn't encouraged his advances but they made dull nights interesting.

Han's infatuation warmed her on this chilly morning. Torrid dreams and fantasies intermingled—she was still an attractive and vital woman and such desires reassured her sexuality. She wouldn't yield, but memories of his hands on her were stimulating when she was lonely.

Hans last night in Bonn had arrived and he started a wood fire in his apartment. Packing boxes were stacked along the walls, ready for the movers. "More wine?" he asked.

"You've been kind to me, Hans."

"I'm happy for both of us. Who knows, maybe, someday...?"

"I don't know."

"Do you remember the first time we met, the very first time, in that restroom?"

"I'll never forget. I was terrified. I thought my life had ended then but now I realize it was just beginning."

The next morning Hans left for Paris and she reported to work as usual, but Anna informed her she had been promoted and was to move upstairs right away. No interviews had been conducted. Anna was taken completely by surprise; she wanted to be considered for that position and Hilda was advanced over her. Even though Hans had told Hilda the job was hers, she couldn't believe it.

She rearranged her few personal things on the luxurious cherry desk, and sat in a soft leather swivel chair. She opened the top drawer and found a note, creased once. She recognized Han's stationary. She opened it, finding a message scribbled beneath the auspicious letterhead—*Congratulations, Hilda. Enjoy the new apartment and your new position. I'll call you from Paris. Miss you already. Be careful. Hans.*

She slipped it in her pocket as the new director of political affairs entered, his hand outstretched. "*Frau* Brunner, I'm *Herr* Guzman. Congratulations on your promotion—and welcome."

"Thank you," she said, accepting his hand.

"*Herr* Globke told me the competition for this position was keen," he said. "You'll have considerable responsibility here. For now, familiarize yourself with the office filing system." He handed her an envelope. "These are the combinations to all the safes. Keep them secured when you're away. Also, your new security classification and access badges are inside. Make yourself at home. We'll have time to get better acquainted later. I have an important meeting with the Chancellor. We have some unexpected and urgent new information to evaluate."

The flowers in the garden Hilda's mother kept would explode into vibrant colors every spring. She hadn't thought of them in years but her memories of that place so long ago oddly returned. The garden hadn't been in England where she lived with her mother, but in Germany before the war. Her father worked in the fields while she helped her mother tend the lovely flowers.

Her father would come late in the afternoon, sit with them on the grass and ask her to name the flowers—he listened tirelessly to her chatter. He would cross his legs and she would sit on the end of his foot, bouncing up and down. They would laugh ... and then the war. Her mother wakened her in the middle of the night, her father kissed her cheek, hugged her mother, and they left by cart, bus, train, boat and finally reached London.

She never saw her father again. Why was she so afraid to go back? She must go there with Kurt before they escaped to Spain. With that settled she felt relieved, one more weed in life's garden tended.

Hilda hummed on her way to work with her indecision resolved. She stopped at a flower shop with a greenhouse to protect the tender plants from the snows blanketing the hills.

"I'd like a mixed bouquet, please."

"Which ones?"

"Two bluebells, please ... and two of the white carnations, a marigold, peony, a pink rose, and one of those lilacs; some greenery please. That'll do nicely."

"You love flowers, don't you? I've seen you here before."

"I feel special today. Thank you."

She had limited such simple pleasures until she saw clearly where her life was going. But she saw her future now and she liked what she saw. The pay raise and the new apartment made each succeeding day brighter while her dream of raising children with Kurt was about to be fulfilled.

Her daily dread of being caught spying had passed and the new office afforded an unsullied sense of identity. For the first time she felt important; she shut her mind to her deception and pampered herself by scheduling an appointment for hair and nails. Surely Kurt would arrive over the weekend and she would be ready—perhaps a concert before they disappeared.

The workload was lighter too, except when the staff prepared for large conferences. Yesterday had been such a day. One of her responsibilities was copying documents on the special machine reserved for classified papers. It was locked in a back room but she had her own key. She copied presentation summaries and staff studies and set up briefing books for the Chancellor and other key staff. She could discretely run extra copies when she found something Kurt might use.

Even better, she signed off on the destruction log for documents no longer needed, giving access to marginal notes jotted during discussions. Espionage didn't get any easier than this. Kurt would be proud and Hans was to thank for it. Hans was expected in Bonn for this meeting and she would see him again.

"Hilda, you've surpassed all my expectations," said *Herr* Guzman. "All the briefing books are in order. You worked late last night and everything is ready so why don't you leave early this afternoon? Take compensatory time but I'll need you here early tomorrow for the meeting."

"Thank you, sir," she said. "But I'm prepared to stay as long as necessary in the event anything else is needed."

"We'll be fine. Go ahead, you deserve it."

She did deserve it—everyone deserved some happiness. She locked the safes and her desk and left with the bouquet in hand. She had purchased a new dress with her pay raise to match her high spirits. The dress was conservative, but new—she felt like a new woman, happier than ever.

As she left the building she noticed a well-dressed, handsome man watching her walk past. His stare was unnerving but she felt a tinge of excitement that brought a sparkle to her eyes. She blushed at her own thoughts—Kurt was the only man for her—yet Han's attention and now this man reassured her femininity and the joys of life.

The sky was dark early as winter stormed in but her mood was buoyant. She decided to indulge herself with a glass of wine at the *weinstube* near her apartment. Perhaps some of her old friends from the typing pool might drop by. She hung her coat beside the door and found a seat.

A draft blew across her calves and she glanced in the direction of the opened door. The same man who had watched her leave entered. She was disappointed when he walked past, taking a table near the window instead of the empty seat beside her. No matter, Hans would arrive tomorrow and Kurt was ready to set a date. She was ashamed of her distracting needs.

She finished her wine, paid her bill and buttoned her coat to the top. She continued along the Rhine walk in a buoyant mood. When she reached her new apartment the security guard greeted her cheerfully.

"*Guten Abend, Fraulein* Brunner."

"*Guten Abend.*"

"I have a message for you." He handed her an envelope. "A courier delivered it this afternoon."

"*Danke.*" She shoved it into her coat pocket, relishing the mystery—was it from Hans, Kurt, or the mysterious stranger? Anyway, it had to be good news. She hung her coat in the closet and tore open the envelope.

She walked near the closed French doors overlooking the balcony for natural light, unfolded the note and read: ***Call this number at eight tonight from a public telephone. I will explain then. Hans.*** The number was at the bottom. She recognized the exchange as Paris, but it was neither Hans' home nor work numbers. The obscurity was disquieting.

She watched snow gathering on the mountains sloping down to the Rhine and—she saw him again! The man who had watched her leaving work then followed her to the *weinstube* was now walking along the street beneath her apartment—stalking! He glanced up briefly then turned his face down and hurried past.

A chill clutched her—the frigid wind that blew through the bar seized her again. Three times within an hour—Kurt did not believe in coincidence. She shivered and started a fire in the fireplace.

A few minutes before the appointed hour, Hilda ducked out of the apartment and made her way to the *Bahnhof*. From a phone booth she dialed the number on the note. Hans interrupted the first ring.

"Hello?"

She recognized his voice but it was different—weaker. "Hans? Are you coming to Bonn?"

"No, Hilda. I'm sorry." His voice was tentative, stifled.

"Are you ill?"

"Worse. I'll explain." She detected a tremor, a slight wavering, and heard him drinking something, or smoking—nervous.

"I asked you to call my friend's apartment because my phone is tapped. I had you use a public phone because I believe yours is as well." He swallowed hard. "That's why I used a courier to deliver the note."

"What?" Her hand trembled as she pressed the phone hard against her ear.

"Hilda, I'm being followed. Have you seen anything suspicious?"

No need to consider—acid dropped in the pit of her stomach. "Maybe."

"Listen carefully. A *Stasi* agent defected. His name was Dieter Haus but that isn't important. He brought files with him. An investigation is underway so we must assume we have both been compromised."

"Oh! Will we be arrested?"

"Yes, I believe so."

"What can we do?" Panic clutched her throat, strangled her—could hardly breathe.

"Fox told me if this happened to go to Switzerland," he said. "You must go there too and turn yourself in at the Soviet Embassy. Ask for asylum."

"Hans, I can't do that. I won't go to Russia. I'm marrying Kurt. We're going to Spain."

"Hilda, please. You must go, but if you won't go to Russia, at least go to Switzerland—not a NATO country. You must go ... tonight."

"Are you going?"

"To Bern, then Moscow—we'll talk about it there. I'm going to the Soviet Embassy—contact me there in a couple of days. I'm taking a circuitous route."

"I must warn Kurt."

"Perhaps you should, but don't call from your apartment phone. You must realize he's likely being followed as well. I'm leaving within the hour on a train. You should, too, call him from Switzerland. Leave now and don't go back to your apartment. I must go now. Good bye Hilda and good luck."

"Good bye, Hans." The tone buzzed. She remembered she had forgotten to thank him—thank him for what?

She racked her memory for the emergency number at Ilse's apartment and dialed it. No one answered. She sat breathlessly in the phone booth until a stranger banged on the door—startling her—only another customer impatient to use the phone.

She hurried away, trying to remember all Hans had said. She walked toward her apartment to duck in, grab a bag, identity papers and the last documents hidden there. She couldn't go to Switzerland without her passport, money, and checkbook. She'd call Kurt when she had a train ticket.

As she approached her building, she saw three cars parked along the curb in a restricted zone. She stepped into an adjacent doorway and saw government license plates on all three. The man from that afternoon was talking to the security guard in her building. Then he got into one of the cars.

She waited for the car to drive away but it remained at the curb. They were waiting for her!

She pulled a scarf over her nose and mouth and raced back to the *Bahnhof,* wondering how she could just leave her entire life behind, and without Kurt.

55

Mounting Desperation

Kurt had slept on the cot in Ilse's basement storeroom, not knowing if Vic would sleep over after dinner. He rose early and patrolled the Wall all morning searching for a new way to the other side, but it was fortified tighter than ever. Ilse had left the phone off the hook all night and had gone to morning rehearsals. They returned to her apartment, arriving at the same time. He was discouraged and she was depressed, both concerned about Vic's reaction. Neither could sleep so they talked.

"I wonder why Vic hasn't called," she said.

"Give him time," said Kurt. "He'll do the right thing. You know, I think he's good for you. You've changed since you met him."

"I'm afraid that's over."

The phone rang but she hesitated to pick it up. "You answer it," said Kurt. It rang again. "Maybe it's Vic; he'd rather talk to you."

Kurt didn't move so she picked it up on the third ring. She listened a moment, frowned, then said, "Just one moment."

She whispered to Kurt, "It's Hilda and she's crying."

He took the phone. "Hilda?"

"Kurt ... it's horrible!" She was sobbing.

"Calm down," he said, giving her a moment to collect her wits. "What's wrong?"

"I'm calling from the *Bahnhof*. I've been here since last night. I don't know what to do."

"Start from the beginning, Hilda."

She wept unrestrained, relating her trauma beginning with Hans' warning to rush to Switzerland, and the man tailing her.

"Go immediately," he said. "As soon as I get Ingrid out of East Berlin my work is finished. I'll meet you there. But Hilda, do not go to the Soviet Embassy."

"Kurt, I don't even have money for a ticket, and I don't have a passport or anything. Everything is in my apartment and the police are there already. I don't know what to do."

"Hilda," he said, "You can access our Swiss savings from any bank. Do you need the numbers again?"

"I remember them."

"Go to a bank you don't normally use, one where they don't know you. They close in an hour. Have five thousand marks transferred to you for cash—wait for it. That amount will not arouse suspicion. Buy a train ticket to Lorrach, across the river from Switzerland. Stay in the *Gasthous* Yellow Rose and use the name Irma Swartz, just as we planned for our escape. Pay cash in advance until I arrive. I'll arrange new identity papers and have them delivered there."

"Kurt, can we do it?"

"Yes, we can. But stay out of sight when you get there."

"Kurt, can you come get me. I'm really scared."

"I would if I could—you know that. But you can't stay there a moment longer—don't wait for me. You can do this, Hilda."

"I'll wait for you in Lorrach, Kurt. Is it finally over?"

"Yes, darling," he said. "It's over when you get to Switzerland. You're very brave, Hilda. You can do this. Go straight to the bank then take a taxi to a small train station out of the city, not the main one. If you see any sign of trouble, hide. Don't walk into a trap. Be careful."

"I will."

"And Hilda, I have something for you as soon as I see you. I have the ring, darling. I want you to know. Be brave for us."

"Oh, Kurt, I love you so much. I can do it, I promise."

"I love you, too."

"And Kurt, I have some good news for us, too. I think ... never mind. I'll tell you when I see you, when I'm sure."

Kurt hung up the phone and explained what Ilse could only surmise. "Now, I must reach Fox immediately. Hilda needs new papers to get out and Ingrid must leave. This is bad!" A knock on the door interrupted.

Ilse answered it. "Vic! How did you get inside?" She took his hand and drew him quickly inside.

"A neighbor was leaving so I just walked in the open door."

Vic sat at the table opposite Kurt while she poured another cup of tea. He said to Kurt, "Something doesn't add up—why did you give those papers to me? You

217

said you are doing this for Germany, so why didn't you give it to a German, Willy Brandt, or the General Staff in Bonn?"

"Vic, you're an American and you acknowledge only the Soviets, discounting Germans. I'm no fool—Germany's only powers are those bestowed by the occupation forces. We hunker in our homes for Soviets to overrun us with tanks, or Americans to protect us by blasting our country with nuclear weapons. We live every day in the last and next battlefield. We must prevent a war between the United States and Russia to save ourselves. Germans don't have that much power. Can't you understand that?"

"I didn't think of it that way."

"You should. You must for your father's country and your own."

"Yeah, well, I guess you want to know what I did."

"We were wondering."

"I gave the document to Colonel Powell. He ripped me good and pumped me for more information about my sources."

"And what did you tell him?"

"...Then I was hauled into the CIA Field Station and grilled some more. They put a tail on me, too, but I lost them. I didn't mention either of you."

"You're sure they didn't follow you here?" Ilse peeped through the curtains onto the street below.

"Oh, I let them follow me all day, but I shook them before coming here. I'm sure of that—they're not as good as *Stasi*. But we can't meet like this. I don't want to slip up and lead them here."

"Vic," said Kurt. "I must go back across. I have urgent unfinished business there. My fiancée and my sister are in danger and I must get them both out of the country. I need help from the other side."

"You're crazy! How can you go back?"

"I don't know. But Hilda's depending on me and my sister is in greater jeopardy than she realizes. I'm finished—just want to protect them."

"I can't help you," said Vic. "We have a two man rule when we go across and Reitz is a straight arrow."

"I realize that," said Kurt.

Ilse turned from the window where she was standing surveillance while they talked. "I can do it," she said. "I'll go over with a visitor's pass or something. No one's looking for me." She walked as she talked, formulating a plan. "I know the way to Ingrid's apartment now and your father could help us out—like before. I know how to contact Fox, too, to get help for Hilda. He owes us that."

Kurt sprang to his feet. "Absolutely not!"

Vic agreed. "No way, Ilse! I won't let you do it."

"It's a good plan," she said. "I can handle Fox while Kurt goes to Hilda. She needs you, Kurt. This would save time. Don't delay this."

"I can't go directly to Hilda," his voice trailed away, tinged with guilt. "If I'm tailed, I'd lead them to her. Besides, she's already leaving Bonn tonight. When she doesn't report to work tomorrow, they'll search trains and planes. There's no more time. Hilda must go immediately and I must ensure Fox cooperates. Then I'll join her."

"You keep mentioning Fox," said Vic. "You're not talking about Mischa Fox are you?" he asked. "Unbelievable!" He walked to the window and double-checked that the police weren't waiting. "Don't you even think about going over there again, Ilse." He massaged his resurging headache. Then he said, "I might know a way to get Kurt through—alone."

"How?"

"We have a tunnel."

"A tunnel?"

"We dug several a few years ago, before the border was closed, to tap Soviet communications. They found one and closed it, but there's another."

"Can I use it?"

"I can get you into it. But finding your way through is your problem. I'm not going with you. I'm in too much trouble already."

"When can we go?" Kurt asked.

"Later, midnight. I'll meet you in *Grunnewald* Park after I lose my tail again."

"Thank you, Vic." She cradled his hand, touched it to her cheek.

"I wish I had run for my life when I first saw you on Ku'damm."

She kissed the back of his hand. "Do you really?"

"No," he admitted. "But I didn't expect you to turn my entire life upside down."

56

The Plumber

Kurt said goodbye to Ilse at midnight, an appropriate time for his dark and doubtful undertaking. The moment carried a foreboding of finality.

"Kurt, promise to be careful."

"I will."

"Is this really the last time?"

"Yes."

"Will I see you again before you go away?"

"Yes, Ilse..." He hesitated. "I want you to safeguard something for me."

"The ring?"

"More than our ring, Ilse—our future." He handed her the ring with a scrap of paper. "These numbers are important, Ilse. These are for our Swiss accounts, investments for our future. Hilda knows them but if anything happens to me, tell her to go to the United States, not Spain. Tell her I said we must leave Europe."

"I will," she promised. "I'll go there too, to Hollywood."

Kurt said, "I'll see you in the movies."

The CIA could never keep pace with Fox's intelligence service in Berlin and they certainly couldn't stay with a professional who routinely eluded Russians and East German secret police. Vic lulled them into complacency then vanished to meet Kurt in the park at midnight. He found only a late-night plumber sitting on a cold park bench. Vic stopped when he heard his name.

"You went overboard with the disguise, didn't you?"

"It was her idea but I've been in tunnels before and they're nasty."

"Come on, let's walk. They'll be watching my parked car."

They cut across city parks, back alleys and side streets to a guarded American military casern. Vic showed the gate guard his military identification card and a forged worker permit. "We have an emergency plumbing repair in the back. This may take a while."

The guard opened the gate and they continued to a small building at the rear of the compound. The sign on the door read, "Entry Forbidden by Order of the Commanding General." Vic opened it with a key and they stepped inside a building crowded with banks of electronics.

"What is this?" Kurt asked.

"Electronics to monitor phone taps. We're still tuning but soon we'll be listening in on some very private discussions."

"This is amazing."

"You can't ever mention this, Kurt. I'm in enough trouble already—they'd send me to Leavenworth for this. Say nothing about this to Fox."

He opened a padlock on a floor hatch and lifted. "This ladder leads to a tunnel connected to the waste water system. Phone cables run overhead. You'll find a stripe painted down the side where you enter the Soviet zone, right beneath the wall. That's the only reference point I know. I don't know where the tunnel goes—you're on your own. There must be a manhole cover, storm sewer, something—just look around. But don't be seen coming out."

"Thank you, Vic."

"Yeah—just don't get caught."

"Vic, I need to tell you something before I go. "Ilse is important to me and my family has somewhat adopted her. You probably know she's in love with you. She may seem strong but that's an act—she's fragile. Don't hurt her."

Kurt stepped into the hole and onto a metal ladder. He switched on a small flashlight when he found footing on concrete beneath mud and two inches of stinking water. He shined the light around—the tunnel was four feet wide and extended beyond the beam of light. As he sloshed he heard the hatch drop with a thud followed by a solid click of the heavy lock.

The top was low forcing Kurt to bend forward when he walked. When he reached a Y-juncture, he tried to get his bearings, straining his eyes against the darkness. The blinking eyes of a sewer rat glinted under his light. Three smaller ones followed along a ridge just above the waterline, sniffed and continued to search for food somewhere.

Further ahead he made out a faint white stripe and hand-lettering that read: *You are leaving the American Sector.*

He switched off the light to test his night vision and look for some hint of illumination from outside. Nothing—he pawed ahead in the dark to retain night vision, pausing to pay attention to any sounds representing a way out. The damp tunnel felt like a tomb, or a leaky U-boat running silent.

Water splashed onto his boots and he saw a steady trickle draining down a side wall. A small stream dribbled from a large opening, a pipe leading up at an incline. Through the opening the echo of gathering rumble was chased by a rush of warm air. He knew the familiar sound of the *U-Bahn*. He gauged his shoulders against the drainpipe. The fit was tight but just large enough to pull in by scrunching his shoulders. He shined the light inside the pipe looking for more

221

rats inside, then went in head first and slithered an inch at a time until he emerged wet and cold onto the subway bed.

He followed the dimly-let tracks and searched for an exit. When he found one, he climbed a ladder to a doorway into the central control zone of the station.

The wall clock read 3:23. Only one attendant was on duty and he glanced up from his pornographic magazine as Kurt sloshed past.

"*Guten morgen.*" The man kept reading, ignoring him. A sign over the exit read *Stetlin Station.*

Kurt slogged directly to Ingrid's flat and arrived forty-five minutes before she rose for work. Leary of waking nosey neighbors by pounding on her door, he shivered in the cold shadows near the factory fence until her light glowed.

He tapped lightly. "It's me."

She yanked the door back and he ducked in. "Thank God! I was so worried."

"I need hot coffee." He was shaking in his wet coveralls.

"Get a towel and dry off. You'll catch pneumonia."

"I'll just get out of these."

He returned from her bedroom in dry pants, socks and a heavy sweater, still shivering. She told him, "Sit down. Coffee will be ready in a minute."

"This is better—freezing!"

"How'd you get so wet?"

"I crawled through a sewer."

"Oh, that's the awful smell! Throw those clothes away; I'm not scrubbing them. How long will you stay?"

"Not long," he said. "Hilda's in trouble. I came for you."

"Hilda?"

"She fled from a dragnet. I need Fox to secure her passage to Switzerland. You must also leave here with me."

She avoided any discussion of leaving her father, changed the subject. "Was the last item I gave you any good?"

"Ingrid, it was *too* good, much too big. I can't use anything that crucial. I gave it to the Americans and they're asking questions. One of Fox's men defected. Hilda and I must leave Europe and you're coming, too. The network is breaking up."

She passed him a chipped cup of fresh coffee. "Have you told father?"

222

He blew over the steaming cup before sipping from it. "Not yet. I'll see him today. I must meet Fox again. Could you help me? I need a guide and the old man's leg.... And you must leave anyway."

"But Fox already knows me!"

"You'll be covered by a monk's robe and hood—the last thing you'll do here."

"Tonight?"

"At the Dom."

"Okay. I'll meet you there. You can tell me what to do then. I have to dress for work. If I don't go, they'll come here looking for me."

"Thank you, Ingrid."

She dressed while he rested. When she came out, he yawned, "Can I use your bed?"

"Only after you bathe with plenty of soap; you stink."

When Ingrid arrived at her office in the Soviet Embassy it was exactly as she had left it—until *Komrade* Sergey, the administrative officer, arrived at mid-morning to inform her of the changes!

"*Frau* Meyer, you'll move to a new job tomorrow. We've been directed to make some staffing changes."

"What changes?"

"You'll move to administrative records. *Komrade* Ivanovich will manage classified records."

"Why?" She shoved her trembling hands into her pockets. "Did I do something wrong?"

"No, no," he assured. "General Rubski came from Moscow to improve security. He wants a Russian handling classified files. That's all. Tomorrow report to room 4 C." Sergey disappeared into the elevator.

Ingrid thought furiously. *I know them too well—Fox had something to do with this. I saw the way he looked at me.*

She had no appetite for lunch and jumped at every sound throughout the day. She stayed late until six o'clock, knowing this was her last chance at the Cuban missile plan—a plan more important than the one to attack NATO. It would be risky to take it but most papers were only filed and forgotten until they were destroyed. She was leaving and could have several days before they discovered it was missing.

She thumbed through the file journal until she found the entry for General Rubski. She studied his signature and practiced repeatedly on a scrap of paper.

She signed the Top Secret plan out to Rubski, carefully forging his signature, verified it using Ivanovich's initials.

She folded the Top Secret plan and slipped it inside her brassier with her practiced signatures. She locked all the safes and called the guard to dismiss her. She just had time to walk to the Dom to help Kurt with his meeting.

She left her office on the beautiful avenue of the linden trees for the last time.

57

Fox Shows his Teeth

Kurt's clandestine meeting with Fox had worked well before, so he replicated it with Ingrid replacing Ilse as guide. He disliked using his sister so close to Fox but he needed a guide and the old man could not do that. It was too late to develop a new plan, time too urgent for Hilda—besides Fox might balk if he detected a trap. Kurt had another sealed envelope delivered by a boy to Fox's headquarters with one document from Hilda about multiple warhead missiles. The note read: *Same place at seven tonight. There are more of these. Chameleon.*

Karl laid out three monk's robes while Kurt briefed Ingrid—only minutes to spare. "Don't speak even if he speaks to you, and don't let him see your face," he warned. He saw she was nervous but there was no time to change—Fox had arrived.

Fox entered the Dom alone. He looked to the passageway, expecting to find the candle. Ingrid, just arriving, lit one and led the man she feared most to the confessional booth. The old man sat in the same darkened corner, his Lugar concealed under his robe and his stiff leg extended. Fox found his seat in the booth.

"Meyer?"

"Yes."

"Have any trouble?"

"Yes."

"I can help."

"Fine, but this is not for me."

"Then who?"

"First, tell me about the defector, Dieter Haus."

"How do you know about him?"

"My ass is in the meat grinder. It's my business to know."

"He took files with him."

"What files?"

225

"His own ... and Abel's," he said. "They were colleagues sharing an office."

"Hilda was compromised, therefore I am as well."

"You need a new identity. But, tell me about Hilda—was she arrested?"

"Security came for her and she had to run."

"Did she spot the trap herself?"

"A friend called from Paris to warn her—then she recognized the trap."

"Hans Globke?"

"His name was Hans."

"Where is she?"

"She's at the Yellow Rose, a pension in Lorrach, across the river from Basil. She's registered as Irma Schwartz. She has money for a few days but she needs papers for Switzerland."

"Our people in Bern will get her a Russian passport and take her to Moscow. She'll be fine."

"She's not going to Russia."

"She must go. It's the only safe place now."

"I said she's not going to Moscow! Switzerland."

"Your interest in her is more than professional."

"That's none of your business!"

"She must go to a safe house. She'll need a Swiss passport. We'll set her up there with Swiss Francs and a job. Don't worry. You'll be able to visit her."

"Okay, but it's critical to get her out quickly. That's the most important thing to me, Fox."

"An affair of the heart," he chuckled. "Love taints your perspective, Meyer."

"Mind your own business. Did you see the paper I sent?"

"Yes. It's good. Do you have more for me?"

"Yes, better than those but the price has increased under the circumstances."

"I'll have the funds transferred after I see the quality of your products. I can double your pay this one time, but I don't know how you'll acquire anything useful without Hilda. I'll only pay for results."

"That's my problem. Send the money to my Swiss account—West German marks. And don't worry about how I'll manage—I've worked independently before. I'm glad she's out of the way."

"Stop freelancing and work for me, Meyer. I'll give you Abel's job, it comes with a two-bedroom state apartment and full bath—we can bring Hilda here. I have two large vacancies in my staff and you're bright and innovative. More importantly, you understand the west. I need you, Meyer. Come over to me."

"You misjudge me, Fox. I value freedom too much. I'll never be one of your goons."

"Well, Meyer, when you're snarled in the barbed wire and soldiers shoot holes in you, remember I offered a better way."

"I have a long memory, Fox."

"Do we have anything else to discuss?"

"No. You'll find the documents on the first pew as you leave. Make the arrangements for Hilda."

"*Guten Nacht, Herr* Meyer."

Fox stepped from the booth, scooped up the envelope, and followed the monk back to the front door of the church. He stopped under the arch. "Until I first came here, I had never seen a female monk, now I've seen two. It's a miracle. Do you believe in miracles, *Frau* Meyer?"

Her knees wobbled—she struggled for balance—leaning against the wall for support. When she could walk, she stumbled to her father's office. She was still pale and shaken when she arrived. "He ... he knew me!" she stammered, finding a wine crate to sit, head between her knees. "He said my name as he left."

"*Scheisse!*" said Kurt. "How'd he know?"

"I was afraid of that," said Karl. "He knew Ilse was a woman."

"He knew my name!" she said.

"I shouldn't have used you," said Kurt. "It's my fault. I was careless, too worried about Hilda to think clearly."

"He remembers me from the Soviet embassy. He went there with General Rubski to read a file about the Russians moving nuclear missiles to Cuba."

"What?" Kurt interrupted her. "Have you seen this?"

"Yes. I have it." She reached into her dress and removed an envelope.

"*Mein Gott*, Ingrid! You should never have taken this. The last one caused enough trouble. This will start a war."

"What if they destroy Washington?" she asked. "Wouldn't that start a war?"

Kurt dropped his head into his palms and rubbed his eyes.

Ingrid crumpled at the waist, her hands clasped over her stomach. "Oh! My stomach aches."

The old man stirred, rusty hinges in his wooden knee creaking. "I lost Inga and my leg to the damned Russians. Now I'm losing my children."

"I'm taking both of you out of here," said Kurt. "Tonight!"

"I'm not leaving," said Karl, "Take Ingrid."

"I won't go, either," she said. "My home is here with you, father. I start a new job tomorrow. I won't steal any more papers."

"A new job?" asked Kurt.

"Yes, one in administration."

"Why are they moving you?" Alarms blared in his head.

"General Rubski reorganized embassy security. He wants Russians handling all secret papers."

"He knows," said Kurt. "Fox was at the office with Rubski before then he recognized you tonight—then Rubski moved you to a new job. They've figured it out, Ingrid—you must get out of here. You're in denial."

"I can't just leave without my things."

"You can't go back to the office, not ever. Just pack one small bag—that's all we can carry. Wear some of my work clothes—pants are easier to run in. Come back here as soon as possible but no later than midnight. Do not go to the embassy under any circumstances."

"You must do this, Ingrid," her father insisted. "I couldn't bear it if anything happened to you. You're so much like your mother. The monks know some people going out—I'll have you both included."

"But who'll stay with you, father?"

"Child, I should have died at Stalingrad. I cheated the devil then but I'll die here when my time comes. The monks and the priest look out for me—they'll hide me. I can never leave here alive."

"Don't say such things, father."

"I can hardly walk on this Russian leg. I want to kill one more before I die."

"Hurry, Ingrid," said Kurt. "I'll stay here with the old man until you return."

Ingrid kissed her father, hugged her brother and left to prepare for a new life.

58

Unraveling

Father and son waited anxiously at the Dom for Ingrid's return. The church retained bedding for winter vagrants and Karl kept the key to the storage locker. They dragged out cots to rest until Kurt and Ingrid linked up with the escapees at 2:00 a.m. Kurt set up the folding cots while the old man tapped into the abundant wine stock. The reclusive old man was unusually talkative this night, perhaps his last with his children.

"Ingrid is just like Inga," he began. "She has the same features, like you only pretty. She carries herself like her mother and is just as determined, a strong will. Her mother and I struggled to survive in Halle, poor, with few pleasures other than our children but we never complained. She made all our clothes and kept the house clean while I worked at the railroad factory. She could pull a few vegetables from the garden, toss them into a pot and create a stew that would bring me running all the way from town. I had both legs then."

Kurt knew the old man had loved his mother, having heard fragments of their early lives over the years, but the old man seldom spoke openly about her. He had seen how he had worshiped her only picture and pined for her.

"She cried all night before I went to the army—broke my heart. When I was released from the *gulag*, I rode the train home. I didn't expect her at the station because she didn't know when I would come. I hobbled down the dirt road past my factory—proud to turn iron into engines—but when I saw it, bombed by the Yankees and ransacked by the Russians, I was alarmed. My factory lay like a dead carcass beside the road, bones picked by vultures. Our future was in that devastation, not only ours but all Germany's. Seeing our industry destroyed was the first time I was truly afraid."

Kurt sat on a crate, leaned against the wall with his glass in his hand. He didn't look at the old man, afraid he might stop talking. He didn't want to hear this painful story but he knew he must listen and learn it—his history, too.

"I hurried but my stump was not healed and I used two crutches—tried to run to her. When I reached our home, it was burned to the ground. I collapsed but couldn't weep. There was nothing left inside me. A neighbor said Inga had been raped and butchered by the Russians. They hid Ingrid in their basement. My mind went white, a film covered my eyes; nothing was out there, nothing was real. The priest said I tried to hang myself in the ruins of our home, I don't remember that, but a monk cut me down and carried me to the monastery where they tended little Ingrid. You had gone away with the Navy—I didn't know that then. I drank myself into a stupor. They wouldn't allow me to see Ingrid until I sobered up. I was one drink from the grave—didn't care." Tears trickled over his craggy face. Kurt faced away to spare them both.

"Finally, I worked one full day in the vineyard, then another, and another. I sweated bitterness during the day and restored it at night until I gradually got control of my anger, but I never gave it up." He thumped his chest with his thumb. "It's still here. It keeps me going—hating the Russians. My life will not be complete until I avenge her."

"It's my fault." Kurt broke his painful silence, thumbed a tear. "I should have stayed and protected them."

"No, son—don't ever think that. You had no choice any more than I. Don't ever blame yourself for your mother's death."

"But, don't you...?"

"No!" Karl slammed his fist on the desk. "When I see you, my son, I see myself. But I don't want you to be like me, a bitter old man. You're doing something good with a clear focus, dreaming about a better world, one that's possible for you but not me. When I see Ingrid, I see only my Inga. I love her with all my soul, but I can't hold her hostage to my misery. You must take her out of here. All I have left of my blessed Inga is this old photograph." He held it up to his failing eyes and was lost in it. "I carry her from my apartment to work every day and bring her home at night. I'll never leave her behind again. All I have left of her is this, and our children."

Kurt wrestled with his control, afraid to speak.

"Take Ingrid out, Kurt. Marry Hilda and have children, my grandchildren. And take care of the little Jew. Make her stop her foolish ways. She's been through too much in her small life."

"I'll try ... father. I'll try."

"I love you, too, Kurt. I love you more than myself. Always remember that."

59

Raid

Karl slept fitfully for a while. Kurt was unable to sleep but was strangely relaxed—everything seemed settled with his father, with Ingrid, and with Hilda. Fox had not refused his request for help or for more money. What had to be done next was clear. He would slip Ingrid out of East Berlin, leave Ilse and the Cuba plan in Vic's hands, and take Hilda to the United States to raise a yard full of kids. The old man would be where he had to be, near his beloved Inga's grave and wallowing in his guilt and hatred.

If this was so simple why couldn't he sleep? He lay awake watching the clock until midnight. He warmed some left over coffee on the furnace and watched the old man tossing restlessly.

Karl woke suddenly, agitated. "Where is Ingrid? It's almost time to go. I must speak to her of her mother; she must never forget her mother."

"This isn't like her," Kurt agreed. "I'll go to her apartment and bring her back. She's probably trying to decide what to take and what to leave—just like a woman."

He scurried through dark passageways, avoiding patrolled areas until he reached her flat. The light was on inside and everything appeared normal at first—until he entered the hallway. He saw her door was ajar, closer he saw it was splintered. "*Mein Gott!*" He rushed inside.

An overturned table blocked his path. Belongings were scattered everywhere. The floor was covered with glass from broken dishes. Mattress and cushions had been slit and feathers floated in the air.

A neighbor appeared in the doorway. "I've seen you here before," she said.

Kurt swirled. "What happened here?"

"The *politzei* came an hour ago. They crashed the door and took her away in handcuffs. For an hour—I've never heard such screaming and shouting. I saw them—a big, mean Russian. His face was red as fire."

Kurt shoved past her and ran all the way back to the church.

When he told his father what he had found and heard, the old man said nothing—sat motionless, cataleptic, plunging to a living death. His eyes were open but unseeing on his journey back to a place he had been before, into an empty desert devoid of life.

231

Kurt found the priest. "Ingrid was arrested. When I told him, he became this way."

"Just like after the war when Inga died. We'll take him back home to the monastery."

"Here," Kurt handed the priest a roll of bills. "This will support him for a while. I'll send more when I can."

"Bless you, son."

"And there is one more thing, please." Kurt held out a second roll of bills with a rubber band around them. "I was planning to see old *Herr* Brunner in Halle. I intend to marry his daughter Hilda, and I wanted to tell him myself. The money is from her. Could you get it to him?"

Kurt held the roll of bills but the priest didn't take it, only bowed his head. "Then you haven't heard?" he said finally. "*Herr* Brunner passed two days ago."

"Oh damn! Hilda will be so...." He pressed the roll into the priest's hand. "Please use this money for a good cause. She would want that."

Monks carried Karl away in an ox-cart that very hour, a journey that took all day. He was returning to where he had lived with Inga and where she was still buried in the vineyard.

Kurt used his father's desk to scribble a note to Mischa Fox. *Come to the same place at Eight o'clock, alone. Chameleon.*

60
In Rasputin's Hands

Major General Nikoli Rubski was a soldier first and foremost. He had led a Russian infantry brigade in defense of Stalingrad during World War II and commanded a tank division in the cold war stand-off with NATO—ever poised to strike west through the Fulda Gap. He was a fearless leader in the ground forces and transferred reluctantly into intelligence.

However, the same traits that made him such an aggressive soldier made him a ruthless operative. His methods were unorthodox even by historic Soviet standards. His exploits harkened to the days of Czar Nicholas II and he carried his earned epitaph proudly—*Rasputin*.

Although Rubski was different from Grigory Rasputin in many ways, legends of their callousness ran parallel. That was what had attracted Khrushchev's attention. He wanted Rubski as his special enforcer, his point man in the cold war. That decision sent a shock wave through Moscow.

But even the hardcore Rubski was worried, more worried than when his back was to the wall at Stalingrad. No one was immune to Khrushchev's wrath. Rubski cracked his knuckles, annoyed by his shaking finger as he dialed up the Chairman's private line. His scar burned bright red.

"*Da.* Khrushchev here."

"It's Rubski."

"Nikoli. How is Berlin?"

"I have bad news, I'm afraid."

"What could be so bad?"

"The ground attack plan, Koniev's top secret plan, has disappeared."

"What do you mean, disappeared?" Khrushchev screamed. "How is that possible?"

"The embassy used a German woman as clerk of the classified files. I believe she took it."

"How stupid! Ulbricht should be made to disappear for this!"

"It's not his fault this time. Responsibility falls with our Ambassador for placing local Germans in critical security positions. I have corrected that problem already by completely changing security at the Embassy."

"But, Nikoli, the ox is out of the barn. How will you recover the plan?"

"Let me explain. When I took Fox to read it he recognized the file clerk as the sister of one of his agents."

"One of his agents defected last week. His team is coming apart."

"That too, but Fox was investigating the woman's brother for killing another agent. That's how he made the connection."

"His agents kill one another? My confidence in Fox may have been misplaced. Has he lost control?"

"No," said Rubski. "This doesn't look good but he's doing a good job, a tough job under very trying conditions."

"Get that document, Nikoli! Make Fox help you. This is the most critical mission you've ever had. Don't fail me!"

"I arrested the woman last night. She's in a *dacha* in Karlshorst."

"Get the paper, damn it! Have you searched for it, questioned her?"

"I arrested her myself," said Rubski, wishing the conversation were over. "I searched her apartment for the document but it wasn't there."

"Has she been questioned yet?"

"Yes, but she admits nothing."

"Nikoli, have you *seriously* interrogated her?"

"Not yet, Comrade. First, I wanted to inform you because she may not survive an extreme interrogation."

"Nikoli, if you don't recover that plan, none of us will survive. That's extreme!"

61

Chameleon and the Fox

Kurt would have to handle his third and last meeting with Fox alone; Ilse was in the west, Ingrid under arrest and the old man crazed with grief. Although Fox had not actually arrested his sister, that did not absolve him of responsibility. Kurt now regretted sharing Hilda's details with him to arrange safe passage. Fox could not be trusted but the he was the only entre to Rubski to save Ingrid. Ingrid's and Hilda's lives depended on compassion from the two cruelest men in Berlin.

Kurt kept the location for the meeting unchanged, but changed the procedure out of necessity.

Dust puffed under his feet as he climbed to the church's old belfry; the old man gone only a day and the place had fallen into neglect. From high in the belfry he had a clear view of the surroundings. He looked for indications of a trap until Fox arrived in front punctually at eight o'clock.

Kurt realized Fox must be under intense pressure and a cornered Fox was dangerous.

Fox bounded the steps into the narthex expecting to find the usual guide monk; instead he found only a candle flickering on a small table. It illuminated a note, which read: *Wait here.*

He shuffled impatiently. This was different and he disliked unexpected changes. He un-holstered his prized H&K 9mm automatic and chambered a round. The metallic crack echoed through the empty sanctuary, announcing his dominance, a sound as out of place in church as the man. Having made his point, he re-holstered his firearm.

A door creaked behind him and he faced a tardy monk.

Fox squinted into the dimness at the familiar brown robe. "Meyer?"

"Follow me."

Kurt led him to a small, dimly lit prayer room in the back of the church, near a rear exit, not the usual confessional.

"Meyer?" he asked again.

"Sit," he said. They took rickety seats across a small table. Kurt pushed back his hood giving Fox a clear look at him.

"You're jerking me around Meyer. What's this all about?"

"Where's my sister?"

"What are you talking about?"

"You saw her at the embassy with the big Russian—Rubski. Then you saw her here last night—right after you left her flat was raided and she was arrested. I hold you personally responsible and I want my sister released, now!"

"Yes, I recognized her from the embassy, that's true. But whatever the Soviets do is their business, not mine. We are an occupied country or have you forgotten?"

"It's your business now—I'm making it yours."

"Is she a spy, Meyer? Are you double-dealing? If you are, I'll kill you myself."

Kurt hammered the table with the butt of Abel's pistol. "I'm calling the shots, Fox. I want my sister."

"I don't know anything about that, I swear. Maybe I can find out something at my headquarters. I'll call Rubski about it."

"I'm not that stupid, Fox."

"Look, Meyer, the only chance you have to get your sister back and ensure *Frau* Brunner's safety is to let me go. I've been straight with you—trust me."

"I did trust you—look what that got me."

"I'll find out what's going on. That's all I can do."

"Listen, Fox," he said. "You and I both know what he wants. I have the Cuban missile plan and I'll give it up, but only when I know the women are safe. If they're hurt, I'll come after both of you."

"You took the Cuban plan? That *was* stupid. So you are a traitor and your sister is in it with you?"

"Yes, that's all true, but it doesn't matter what I've done. You can kill me, I don't care anymore, but I want Ingrid and Hilda safe."

"I'll deliver your message to Rubski."

"Okay, let's go." They stood together, scraping chairs backwards.

Kurt opened the rear exit.

Fox protested. "My car is in front. If I don't return in five minutes my driver will call out the storm troopers. No one has forgotten what happened to Abel. Let's go to my office."

"No. We'll do this my way." Kurt shoved the muzzle into Fox's ribs, reached inside his jacket and removed the chrome H&K. He dropped it into the deep pocket of his robe and shoved Fox into the dark ally, concealing the pistol under the robe but pressed firmly against his captive. They hurried through narrow alleys to Stetlin Station. Kurt shoved him into a public phone booth and blocked the door.

"Make the call."

Fox fumbled in his pockets for change and dropped coins into the slots. He spoke to the embassy operator in Russian, using Rubski's name in the conversation.

Kurt pressed the gun against his chest, listening into the receiver. He couldn't follow the conversation in Russian. Fox held his hand over the receiver and said, "They're trying to locate him. Be patient."

Kurt glanced at the station clock and watched the second hand tick around. After another minute, no one had come on the line. When another thirty seconds ticked away, he shoved Fox against the back of the booth.

"You're stalling." He slipped a hand into Fox's suit jacket; found a wire attached to a small transmitter with a blinking light.

He snatched it. "You're wired!"

He glanced around and spotted a *Stasi* agent in an overcoat scanning the bay with a signal receiver; others followed. Kurt stomped the device with his heel and ran into the crowded station.

Fox shouted, "Stop him!"

Agents appeared out of concealment to pursue. A ticket collector jumped away from a monk charging with a pistol in each hand. Kurt hurtled the turnstile with robes flowing behind.

Men in dark suits chased him with pistols drawn; uniformed *politzei* with submachine guns joined the chase.

Kurt brushed passengers aside and jumped onto the subway tracks below the platform. He dashed along the rocky track bed, shedding the robe behind.

A shot rang through the tunnel and ricocheted off the wall with a zing. Two more cracks followed—too close!

A light broke through the blackness in front of him—faint at first and becoming brighter as an oncoming train rounded a curve in the tunnel. Kurt was blinded but ran directly at it. The engine filled the narrow space between the walls, illuminating Kurt's silhouette, a perfect target but moving fast.

The engineer yanked the brake cord with one hand, an ear-splitting whistle with the other. Brakes squealed—smoke and fire trailed from the tracks when the wheels locked and the engine slid forward with unstoppable momentum. In a split-second, Kurt lunged—hurling his body on the track bed tight against the wall.

Iron rims screeched near his head, throwing sparks in all directions.

After the blinding headlights passed he was in utter darkness and clawed frantically along the walls with both hands bruised on the rocks as the cars rolled past, scattering his pursuers.

His hand found the emptiness he was seeking. He squeezed inside the drainpipe, propelling himself headfirst with the water runoff. He smacked down headfirst into two inches of sewage. *Stasi* agents ran noisily along the tracks above, shouting. He breathed deeply of the fouled air and listened.

When he heard they had found the monk's robe he moved on, kicking a sewer rat from his path.

62

Closing in

Fox hammered his fists against his desk so hard the drawers rattled. He pulled one open, grabbed an old automatic and snapped a full magazine into it. He chambered a round and shoved the pistol into his empty shoulder holster. Marshal Koniev had personally presented that chrome pistol when he left Moscow for Berlin. Koniev told him it came from a Nazi defending Hitler's bunker and said, "General Fox's family fled that tyrant for Mother Russia. Now he has the pistol of the guard who protected *der Führer*."

Instead, Meyer threatened to kill *him* with that pistol. Fury at losing his pistol was overshadowed by the humiliation of being hostage to one of his agents. He would never live this down.

"Major Ebert!" He bellowed loud enough to be heard throughout the building. He had seen no one in the halls when he entered; they avoided him for good reason.

"General, are you all right?" Ebert asked.

"I want a full alert for Meyer at all border crossings. Don't trust the *grepos;* use our own men. Wake them up! Circulate his picture everywhere. Inform the *politzei* I want him brought here. If he somehow gets across the border, kidnap him and bring him back. Notify my specialist in West Berlin to find him."

"Why did he do this?"

"He said something about his sister being arrested. Do you know anything about that?"

"There was a raid, I know that much, but I've heard no details. General Rubski called earlier and said it was important for you to return his call the moment you arrived."

"I tried to phone him when I had Meyer. He wasn't at the embassy."

"He is now. Shall I get him on the phone?"

"Yes." Ebert dialed the number, handed Fox the phone, and left the room.

Rubski blurted, "Fox, find Meyer immediately!"

"I have an all-points bulletin out for him. He has the Cuba plan and wants to exchange it for his sister. He also wants papers for *Frau* Brunner to go to Switzerland. Those are his conditions."

"Who is *Frau* Brunner?"

"She's his lover, his main resource in Bonn, but she was exposed and now she's running, too."

"Then she knows too much. We can't allow her to be captured. Where is she?"

"She's at the *Gasthaus* Yellow Rose in Lorrach under the name of Irma Schwartz. She's headed to Switzerland but ran without her passport. We need her out of Germany immediately and all my agents are in hiding because of the defector. Meyer won't cooperate without her safety."

"I'll get her out. I have a team in Bern. We'll take her to Moscow."

"She won't go to Moscow. Leave her in Switzerland."

"We'll see about that."

"Did you arrest *Frau* Meyer?"

"Yes, but you just said her brother has the plan. Did he have it with him?"

"I didn't see it."

"He's going west," declared Rubski. "Do you know where he stays?"

"No, he has no address but he has a girlfriend somewhere in West Berlin. Perhaps *Frau* Meyer will tell us more about her."

"I'll make her tell me. Meyer seems to attract woman, three of them. I'll cut his balls off when I get my hands on him."

"Nikoli," said Fox. "Meyer said he'd come after us if the women were hurt. He killed Abel, you know."

"I'm quaking in my boots," Rubski laughed. "I'm going after him before he comes looking for me. Have you alerted your people?"

"Everyone is on full alert."

"Not good enough. This isn't for me, Fox. Khrushchev has been briefed and he wants Meyer and everyone else who have seen the plan. He wants it back and he wants them dead. Khrushchev gets what he wants."

63

Muddy Slime

Kurt sloshed through muddy slime until the battery in his light faded then went out. He tossed it. His race to freedom slowed to a crawl as he felt his way along the dark tunnel walls.

He bumped his head on a pipe running through the tunnel, dropped Fox's pistol and had to fish it from the sludge. He bent lower after that, back aching, remembering Vic's warning not to use the tunnel to return. No choice.

He overshot the painted line in the dark but knew he had gone at least that far. In the darkness he saw nothing and heard nothing but the groans of the underground—a creaking submarine at crushing depth. He was under the city with nowhere to rest except in the mud so he exerted exhausted muscles in a last effort.

He surmised he was in the west and near the ladder when he bumped it in the dark. Above, he heard muffled voices speaking in English. He climbed hand-over-hand, pushed against the hatch but it was locked. He had left the plumber's tool belt at the church. His only tools were a pistol, his hands, and his wits. He concealed the pistol and rapped his knuckles against the hatch until the talking stopped.

"Who's there?"

He thought about Lyndon Johnson. "Ya'll let me outa here, goddamn it all! Sons of bitches left me down here."

"Who are you?"

"I'm Billy from plumbing. They called me to fix a leak and left me here. Damn flashlight quit on me, too."

"I'll need to verify that."

"Open the goddamned door, sum-bitch!" He banged harder with the heel of his hand. "Rats down here. I'll show you my ID when I get outa here."

"Hold on."

He banged harder for emphasis.

"Hold your frickin' horses, Tex!"

A key rattled in the lock then the hatch swung open. Blinding light stabbed his eyes.

"Let's see that ID, buddy."

"It's Billy and keep your pants on." Kurt shoved his head and shoulders out. "I need both hands right now. I'll get it when I'm out of this stinking hole."

An army lieutenant stood aside as Kurt climbed into the dry communications center, dripping sewer water. "You don't look American," he said. "Let me see your ID."

Kurt reached deep into his pocket. "Here's it is." He shoved Fox's H&K at the officer's nose. Chrome gleamed in the bright lights. "No one move or the lieutenant dies."

"What the hell?" said the lieutenant?

"I'm on your side," said Kurt. "But right now you're going to escort me out." Kurt shoved him toward the exit.

"Hell no, I won't." The macho young officer's voice quavered, but no one noticed—all were focused on the shiny pistol. "Call the MP's," he ordered, but no one moved.

"Do you want to die now?" Kurt asked him calmly. Kurt thought of one of the James Cagney movies Ilse had dragged him to against his will. "The sergeant can walk me out of here." Then to the others, "If anyone moves before the lieutenant gets back here, I'll kill him. Don't make me prove it."

Kurt shoved him out with the muzzle in his back. He stuck to the lieutenant as they walked to the main gate with the pistol concealed in his pocket. "When we get there, say you're escorting a worker. When I'm on the sidewalk you can yell all you want. Understand?"

"All right, damn it." The lieutenant did as he was told. As soon as Kurt cleared the gate he sprinted for an alley.

The lieutenant shouted, "Intruder! Call the MP's."

Kurt covered two blocks before the first siren was heard and military police jeeps ran about helter-skelter. He couldn't go directly to Ilse's with the military searching for him so he hitched a ride from a West Berliner eager to help an escaping *Ossie* get to the refugee center at Marienfeld.

He registered there under a false name and ate a long overdue meal of U.S. Army C-rations. No one doubted him—he looked and smelled like thousands of other refugees who had snuck across. He showered and accepted some second-hand clothes. The cashier paid him one hundred marks as fresh-start money, which he couldn't refuse without raising suspicion.

Kurt was buried in an avalanche of problems. East German *Stasi*, West German security, the American military and CIA, NATO security, and the Russian KGB were all after him. Hilda, Ingrid, and the old man were ensnarled in the net thrown for him. Only Ilse could save herself and he had yet to convince her to go.

He walked to the front door of the refugee center to leave. A volunteer counselor draped an arm over his shoulder. "It's going to be fine," he said.

"We'll help you find a new job, a new home. You're a free man now. Welcome to West Berlin."

Kurt stepped into the dusk and a cold, drizzling rain. The weather was suitable.

64

Irma Swartz

Hilda Brunner, a.k.a. Irma Swartz, was as much a prisoner in her small room at the *Gasthaus* Yellow Rose as in the Karlsruhe prison. She prayed for Kurt to come but knew it might be a stranger instead. She would go to Switzerland and Kurt would whisk her away to their new lives. They would change their identities to the outside world but never to themselves—bound forever by a common history. For several days she had left her tiny room only for meals and was feeling claustrophobic.

The dinner hour had almost ended when she walked downstairs to the dining room. She waited late to avoid conversations with other guests. Several still lingered over coffee and dessert when she arrived but they were occupied with one another. She saw some newspapers and picked up a copy of *Die Welt* and chose a table away from them. She hid behind the paper.

Frau Shiller, the proprietor, approached for her order and waited until their eyes met. "Our special tonight is *sauerbraten*. Will you have that or something from the menu, *Frau* Swartz?"

"*Sauerbraten*," she said. "*Danke*." She ducked behind the paper again.

Frau Shiller lingered.

"*Ja?*" Hilda inquired.

"Would you like some red wine with dinner," asked *Frau* Shiller. "It's my gift."

"*Ja, danke*." Hilda needed the wine but she assumed there were strings attached. She knew *Frau* Shiller would use it to pry.

Hilda could scarcely believe the little girl who had fled with her mother to England and worked at the pinnacle of the German government could be in this mess. Hilda Brunner, who wanted only to be Hilda Meyer or whatever names they used, the same woman who only wanted a normal life—how could she be here? How could she be so afraid? How could she be a fugitive? She had only wanted to do right, how had that gone so wrong?

She stared at the sports page without seeing it—not interested in soccer scores. *Frau* Shiller returned with her dinner, arranging it on the table. "I'll bring the wine." Hilda prepared the silverware; she was a guest after all, not a criminal.

Frau Shiller brought a bottle of nice *kabinett* and two glasses, not the usual ones but crystal from her personal cabinet.

"The wine comes from my family vineyard, *Frau* Swartz." She poured two glasses half full. "You've been with us five days now. May I sit with you?" She pulled out a chair without waiting for an answer.

She wanted to say no, but said, "Of course."

Frau Shiller sipped from her glass, allowing Hilda time to begin eating. "I usually know my guests well in two days, but I hardly know you at all, Irma. May I call you Irma?"

"Of course," said Hilda.

"Please call me Ellen."

"Thank you for the wine, Ellen. You're very gracious."

"I'm glad you've kept your appetite. How do you do it? Up in your room all day?"

"I exercise in my room."

"You should get out more. It's not healthy staying inside all the time. You need fresh air. I walk every morning. Would you go with me tomorrow?"

"I must wait here." Hilda felt the acid building in her stomach. "I'm expecting someone. We'll be leaving soon but I don't know exactly when he'll come."

"Where are you going?"

"Switzerland ... on a holiday. We planned to meet here, but business delayed him unexpectedly."

"I see. Others are phoning for reservations and I don't know what to tell them. So you don't know how long you'll stay?" *Frau* Shiller stood to leave.

"Not exactly, but I'll leave very soon I hope—a day or two longer at most."

"Enjoy the wine." Ellen left with her empty glass and an edge on her voice.

Hilda inhaled deeply as if she had been holding her breath. She pushed the half-finished meal away and refilled the wine glass, the crystal reminding her of Hans. He had been loyal to wait in Paris to warn her. Her appetite had vanished but her fears remained. She nervously flipped the pages of the newspaper, looking for anything but sports. She found it, but it was not what she wanted to see. She choked and a drop of red wine spilled onto the paper.

She was lightheaded, almost fainting. She stared at the paper trying to absorb the picture of Hans on the front page. His eyes looked back from an official photograph she had seen before, framed at the Chancellery. She forced her eyes to the headline and made her mind comprehend: *NATO Spy Caught. Others Sought in Paris, Bonn, Berlin.*

She willed one foot ahead of the other and walked unsteadily to her room. She didn't hear Ellen wish her a good evening. Hilda collapsed on the edge of her bed, doubled at the waist with her head against her knees. Her breathing was shallow. She felt she was drowning, being pushed under, unable to breathe.

A loud rap at the door startled her.

"Who is it?" She jerked straight up. "Ellen?"

"A friend." It was a man's surly voice. "I have papers for you."

Her heart raced and her mind tried to catch up. "What papers?" She challenged him. Kurt had warned her never to open the door to strangers; he always knew what to do.

"The papers you need for Switzerland, *Frau* Swartz."

She breathed again and a wave of euphoria lifted her. She unbolted the door to a large man in a crumpled dark woolen suit and hat, overcoat draped over an arm and hand that held a brown envelope. He was not a romantic hero but he was there for her so he would do.

"Are you ready to go?" he asked, his accent Slavic.

"Can I see the passport?" she asked.

"Of course," he said, and handed her the envelope. "It's not perfect, you're much prettier than this one, but it'll get you across. We'll make a new one in Switzerland with your picture. But, you can see the resemblance, with a few...."

Hilda studied the picture, looked over the visa stamps—the former owner had gone to Russia many times. "Who is this?" she asked.

"No one," he said. "It's from our special supply. Memorize the name and address. We'll go to a safe house to prepare your personal documents."

Hilda propped the passport against the mirror. She styled her hair to the photograph and applied lipstick, making her lips wider, more rouge and eye shadow, heavier eyebrows.

"While you're getting ready I need to ask you some questions. We must help your boy friend escape was well. Do you know where he is?"

She stopped brushing and thought about the question. What would Kurt have her say? She had already warned him of the danger and they had a secret escape plan apart from all these people. The only way this man could know she was here was if Kurt told someone.

"My boy friend?" she tested. "Do you know him?"

"Yes; *Herr* Meyer, Kurt Meyer. The authorities are on to him, you know. There was a defector. How can we reach him?"

"I don't know where he is," she said honestly. "He's away on business. I left Bonn very quickly and I haven't talked to him since."

"He told us how to find you."

"Well, I suppose you've talked to him since I have. How was he?"

"Can you reach him? An address, phone number perhaps, anything? We must contact him right away. His life may depend on it."

She began brushing her hair again to give her trembling hand something else to do. Kurt said he would meet her in Switzerland in a few days and they would disappear together. "Don't get trapped," he had warned. If he wanted to be found, he could easily arrange it.

"No. I'm sorry; I don't know how to contact him."

"You do know he has a girl friend in Berlin, I suppose?" The way he said it made clear that he hoped to surprise her, arose anger.

She swallowed hard. Kurt's affection for Ilse, and hers for him, was painful. "Yes," she said. "I know he has a girl friend."

"Do you know how to contact her?" he asked, then a jab. "Perhaps he's sleeping in her bed?"

"No, I don't want to know," she said. "He only sees her occasionally. When he's away a long time he has masculine needs. I thought a man would understand that."

"Then you must be a very selfless woman," he said. "I wish my wife was so accepting."

"Perhaps I'm naïve," she said. "I'm trusting *you*."

He stood. "I'll settle your account with the innkeeper so you won't need to stop at the desk," he said as he walked to the door. He looked back at her still working before the mirror. "I don't want her to see you since you've changed your appearance. She already knew that you are going to Switzerland. Did you tell her that?"

"She asks many questions," she explained. "I've been here much too long already."

"I'll return for you in a few minutes." Hilda listened to his steps in the hall and she heard them stop near the telephone to place a call. She couldn't make out any of the conversation, which was entirely in Russian.

247

In forty-five minutes they crossed the Rhine River at Basil in a sedan. Two and a half hours later, they reached a country safe house outside Bern. It was late when they arrived.

The furnishings were rustic but far more spacious than her small room in the Yellow Rose. She felt released from a life sentence. Forests surrounded the estate and she couldn't wait until morning for a long-delayed walk alone in the cold, fresh air. Ellen had been right, exercise was important now that she was pregnant; she was sure about that now. She thought about being one more day and several hundred kilometers closer to Kurt's coming for her and her spirits soared. That was all that really mattered now—Kurt would come, their escape, and the baby.

"Hilda, I have a camera and a backdrop set up in the basement for a new passport photo. Shall we take care of that before relaxing? I brought a bottle of champagne to celebrate your freedom."

She followed him to the staircase and beside it was a table with a vase of freshly cut flowers. A woman's touch, but she hadn't seen a woman—perhaps a maid had placed them. She sniffed the arrangement and selected a tulip to carry with her down the stairs.

At the bottom of the stairway a bed sheet was fastened to the brick wall with duct tape. A camera rested on a tripod. Beside the camera a bright light bulb on a pole made a passport photo possible in the shadows of the underground. The man positioned her toes along a strip of tape in front of the sheet and then moved behind the camera.

When he was ready to snap it, he raised his head and asked, "Hilda, the passport photos for Switzerland and Russia are different sizes. I've been instructed to ask you once more to accompany me to Moscow before I take the shot."

"No, thank you. I want to stay in Switzerland. I'll wait for my boy friend here. Then we'll decide together."

"As you wish," he said, switching on the blinding light.

She didn't hear the crack of the bullet, or feel it. It split her skull, disfigured her face and splattered blood and brain matter on the white sheet behind her.

A woman materialized from the shadows and blue smoke rose from the small bore of her silenced pistol. They worked together, rolling Hilda's warm body into the sheet. When they were done, they dropped her into an open septic tank. The woman picked up the tulip and tossed it in after her.

"Pity!" she said.

He opened the champagne.

65

Braver than Rubski's Soldiers

Rubski sat ramrod straight in the back seat of his black sedan, cracking his knuckles as tires crunched gravel and ice on the unpaved road. The sedan stopped at an isolated *dacha* near Karlshorst, East Germany, near the main KGB field station. Two Russian soldiers stood guard outside, alternating with two others keeping warm inside. All four wore great coats and pile caps, armed with assault rifles.

Rubski slowly climbed the steps of the *dacha*, contemplating what lay ahead. His mission from Moscow was to extract vital information from the woman. Inside, Ingrid was strapped in a hardwood chair at the center of a nearly vacant room. Her arms were bound tightly behind her, each leg tied to a leg of the chair. Tears tracked her cheeks but her eyes were wide with terror. Duct tape covered her mouth.

"*Guten abend, Frau* Meyer." Rubski tested his rough German on an unwilling participant. He stood close, leaned closer then snatched the tape from her mouth.

She gasped. "I need to go to the toilet." She looked down, embarrassed. "The soldiers wouldn't let me."

Rubski stayed close, pulling on gloves. With a lightning strike he buried his fist into her stomach, propelling her backwards onto her back, wrists still bound to the chair. The impact broke them both. She lay on her broken wrists, her head against the floor and legs still strapped to the chair. Urine soaked her dress as she gasped for air until she passed out.

Rubski went to his sedan, passing the wide-eyed guards watching him as they warmed inside. He returned with a bottle of vodka. One guard was bent over vomiting from what he had witnessed.

"What kind of soldier are you?" Rubski kicked him in his buttocks, propelling him into his own vomit. "Get outside! Stay there!"

He then turned to the other, also pale and shaken. "You're no better!" he shouted. "Get out there with your comrade."

Rubski, alone with the unconscious Ingrid, turned the Vodka bottle up and drank. Then he righted her chair as she hung limply lashed in it. He pulled another chair beside her to wait while finishing the vodka and a pack of cigarettes.

She slowly came to. He moved closer, avoiding the urine on the floor. "Ingrid," he whispered. "I know you took the document. Your brother has already admitted that so tell me where he is and this will end."

She shook her head, squeezing her eyes closed.

"Ingrid, where does Meyer live in West Berlin? Who is his girlfriend? Where is she?"

She shook her head again through spasms of pain from her broken wrists and swelling from the tight bindings.

"Ingrid, I don't enjoy this. I've been ordered to get certain information, that's all." He lit another cigarette and blew the smoke away. "Just tell me where the girl lives and I'll let you go."

She kept her eyes tightly closed and continued shaking her head from side to side. He walked behind her, took her hands in his, and snapped. The broken wrist bones cracked. Ingrid passed out again.

When she came to an hour later she was horrified. She was on top of the dining room table, broken wrists dangling over the edges, elbows tied to the table legs at one end, ankles bound to the table legs at the other. She was spread eagle and naked.

The windows in the *dacha* were opened wide and an icy wind blew through, the outside temperature well below freezing. Her skin was bluish and she shook in convulsions from shock and approaching hypothermia.

Rubski wore his greatcoat, buttoned to the neck, and a wool pile cap on his shaved head. The red star with hammer and sickle on the front of the cap filled the room. His burn scar was deep purple. An empty vodka bottle lay on the floor; another half empty stood on the edge of the table.

"Unless you tell me what I must know, I'll have the soldiers rape you. The choice is yours." Rubski crushed his cigarette on her nipple.

She whimpered. Then she opened her eyes, looked right at him and said through clenched teeth, "I'll tell you nothing. Kill me. Do It now!"

Rubski raised the vodka bottle and swallowed again before he leaned close to her ear. "Only you can end this, Ingrid. Tell me where Meyer and his girlfriend are."

She turned her head to make hard contact and said, "A Russian pig raped and murdered my mother. Were you the one?" Then she spit blood in his face.

Rubski tried to dodge but failed. He wiped at his face with a handkerchief, grabbed the vodka and finished it, then smashed the bottle against the wall. Shards of glass flew back and cut his cheek. He saw her watching defiantly. Her eyes were not those of a broken woman, but burned with a fire unlike others he tortured in the war. She watched, challenging him. Her jaw was set and she was prepared for what followed. He drew his pistol but she showed no sign of fear.

"D, Do it, b, bastard," she stuttered, teeth chattering from the cold. "D, Do one human thing in your l, life. I don't think you can." She faced the ceiling with eyes open.

Rubski stuck the pistol against her temple and his hand shook. He gripped it with both hands to steady it and squeezed.

When it fired he staggered backwards. His overcoat was spotted with blood and other matter. He leaned over and vomited over his own boots.

He lit a cigarette, closed the windows and paced back and forth, avoiding his mutilation. He used her dress to wipe his boots and overcoat then spread it over her naked body. Then he opened the door and found four dazed soldiers standing there.

"Go to the barn and find shovels," he commanded. "Dig a hole in the woods to bury this woman."

"The ground is frozen, General," protested the one he had kicked. "We can't dig today."

Rubski raised the hand that still held the pistol and fired into the soldier's chest. He watched him flip backwards; his eyes open this time.

The others ran to the barn and found picks and shovels to scrape at the frozen ground.

He muttered. "She was stronger than any of you."

66

Amateurs in a Professional Game

Nervous soldiers needed three hours to scrape out a trench deep enough to bury Ingrid. When they finished that one, they dug another for their dead comrade. Rubski waited patiently until the job was done. He dreaded his next duties.

When he reached Berlin he made two stops. The first was at the embassy to report to Khrushchev. "Mr. Chairman, I interrogated the woman. She admitted her brother has the document but didn't reveal his intentions or destination. She did not survive interrogation."

"Tell Fox to find the spy. Recover the plan. Kill him. No more delays."

Rubski rubbed his splitting forehead then dialed Fox's number at home. "Mischa, I'm coming to your apartment. Come out to my car. It's important."

When Rubski's sedan stopped at the curb, Fox rushed out of the building in his hat and coat, scarf around his face. Rubski pushed open the door for him to climb in the backseat next to him. "Drive around the block while we talk," he instructed his driver. "Keep the heat on."

"You look ill, Nikoli," said Fox. "What's that smell? Have you been sick?"

"This is a filthy business," he said. "I don't like killing women. I don't like gutless soldiers. I don't like peacetime. I'm quitting when this is finished. I'm going to the Black Sea and to hell with Khrushchev."

"Nikoli, did you kill *Frau* Meyer?"

"She left me no choice."

"Did she know where to find the document, or Meyer, or any information about the other woman?"

"That's the worst part. We already knew she gave it to him. Even though she knew that I knew, she told me nothing, not a word. Facing death, she spit on me. She said something about my troops raping her mother. Fox, she died like a soldier—better than many of my men in battle. I had her buried."

"What should I do?"

"Khrushchev wants Meyer tracked down. Let me be very clear, Mischa. If we don't get Meyer, there will be a firing squad in our future. Find him and get that plan—that's our sole mission."

"I've sent a specialist after him." Fox opened the door to get out but Rubski grasped his arm and held him. Fox closed the door against the cold.

"One more thing," said Rubski. "Did the Meyer woman have any relatives, other than her damned brother?"

"Her father is a one-legged man who works at a church."

"Give him this." Rubski passed him Ingrid's purse with her identification papers and personal effects. "Tell him she was brave."

Fox ran back into his apartment. He thought about their conversation as he spilled the contents of Ingrid's purse over the kitchen table. He shuffled through her personal things, looking for clues why she would die protecting her brother. He found nothing of interest so he scooped the contents back into her bag. When he looked up he found Emmi watching.

"Mischa, whose purse is that?"

"I didn't know her, Emmi. I only met her twice."

"You speak of her in past tense. She's dead. Did you have her killed?"

"No, not intentionally. But she made her own choices, signed her own death warrant." He massaged his temple with his thumb. "Why are you so concerned?"

"You look disturbed, that's all. I've never seen you distraught over a lousy spy, not even Abel. What did she do that was so terrible?"

"She broke all the rules. She stole information from the Russians while her brother was working for me. When she was caught, she resisted—that was pointless. Had she cooperated she might have lived. I suppose we'll never know why they do it. They're amateurs in a professional game."

"You talk as if it were a soccer match. This is no game."

"Still, there are rules. Everyone should know how the game is played before they begin. When you cross the line you must pay the penalty."

"They were both spies?"

"The worst kind—idealists. They cling to a hopeless morality, a stupid romanticism, like the resistance during the war—no one controls them. They work for their own ends and are willing to die for who knows what. That's why it bothers me—I don't understand it."

"You're an idealist too, Mischa. You are, you know? You sound almost envious. Sometimes I don't understand you at all."

He stood up, buttoning his overcoat over his suit. "What pains me most is that I like him. Now I have to kill him."

"Where are you going? You haven't had breakfast yet."

"I'm not hungry, Emmi. I have to find an answer." As he left, warm air followed creating a vaporous cloud in the icy outside.

His driver waited at the curb with the heater running. "The Dom," he told him. It was Sunday morning and a few worshippers were leaving after early prayers. Fox sat in the car, searching the grim faces of those leaving the church. "They all look unhappy to me," he mumbled to himself. "I thought the church was supposed to lift their spirits."

"Sir?" asked his driver.

"Never mind. Wait here."

When the small stream of people ended, Fox started toward the priest standing just inside the doorway, not quite sure how to address him. "Pardon me, sir. May I have a word with you?"

The old priest turned slowly to face him. "How may I help you, my son?"

"An old man works here, Karl Meyer. I need to have a word with him."

The priest looked Fox over. "And why do you need to see *Herr* Meyer, sir?"

"I have something for him and I hope he'll have something to tell me in return."

"Are you representing the government, sir?"

"Yes."

"Brother Karl is no longer the concern of the government."

"He left?"

"He's in the care of the church. God has taken him out of his pain until he is strong enough to accept his will."

"Then you can still reach him?"

"I know where he is, but I don't know if I can reach him."

"I came to give him this." Fox reached under his overcoat and withdrew Ingrid's purse. "Would you see that he gets it?"

The priest accepted the purse without looking at it. "This is Ingrid Meyer's purse. Is she dead?"

"I'm afraid so."

"Was she given last rites?"

"I don't think so."

"Where is she buried?"

"I don't know." Fox lowered his eyes.

"You seem to be carrying a heavy burden, *Herr* Fox. Do you want to make a confession?"

"I can't do that. I don't believe.... How did you know my name?"

"You've been in my confessional before, haven't you?"

"Would you just give these things to *Herr* Meyer, please?"

"You no longer want to meet him face-to-face?"

"No. I hope I never see him again."

"Ingrid was the only precious thing left in his life. What can I tell him about his child?"

Fox shuffled uncomfortably. "Why do they do it? Why do they persist in treasonous acts against their own state? Why do they break the rules?"

"Treason, *Herr* Fox? I believe you're the proponent of treason."

"But what I do is helping my country."

"Perhaps you don't understand their motivation. Consider the possibility that others may believe something is more important than man-made chasms, especially concrete walls separating people. Most people don't see the world the same way as you. Many are driven by higher principles, although only a very few ever act on their beliefs. Ingrid was one of those who did."

"I have principles—I do. I wasn't there when she died. I didn't have her arrested, either. A Russian gave me her things to return to her family. He regretted how it ended. He told me she was very brave, braver than his soldiers."

"Yet he killed her anyway?"

"Yes. It was his job."

"His job *Herr* Fox? That's God's job."

When the priest gave Ingrid's purse to Karl at the monastery the old man didn't move nor even blink. He clutched it tightly to his chest; his eyes dry and face expressionless—seemed to recognize her smell on the leather.

The priest described Fox's last visit but the old man gave no visible signs of understanding the words. He sat holding her purse against his heart.

After three days he rose from his bed, ate a hearty breakfast, and joined a work party cutting wood as if nothing had happened. He worked day-after-day swinging a heavy ax without speaking and drank wine late into the evenings. It was rumored among the monks that the old man had finally lost his voice in addition to his mind and his leg.

Perhaps he had—worse, he had lost his soul.

67

A Ring and a Note

Kurt reached Ilse's apartment as she prepared to depart for the Hilton, only two hours before her performance. She had been afraid he would not return though he promised to come for the ring. She clung to him and cried on his shoulder.

"You'll have to redo your makeup," he said.

"I don't care," she sniffled. "I'll phone in sick and just stay here with you."

"You must go on," he said. "Life goes on."

"Are you finished with this unsavory business, Kurt?" She looked for an answer in his face. "You said this was the last time."

He hesitated. "There was more trouble."

"Vic told me about your ruckus at the American casern. He's in trouble with the authorities over that, too. He's under investigation."

"I need to see him to give him something," he said, pulling the Cuban missile plan from his pocket.

"Kurt, he can't stand any more trouble. The last one.... And exposing their secret tunnel, and pointing a gun at an officer—that was over the line."

"Vic has no choice." His tone, one from the grave, chilled. "Ingrid may have died for this. This is a war and the Soviets are already moving to strike."

"Ingrid?"

"She was kidnapped by that goddamned Russian."

"Oh no!" She barely breathed. "Not Ingrid."

"Ilse, I'm worried they're torturing Ingrid to get information about me. The old man lost his mind when I told him she had been arrested. What have I done?"

"Oh no!"

"And I told Fox about Hilda before Ingrid was taken. He tried to kill me and now I can't trust him."

"What can you do?"

"I must put this in Vic's hands and tomorrow find Hilda either in Lorrach or Switzerland. We'll get out of Europe somehow."

"Go," she said. "Go now. "Find Hilda and just go. I'll give Vic that document."

"I can't go now. I'm exhausted and need to rest. I'm too tired and I'd make a mistake. Besides, I don't want you involved anymore."

"Then stay here and rest. I'll bring Vic here after the show."

"Hide this."

She took the envelope and scouted for a suitable hiding place.

"Okay," he said. "Bring Vic here after your show but be careful you're not followed. I'll give it to him then leave. It's settled."

She went to the fireplace and slipped the envelope behind the Dietrich poster. "You see where it is?" she asked. "And right beside it, in this vase, is Hilda's ring and the note you had me keep, with the account numbers. Don't forget to take them."

"Thank you."

"Kurt. Just rest and then go. Don't wait for us."

"I am tired," he admitted. "But I want to see you sing one last time. I may never see you again."

"No! Don't go there!" She said. "I'll bring Vic here. Sleep on my bed and we'll wake you."

"Ilse, whatever happens, in one month check on the funds in that Swiss account. If there have been no withdrawals it means that Hilda and I ... it means the money is yours."

"Don't you dare say that to me, Kurt Meyer!" She struck his chest with her fist. "I don't want your damned money. That's your future, and Hilda's. You've given me so much. I'd be nothing without you."

"Ilse...."

"Kurt, Vic has my heart but you're my *soul*. Wherever you go I'll find you. I promise. I'll find you."

When Ilse left, Kurt was exhausted but unable to sleep more than a few minutes, the chaos of his life interfering. "I must hear her sing one last time then I'll find Hilda. I don't give a damn what Vic does any more. Damn all these secret plans!"

He shivered before the cold fireplace. He wondered if he had pneumonia from the sewer. He stacked broken twigs and laid black coal on top. He lit the fire and settled into the warmth, thinking of Hilda.

He took the vase from the mantle and emptied it into his hand, light fairies sparkling off Hilda's diamond danced on the ceiling.

Then he opened the small slip of paper and looked at the numbers. He dropped both back into the vase and curled by the fire until time to go.

68

Snowflakes Swirled

Snowflakes swirled around Vic as he hurried along Kurfürstendamm to reach the Hilton. A latent promise of excitement was always present along that busy boulevard—anything could happen there, but he had seen enough in the past weeks to last him a lifetime.

He turned the collar of his topcoat against the wind, beneath it he wore his only gray suit, under that he carried a service Colt .45 automatic, fully loaded. He would be ready for anything.

He checked a glossy photograph of Ilse in a man's suit and fedora near the entrance, using the reflection in the glass to ensure he had lost his CIA tail. He was anxious to hear Ilse sing again and meet her afterwards. He buttoned his suit jacket to conceal the unauthorized weapon before checking his overcoat.

The piano bar was packed. She was already on stage but smiled as he settled onto a barstool. He watched her reflection and the crowd in the bar mirror and ordered scotch on the rocks. As the bartender delivered his drink, he saw Kurt coming his way. He couldn't believe he had the gall to come.

Kurt was dressed as an off-duty sailor and looked tired; he surveyed the room as he walked to the bar. He leaned against a barstool at the curve of the counter and ordered Schnapps and a Lager, ignoring Vic.

The bartender delivered Kurt's drinks with a paper napkin, thumping the bar with his knuckle. Kurt studied the napkin, turned slowly and swept the room again with his eyes. He drank his Schnapps and crushed the napkin, rubbing a finger over his eyebrow. Then he dropped the napkin on the bar, slid off the stool and walked toward the men's room.

Vic reached across and snatched the napkin before the bartender collected it. He read: "*Gefahr!*" Danger!

Meanwhile, Ilse's songs had captured everyone's attention—everyone except for one heavy-set man studying Kurt from across the room. He was older, late-fifties maybe. He looked familiar to Vic and he looked him over carefully. He did know him—Major General Nikoli Rubski, former commander of a Russian division at the Fulda Gap, now on special assignment for Khrushchev. The gasoline burn on his neck blazed red, a bloody claw that crept up his cheek. Vic knew the scar brightened when he was mad, and he was sure mad as hell! His job was watching Russians so he would keep an eye on this one.

Kurt returned after a few moments wearing a short red waiter's jacket belonging to the Hilton. His hair was slicked back and he wore wire-rimmed glasses, altering his appearance. He stood near an exit and held a tray as if collecting glasses.

They were both waiting for Ilse to finish her routine. Vic already knew they would meet at her apartment afterwards. He had almost lost himself in her number when he heard glasses rattle. An East German, an obvious *Stasi* agent, was whispering into Kurt's ear and jammed a pistol against his ribs.

Ilse also saw the pistol from the stage as she reached the last stanza of *Lili Marlene*. She stopped singing in mid-verse. The pianist played on a few bars then he stopped too. Silence filled the room. Patrons stared in disbelief. She screamed. "Fire! *Feuer! Ausgang schnell!*—Get out fast!"

A hundred people leapt to their feet—rushing doors in pandemonium. Women screamed, men shouted. The bartender pulled an alarm and sent an ear-splitting wail throughout the entire hotel.

Kurt slammed an elbow into the throat of the East German. Before Fox's specialist hit the floor Kurt was through the lobby. He whipped from the main entrance onto a hallway.

Vic lost sight of Kurt and dashed into the street ahead of the shoving crowd. He looked back for Rubski but had lost him, too. A black diplomatic sedan passed him spraying slush and he looked in the direction it was going.

Kurt crashed through an emergency door, right into Rubski's fist. Kurt collapsed on the snowy sidewalk under the ugly Russian. Vic waded through the slush in their direction. Still a block away, he saw blood from Kurt's broken nose dripping onto the white snow.

Rubski said, "Meyer, I need a word with you. *Komrade* Khrushchev has some questions." He snatched Kurt onto his feet.

Vic shouted, "Hey, Rubski ... hold on!"

The Mercedes slid to a stop beside the Russian—engine revved. Rubski shoved Kurt but he tried to break away. Rubski grabbed his collar, slammed a blackjack against the back of his skull.

"Hold on, General," yelled Vic again. "I need to talk to you. Stop!"

Rubski lifted Kurt easily and tossed him into the trunk. He dived into the rear seat and the Mercedes spun snow and gravel into Vic's face.

"Stop, you Goddamned Russian! Stop!"

He stopped running. "Shit. How did I get into this mess?"

69
Facts meet Fantasy

Vic kept Rubski's sedan in sight until it disappeared around a corner. His personal car, a 1959 Ford Mustang, was concealed nearby so he ran to it and jumped in. He turned the ignition switch and revved the engine for a fast warm up. The passenger-side door opened and snow and cold air blew inside, followed by Ilse still wearing her Dietrich outfit, complete with hat and cane.

"What are you doing?" he demanded.

"I'm going with you."

"No way in hell!"

"Hurry, damn it—he's getting away!"

Vic stomped the accelerator and his Mustang skidded into the street, narrowly missing a merging BMW. He navigated around people milling aimlessly outside the hotel. Once clear, the muscle car lurched in hot pursuit of the Mercedes. They gained ground but not nearly fast enough. Rubski headed north toward Oranienburg, away from crossing points manned by Americans. Rubski would easily reach the border before they caught up. Vic knew he couldn't cross without his credentials.

"Don't lose him," she begged.

"We can't possibly catch him. What would you do anyway—hit him with that cane?"

"I don't know," she admitted.

"He has a big head-start," he said, then tapped the brake and skidded on the slick road. "Checkpoint ahead—we can't go any further. I don't have my pass and this car isn't registered." He stopped in a line of cars being checked, well behind the Mercedes. A policeman waved Rubski's car with diplomatic plates ahead of the others and the Mercedes vanished. The border guards had been expecting him.

A policeman shouted through Vic's window. "Papers!" Three armed soldiers encircled the Mustang.

Vic warned Ilse, "Keep your mouth shut!" Then to the guard, he said, "I made a wrong turn. I want to turn around."

One guard motioned Vic into a U-turn with his assault rifle. "Take your whore back home."

"That's the second time I've been called that," she said.

Vic circled back towards city center. He glanced over and saw her shoulders were shaking and her makeup was smeared.

"I begged him not to come," she said. She used her shirttail to wipe her eyes, further smearing her mascara and leaving black traces on the white shirt.

"No one tells Kurt what to do, not even you."

"Where are you going?" she asked.

"I'm taking you home." Vic turned the heater higher.

"You're just giving up?" she said. "You're quitting—just like that?"

"There's nothing else we can do."

"I can't believe you! No wonder the Soviets push you Americans around; you don't push back."

"Okay, what do you suggest, an invasion?"

"Take me back to the hotel. I need to change clothes."

"You won't be welcome there. False alarms are illegal, you know. There might be a cop waiting for you there."

"Frankly, my dear, I don't give a damn."

"Okay, Scarlet."

70

Changing Gears

Vic double-parked at the front entrance of the hotel. A policeman and a fire marshal stood inside the glass doors talking with the manager. "They're waiting for you," he said. "Let's go home and come back tomorrow when it cools off."

"I need my purse," she said opening the door and walking straight toward them.

Vic watched—he couldn't hear from inside the car but he remembered watching drive-in movies with broken sound boxes, sometimes staring Marlene Dietrich. Ilse, still wearing her Dietrich costume, spoke to the fireman, then shook hands with the policeman, and hugged *Herr* Eichmann before moving off stage. A few minutes later she returned in street clothes, no longer Dietrich. Ilse spoke to the policeman and fireman again and kissed Eichmann's cheek. He beamed as she walked away—newspaper entertainment sections would be all over this, drawing even more customers. Vic wondered if he was only supporting cast for her fantasy life.

"Where to now, gorgeous?"

"Let's talk to your boss."

"Are you crazy? I may already be going to Fort Leavenworth." The last person Vic wanted to see was Colonel Powell, especially in the middle of the night. But she made him do irrational acts—Alice in Wonderland in a spaghetti western. He parked the Mustang in Powell's driveway, shaking his head in disbelief. "Are you sure you're ready for this?" he asked. "He's really pissed."

"That makes two of us," she said. "Let's go."

Vic pressed the front doorbell several times.

A dim lamp came on in an upstairs bedroom and a scowling face appeared in the window. Two minutes later the porch light illuminated and the front door flew open. "Werner! What the hell has gotten into you? It's the middle of the fucking night! Have the goddamned...?" He stopped short when he saw Ilse. "...Come on in." He backed up to give them room to pass through the doorway. "I've got to hear your explanation for this, Werner."

Powell was still in wool plaid pajamas under a gray West Point robe and leather slippers. His hair was disheveled. A woman shouted from upstairs. "Who is it, John? Are you coming back to bed?"

"Go back to sleep, Hon, this might take a while."

Vic and Ilse hung their coats on hooks in the foyer as Powell studied them. He spoke first to her, "Excuse my language, ma'am. He brings out my worst side."

Then, "Will one of you explain what the hell this is all about?"

"Ah'll try suh." Ilse used her southern drawl.

"Well.... Come into my study, little lady." They followed him through a formal living room filled with antiques, past a winding staircase, down an endless hallway, and around a garden chock with masonry statues.

Ilse whispered, "I'll do the talking."

Vic shrugged. "This is your party."

Inside Powell's office he indicated a leather sofa angled to the desk where he held court at home. "Well, I'm waiting...."

"It's quite simple, sir," she began. "A Russian kidnapped my best friend and took him to East Germany. I'm afraid he'll kill him."

"Well, is *that* all?" Powell said with sarcasm. "I'll just call President Kennedy and tell him to blast Moscow back to the Stone Age. Is that what you want, ma'am?"

"No, sir," she said. "I just want my friend back."

"Why'd they do it?" he asked. "Why'd they snatch him?"

"They think he's a spy. The Russian thinks he has something of his."

"Well, judging by .... I suppose he's the one who ... what Captain Werner turned in last week, from what I've seen, I'd say they're right."

"It's not that simple, sir."

"I know it's not simple, ma'am. It's a total goddamned mess. This is a matter for the CIA, or police, not the army."

Vic stepped in. "I know who the Russian is, Colonel. It was General Rubski."

Powell raised his eyebrows. "And just how do you know that, Sherlock?"

"I saw him do it, sir, and we followed him to the border."

Powell thought for a minute. "Rubski's a bad case, but there's nothing I can do about him. Tell the German police. Tell the Embassy; you're an American, aren't you?" he asked her. "How'd a nice lady like you get mixed up with a German spy?"

"I just want my friend to be safe," she said. Ilse puckered her lips as if about to cry.

"But my hands are tied. I track Soviets but I don't arrest them. I have no authority for that. And you, Captain," He pointed an accusing finger. "Need I remind you that you're a United States Army officer and duty-bound by that too?"

"But maybe there's something you could do, Colonel."

"Yeah? Well, I'm just dying to find out what. I can hardly wait for you to tell me."

"Call Marshall Koniev," said Vic. They both looked at Vic, wanting him to continue. "Ask him to get Rubski to talk to me."

Powell rubbed his chin. "Well, I'll think about that one. Maybe I could, but not now. I'm not calling the Commander-in-Chief of Soviet Forces in the middle of the night. My manners are better than yours."

"But, sir...." Ilse pleaded.

He cut her off. "I'll see you both at my office, my real office, at zero-eight hundred sharp. That's that. Now get out of here. I'm going back to bed."

They lingered in the driveway after the porch light went out, alone and in the dark with their problem. "Now what?" Vic asked.

"Get in the car," she said. "It's too cold to stand out here."

When they were inside, he started the Mustang and goosed the engine until the heater warmed. "OK?"

"I'm thinking," she said. "What would you tell Rubski?"

"First, we don't even know if Powell will call Koniev. And if he does, we don't know if Koniev will agree to talk. Rubski works for Khrushchev."

"Think positive thoughts, Vic."

"Well, assume it all positively works. I'll tell Rubski the game is over. We want Kurt back and that's that."

"He'd laugh at us," she said. "Tell him we want a face-to-face meeting. Tell him we have what he wants and we'll swap. See what he says to that."

"He won't come to a meeting. Besides, what does he want? I've already turned in what Kurt gave me, the Warsaw Pact ground plan. That's what got me into this mess in the first place."

"I think he'll meet with us. He still wants *something*."

"You're not listening, beautiful. The plan Kurt gave me has already gone to Washington and I can't get it back. I wish I'd never seen it."

"A face-to-face meeting," she repeated.

"It'll never work," he argued. "I guess we can give it the old college try, but it won't fly." He put his hand on the gearshift and stomped the clutch. "Are we going to just sit here until morning?"

"No, let's go to my place. I'll make coffee and we can warm up until we go to your boss's office," she said. "He's not so bad, really—just a big teddy bear."

71

Goose Bumps

The aroma of fresh coffee filled Ilse's apartment, bringing further clarity to a situation that was all too clear already. Vic excused himself to go into her bathroom. Ilse left her coffee on the table and went to her Dietrich poster, reached behind it and removed the envelope. *So Rubski kills for this,* she thought as she slipped it into her pocket.

She took the vase with Kurt's personal things, and emptied the contents into her hand. She rubbed the diamond over her sleeve and shoved it deep into her pocket. Then she opened the scrap of paper for the first time. She'd always been more interested in Hilda's ring than a row of numbers.

As she opened it she heard Kurt's words: "If the money is still there in month ... it belongs to you."

Goose bumps climbed her arm and her hand trembled. She was dumb-founded—the numbers had meaning. She unbuttoned her left sleeve, rolled it up and removed her wide watchband. She compared the numbers on the paper with those tattooed on her wrist: *767664252 – 767664252.*

The numbers were those Nazis had branded her with, and below them was written his secret password: *Lili—Lili Marlene.* His name escaped her lips—"Kurt!"

"What?" asked Vic, emerging from the bathroom.

"Nothing," she stammered and tossed the slip of paper into the embers of Kurt's dying fire. "I was wondering what has happened to Kurt. Are you cold? I am."

She tossed on more coal and stoked the sparks until the flame brightened. She saw Vic looking at her one rolled sleeve. "I was winding my watch." She returned her watch to her wrist and buttoned her sleeve over it. "Vic, I left my coffee in the kitchen. Would you bring it?"

"It's cold by now," he said.

"Just bring it, please."

Vic brushed her when he sat near on the rug near the fire. "I need to ask you something," he said. "Would you answer honestly?"

"No promises." She watched as the rising flames consumed the scrap of paper. "I haven't heard the question yet."

"That's what I thought."

"Ask the damned question!"

"Before Kurt went into that tunnel he said I should take care of you. He said you loved me. Do you?"

"Vic, this isn't the time to discuss us," she said. "I think I'm in love with you, but right now my heart aches for Kurt and his family. That's all I can handle right now. We can talk about us after this."

"I wonder if this will ever be over. I just wanted you to know I love you now, no matter what happens after this. I'm with you either way but I want to know if we might have a future together. That's all."

She took his hand. "Vic, I'm not using you, if that's what you're worried about. If you don't help me—for any reason—I'll understand. I owe this to Kurt."

"I hope you'll feel that way about me someday."

"There are volumes you don't know about me, Vic." She patted his hand and started for her bedroom. "I'm wearing boots," she said. "I'll be right out."

She slipped off her blouse, replacing it with a wool sweater, found her boots under the bed then went to the dresser for Kurt's heavy wool socks. Beneath them was Abel's Walther—she recoiled. She gathered her courage and lifted it by the handle with two fingers and laid it carefully on the dresser.

A knock at the door startled her.

"Are you all right in there?" Vic asked.

"Just a minute!" She checked for the ring in one pocket, the Top Secret plan in another, pulled the socks on her feet, tied the boots and stood. Then she dropped Abel's pistol into her coat pocket, took a deep breath and walked out.

"Are you coming?" she called as she opened the front door.

72

Little Hope for a Brighter Day

Rubski's car slipped into the familiar frozen ruts at the KGB *dacha* near Karlshorst, East Germany. The sun, diffused by a hanging fog, offered little hope for a brighter day. His driver opened the trunk and Rubski checked that his unconscious prisoner was still alive. Rubski inspected the fresh guards. These wore crisp uniforms and stood at attention. These were soldiers—more formidable than those now en route to Siberia.

"Take him inside and secure him," Rubski ordered.

"*Da*, General!" They lifted Kurt and carried him in, dropped him on the floor, handcuffed his hands behind and bound his feet with rope by looping it around a cold radiator. They stood back for Rubski to check their work. He nodded his approval.

Kurt's broken nose was blue and dried blood caked his cheek. Rubski rubbed his sore knuckles then checked the back of Kurt's head. He knew the blackjack would cause a concussion without breaking the skin; he liked blackjacks. He felt for a pulse on Kurt's throat and stood back; satisfied his prisoner would be talking soon.

"Don't harm him or talk to him," he instructed the guards. "And don't release him for any reason. No food, no water, nothing. I'll return this afternoon for questioning."

"*Da*, General."

He started outside but turned around at the door. "If he escapes ...." He aimed a thick finger at each one and cocked his thumb. "I'll personally shoot all of you." They snapped to attention—word spread quickly about the other guards. He liked it that way—Rasputin was back.

"Where to, general?" his driver asked.

"The embassy—I must phone Moscow," he said, and rode in silence all the way into East Berlin. The sedan turned off *Unter den Linden* into the underground garage, where he left the car for a private elevator reserved for diplomats and generals. At his office, he checked the time in Moscow and dialed the phone.

"Khrushchev."

"This is Nikoli, *komrade*."

"Did Fox catch the spy?"

"I snatched him myself but he doesn't have the plan with him. I hit him too hard—he's unconscious. I will thoroughly interrogate him this afternoon—before I kill him."

"Keep me informed, Nikoli. Missiles have already reached Havana Bay. We must protect Koniev's ground attack plan until we are prepared to launch the missiles. Do your job!" Click.

Rubski sat paralyzed in his seat until someone knocked on his door. "Enter."

Komrade Sergey, embassy administrative officer, came in. "Excuse me for interrupting, general. I have some bad news."

"How can there be more bad news?"

"Well, after I replaced *Frau* Meyer with *Komrade* Ivanovich, I had him do a complete inventory. There are other documents missing going back for almost a year."

"A year?"

"Yes. One is the plan Marshall Koniev filed here last month."

"So I have learned," said Rubski.

"And another," said Sergey, "is the plan to move missiles to Cuba."

"Both are missing?"

"Yes, General."

Rubski's burn blazed and he started to stand before his knees turned watery. "Sergey, we'll keep this between you and me for now. I'm investigating this and I don't want anyone outside this room to know. Understood?"

"*Da*, General."

Rubski flicked his hand and waved him out then massaged his temples with his thumbs, swallowed a pill, checked his watch again and walked upstairs for a cigarette. The restaurant would open soon for breakfast.

271

73

Kick the Bear

Vic and Ilse arrived at Powell's office several minutes before eight that morning and he was already behind his desk. "Come on in," he called, his mood lighter than when aroused a few hours earlier. He smiled at her New York Yankees baseball cap. "Are you a Yankees fan?"

"Why yes I am, colonel." She retained her southern accent as it was paying off. "Are you one, too?"

"Hell, no!" he said. "I don't like anything about New York, not even West Point. Where are you from, not New York I'll bet?"

"Biloxi."

"I'll swear. You talk just like my Aunt Sadie, she's dead now—God rest her soul. She lived and died in Gulfport—don't think she ever left except to go to Mobile once."

Vic interrupted, "Colonel, can you make that call now?"

"Keep your pants on, Captain. I've already called Marshall Koniev. Now, there's a real commander. He was up early exercising; his staff patched me right through an hour ago. He usually doesn't take calls but he made an exception for me. We need more like him in our army."

"What did he say?"

"I'll tell you what he said. He gave some damned good advice and I'm passing it on to you. He said: 'Stay out of politics!' Good idea—why didn't I think of that?"

"That's all?"

"No, that's not all. He said he'd call Rubski and tell him to accept your call. Here's the phone number for the Soviet Embassy. The switchboard will connect you. The general is having breakfast so wait until nine o'clock. You can use your own office for this, but Vic, if you don't stay out of politics you'll ruin a damned fine career. That's more free advice." Powell leaned back in his chair, hands behind his head. "I like that Koniev fellow more every time I talk to him—reminds me of Georgie Patton. Did I ever tell you ... never mind."

"Thank you, sir," said Vic.

Ilse said, "Thank you so much, Colonel Powell. I'm so truly indebted to you."

"You should be," he said. "Now get the hell out so I can do some real work. And try not to make an enemy of General Rubski."

272

Ilse couldn't relax. She paced prowled the crowded basement office, nerves on edge. Vic filled two mugs with strong army coffee. "Have some java," he said and offered her one. He settled behind his desk and synchronized his watch with the wall clock. "Twelve minutes to go," he said.

She sniffed the coffee, "I can't possibly drink this." She slid the mug to the edge of his desk.

"Let's go over this again'" he said. "Your bright idea is to try to set up a face-to-face meeting in West Berlin?"

"Rubski will never come here, not with Kurt. He'll stay on his own ground."

"Yeah, so what's Plan B?"

"The backup plan...." She thought for a minute. "Does he speak English?"

"I don't think so, but his German is fair. Why?"

"Then I'll do the talking."

"No way!" he said. "You'll get me thirty years in prison."

She snatched the Embassy number from his fingers and lifted the phone. It was still four minutes early but she placed the call.

"*Herr* General Rubski, *bitte*." The East German switchboard operator at the Soviet Embassy patched her call through. She cleared her throat while waiting.

"*Da*. Rubski here," he answered in Russian.

In a deep masculine German voice she said, "*Herr* Rubski, this is Captain Victor Werner of the United States Military Liaison Mission. Can we speak in German, please?" She was sure Rubski wouldn't recognize Vic's voice.

"Didn't I see you running in the snow last night, Captain?"

"I saw you, too. Kidnapping is a crime, *Herr* General."

"I made a legal arrest, Captain. I apprehended a spy in the Soviet city of Berlin. He'll be tried, found guilty, and executed. We all know he's guilty, don't we? Even he has admitted it."

"True or not, if you kill him without getting what you need, your life won't be worth your weight in salt, General. You know that, don't you?"

A moment of silence, then, "You know about it?"

"Yes ... I have it."

"Has anyone else seen it?"

"No."

"Why should I believe you?"

"I'll exchange his life for yours. If you get it back, you can tell Khrushchev anything you want. The document is your protection as long as you have it—without it, salt mines."

"Exactly what do you want?"

"I want Meyer back. He'll retire and you'll have your paper. We'll all live happily ever after."

"Ha!" he laughed. "You Americans are too sentimental. Only fools believe those dreams. It never works that way."

"What's the difference between reality and dreams? After all, we're only dreaming this conversation is happening."

The phone hummed until he said, "What do you suggest?"

"Meet me at the West Berlin Zoo, only you and Meyer. I'll bring the document. We'll both get what we want, a happy ending."

"Never! I won't go into West Berlin again, not with Meyer!"

"Do you have a better idea?" she asked. "I'm giving it to the CIA in twenty-four hours if this isn't resolved by then. Think fast."

The phone hummed again as he thought about it. "Okay, I'll meet with you, but it must be in East Berlin, at the Soviet Embassy."

"East Berlin, then," she said, "but on neutral ground. I'll call you later and I'll set the place and time. That should be fair, don't you think?"

"Stupid Americans, you think everything should be fair. I have news for you—life is not fair."

"I agree with you, General. You see? We've found common ground already. I'll call you again tomorrow, but if Meyer is hurt ...."

"His nose is broken but he is not dead," said Rubski. "But you better have what I want or both you and Meyer will wish you were dead." He slammed down the phone.

Vic gnashed his teeth. "You're crazy," he said, shaking his head. "I can't believe what I just heard. You just made that up. This is suicide."

"I can do this without you Vic, but I want your help. Someday you'll understand this is bigger than us."

"I hope we live to see that day. You just kicked a bear, and that document you were talking to him about isn't the one you gave me, is it?"

"There's another one," she said and absently touched her hip pocket, verifying it was still there. "We'll look at it later but we don't have time now. Let's go to your apartment and get ready."

"Get ready? How can we get ready for this?"

74

Hearts in a Fog

Vic and Ilse went to his Grunewald apartment, without even trying to dodge the CIA stakeout. They sat at his small dining table and considered their next steps.

Ilse mused, "I crossed over with Kurt right after the fence was put there but we could never do that now."

"We sure can't use that tunnel under the casern again. And It's a violation of policy for my team to go into East Berlin anyway," he said.

She looked as though he said the dumbest thing she had ever heard. "Policy...?"

"I know that was stupid. I said I'd help you and I will. I'd have to steal the official car to take it around Berlin but you don't have a pass to get through the checkpoint."

"I'll hide in the trunk."

"There must be two people with passes in the car. Someone else with a pass would have to sit up front."

"How can I get a pass?"

"That's impossible."

"Let me see yours."

He removed his USMLM card and handed it to her. She studied it and said, "I'll use this one. You can get another."

"Damn it, Ilse!"

She left the table, went into his bedroom and rifled through the closet and drawers, flinging clothes across his bed.

He followed her. "Why are you trashing my place?"

"Do you have a sewing machine?"

He held up both hands. "Do I look like someone who would own a sewing machine?"

A soft tapping on his door interrupted. Vic opened it to his *hausfrau* holding fresh sheets, towels, and cleaning supplies. "Later, please—come back in an hour." He started to close the door.

"Wait," Ilse called. "Can you sew?"

"Yes, *fraulein*. But my husband is a tailor; he has a little shop to make repairs, hem uniforms, make drapes, things like that."

Ilse handed her twenty marks. "Bring him here please, with his sewing machine. And do you know a barber?"

"Yes, *fraulein*. My brother."

"Bring him, too, with his clippers." The maid hurried away on her assignments, inspecting the money as she walked away, stuffing it into her pocket before she reached the street.

Ilse swirled, smiling. Vic ran his hands through his hair.

The maid returned with two middle-aged Germans—a tailor and a barber. Ilse took charge. She selected one of Vic's uniforms and a civilian shirt. She instructed the tailor to alter the uniform to fit her, adding padding in the shoulders.

The tailor sewed, and the barber clipped, snipped, and buzzed leaving long, curly strands at her feet. "Just like his," she said, pointing to Vic. In two hours, they were both finished and well paid for their services.

She changed into the uniform and had Vic stand next to her while she applied makeup, adding a five o'clock shadow, crinkles around her eyes, thicker eyebrows. "Good enough for government work." she said.

"Shit. You look like a man."

"We need another of those special passes—then off the meet the wicked witch of the East."

He asked, "You'll be pretending to be my driver?"

"Drive? I can't drive. Besides, I'm Vic Werner—you're the driver."

"Jesus Christ."

"Don't say that! Just say '*Scheisse!*'"

Vic gave Ilse instructions on where to meet him in a wooded park near Gleinecke Castle, across the river from Potsdam. She covered the uniform with her coat and proceeded alone by subway since the CIA agent wasn't tailing her. Vic drove alone across the demarcation bridge in his stick shift Mustang and the CIA fell away as they had no authority to cross the bridge. He parked it at the motor pool and took Reitz's super-charged '57 Chevrolet. The speedometer was calibrated for miles-per-hour. A mechanic had used a grease pen to mark the kilometers-per-hour on the glass so the driver would know if he was speeding on European highways. Vic intended to break every posted speed limit anyway.

He lifted Airman Reitz's badge from the pass box and pinned it to his uniform, then he removed his silver captain's bars and dropped them into the ashtray and his badge on the passenger seat. He pinned Reitz's stripes to his collar. Reitz was meticulous about his badge and his car and would be irate when he found out someone had taken them.

Vic eased the Chevy back over the river bridge from Potsdam into West Berlin where Ilse waited in a clump of trees in the park. She looked nervous in his uniform, but wore it well. The tailor had done a good job on the cloth—God performed a miracle with the rest. She was sexier in military uniform than as Dietrich and had reentered her other world, the world of fantasy.

She jumped into the car before it completely stopped. Vic took his silver bars from the ashtray and leaned over to pin them to her collar. Their eyes met, inches apart. She took his cheeks in her hands and kissed him. It was warm, wet, their tongues touching. He slipped his hand behind her neck and ran it up through her clipped hair. He pulled her close and she gave in easily.

The engine was still running but he found neutral and the emergency brake. Her glassy eyes and parted lips were unmistakable evidence she felt something. The front seat slid all the way back and reclined in one move. They touched from lips to thighs. The windows fogged over, shutting out the world beyond the Chevy.

He worked the buttons on her shirt. Her hands slid under his and she drug her nails across his chest. Both shirts were open but he couldn't quite reach what he wanted. She guided him there and he almost lost control.

She pushed her pants down to her knees and Vic worked them to her boots. She spread her knees as wide as possible. Everything he wanted was there. Her breathing was fast and heavy but came in soft moans. They lay in a tangle of semi-naked arms and legs, catching their breath, afraid to speak. Maybe this was all there was, the best life had. Neither moved for a time until Ilse touched a single finger to the windshield and drew a heart in the fog where their breath had blended.

75

Cross the Rubicon

They re-dressed in the cramped car, not quite sure of the meaning of where they had just been or where they were going. Vic backed the car from the park and they re-crossed Freedom Bridge from West Germany going east. He had crossed the bridge once to get the car, then back to pick her up. This was his third crossing in an hour but the rules of the Heubner-Mallinin Agreement were to enter the Soviet zone only from Potsdam.

Ilse had never learned to drive, so she sat in the passenger seat. She looked like another man, despite what had just happened between them. They didn't speak of it. Vic knew what had happened was significant to both of them but focused on the job ahead. "We'll get through the West German side without any problems," he said, "and the Soviet guard will wave me through. Remember, ignore the East Germans—they have no authority over us. The problem starts when *Stasi* follows us in the Soviet zone. Rubski and Fox will have already made special arrangements for that." He glanced over at her. "Are you nervous?"

"Just stage fright," she said. "But it goes away as soon as I start performing."

"Were you ... never mind."

They flashed their identification and cleared the checkpoints quickly. Vic weaved between the barriers and they were across. "We're being followed already," he said. She glanced in the outside mirror. "They brought the BMW," he said. "Where to my lady?"

"We need to get to East Berlin fast," she said. "It's right over the wall, so why are going the long way?"

"I must leave from Potsdam—it's one of the rules."

"Forget the rules, Vic."

"I must circle around. We can't cross the Wall."

"That'll take all day," she said. "We need to find a place to meet Rubski."

"You've never been in one of these babies," he said. "Fasten your seat belt!"

As her fastener snapped over her lap, her head snapped back. "Oh!" The landscape outside her window was instantly blurred. The engine thundered onto a paved highway, overtaking Trabants, Wartburgs, and Opels—tractors and oxcarts were nearly blown off the road. The BMW fell behind initially but gradually gained on them after several kilometers of open road.

"Be careful, Vic!" she cried. "I've never been this fast. Don't kill us before we get there."

"We have to lose them. Hang on, this may get rough." Vic swung the wheel and the Chevy swerved sharply to the right and off the road. She jammed one hand against the dash and the other clung to the handhold above the door. They bounced hard on compressed shock absorbers, crossing a potato patch. Vic steered the tires into the furrows, scraping dirt under the car and leaving a trail of heavy dust. The BMW tried to follow but quickly bottomed out in the deep ruts. Leaving the BMW hopelessly stuck, Vic swung back onto the highway. They circumnavigated the city at high speed, but without a tail.

"How far can you drive this way?"

"It has a forty-gallon tank, so four times as far as their car," he said. "What will we do when we get there?"

"Look around first. I need to get my bearings. Go past the Berliner Ensemble then drive past the Café Gazebo, Emil's bakery, and the Dom Cathedral. I'm familiar with those and one may do for a meeting."

"We'll pick up another tail as soon as we hit the city limits."

"Can you lose them?"

"Yeah, but not in town." He looked in the rear view mirror. "They're here already." She looked in the side mirror, gnawing her lower lip.

They cruised East Berlin, permitting the *Stasi* car to follow them easily, spoke little and tried to get their bearings, mulling different plans. Ilse considered what she had to do—exchange a document for Kurt, and get away alive. Vic concentrated on driving and memorizing unfamiliar streets.

They hadn't eaten all day. "Are you hungry?" he asked.

"I hadn't thought about it, but yes."

"Let's get out of town. I know a good place for soup."

Vic sped out of Berlin toward Lake Muggelsee and stopped at a quaint resort. A brown coal fire burned in one corner of the restaurant, yet it was nearly deserted. He parked the Chevy near the front and they entered the dining room. He took a seat near the window where they could watch the car. The *Stasi* agents parked alongside the Chevy but remained in their BMW.

He ordered soup while she went into the men's restroom, locking the door behind. When she returned, hot soup, fresh bread and cheese were waiting.

"Oh! I was hungrier than I realized," she said.

"Take your time. We need to make our friends outside uncomfortable." Vic signaled the proprietor and she approached the table suspiciously, glancing out at the obvious *Stasi* car.

"The soup is *wunderbar*," said Vic.

"*Danke*."

"I'll pay you now. We may leave in a hurry."

"*Danke*."

"I want to buy some soup and hot tea for our friends parked outside in the cold. But don't tell them I paid for it. Say you felt sorry for them. I'll leave a nice tip on the table for you," he said. Then he added, "Oh, and drop this into the soup please." Vic handed her several small white tablets, along with one hundred West German marks, more than the restaurant would make all winter. He aligned a pack of Winston cigarettes and two Hershey bars beside his plate.

"*Danke*. God bless America!" She hurried to the kitchen to prepare a tray with soup and a pitcher of hot tea.

Ilse asked, "What were those tablets?"

"A strong laxative for extended field trips. Be ready to leave in a hurry. Have you decided where to make the swap?"

"I need to check a couple of places more closely. Getting away with Kurt might be a problem if he's injured or tied up."

"I hadn't thought of that."

They watched the waitress carry the tray to the chase car. "They've been out there an hour already. That laxative will work fast. When they come inside to the bathroom, we'll run for the car."

Half an hour later, one of the *Stasi* agents stepped out of the car and shuffled inside. He glanced at Vic and Ilse as he hurried into the restroom.

Vic handed her the car key. "Jump in the car and start it. I'll be right behind you. Hurry."

Ilse ran to the car, jumped into the driver's side and started the engine. She slid over to the passenger side, leaving the driver-side door open.

Vic jammed a chair under the handle of the restroom door and ran to the car. He jumped behind the wheel, gunned the engine and checked the gauges. Tires squealed as the Chevy jumped onto the road, spewing rocks behind. The lone agent in the BMW blasted his horn, signaling his partner to hurry.

The man inside ran from the front door of the restaurant, still hitching his belt while the driver raced his engine and leaned on the horn. Vic sped on the dark road with headlights out. The '57 Chevy was painted olive drab including the chrome, and it had almost disappeared into the fading light before the chase car got underway. The tail car found the pavement as Vic swerved onto a narrow farm road out of sight. He braked behind a weathered barn and killed the engine. The BMW roared past them on the dark highway.

Ilse shrugged. "What now?"

"We can't go into Berlin with this car. They'll have an alert out and we'll get clobbered now for sure. I know this farmer—he'll give us a ride part way. He smokes like a chimney and his wife would kill for chocolate."

The farmer gratefully accepted a carton of cigarettes and a roll of bills. Ilse guided the car while Vic and the farmer pushed it into the barn and covered it completely with straw. They took their spare clothes into the farmhouse where the farmer's wife admired the chocolates, some already missing.

Vic and Ilse changed clothes, tossed uniforms into the rear seat of the car, and restored the camouflage. They climbed onto a hay wagon and covered themselves with more straw. The old tractor rattled and the wagon bounced behind it.

"I'm itching. There are bugs in here!"

"Hush. You got us into this."

The distance from the farmhouse to the bus stop was only three kilometers along a rutted farm road but seemed further under the straw. The farmer stopped short of the bus stop and they climbed out brushing hay. Vic gave the farmer a few more bills. "This is an advance. Meet us here tomorrow night. We'll have someone else with us." The farmer made a wide U-turn and headed home, already counting the money. He slipped one bill off the roll and stuffed it into the top of his shoe.

Ilse looked around and said, "This isn't Berlin, Vic. What now?"

"We'll walk two hundred meters to the intersection. The bus stops there for passengers. In town, we get around like everyone else."

"How will we get back out?"

"We'll solve that when the time comes," he said. "We'll improvise, isn't that what you do best?"

They got on the bus and off at the center of the city. It was cold—even the fog was freezing, coating streets, rooftops, and signposts with thin invisible ice. Few pedestrians were out so the streets were nearly deserted. They stood before Emil's old bakery.

"Looks like it's closed," said Vic, "Are you hungry?"

"I know they're closed—out of business. Kurt and I escaped through a tunnel in the basement that connects with a sewer. "

"A sewer? Kurt seems to always be in a sewer."

A late shopper approached clutching a shopping bag to her chest. She slipped on the icy sidewalk. Ilse took her arm to steady her. "Be careful!"

"You be careful, *fraulein*. Don't linger here."

"Why not?"

"*Volkspoltzei* raided the shop a few days ago. They found a tunnel in the basement."

"Did they close it?"

"*Natürlich*. They hauled enough bricks and mortar here to build another wall." She hurried along her route, drawing her coat close around her throat.

"Damn it." Ilse stomped her foot. "That was our best way out."

"What now, Einstein?"

"The Dom Cathedral."

"To pray?"

"Good idea."

76

Ideology vs. Idealism

General Rubski stopped at Fox's headquarters for a situation update while waiting for Kurt to recover from his beating. Fox emptied an ashtray and offered him a Marlboro. Rubski broke the filter off before lighting it.

"I had Werner tracked from the border," said Fox, in a cloud of smoke. "He's a reckless driver. He'll get killed on the highway some day."

"Don't worry—I'll kill him first but I need what he has before I do."

"We'll get it."

"The situation is worse than you know, Fox. Your spies have been taking papers from our embassy for a year."

"No!"

Rubski said, "Koniev's ground attack and the Cuban missile attack are the combined strategy for World War III. I want to make one thing very clear, Mischa—I won't leave anyone to leak this story." That thought hung like a gathering storm. He smashed out the cigarette, pulled on his wool hat, and headed straight back to the *dacha*.

Kurt was emerging from the fog of his concussion when Rubski's heavy steps disturbed the quiet cottage. "So the Chameleon has awakened from his nap. Why don't you become a snake and crawl away?" Rubski laughed and flung his overcoat onto the scrubbed dining room table. "Are you ready to talk?"

Kurt had been unscrambling his mind and reassembling the pieces of his capture—Ilse, Vic, the Hilton, *Stasi* agent, Fox, Rubski, KGB, safe house, East Germany, Hilda, Ingrid, documents.

"Put him in that chair," Rubski said to his men. "We need to have a friendly chat." The soldiers unlocked his handcuffs and lifted him into the same chair where Ingrid had sat. His image of Rubski was fuzzy as the soldiers snapped the handcuffs on his wrists and threaded a long chain through the slats behind the chair.

"Talk to me, Meyer! Where are the documents Ingrid gave you?"

Kurt grimaced at his sister's name on Rubski's tongue, his vision clearing, his disgust driving away clouds. He concentrated on Rubski and realized how his father's hatred had driven him when all seemed lost.

Rubski slapped his face. The chair toppled and he bumped his tender head on the floor.

"I asked you a question, Meyer. Where are they?"

"Go to hell!" His voice mushy and tongue thick.

"Set his chair up," Rubski ordered. "I'll ask him again."

When the chair was upright, Rubski shoved his face close and whispered, "Where are the documents, Meyer? Did you sell them to Werner?"

The question confused him. He hadn't given the document to Vic—why would Rubski suspect that? Had Ilse gotten caught with it? Before he worked it out, Rubski's fist crashed into his broken nose. His chair plummeted back and his head struck first on the floor, hard. Kurt saw another flash of light, then nothing.

Rubski's temper was nearly out of control. His fury included Khrushchev and the Soviet Ambassador, Werner and that singing woman, Fox and his errant agents, but especially Kurt Meyer. He was primed to kill. *Damn! I have to keep him alive.*

He ordered his men, "Watch him—keep him alive but don't give him a chance to escape—he's a slippery bastard. I'll return soon."

His driver raced back to the embassy and Rubski watched the countryside flash past his window in a kaleidoscope of barren farms, empty factories, vacant smoke stacks, people doing nothing of value. His mood lifted at luxurious Embassy row. He lit a Russian cigarette in his office and dialed Fox.

"Mischa, I just talked to Meyer."

"Good."

"I forgot to mention before," he said. "He had a nice pistol when I arrested him. Funny thing—it's inscribed to you from Marshall Koniev. How did Meyer get it?"

"He's a thief—you know that. He stole your plans, didn't he? Did you get them?"

"No, I'm sure the American has it—he proposed an exchange, the document for Meyer. What do you think?"

"The American has it?"

"Apparently, yes."

"How is that possible?"

"I don't know, but Captain Werner called me and claims to have it. He said no one else has seen it."

"Do you believe him?" asked Fox.

"Who knows?"

"I have a dossier on Werner," said Fox. "He's an American but he was born German."

"So that's why he spoke in German," said Rubksi, rubbing his bald head. "That's bad—Germans are crazy!"

"This doesn't make sense," said Fox. "Why would an American who knew your plan waste one minute on a German spy when the United States is threatened with a coordinated strike?" He ran his hand through his hair, considering. "Unless ... unless he's behaving as a German, not an American. If that is why, perhaps he hasn't shown it to the CIA, not yet anyway."

"You're losing me, Fox."

"The first German concern is to avoid war on this soil. Germany would be destroyed."

"So, this is maybe possible—but only if he's really a German instead of an American? This is too much for me! How can one person be two people? I don't even want to think about this. I only want Khrushchev's plan back. Then I'll kill all of them."

"It's possible, Nikoli. What's his proposal?"

"Werner wants to swap Meyer for it, in East Berlin but he'll decide where and when."

"Is he alone?"

"You said he has a driver," said Rubski. "But the agreement is just us."

"My agents saw two of them...." Fox considered then said, "My special enforcer told me you took Meyer at the Hilton."

"Yes. He was running from a fire, like everyone."

"Nikoli, there was no fire," he said. "My agent had a gun on Meyer when that singer cried fire and started a riot."

"The fire was faked for his escape? I saw that singer," Rubski said. "She chased us in her bare legs in the snow. She's another crazy German."

"I have more news for you," Fox said. "She's Meyer's other girl friend—the one we're trying to find. If Werner doesn't have the paper, she has it. Or perhaps Werner got it from her. She's very seductive and might have enticed Werner into helping her. There are possibilities within this *ménage a troi*. This is very interesting, indeed."

"What is it about you and women, Fox?"

"Women, my friend, they keep us on our game or throw us off. Behind every success or failure in this business lies a woman, often a beautiful one."

"No wonder Khrushchev likes you, Fox. You think like a Russian."

"I hate to disappoint you, old friend, but I understand this only because I'm a man. Tell me when the meeting is set. We'll collect them and the plan, all at once."

77

Church Revival

A rusty iron handle served the side entrance to the old church, the same place the monk had snatched Ilse from the clutches of the *Stasi*. Kurt had led her through that door to meet Fox. Karl Meyer had worked behind it. When she touched the door's handle a tidal wave of memories washed over her.

"What's wrong?" Vic asked.

"Nothing," she said, and then pulled with both hands.

When they were both inside she closed the door to total darkness.

"Shit. I can't see," he said.

"Watch your language! This is a church. Just hold my hand—I know the way." She led him through familiar passages into the musty candle-lit wine cellar, pulled a bottle of red from a rack and continued to Karl's small office. She stopped abruptly at the entrance.

A giant hooded monk sat at Karl's place, a specter where the old man should have been. "May I help you, children?" he asked from behind a full gray beard.

"We were ... we were looking for *Herr* Meyer," said Ilse.

"*Herr* Meyer isn't well," he said. "I'm handling his duties until he returns. Are you his family?"

"Yes," she said. "He's ... like my family."

"You must be Kurt's special friend."

"Yes, we're best friends."

The monk noticed the bottle in her hand. "I see you found the wine. Karl *was* fond of the grape."

"I ... I wasn't stealing it," she stammered. "I thought ... I just thought Karl was entitled ...."

"If you find comfort child, take all you want. Karl did. Wine nourishes a German soul. Here, give it to me."

He took the bottle and fumbled around the desk until he found a well-used corkscrew. He drilled and popped the cork then filled three glasses, examining each by holding it near the candle. "God's finest creation," he said, raising one glass. "Better than mankind, I believe. I'm proud to help him create this treasure."

"Where is Karl?" Ilse asked.

"He hasn't spoken since Ingrid was taken, the same as when Inga Meyer died in the war. God will hold his mind in his hand until he can accept this hell on earth." The old monk raised his glass. "God's will be done."

"God's will," Ilse said, drinking. "Is there news of Ingrid?"

"She's gone to a better place, my child."

"Oh no! Oh, *Mein Gott*! No!" Ilse fell to her knees sobbing. Vic kneeled beside her and wrapped an arm around her. Her tears rained over his shoulder and he helped her to an overturned wine crate to sit. During this episode the old monk vanished, replaced by a priest in flowing white robes. He spoke gently, "*Fraulein*, I'm sorry for your loss. I must ask if you know where to find Kurt?" he asked. "I think he could help Karl's recovery."

"I came here to find him," she said, drying her eyes. "The ugly Russian kidnapped him ... I'm trying to get Kurt released."

"So you have been in contact with the Russian?"

"Yes."

"Be very careful, my child," he said. "He murdered Ingrid."

She looked at the priest. "It wasn't Fox?" Vic gave her his handkerchief.

"Fox returned her purse with the sad news, a compassionate gesture in his strange way. He told me the Russian was responsible and I believed him, Ilse." He moved around them to sit in Karl's chair.

"How do you know my name?" she asked.

"Karl told me about you—we are very close friends. I was the only one he would talk to after Inga died. I miss my friend now."

"Rubski killed Ingrid and now he has Kurt," Vic recited what he had heard. "That cold-blooded bastard!" Ilse gave him a warning look.

"How do you propose to have him released?" asked the priest. "Will it include violence?"

"I hope not," she said. "I'll swap a document Rubski wants for Kurt."

"A paper for a life," said the priest. "Will you use the church?"

"Could we?"

"This is God's house, *fraulein,* not mine," he said. "Let's ask him." The priest gathered one of her hands and one of Vic's into his. The priest's hands were rough as a carpenter's. They stood quietly in a small circle with heads bowed and the priest intoned verses in Latin. When he looked up, he said, "I heard no objections." He still held their hands.

Ilse said, "I must phone the Russian at nine o'clock in the morning. Can we stay the night here?"

"Yes. We have cots and blankets for vagrants. I'll have fresh bedding delivered. When will you meet him?"

"I'll set it for ten o'clock tomorrow night, but I won't tell him where until just before then."

"Good," said the priest. "I'll ask some watchers to be alert for any traps. We'll help God on this one."

"Thank you," she said.

Vic added, "My greatest concern is getting away afterwards. Once Rubski has what he wants and knows where we are, we'll be in the greatest danger."

"I'll meditate about that. God will tell us what to do. Meanwhile, get some rest; you'll need it." The priest released Vic's hand and wrapped both his around Ilse's. "Are you well, my dear?" He studied her eyes.

"I ... I think so."

"Karl told me what happened to you in the war, child. He asked me to pray for you."

"But you know I'm Jewish?"

"I know you're God's child," he said. "And I know you're in a race with the devil. I'll say a special prayer for you. *Guten Nacht.*" He kissed her hand, released it and left.

The old monk returned with folding cots and blankets as if he had been waiting. Then he left, leaving them alone with what had been said.

Vic refilled their glasses with the last of the wine.

"What was he talking about?" he asked. "I didn't even know you were Jewish. And what did he mean about the war?"

"That isn't important," she said then whispered. "He said the old man liked me." Her eyes watered again and she wiped them quickly. "If my being Jewish is a problem for you Vic, just tell me now."

"No, it isn't a problem. I just...."

"I told you before there are things about me you don't know, so don't fall in love with me too fast. For your own sake, don't until...."

"Ilse...." he interrupted. "Was that the first time for you? You know, back there ... in the car?"

"So what!" She drew her knees close, defensive and defiant, and clinched her eyes.

"I'm sorry," he said. "I just didn't think...."

"You couldn't believe ... at my age?" She kept her eyes closed and turned away.

"I'm just ... I guess I'm trying to say I'm honored that I would be...." He dropped on his knees behind her and wrapped his arms around her.

"Vic, I have some issues ... some problems. I'm making progress, though." She turned and faced him. "I'm glad it was with you too, but my problems may be too much even for you. We must wait until after this is over to discuss us. Is that all right?"

"I just want to protect you, that's all."

"We must concentrate on this meeting with Rubski. We need to rest tonight, as the priest said."

"But there's one more thing," he said. "Isn't it time you showed me that document. The one I'm risking my life over?"

"I wish I'd never seen it, and you will, too." She slid the folded envelope from her pocket and handed it to him.

Vic's skepticism about the thin document was evident. He unfolded it and smoothed it over the desktop and moved the candle to read. After a moment he snapped, "God Damn! Do you know what this is? Holy shit!"

"Language, Vic," she said, "remember where you are."

He stared at her and read it again. "God damn Khrushchev!" he said. "I have to get this to Powell right away. Let's go to the car!" He stood up, grabbed for his coat and thrust one arm into a sleeve.

Ilse uncorked a roundhouse that caught him square on the chin. He stumbled over the wine crate and sprawled on the floor on his back, tangled in his coat. She straddled him, snatched the document and stuffed it into her bra. "I know precisely what it is," she said in measured cadence. "This is Kurt's life. I'm trading it for his life. Ingrid already gave hers for it."

"Let me up," he said rubbing his jaw.

She didn't move. "They'll believe you in Washington but they'll never believe me. You can make them believe it." After a few seconds, she said, "Vic, I do love you. I'm sorry about that." She extended her bruised hand.

He rubbed his chin and flexed his jaw. "Damn. You hit hard for a girl."

291

"I'm sorry I hit you, Vic. But, you really scared me, acting crazy like that."

"*Me?* You're the crazy one. But we can't just give it back."

"Yes, we can."

"You don't really think he'll let us leave after they have it, do you? I don't."

"Well ... we need a plan," she agreed. "That's my main worry, too."

"Any ideas?"

"I'm counting on the priest for divine intervention."

He studied her. "You're just flying by the seat of your pants, aren't you?"

"It's called improvisation, Vic," she said. "An acquired skill—I have a talent for it."

"This isn't some drama, you know? We have to actually call Rubski. What will you tell him?"

"Open another bottle," she said, "I'll think of something."

78

Star of a Tragedy

Rubski was agitated and stomped from one end of his office to the other. He hated mindless waiting, especially waiting for his enemy. He would never wait for an American army captain if Khrushchev weren't holding a gun to his head. When the phone finally rang, he let it ring three times and his burn reddened with each one. Finally, he picked it up. "General Rubski, here."

"This is Captain Werner," Ilse lied in her deepest voice. "The meeting is at ten tonight."

"That's not enough time!"

"Twenty-two hundred hours! That's all."

"Where?" Rubski asked, "Where will we meet?"

"I'll tell you where just before the meeting. Have Meyer with you—only the two of you. The deal is Meyer for the plan. Agreed?"

"*Da*." As soon as Rubski clicked off he dialed another number which was answered immediately.

"Fox."

"Mischa, this is Nikoli."

"Where's the meeting?"

"He wouldn't say, but it's at twenty-two hundred hours. He'll call just before to tell me where."

"I'll have my teams surround them. As soon as you get what you want, we'll arrest them."

"There won't be time to set a trap. That's why he's keeping it secret until the last moment."

"There's plenty of time," Fox said. "I know precisely where the meeting will be."

"How could you? He hasn't even told me."

"I know them. They have limited options here—this still is my city. Just play along and get your document. I'll handle the rest."

"I'll call you as soon as I hear from them." The phone clattered when Rubski dropped it. He pulled on his overcoat and dashed for his sedan. "Karlshorst," he shouted at his driver. "The *dacha,* and step on it!"

When Rubski reached the cottage Kurt was conscious again but his eyes were glassy, pupils dilated, and his face a pattern of deep purple bruises. His twice-broken nose was swollen and smeared oddly to one side. He breathed only through his mouth. The cottage was icy cold. "Untie him so he can walk," Rubski instructed the guards. When Kurt was out of the chair, guards helped him balance on wobbly legs until he stood alone.

"Let's go, Meyer." Rubski shoved him toward the door but he fell to his knees. The guards stood him up again and he took a few shaky steps.

"You!" Rubski pointed to one of the soldiers. "Put your coat over him." The soldier reluctantly removed his greatcoat and draped it over Kurt's shoulders. Rubski pulled the cap from Kurt's pocket and pulled it over his head.

He pushed him again, this time toward the woods behind the cottage. Kurt tripped over a fallen branch but regained his balance without help. They continued for several meters into the trees to an empty grave chiseled from the frozen earth. Two covered mounds were basted with frost and a sprinkling of powdered snow.

Rubski walked around Kurt and stood on top of one mound. "This one was a coward," he said. A Russian pile cap lay in the snow and Rubski stepped on it. "I killed him. I do not condone weakness in soldiers."

On the other mound, two sticks were lashed into a wobbly cross. It had been hammered into the frozen ground and rocks piled around it. "This one is your beloved sister, Meyer."

Kurt knew that already. He had known he couldn't save her and he was responsible for her death. It was the reason the old man had lost his mind again. He collapsed over her grave, his face against the frozen dirt, his shoulders shaking under the heavy coat. No tears could come to his damaged eyes, no sound to his parched throat; he wanted it to end and he was ready to die. He was sure he would never see his beloved Hilda again. Kurt Meyer was finished with this life.

Rubski backed away and turned his back. He left Kurt with his grief while he smoked a cigarette—the ultimate torture working well enough. Rubski eventually spoke in an even manner. "She didn't have a priest," he said. "But she did have a proper burial, the best we could do under the circumstances. I wanted you to know."

"Why did you do it?"

"No choice, Meyer. *You* left me no choice. The security of my government depends on keeping the secret she stole. Power, Meyer, it's all about power. It's about the world and who rules it. You can't change that—you're up against overwhelming odds."

Rubski's words struck a spark within. "Russia will never rule the world, you idiot!" Still on his knees, he tried to spit on Rubski's boots through his broken teeth. His voice was hoarse. "You built a monument to your own failure—that wall is a parody of defeat. It'll collapse of its own weight, just like communism."

"Ah!" Rubski sighed. "But it doesn't really matter, Meyer. By tomorrow night, you'll be buried beside your sister. The American, Werner, will lie beside you. I'll order my guards to dig another one tonight—no, two more—one for the singing girl."

"I don't care what you do to me," he coughed up more blood. "I'm only sorry I won't be here to see you die."

Rubski struck a match but the wind blew it out before he could light his cigarette. He struck another inside the folds of his greatcoat and inhaled deeply. "Oh, I almost forgot to tell you, Meyer, about your fiancée," he said, "not the singing whore from Berlin, the one from Bonn, Hilda Brunner." His words terrifying than any other threat.

"Fox asked me to help her out of Germany," he said. "You'll be happy to know she made it safely to Switzerland. I offered her passage to Moscow, but she refused. She said she would wait for you there." Rubski blew smoke at him but the wind blew it away. "She still waits for you, Meyer, but the maggots have stripped flesh from her bones. I'm afraid the same fate met your unborn child."

Kurt went vacant, overwhelmed by the same white space as his father. Hope was gone, life was over; he still breathed but no longer wanted to. With certain clarity he knew what his mother's death had done to his father; the only compelling force that remained within him was to kill the Russian.

Rubski signaled for the guards. "Take him to the car," he said. "Put him in the trunk." The shivering guard pulled his greatcoat on over his uniform before he lifted the body of the living dead man.

As they carried him away, Rubski said, "You're the star of this tragedy, Meyer. I see why Fox is amused by you."

79

Tracks to a Grave

At the Dom, Ilse squinted into a ray of light when the door cracked open. The coal-fueled furnace had warmed and dried the room in the musty cellar where they had gained some needed rest. The giant monk set a tray of butter, bread, honey, and hot tea on the desk and left.

"Room service," Vic muttered, swinging his feet off the canvas cot. "Hope I can eat with a broken jaw." He flexed it, grimacing.

"I'm sorry," she said. "My hand hurts too, if it makes you feel any better." She poured tea from a kettle while he broke the loaf and pinched a soft piece from the center.

The priest entered the room as they were beginning to eat. "I wish we had more to offer," he said. "But I do have some news." He turned a wine crate on end and smiled as he swept his robes aside to sit on it.

"I hope your prayers were heard," she said.

"God acts in *mysterious* ways. I have a way out if you're not afraid of ghosts."

"I am," she said. "But I've learned to live with mine."

"Then this will suit you. There's a tunnel in the cemetery near the wall. It's necessary to enter through an open grave to reach it. Both were dug today and will be sealed tomorrow when *Frau* Oberlin is buried. It's covered with boards now to keep the snow out."

"That's wonderful news. Thank you."

"But, how do we get from here to the graveyard?" asked Vic. "That's the problem. We can't just walk out of here with Kurt and hail a taxi." The stones under their feet shook again—they had been awakened several times during the night by such irregular rumblings.

The priest closed his eyes and waited for the disturbance to pass. "I'll start at the beginning," he said. "This building is more than two hundred years old, but it was built over the ruins of churches going back many centuries. At first people relied on walking or animals for transportation. Over time, other means appeared, like motorcars and the airplanes that bombed it, and finally the *U-bahn* you just heard. Our sanctuary was in the path of the planned tunnel—authorities wanted to dig it directly through the church, right where we are now. Had it not been for the mausoleum under our feet, they would have." They gazed down at the stones under foot. "We still furnish a monthly gratuity of wine to the official who made that decision and an annual cash Christmas bonus. God sometimes works in *material* ways."

After a moment of apparent silent prayer, he continued. "Our accommodation with the government resulted in the tunnel being diverted to run alongside our foundation instead of through it and a hatch was cut to allow maintenance crews access to the tracks. The door is in the furnace room. A worker was badly burned on it several winters ago and no one has used it since."

"Are you saying we can catch the subway right here?" Vic asked.

"Not exactly," said the priest. "But you can get on the tracks. Of course, there are dangers. First, you must not touch the furnace, it'll be red hot this evening. Once inside the tunnel, the door will be locked behind you and the key misplaced for several days. You'll have to find the way to the cemetery on your own, but there is a station nearby. A partisan has already walked the route above the tracks and prepared a rough map." He handed Vic a hand-drawn sketch map.

"There are other dangers, as well. The train still uses those tracks as you've just heard, and the space is quite confined. The middle rail is electrified and will kill you if you touch it."

"But it would be possible," Vic mused.

"All things are possible with God's help," said the priest.

"So," said Ilse, "if we swap the document for Kurt at ten o'clock, we'll get into the tunnel immediately. Then we'll follow it to the cemetery, find the grave, go underground, cross under the Wall and reach the other side by morning—all three of us."

"That's the way I heard it," said Vic.

"It is a reasonable plan, but sometimes plans are disrupted," warned the priest. "Friendly eyes and ears will warn us of a trap if they detect one. They'll use lanterns to signal the belfry if one is discovered. The bell will ring a single time. Only once, and then the bell-ringer will stifle it immediately so he can confess to an accident. If you hear the interrupted bell you must run for your lives. There will be only seconds to spare."

"An underground railroad," said Vic, "with Paul Revere as engineer."

"One of our monks will meet you at the cemetery and lead you to your grave," said the priest. "God bless you." He left them alone with the map and their unspoken doubts.

Vic studied the hand-drawn map, memorizing routes, directions and distances as he did before every mission. He was engrossed in his work and at first didn't hear her say, "It's time to go." Ilse pulled her sleeve over her watchband and nudged him. "I said, "We have to call Rubski."

"Are you nervous?"

"More than I've ever been in my life."

He was surprised by that admission. "You're the bravest person I've ever known," he said, taking her hand. "We'll make it through this."

"It may not go the way we've planned, you know." She looked worried. "If anything goes wrong, Vic, my first concern will be Kurt's safety. We came here for him and he may be hurt. But I want you safe, too. I'm worried about you both."

"I can take care of myself," he said. "You just be careful. We're pushing Rubski into a corner and he'll certainly strike back. He has a bad reputation in these situations."

"I'd gladly kill him," she said. "But I've never shot a pistol. Do you know how to use this?" She held Abel's P-38 in her fingertips. He took it from her.

"Where did you get this?"

"Kurt had it—he took it from a dead Nazi," she said. "Do you know how to use it?"

Vic slid back the action, saw a round was already seated and it was in working order. "Hell, yes," he said. "If it's a gun, I can shoot it. Are you sure you don't want to hold on to it?"

"I don't like it," she said.

He stuffed it into his belt and buttoned his coat over it, but he left the two at the bottom unfastened for easy access. She didn't see the Colt .45 caliber service automatic he already carried. He was well armed for a church meeting.

Ilse led the way out and Vic followed close, alert for trouble, his hand on his own .45 inside his pocket. They ran to a phone booth on the next block. She dropped coins and dialed Rubski's number.

"General, this is Captain Werner," she lied again.

Vic faced away, watching for anything out of the ordinary. Three citizens huddled near the bus stop but the street was deserted otherwise. A bus rolled up the street collecting passengers along the route. A few people sat in the lights of a café across the street, talking and drinking coffee. Otherwise, they seemed to be alone.

"Do you have him?" she asked.

"*Da.* Where is the meeting?"

"Come inside the front of the Dom at ten o'clock," she told him. "The wind was frigid and she shivered, but she fought to keep the tremor from her voice. "Bring Meyer and don't be late!"

She hung up and backed into Vic. "Let's go." They ran past the bus stop to the Dom and ducked inside.

Two passengers at the bus stop boarded a bus, leaving a lone man with his chin buried in his overcoat and his hat pulled low against the cold. He watched them run away. When they were inside, he rejoined his team in the café.

80

"Do it to Survive"

Fox was waiting in his office for a report from his surveillance team. He had taken Rubski's report of Khrushchev's ire seriously and was ready to do his duty even though he didn't like it. He looked at the clock—9:02. His hand was on the phone when it rang and he snatched it up. "Fox!"

"There are two of them—a man and a woman dressed like a man. Her hair is cut short. They came from the church and ran back there after using the phone. The woman did the talking while he kept watch. I didn't see a gun but he looked like he had one in his pocket."

"Did they spot you?"

"*Nein*, I'm invisible."

"Get in position." Click.

As soon as Fox hung up the phone rang again. "Fox."

"It's Nikoli." He sounded irritated. "Your phone was busy."

"Where's the meeting?"

"At the Dom at ten—twenty-seven minutes from now."

"Just as I thought. I have the church surrounded. Only a miracle can save them."

"I have Meyer ready."

"No," said Fox. "Don't bring him. They're playing a game but they're amateurs. There are two of them. With Meyer, that's three against one. Even hurt, he can be trouble when you least expect it."

"What are you saying?" Rubski hated last minute changes. "I want that document tonight, Fox. We can get Meyer back later if we have to, or I'll just shoot him. But I have to get that paper. Khrushchev is not a patient man."

"I know them too well," he said. "They have a scheme."

"What then?"

"Surprise them, as they're trying to surprise us."

"But I only want the document—everything depends that. After I get it you can arrest them."

"We need to adjust. Think about it, Nikoli, they've already read the plan and they'll leak it if they get away. Meyer is the cork in the bottle—as long as we have him, no leaks."

"I don't like it," he said, "but you may be right. We don't have time to argue."

"Nikoli, by midnight you'll have the document in your pocket, Khrushchev will think you're a hero, the spies will disappear, and I'll have Meyer. By midnight we'll be drinking champagne."

Rubski was quiet for a moment. "Mischa, when I showed Meyer his sister's grave, do you know what he said?"

"What?"

"He said communism would collapse. He was crying over his sister's grave and he said that. Who is this crazy man?"

"He isn't crazy but he is tough," said Fox. "Let Kennedy and Khrushchev worry about history. You and I should only worry about tonight. We have only twenty minutes left."

"*Da.* Tell me your plan, but hurry."

Fox's driver parked the Mercedes so that it was inconspicuous yet had a clear view of the church. Fox was familiar with the layout and he imagined scenarios while he waited to see what would unfold. His teams were situated near every juncture and out of sight until he gave the radio signal to cordon the church. Rubski's car came into view and his driver parked at the front steps. The operation was in motion.

Rubski climbed out, looked around and spotted Fox's car. He ignored it and he whispered to his prisoner, whose hands were behind him and his face concealed by a ski mask and hood. Rubski followed him inside. "Werner!" he growled, and the echo doubled back at him.

"Over here," Vic called from his left, barely revealed by a flickering candle.

Ilse, concealed in the shadows on the opposite side, recognized Rubski from the Hilton but concentrated on his prisoner—his size, shape, clothes, and the way he stood.

"I have Meyer," shouted Rubski. "Where's the document? Let's finish this."

"I have it," Vic said. "Send Meyer to your right." Ilse waited in the shadows to rush Kurt to the escape hatch.

"I want to see the document first," said Rubski.

Vic shook the folds out of the papers, holding them high. "Here. See it? I'll leave it on this pew and back away. When Meyer is over there, you can come get it." He dropped the papers on a bench.

Ilse studied the prisoner. She wanted it to be Kurt, but her mind was playing tricks—something was wrong. The prisoner looked toward Vic so she didn't have a good view of him. She felt in her pocket for Hilda's ring. She wanted to give it to Kurt—if Rubski would only remove the mask she could be sure. She had to resolve all doubts before Rubski got the papers. The man's stance was wrong and he shifted from foot to foot, the clothing was not Kurt's. Why the mask? She needed to hear his voice—voices never failed her.

She stepped into the light and called in German. "Come Kurt! Hilda is waiting."

On the darkened streets outside, *Stasi* agents moved to block every street and alley around the church using their vehicles and uniformed *volkspolizei*. A cordon of armed men closed in on the church, tightening the noose.

The prisoner was confused; he didn't even understand German! The gong of a giant bell shook the belfry and was instantly muffled.

"Run Vic!" she yelled. "It's a trap!"

Vic bent for the papers. A shot cracked over his head. Gray smoke circled Rubski's pistol. Vic ran, heavy heels pounding behind. He swirled and fired his .45 wildly, then dived into the stairwell. The ricochet missed Rubski by a meter but slowed him for precious seconds. Two shots rang out across the sanctuary in Ilse's direction.

Vic glanced back, snagged his toe on a nail at the top of the stairs. He stumbled, grabbed for a railing, caught his balance. But he dropped the .45. It clattered on the stones below. He groped in the dark on hands and knees, but couldn't find it. He looked up as a figure appeared in the shadows. He pointed the P-38 at center of mass and squeezed the trigger. Misfire.

"Shit!" He ejected the round and chambered another.

"Don't shoot!" cried Ilse. "It's me."

Heavy heels were running again, then a crash. Falling bottles burst over stones in the dark cellar. The smell of wine saturated the air along with Rubski's curses.

They ducked into the furnace room and closed the door. Vic slammed the dead bolt, buying at least three more seconds. A monk stood beside the glowing furnace—Dante at the gates of hell! The grate was open and flames leapt from a heaping pile of coal.

Ilse nearly fainted at the vision she saw in the fire. *Her mother's face was in the oven, a scream on her lips. Her sad eyes fixed on her. She spoke: "Do what you have to do to survive. Do it for me, Ilse."*

She slumped to the floor; Vic slapped her and pulled her to her feet. A narrow iron door stood open behind the furnace, a rusty padlock hung from the hasp. The giant monk wore heavy leather work-gloves to protect his hands. They had to get past the open furnace to go behind it. Vic shoved her.

She squeezed behind the red-hot boiler and climbed through the rusty doorway. Vic held her hand and lowered her three meters to the track bed. Then he jumped. He hit the gravel, slipped, and stumbled straight for the center rail. She grabbed blindly and caught his coat in her fingers, pulled back hard and they fell in a heap against the wall.

The iron hatch above creaked and slammed shut. A rusty padlock grated as it locked. They heard pounding on the outer door but they were alone under East Berlin while hundreds of *Stasi* officers and soldiers searched for them above.

"This way," said Vic. "Let's get out of here."

He hurried through the dark, following the route he had memorized, relying on his trained sense of direction and distance. He counted his steps and felt his way while she clung to his coattail. They had moved a half dozen underground city blocks when the earth shook. The noise was amplified in the tunnel, a deafening roar that rolled over itself, swelling until the vibrations shook their bones. The headlight of the train, dim at first, brightened fast.

"Lie down!" Vic shouted into her ear. "Get into the corner, flat." He shoved her down and against the wall of the tunnel. "Don't lift your head," he shouted into her ear. She didn't hear but she was already doing it. They pushed fingers into their ears and waited. The train was upon them, only five cars—seemed like fifty. Sparks and stones ricocheted about the tunnel walls, falling back with dust and debris.

As soon as it passed, Vic said, "Let's go."

"No. Wait." She held his sleeve. "I need to rest a minute."

They leaned on the wall and let their nerves settle. After a moment, he asked, "What happened at the church?"

"It was a trap," she said. "You heard the bell. They wanted to arrest us and keep the document."

"What did you say back there, something about Hilda?"

"That wasn't Kurt—I wanted to be sure. Rubski had no intention of releasing him."

"That son-of-a-bitch!"

"His father warned me never to trust a Russian."

"Ilse," he said, "you do realize Kurt may be dead, don't you? That may be why he wasn't there."

"No!" She screamed and covered her ears. "Don't ever say that to me again, Vic. Never...."

"We have to get out of here fast. Everyone in this city is looking for us." He pulled her up.

"We'll have to find another way to get him," she said. "Do you still have it, the document?"

"Yeah, but I don't know why. It's useless now."

"No. It isn't! Rubski's life depends on it even more than Kurt's. It's his only hope. Khrushchev will kill him if he doesn't get it back."

"Do you really think he would waste Rubski over this?"

"You're the Russian expert—what do you think?"

81

Meet *Frau* Oberlin

Rubski ran from the church waving his pistol. Fox had heard the shots and was already running toward him. "What happened?"

"They escaped with it—vanished!"

"Impossible!" said Fox. "I'll have my team tear the church apart stone by stone," he said. He shouted to his driver "Tell Ebert to get down here with a search crew." Then to Rubski, "The church is completely surrounded. When they come out we'll nail them."

"Damn it, Fox!" Rubski's scar was redder than ever. "I should have brought Meyer. The girl smelled the trap. This was all your idea. This would be over if I'd brought him here."

"It wouldn't be over," Fox said calmly. "They escaped, didn't they, right before your eyes? You might have the document, or maybe not, but they've all seen it and they still escaped. Worse case, Meyer would have escaped, too. I warned you they were scheming. We'll still get them."

Vic and Ilse walked until they saw lights from the train station glistening along the well-polished tracks. Fresh air whistled into the tunnel, replacing the noxious gasses that burned their lungs.

"We have to time this," Vic told her. "Wait here for another train."

"Not again—let's get out now."

"They'll be expecting us to board a train. They won't expect us to leave one. The next one will stop at this station. We'll run behind it and climb onto the platform. We'll blend with passengers crossing the street to the cemetery."

"I hear it coming," she said.

"Get ready."

In the lights on the platform they saw passengers gathering to board the next train. The engine passed, slowing for the station. They ran behind the last car and when it stopped, they climbed aboard and followed the passengers through the car as they left the station.

Upon exit, they breathed deeply of fresh air and Vic double-checked his sketched map under a streetlight before they crossed at the corner. The cemetery was a welcome sight—until a dark figure stepped from behind a grave stone to block them. Vic yanked his pistol but held his fire, remembering how he had almost shot Ilse. She was already flat on the ground this time.

"Go with God!" said the monk. "Come quickly, over here."

Vic put the gun away. "It went badly at the church," he said. "We must hurry."

"I'm afraid the news here is not so good, either," he said. "The grave has been closed."

"Oh, no," she said. "That's our way out."

"I'm sorry. Twenty-nine people escaped through that grave. Unfortunately, one woman brought her child and left the stroller behind. The police saw it and discovered the tunnel. Poor *Frau* Oberlin—we couldn't even bury her."

"Damn. That was our only chance," said Vic.

"What can we do?" she asked, wringing her hands.

"There's one way out of town," said the monk. "The hearse is over there. The driver will take you out of the city. That's all I can offer."

"God bless you," she said.

"Go with God, children."

The hearse driver swung open the rear doors. A single coffin filled the narrow rear compartment. The driver lifted the lid.

"Climb in," he said.

"In there?" She convulsed at the notion.

"It's the only way," said the driver. "I'll close the lid with a seal which can't be removed by the police."

"I don't like this," said Vic. "A tunnel in a grave was okay, but a coffin?"

"Come on," she said. "We'll be cozy." She put her hands inside the dark box. She screamed and jumped back into Vic. "My god! She's still in there!"

"They closed the grave," said the driver. "We couldn't bury in the grave her and the ground is frozen. We couldn't dig a new one."

"Oh my God!" she said. "I'm not getting in there with a dead body!" She sat on the ground and buried her face in her hands.

"We'll have to remove her," Vic said to the driver.

"I don't have a place for her," said the driver. "She's my responsibility."

"We'll have to leave her here," said Vic. "It's freezing, so no problem. You can come back for her later."

"I have no instructions about that," he said.

"The monk said you would take us out," said Vic. "So the church has approved."

"But I work for the funeral home," he said. "I'll have to ask my boss about leaving the body."

Vic pulled out a roll of bills and pulled off several of large denomination. "Now you work for me," he said. "Help me lift her."

The driver stuffed the bills in his pocket and shrugged. They lifted the body from the casket and concealed it in the hedge. When that was done, Vic went to Ilse.

"Let's go," he said.

She shook her head. "I'm not getting in there," she said. "I'm not getting in a casket where a dead woman was."

He pulled her up. "Get your ass in there right now!" It was tight, but lying on their sides facing each other, they fit.

"Where to?" asked the driver.

"The Spa at Lake Mugglesee," said Vic. "We have a car there."

"You'll have enough air for one hour," said the driver, closing the lid and snapping it shut.

"What if...."

"Shut up!" he said. "Save our air."

82

Busting Freedom Bridge

In just over an hour, the top of the casket snapped popped open. Vic and Ilse sat up, gasping. "Sorry, I got lost but we're near the spa," said the driver. "Is your ride there?"

"No," said Vic, "there's a farmhouse nearby. But I'm not getting back inside this damned thing. I'll sit up front and show you the way."

"Me, too," said Ilse, eyes wide. "That was horrible!"

"There's not enough room up here," said the driver. "One of you will have to stay in back. I'll leave the lid open."

"Then you get back there," said Vic. "I'll drive."

The driver shook his head and climbed behind the wheel. Vic climbed into in the passenger seat with Ilse right behind.

"I'll sit on his lap," she said. "Let's go."

The hearse stopped at the farmer's house and he came out on the porch with a lantern in his hand. He said to Vic, "I waited at the bus stop as you asked."

"We were delayed." The hearse left in a cloud of dust, the only evidence it had been there. "Do you have any paint?" Vic asked the farmer.

"A little," he said. "Paint is scarce, like everything."

"I'll buy it." Vic handed him a hundred Deutsch Mark bill. "I need a brush and some tools then we'll leave."

"Help yourself," said the farmer gesturing toward the barn. "My wife is awake. She'll warm something to eat."

They brushed straw off the car and Vic spattered it with white paint. He dented the fenders and hood with a hammer and used a screwdriver to scrape the finish. He couldn't change that it was still a 1957 Chevy in a country with cars made of tin but he pried off the Chevrolet emblems while he worked.

"It looks dreadful," said Ilse.

"I'm just trying to change it some."

"It was a new car," she said. We still can't get through the city in this."

"We're going around again."

"We need to make a call soon," said Ilse. "I must talk to Rubski before he does anything drastic."

Vic pounded the Chevy until it looked like a wreck but the overpowered engine still roared under the hood. He stood back and examined the dents. Powell would have the damage to the car investigated, as well as his lost .45, the stolen USMLM identification badges, his absence without authority, violating restrictions, consorting with spies, and everything else he could imagine. Reitz would hate him for heisting his badge and car. But those were only minor inconveniences until his court-martial for treason.

Vic noticed Ilse sitting on a bale of hay lost in her own thoughts. He had joined this foray knowing it could only be trouble. Above all, he came for her sake but was convinced he had already lost her. He opened the car door and beckoned her to get in. He scratched off on the gravel, beginning a race to freedom. When they reached the small village of Grünheide, they hadn't picked up a tail so he stopped for Ilse to place her call. Vic locked the car and followed her to the small phone booth. She was already dialing.

"General Rubski."

"This is Captain Werner, General."

"Ah, ha!" he said. "I know who you are *fraulein*. Let me speak to the real one." Vic had his ear near the phone and overheard.

"Liar!" She screamed, her disciplined voice cracking. "Why didn't you bring Kurt?" Her voice broke. "...This would be *over* if ... if you kept your promise."

"Well, well," Rubski said. "It seems the tough act is over." He slapped his hand on his desk. "I don't have any more time for a whore. Put Werner on the phone."

"Bastard!" She shouted again. "Unless I speak to him, I'll blab your precious secret to newspapers. You'll have nowhere to hide, you, you...."

"What do you want? I'm tired of this."

"I want to talk to Kurt, to know he's alive," she said.

"And then?"

"I'll still make the trade."

"All right," he said. "I'll let him speak. But then I want to talk to Werner. Agreed?"

"Yes." She waited.

"Ilse?" Kurt's voice was mushy. "Are you all right? He killed...." He sounded dazed, beaten.

"Kurt, are you hurt?"

"I'm...."

"Kurt?"

Rubski had the phone again. "You talked. Put Werner on."

She broke and sat on the ground crying. The phone dangled at the end of its cable. Vic snatched it and spoke in Russian.

"This is Werner, Rubski. I demand you release Meyer, now."

"You're in no position to make demands, Captain. A death penalty awaits you for spying."

"Death might look good to you when you have to explain this to Khrushchev."

"What are you getting at?"

"We'll still trade his life for yours."

"No, you've already read the plan."

"Doesn't matter," he said. "That shouldn't concern you. If you have it, your hands are clean. If it leaks, you still have denial. Besides, who would believe us? If you have it, it will be one person's word against another's. You'll be a live hero, not a dead fool."

His silence signaled he was considering, so Vic waited. Finally Rubski asked, "What is your new plan?"

"I'll call you in an hour; stay near this phone. And keep Meyer alive." Vic hung up quickly.

Ilse had recovered enough to ask, "Why'd you hang up?"

"He was tracing us—keeping us here until he could get a fix and send someone to get us. We must go right now. We'll call again later."

They ran for the car, which was surrounded by a crowd of admiring young men. He raced the powerful engine and roared out of town, leaving them clapping and hooting in the dust. Vic resumed a wide arc, circling south of Berlin.

"Where are you going?" she asked.

"Potsdam."

"No!" she argued. "Kurt's in East Berlin. We can't desert him. We must go back."

"Your plan didn't work, even with divine intervention. We need a military solution."

"What solution?"

"I'm working on it."

He broke speed records to Mittenwalde, where they stopped at a small bus stop with a phone. "Let me have the number," he said. "I need to keep this short and unemotional. If he figures out where we are, he'll have us."

She handed him the paper. "You mean … I didn't handle it well?"

"He wants to talk to an army officer—maintain a semblance of prestige." Vic stared at the phone number. It was in Powell's handwriting—reminded him that he would have to answer for this. His career was over, or worse. He looked at her again—the reason he kept going. He ran to the phone before he changed his mind.

"Rubski, this is Werner."

"I know who it is. What's your plan?"

He stalled. "Details later. We swap at midnight. Be ready on short notice. Keep Meyer alive." He barked orders in clipped military fashion. "No more double-crosses or the deal is off. Try explaining this from Siberia."

"Let's discuss this, Werner. I'm not going into West Berlin with Meyer. I need more details so I can prepare."

"Later." Vic cut him off and rushed back to the car. He wanted to get away without drawing another crowd.

Ilse looked at him, questioning. He only said, "We're out of here."

They reached the highway quickly. "If they're any good at tracking, they'll know we started at Lake Mugglesee where the *Stasi* lost us, then to Grünheide, now Mittenwalde," he said. "All they have to do is connect the dots to see that we're headed for Potsdam. They know that's my home base and the only legal crossing point. We need to get there fast and lay low until midnight." His short-term plan was clear, but it had two major holes—crossing the bridge at Potsdam, and everything after that.

"Vic, do you even have a plan?"

"It's coming together, in here." He tapped his head. "I'll explain when I get it worked out. Do you have any ideas where we can hole-up until midnight? My apartment is under surveillance."

"We can't go to mine," she said. "Fox will have it staked out by now if he hasn't torn it apart already. Let's leave this car and use the streetcar. There is someone who might help."

"Okay. But, first we must get back into West Berlin. Get the uniforms from the back seat."

"Why?"

"Maybe we can bluff our way across the bridge. Just slip the shirt over your other clothes and wear my hat. Have your identification card ready."

She complied.

"Now hold the wheel," he said, "while I pull my shirt on." He slowed so she could hold the car on the road until he took the wheel again.

The lofty arches of the long bridge connecting Potsdam with West Berlin towered directly ahead. Fortifications had been increased, the bridge militarized. "What will we do?" she asked, alarmed.

"Fake it as long as we can," he said. "Just act like we belong here. And, smile for the camera!"

The checkpoint was reinforced with a gun jeep and a squad of armed soldiers along with increased border police. A policeman pointed to the car as it came into sight. He stood with legs spread wide in the center of the road. A soldier leveled an assault rifle at them.

"Just keep smiling until I tell you," said Vic. "Then get flat on the floor!"

"Why?"

"Do as I say, damn it!"

Vic held his pass out the window as the car rolled toward the guard. The guard reached for it as the gun jeep pulled forward, blocking the road.

"Down!" he shouted, and stomped the accelerator to the floor while leaning on the horn. The sudden acceleration and the rising roar of the supercharged engine surprised the guards. The Chevy attacked and clipped a policeman. Vic aimed the front bumper at the jeep's rear axle. The gunner swung the machine gun around as the jeep driver sprang out. Most dove from the path of destruction.

Ilse curled on the floorboard beneath the dash and behind the engine block. Three machinegun rounds shattered the windshield where she had been sitting. More bullets ripped metal. Others cracked close by. The car hit the jeep squarely, spinning it around, slinging off the gunner. The passenger side of the car skimmed the bridge railing, spraying sparks and leaving paint trails. Vic accelerated from ten miles-per-hour to sixty over the 140-yard span to the West Berlin side. He drove straight through the long barrier pole, snapping it off. Cold air stung his face through the vaporized windshield. Blood from glass cuts stained his cheeks and dripped into his lap.

Ilse crawled onto the seat. Wind whipped her short hair. "You're hurt!" she yelled.

He didn't reply.

"God! You were *wunderbar*!" She dabbed the blood on his forehead to keep it out of his eyes.

"Take off the uniform," he said. "We're civilians again, but keep my ID." He screeched tires turning into a nearly vacant parking garage. "Let's go—they'll be after us." He tossed his army shirt in back with what was left of his career.

They ran to the subway station and hopped the first train to anywhere. It took them to the zoo. She found a phone while Vic wiped the blood from his face. She dialed a number from operator assistance.

After one ring, an answer: "Mayor Brandt's office."

"Trudy, this is Ilse."

"*Fraulein*, where are you?" asked Trudy. "He's been trying to sign you for a party. Did the Hilton tell you?"

"Actually, I haven't been to the Hilton for a while. They've probably fired me by now."

"Oh, I don't think so. They would never fire you."

"Trudy, I called because I need help."

"What is it?"

"I *must* speak with the mayor."

"He's out of town, in Bonn." She rustled papers. "He'll return tonight, about ten-thirty."

"Oh no!"

"Can I help?"

"I ... we need somewhere to wait for him."

"I thought you had an apartment?"

"Well ... actually ... it's being renovated and the electricity and water are off," she lied. "I've been away but I returned before the work was finished. I, we, need somewhere to stay for a few hours. Can you help?"

"Are you with *Herr* Meyer?"

"Actually, I'm with an American officer right now. We're meeting Kurt later."

"Would you like to go to my apartment?"

"Could we?" She had prayed for that. "That's so considerate of you."

"Write down this address."

She copied the address, already knowing the nearest subway stop. "How will we get inside?"

"There's a key under a stone in the flower pot near the door. You'll find it. I'll be home at six. I'll phone the mayor to update him at ten thirty tonight. You can talk to him then."

"Thank you so much, Trudy. I owe you." She replaced the phone, checked her watch then said to Vic, "not much time. I only hope it's not too late for Kurt."

"It'll be too late for us if we don't get out of sight," he said. "Let's go."

83

The *Burgermeister* Reacts

Trudy's key was hidden under the rock as she promised—first place anyone would look. The door closed behind them, creating a false sense of security in a situation growing more dangerous hourly. Ilse soaked in a tub of warm soapy water while Vic catnapped. After they had both cleaned up, Ilse made tea wearing Trudy's robe. She said, "I'm washing some of my things; can I wash your shirt or something?"

"No thanks. I'll just trash everything after this."

She ran water into the kitchen sink. "Tell me your plan."

"It's simple," he said. "We'll make the exchange at midnight on Freedom Bridge."

"Glienecke Bridge, we just crashed through it!"

"We've made prisoner exchanges with the Soviets there before. Francis Gary Powers for William Fischer, alias Rudolph Abel, was the biggest. Rubski knows how it works already. We'll keep one foot on our own side and he can do the same."

"He'll set a trap for us," she said. "We can't trust him. We'll be exposed."

"They've already increased security and that should work to our benefit. I'll call Powell at the last possible minute and he could roll out the Army Brigade to even the odds if he wants to."

"What if he arrests us instead? He won't give up that plan for a German spy."

"Yeah—that's a problem," Vic agreed. "We'll stay out of sight until it's too late for him to screw it up."

"But Vic," she said, "When this is over you know they'll arrest us anyway. If you want out now I'll understand. I can do this alone."

"We crossed the point of no return a long time ago. This is your last chance to get Kurt. But you know this might not work. Rubski might cut his losses."

"Cut his losses?" she said. "You mean kill him?"

"Yeah," he said. "…All of us."

"I don't like this plan very much."

"Got a better one?"

"I'm thinking," she said. "Maybe we can improve it."

"We'll have to explain why we did this soon," he said. "I hope somebody believes us, otherwise this is all wasted."

"It's not wasted! And who *would* believe it? It's unbelievable to me and I'm in the middle of it."

Trudy arrived late at seven, laden with shopping bags. She was breathing hard but her eyes sparkled. Ilse had seen the photograph Trudy asked her to sign for her phony neice, framed and conspicuously displayed on her mantle. "Ilse, I'm happy to see you," she began. "But you look tired, dear. Is anything wrong? And whatever happened to your lovely hair?"

"I'm fine, Trudy. Thank you for letting us wait here."

Vic, standing aside, cleared his throat. "Oh, I'm sorry," said Ilse. "This is Vic Werner. He's my friend, more than a friend. Vic, this is Trudy, the mayor's assistant."

"It's nice to meet you, Vic." She set her bags on the kitchen cabinet. "I'm only the mayor's secretary. I'll prepare dinner. Why don't you open the wine, Vic?" She checked the cuts on his face and hands and his soiled clothes, but said nothing.

"We're having only coffee tonight," said Ilse. "We have a late meeting. We need to be alert."

"This sounds interesting," said Trudy.

"I'll explain it all to the mayor later, Trudy, but please keep it quite."

"Oh, I will."

"The KGB kidnapped Kurt," she said. "We're trying to get him back."

"Like that Flowers man, the U-2 pilot who was shot down over Russia?"

"Yes, just like that."

"That's dangerous." She held her hand over her mouth. "I'll help if I can, but I'm not a fighter." She glanced back at Vic who looked like he had just been in battle.

"You've helped us already," he said. "But we'll need to use your telephone to make the final arrangements."

"Of course." She lifted the receiver to test for a dial tone. "I use it for official business. The mayor is always thinking of something that needs to be done in the middle of the night. He just calls me with the details before he forgets."

"Not now," Ilse said. "We'll do that after I speak with the mayor."

"I'll start dinner."

At ten thirty, Trudy dialed the Mayor's private number. When he was on the line, she covered a few minor scheduling matters, told him about someone crashing across the bridge, and then informed him someone wanted to speak to him.

"Mayor Brandt, this is Ilse Braun."

"Ilse, I've been trying to reach you," he said. "I booked you for an official party. You're the talk of the town, young lady, but where have you been? You must stop disappearing."

"I desperately need your help," she said. "The KGB kidnapped Kurt. I'm afraid they'll kill him."

"Kurt? Is he the man you brought to my office, your manager or something? I remember he was an advocate for German unity? There was something else about him...."

"Yes sir, he's the same one."

"What's he done?"

"He discovered information the Russians want to keep secret. We'll exchange a document for him tonight."

"This is a matter for the military, or the police, or more likely the intelligent services—not the mayor. And who do you mean by 'we?'"

"Please believe me, this is immensely important but I can't explain it over the phone. I can't even say what it is about until he's released or they'll kill him. They'll kill all of us."

"Who else is involved in this?"

"An American army officer is helping me."

"Then why doesn't the U.S. Army handle this, or the CIA? They're equipped and trained—not the mayor's office."

"If the Americans get involved, they'd just kill Kurt. They'll do anything to keep this from the CIA. For now it's a matter of greatest concern for Germany. You could deliver this important information to President Kennedy after Kurt is released. Please help us."

"How can I help you?"

"Armed police, out of sight, just to cover the exchange, keep the Russians from doing anything rash, from coming into West Berlin. Just back us up, and don't let the West German guards stop us at the checkpoint."

"Are you trying to start World War III?" the mayor asked. "All the allies will be in an uproar—not only the Russians. The French! Berlin is still an occupied city, remember?"

"We're trying to stop a war—besides where was the uproar when they built the wall?"

"That was different."

"The Americans will get over it when they find out what this is, I promise. And, if they don't—Berlin, Washington, and Moscow will be gone anyway."

"I'm sure you exaggerate. And you said you were returning it anyway."

"We know what it is already. Only you can help us, mayor. Don't fail us. Please?"

"I don't know.... You're putting me on the spot. Where is this to happen?"

"On Glienecke Bridge at midnight."

"I might have guessed."

"Will you help us?"

"I'll be there," he said. "I'll be held responsible anyway. I wouldn't miss my own funeral."

As soon as Ilse hung up, Vic dialed another number and spoke in Russian. "Rubski, its Werner. The exchange is at midnight at Glienecke Bridge. We'll walk from the west to the center; you come from the east. We'll swap in the middle. No tricks."

84

End of Delusion

Rubski slammed down the phone and turned to Mischa Fox, standing beside him, "You heard?"

"Yes. They're very predictable. I'll have men on both sides. If we can't arrest them, we'll kill them."

Rubski shouted to his aide. "Get the cars started. Have the guard bring the prisoner here."

Shortly, the guard shoved Kurt into the room ahead of him. His eyes and mouth were covered with duct tape, hands and feet shackled. Rubski peeled back a corner of the tape over his eyes and snatched it.

Kurt grunted as the tape pulled most of the hair from his eyebrows, exposing an old scar from another war. He blinked in the bright light.

Rubski snatched the tape from his mouth.

"Any final words before we meet your friends, Chameleon?"

He only glared back at them.

Fox chided. "I warned you about getting tangled in the wire, Meyer. What have you to say for yourself?"

"You're a traitor, Fox," he said, his voice was stronger. "These stupid games only delay the end of your delusion. The wall proves you can't govern."

"That's only your opinion, Meyer. You don't know all the facts."

"My opinion is you helped the devil turn Germany into hell on earth."

Rubski had heard enough. "Tape his mouth," he told the guard.

"Shutting me up won't change reality," said Kurt. "You're a murderer and you're starting a war."

Rubski lost his temper again and swung his fist, breaking another tooth and cutting his knuckle. The guard ripped a strip from a roll of duct tape.

"Shoot me now," said Kurt, spitting blood and tooth fragments at Rubski. "Werner will never give you what you want." Duct tape ended the argument.

"Leave his eyes uncovered and lengthen the shackles. He'll walk to his death."

Rubski's aide slapped tape over his mouth and lengthened the chain on his ankles.

"It's time to go," said Rubski to his aide, "Take him to the car. Put him in the front seat so I can keep an eye on him." Rubski left the room first and Fox followed a few seconds later.

Fox whispered to Kurt as he passed, "It could have been different if you'd only listened to me."

85

Gleinicke Bridge

Gleinicke Bridge connects Potsdam with West Berlin. It was known as Freedom Bridge in the west and Bridge of Unity in the east—it was neither. The bridge was first built in 1660, a wooden span over the Havel River's most narrow point between two river lakes, the *Jungfernsee* and the *Tiefensee*. It originally gave Grand Elector Friedrich Wilhelm access to Berlin from Imperial Prussian Potsdam.

In 1687 it was widened into an avenue, *Berlinallee*, and in 1777 it was converted to a drawbridge, a vital link in the 1,000 kilometers from Aachen to Königsberg. Steel girders replaced the brick and wood Roman arches in 1908—art sacrificed for modernization. Berlin began or ended at Gleinicke Bridge, depending on which direction one faced.

Captain Ralph Harker was prepared to begin a routine reconnaissance tour for USMLM in East Germany. En route to Potsdam from his quarters in Berlin, he reached Freedom Bridge at eleven thirty-five. He was a skilled observer and saw the heightened security on both sides. The abutment was damaged in the east and the pole gate broken on the west. He smiled at a battered soviet gun jeep overturned beside the road. Sometime after he last crossed, the bridge had become a battleground.

Official sedans faced off on each end, clearly indicating the trouble wasn't over. Harker directed Reitz to U-turn and rush to Powell's residence, where he charged up the steps and pounded on the door until Powell answered. He came out in stocking feet, his shirttail hanging out.

"What the hell is it, Harker?" Bourbon reeked on his breath.

"Something's going down at the bridge, sir."

"Tell me, son."

"It looks like the bridge is being closed, sir. I saw a big black sedan, I think it was the mayor's, parked on the west. He had police with him. I swear to God, *Stasi* agents were in the trees behind them. And a Mercedes with Russian plates was on the east side. Two trucks with Russian infantry were behind that sedan. The Russians had set up a machine gun. *Stasi* were on that side, too. Looks like a standoff."

"That's preposterous—the mayor in a standoff with the Russian army?"

"This could be a secret prisoner exchange like the CIA did—only the mayor is involved."

"Damn the CIA! I'm supposed to know about these things. I'll call them first, but we're going there. Keep the car warmed up." Powell stuffed his shirttail in as he shuffled to the phone.

In the car a few minutes later he told Harker, "CIA didn't know anything about it—wish I hadn't told them." He laced his shoes as Reitz sped away in a new car. Powell stuffed half a pack of fresh chewing gum in his mouth.

"What will we do, sir?"

"Observe and report, Harker," he said. "That's our job, isn't it? I don't know what's going on but we'll find out, won't we? Just stay out of sight—we weren't invited to this party. Hand me those field glasses."

Vic had dialed Powell's number twice in the final minutes before they left Trudy's apartment. Explaining this was distasteful but his career was finished anyway. The phone was busy the first time and no one answered the second call. His concern now was for the three endangered lives—Ilse's, Kurt's, and his. He led her into the dark night without completing his call for help. He flagged a taxi and gave an address near *Gleinike*. "I wish I'd called Powell sooner."

"I'm glad you didn't," she said.

"He could help," said Vic. "He obeys the laws. We've broken them all."

"I hope the mayor will help."

"He'd be crazy," said Vic. "But he *is* German."

"You are, too," she said, taking his hand. "Don't forget why you're doing this."

"Look Ilse, I'm doing this for one reason—you. All that bullshit about reunification—we won't live long enough to see that, if it ever comes. Prevent a war? We may not even see the sun rise tomorrow."

She moved closer. "I'm scared," she said. "I know this won't go according to the script. I don't know how to finesse it anymore."

"If it goes bad," he said. "I want you to get out of there fast. Don't wait for me to tell you to run. I'll use the Nazi pistol on Rubski—that's all we can do. Just run to the mayor and tell the Americans about the plan."

"This has to work. It has to."

Their taxi stopped a block from the bridge. Vic prepared to pay the driver, but he saw the developing situation and sped away. Vic checked his watch. "Let's walk to the end of the bridge and wait there."

The mayor was sitting near the bridge abutment in the back seat of his sedan. She saw him. He rolled his darkened window down and flicked his fingers in a salute. She waved anxiously but kept walking. Vic scanned the far side of the bridge as his night vision adjusted to the darkness.

"I see a car," he said. "It's an official Soviet sedan and it's creeping toward us. Has to be them ... there's another behind it, *Stasi*."

Rubski's car stopped at the edge of the bridge, where Vic had bounced the Chevy off the abutment. The car lights were on high beam and illuminated them. The lights went off but not the engine. Rubski stepped out, followed by Fox from the second car. Ebert fell in behind but hung further back.

Rubski pulled Kurt from the front seat and shoved him ahead. Kurt took choppy steps with his ankles shackled, his hands locked in cuffs and a chain in front. His head was uncovered so he could be recognized. The tape had been removed and blood was crusted around his nose and mouth.

"It's Kurt!" Ilse gasped. "He's alive...."

Powell followed the unfolding scene through field glasses. "That's Willy Brandt on this side. I recognized him when he rolled his window down. But, I can't understand why he'd be out here in the middle of the night. And that's Rubski on the far side coming this way, I'd know that ugly face anywhere, and he has a prisoner with him. I don't recognize that poor fellow—his face is mincemeat. And I can't make out who that is further back getting from the second car. Wish I had the telephoto lens to take a picture."

"Look!" said Captain Harker. "There's someone else on this side, two of them walking together."

Powell changed the perspective of his glasses and swept the near side of the bridge. "Damn it! That's Werner and that crazy girl from Mississippi. I'd know that ass anywhere. Screwed up her hair. What the hell are they doing? I ordered him to stay out of this."

A black BMW stopped beside Powell's car and the window lowered. Powell recognized the CIA's field station chief, codenamed El Supremo. They acknowledged one another with silent nods, and waited.

86

"Save the *fraulein*"

Ilse clung to Vic's left hand as they stepped onto the edge of the bridge. He touched the pistol in his belt with his right then verified the document in his pocket. They walked east toward the center of the bridge, seventy-five meters away. Rubski stopped one-third distance from the east and Vic stopped the same distance from the white paint marking the center of the bridge—division between the American and Soviet sectors. Everything was going according to plan.

Rubski made the first change. "Only one of you from there," he shouted in Russian.

"Me," Vic shouted back. He told Ilse, "He's using Russian. Stay here."

"Be careful," she said. "Don't trust him, Vic. Do you have the pistol?"

"Yes. I'll let Kurt get to you before I give him the document."

"I love you." She squeezed his hand and dropped it. Then with ice in her voice, she said, "Kill him if you can."

Vic walked forward alone, slowly closing the distance. Rubski shoved Kurt ahead of him in painful slow motion. Ten meters divided them when Rubski stopped. Vic waited for him to make the next move. "Show me the document," said Rubski.

Vic held it high. Rubski waved his left hand above his head and his driver switched his headlights to high beam. Rubski inched closer to verify it in the light. He waved again and the headlights went off, but not before wrecking Vic's night vision. He blinked several times.

"Send Meyer ahead," Vic said. "When he reaches her, you can have it.

"Come closer first. I don't trust you."

Vic took one short step, feeling with his toes, then another. Rubski eased closer until they could almost touch. Kurt stood beside Rubski. Only the white line and a few feet separated them.

"Close enough," said Vic. "I know you're armed."

"How clever!" said Rubski. "I found your pistol at the church."

Vic's vision was improving but he blinked again, still trying to clear the blind spots before him. He could make out Rubski and Kurt but not clearly enough for a shootout.

Rubski recognized his problem and smiled. He raised his hand again and his car's high beams came on. Rubski pounced, snatched the document, torn but intact.

Kurt saw Rubski step back in line, eye on the paper. He smashed his shackled wrists upwards into Rubski's face. Steel chains cracked cartilage and enamel. Rubski howled through broken teeth and a cut tongue. Blood drained from his nose and mouth, over his overcoat and boots.

Rubski leaned forward, holding his nose. Kurt struck again. Heavy chains clattered against the base of Rubski's skull. Rubski fell to his knees clawing for his pistol.

Bright car lights illuminated Kurt's lightning strike—but blinded Vic. He heard the struggle, drew the pistol and stepped into it.

Ilse saw Rubski reach his gun. "No!" she screamed. She ran past Vic into the melee.

Kurt struck Rubski's arm and he fumbled his pistol.

Kurt and Rubski both dove for it. They sprawled on the bridge locked in a struggle for control.

Ilse piled on Rubski. Her fists flailed, she clawed at his burn scar with vengeance. Rubski and Kurt both had hands on the pistol. Rubski released one to grasp Ilse's short hair—pull the harpy off.

Vic pointed his pistol at the scuffle—no clean shot—might hit Ilse or Kurt. He did detect silhouettes of East German soldiers running toward them. Better targets in the lights.

Vic pointed his pistol in their direction and warned, "Halt! I'll shoot." He fired one round over their heads.

Then Rubski's pistol fired—point-blank. Ilse screamed. Rubski struggled to his knees, chest covered in blood. Kurt lay flat on his back in a pool of blood. Rubski lunged for Vic, grabbed his coat, and fired. The round tore through his coat but missed.

Vic fired the P-38 at close range—the muzzle pressed against the Rubski's torso. Rubski spun, lost his grip, and fell across his pistol and the document.

Kurt's chest was wet and sticky. Ilse kneeled over him, pleading. He didn't respond—she started artificial respiration.

Vic tried to flip Rubski for the document but he was heavy and bloody. Troops were coming again—fast. Vic knelt between them and Ilse. He fired once and they dove for cover.

Rubski's Mercedes passed the prone troops with another close behind. They skidded to a stop thirty meters away. Two men exited.

Storm troopers ran toward the center of the bridge carrying assault rifles. The soldiers fired toward Vic but were met by heavy fire from the west.

Vic dropped flat beside Kurt and Ilse. They were caught in crossfire passing low overhead.

Fire from the west raked the cars and the two men in suits ducked for cover behind them. Rubski's driver threw his car in reverse, smashed into the other and stopped. Both drivers then reversed, finding protection with Russian and East German troops. An officer shouted, the lights went out and the firing slowed, and then fell silent.

The silence was only broken by Ilse crying Kurt's name, begging him to speak, to live. He didn't move. Blood was thick around him—she was saturated with blood from Kurt and Rubski.

Three soldiers snaked closer with automatic rifles cradled in their elbows.

Vic saw them coming, stood, and pulled Ilse's coat. "We've got to get out of here—fast!"

"No!" she sobbed. "I won't leave him."

"They'll kill us!" Vic shouted. "Kurt's dead! You can't help him now."

"No!"

Vic uncorked a fist hard against her head. Ilse dropped beside Kurt. He scooped her up in his arms and stood. His knees nearly buckled at what he faced.

He had never seen the man, but he knew immediately it was Fox. He stood only inches away, between them and the soldiers, impervious to disaster, his chrome H&K inches from Vic's forehead.

Rubski stirred at Fox's feet, his own pistol just out of reach. "Kill them, Fox," he groaned. "Finish it." Fox flicked his toe and the pistol skidded away. "Kill them." Rubski groaned and passed out.

Fox's face was carved stone. "It's your move, Werner. What will you do now?"

Vic turned his back on Fox and walked to the edge of the bridge. He tossed Ilse over the railing and waited for his execution. He heard her splash into the frigid waters and turned to face death.

Fox said quietly, so softly Vic thought he was dreaming, "Too many Germans have died for Russia." He lowered his pistol. "Save the *fraulein*."

Vic jumped from the bridge as Russian bullets sprayed the steel girders.

While Vic and Ilse were in the water Fox was busy on the bridge. Rubski was unconscious and had lost blood from Vic's gunshot. Fox ordered Rubski's driver to rush him to a hospital, his life might be saved. The Mercedes roared away.

Russian soldiers held the center of the bridge while West Berlin police held only the west end. Fox's driver stopped beside him. "Toss his body in the back seat," he instructed loud enough to be overheard. "We must get rid of the evidence."

He told Ebert to stay and oversee the cleanup. "I'll see you at headquarters later. Bring that document and General Rubski's pistol."

Fox's car turned and sped off the bridge. "The morgue?" asked his driver.

"No," Fox said, "my personal physician." He turned in his seat as they roared over the deserted streets. "Step on it," he ordered.

87

Berlin's her Home

The slap of cold river water jolted Ilse. She struggled against the wet coat dragging her under, gasping. "I can't swim." She gulped air before going back down.

Vic hit the water nearby and hooked one arm under her chin, holding her head above water. He kicked toward the west bank. The bridge above had become quiet, except for Fox's barked commands and cars and trucks speeding east.

When his feet found the muddy bottom he dragged Ilse until she got her feet down, her arms cinched tightly around his neck. Brandt and his driver waded to their waists and helped them ashore. Brandt pushed her into the rear seat and Vic followed. Brandt jumped in front, shouting to his driver, "Run the heater as high as it'll go." They all shivered.

Tires screeched to a stop beside them. "Mayor!" yelled Powell. "Those are Americans, one's an army officer. I'll take custody."

Another car slid to a stop on the other side. "CIA, Mayor. That man's a spy! I'll take over here." Both men were out of their cars.

Brandt commanded his driver, "City Hall! Forget the speed limit." His sedan left Powell and El Supremo running back to their cars. They stayed close in a convoy of three. His driver entered the garage at City Hall with Brandt shouting, "Lock the gate!" Powell and El Supremo could only watch as Brandt hustled the drenched fugitives inside.

Ilse lashed out at Vic in the mayor's office, "You left him, damn it! Do you think you're God?" Vic stared stoically ahead but there were no answers there.

Trudy brought in blankets and dry coveralls from the cleaning crew's storage closet as Ilse still ranted. "My, my!" she said. "Hot tea will be here momentarily."

Brandt followed her, shaking his head. "I'll be back here in a few minutes to deal with you two," he said, pointing accusing fingers at them. "First, I must appease the Americans before they impose martial law. I want some straight answers when I return, and they better be good." He stomped out, leaving them in Trudy's care.

Brandt returned from half an hour of exchanging profanity with the Americans. Vic and Ilse could overhear and it seemed more like eternity. They sat against opposing walls, covered in blankets and sipping hot tea. Brandt sent Trudy from the room and slammed the door. "The hounds are baying—they smell blood. Tell me everything now or I'll turn you over to them."

Ilse dried her eyes as Vic began. "The Russians put nuclear missiles in Cuba. They're planning to attack Washington then launch a ground attack on NATO."

She added, "They killed Kurt and his sister to keep it secret."

"I hope you don't expect me to believe this without proof," said Brandt. "I saw them take a document on the bridge."

"We know what it says," Vic said. "Colonel Powell won't believe this, or the CIA. They think I'm crazy and they're ready to lock me up. I broke every law in four countries, lost a car … and a pistol ... shit."

"I think they're right," said the mayor. "This is crazy." He lit a cigarette and found a flask of Scotch in his desk. He sipped from it and handed it to Ilse. "Try this," he said. "Anyway, you're right about one thing, this is for someone higher than us, higher than the army or the CIA." He checked his watch and reached for the black phone. "Place a call to Washington, Vice President Lyndon Johnson."

They sat around quietly until the mayor's phone rang back. "The White House operator is on line one, Mayor. They'll connect you with your party."

"Willy, this is Lyndon. Are you starting another damned war in Berlin?"

"Not exactly, but you may have one in Washington—you just don't know it yet."

"What the hell are you talking about, Willy?"

"I have two people here you need to listen to, fast. They need to see the president."

"Well who are they? Put them on."

"In person, Lyndon—we can't discuss this over a phone. It's too big."

"Well, I reckon we'll just have to get 'em over here quick."

"I need them out of Berlin right away. If I get them to Templehof, can you take it from there?"

"I believe the United States Air Force can handle that. I'll have a ride waiting. Exactly who are we talking about, Willy?"

"One's an American officer, part of your Soviet military team. And the other one ... well, do you remember Marlene Dietrich? She sang for you when you were here."

"Well, well, you're sending her home?"

"Berlin's her home, Lyndon, but I'll loan her to you for a while—she's having a bad hair day, though. Listen to them, Lyndon. Their story may be hard to believe but the Russians just tried to kill them so they couldn't tell it."

88

Farewell to an Old Friend

Rubski survived his beating, arm and chest wound, but the chaos on Freedom Bridge unnerved him. When he passed out he missed Fox's confrontation with Vic and Ilse. He was angered by their escape and couldn't understand how Fox could have allowed it. His soldiers reported the events and Fox didn't refute it. Rubski felt betrayed by his friend, but at least he had the bloody document locked in his attaché case. The blood stains on it and his wounds were evidence of his courage in recovering it. At least he had three bodies to his credit—Meyer, his sister, and his fiancé.

His shoulder was patched and his left arm slung securely over the hole in his chest. A metal splint taped over his broken nose held it straight. His teeth could be fixed later, or replaced. The scars from the chains might be permanent, but the deep fingernail scratches on his burn scar were especially painful. He held the document as a measure of security when he called Khrushchev in Moscow.

"Khrushchev."

"I have the document, sir."

"How about the spy, Nikoli?"

"Meyer is finished."

"Excellent," said Khrushchev. "Are there any loose ends?"

Rubski had thought about Werner's advice: "Blame leaks on others." He had already decided his answer to that question. "No, *komrade;* the case is closed."

"Come home, Nikoli, come home to Moscow. I'll personally decorate you with a medal for your extraordinary courage. We'll have a ceremony in Red Square. Of course, we can never reveal the true story—we must dream up one for the citation."

"Thank you, *komrade,*" he said with a sigh of relief. "I'll leave tomorrow."

"I'll be waiting with open arms, my friend."

After Khrushchev spoke with Rubski, he called Mischa Fox.

"Mischa, this is Nikita Khrushchev."

"It's an honor, Mr. Chairman."

"Are you aware of the ruckus over stolen documents by one of your agents?"

"Yes, I'm sorry. General Rubski showed great courage in recovering it last night."

"I understand the agent was killed—you saw it?"

"I saw General Rubski shoot him," he said.

"What is your assessment?" Khrushchev asked. "Will there be any fallout?"

Fox was unprepared for that—had not anticipated a phone call from Khrushchev to verify Rubski's story. He hesitated to answer.

"Mischa ... I want the truth," Khrushchev said. "You're a Russian—missiles are at their destination and more are on the way. I need to know if there will be repercussions from Kennedy before we strike."

"Two other people are aware of the plan, sir," said Fox, "a German woman and an American officer."

"That's unfortunate, Mischa."

"Do you have any instructions for me?"

"Mischa," said Khrushchev. "Nikoli is returning to Moscow tomorrow. Perhaps you should say farewell to your old friend."

89

Beyond Brandenburg Gate

Karl Meyer sat slump-shouldered on the edge of his cot at the monastery. He strapped his wooden leg onto his stump and pulled a stocking cap over his head. He tenderly removed the picture of his beloved Inga from the frame which had protected it for fifteen years. He studied the image of his wife from happier times and brushed his cheek with his sleeve. Then he peeled Ingrid's picture from her identity papers, carefully pinching off bits of paper from the edges. He held the two pictures side-by-side and studied them together then slipped both into his coat pocket.

A wine wagon, fully loaded and heavy on wooden wheels was bound for Berlin. A team of oxen stood prepared to pull it. Karl silently accepted the hand of a strong monk who pulled him aboard. The hard journey into Berlin would take all day.

When they arrived in the alley beside the Dom, Karl went directly to the wine cellar and selected a bottle of red which he carried into his old office. He closed the door and pulled the cork, raised the bottle and drank deeply then poured a glass and drank all of that. He filled the glass again and left it on his desk.

He ran his hands along the stones of the familiar old church, feeling with his fingertips, tapping his knuckles until he found the one. He poked his gnarled fingers into the crevice and pulled the heavy stone away. Behind it was the package he had hidden there. He removed the oilcloth from the policeman's Lugar and inspected the chamber for a round, examined the full magazine and reseated it.

Karl Meyer laid the pistol on the desk next to the half-empty wine bottle. He removed the two photographs from his pocket and aligned them side-by-side on his desk. His entire world was before him. He looked from the pistol to the wine then to the pictures of Inga and Ingrid. Then, he looked again at the wine, then the pistol. Finally, he picked up the wine, drank it all and opened another bottle, then another.

Three kilometers from the old church, a farewell was underway at the Soviet Embassy on *Unter den Linden*. "I came to say goodbye, old friend," said Fox. "How are your wounds healing?"

"Small problem for an old soldier," he said. "It takes more than a single bullet to stop me. How did you know I was leaving today?"

"It's my business to know things," said Fox.

"I was planning to phone you before I left," said Rubski. "But now that you're here let's drink to our long friendship." He unscrewed the top of the vodka with his one free hand and filled two glasses. He handed one to Fox and lifted the other. "To Mother Russia."

Fox drank all of it.

Rubski cleared his throat. "Thank you for your help, Mischa."

"I'm afraid I didn't do enough to help you," he said.

"Listen, Mischa; I'm retiring to my *dacha* at the Black Sea as soon as I see Khrushchev. My son Ivan will spend his annual military leave there with me and we're going hunting together. I hate Moscow's winters—I hate Moscow."

"Just like that?" asked Fox. "Just leave the army you love?"

"I don't have the stomach for it any more, Mischa. This cold war bothers me. I'm a soldier. I don't like fighting civilians, especially women."

"Surely, you killed many more in the war, Nikoli?"

"That was different. That was war. This is something else."

"This is war, too, my friend. It's a different kind, maybe more inhumane, but it is war nevertheless."

"Tell me, Mischa," said Rubski. "If this is war, why did you let the German woman escape ... and the American? I wish you hadn't done that."

"I suppose there comes a time in every life when we discover who we really are, as you're doing now. I realized I was first a German. That's all I can say."

"Khrushchev will be disappointed to learn that."

"I know," said Fox. "I'm sorry to disappoint him and you. I'll walk with you to your car, my friend."

Rubski picked up the locked attaché case containing only the torn and bloodstained pages of the Cuban missile plan and they walked side-by-side to the underground garage.

"When will I see you again, Mischa?"

Fox blinked and looked away.

"What's wrong?" asked Rubski. "Is there something you're not telling me?"

Berlin Connection

"I just remembered something you once told me, Nikoli." Fox lit a Marlboro and inhaled deeply, then blew it out in a cloud of white smoke. "It was when you first arrived here," he said, inhaling again. "When I told you I was afraid you had come for me, to kill me. And you said you'd tell me to put a pistol in my mouth." He let more smoke escape through his lips. "Be very careful in Moscow, Nikoli."

Color drained from Rubski's ruddy face, leaving him more ashen. His scabby scar brightened and a trickle of blood oozed from one of the nail scratches. He leaned against the car, swallowed hard then climbed in.

Fox drew deeper on his cigarette as the sedan rolled slowly from the garage onto the avenue under the linden trees.

Rubski's car stopped suddenly, tires squealing on the divided thoroughfare. An old man stood in the middle of the busy avenue waving a cane in the air, blocking all traffic. Rubski got out of his car, shouting, "Get out of the street old man. Get out of my way!"

The old man faced him. "Get out of my country, Russian."

He stepped closer. Then he pulled an old Lugar from his coat and pointed it at Rubski. "This is for Inga." He fired the first bullet into his stomach. Rubski staggered backwards, reaching under his sling, clawing for his gun.

"This is for Ingrid." The old man fired again into his chest. Rubski slammed back against the car. Pedestrians ran for cover; gates of the Embassy opened wide. The old man fired again into the bloodstained chest. "That was for Kurt, you bastard." Rubski's knees buckled and he slid down, leaving a trail of blood on the fender.

The old man dropped his cane and hobbled closer, stuck the muzzle between Rubski's wide eyes, and squeezed. The back of his head exploded, covering the side of the car with mush. "And that was for me, you stinking Russian bastard. Die!"

A rain of bullets from embassy police tore into Karl Meyer, some hitting the fallen Russian and his driver before the fuselage ended. At the end of the shooting, there was only smoke and silence. Fox stood by the garage entrance and watched. He lit another Marlboro.

Spectators had already gathered on the wide sidewalks around the old man, his wooden leg splintered and detached from the hail of bullets. Russian soldiers and *volkspolitzei* barricaded *Unter den Linden* from end to end. The old man lay beside the Russian General, their blood mingling on the beautiful tree-lined avenue. At the end of it, the sun was setting beyond Brandenburg Gate.

Berlin Connection

Part III

Close Connections

1962-1989

90

Washington, D.C.

A United States Air Force C-141 Starlifter flew nearly empty from Templehof to Frankfurt, West Germany. The same aircraft roared off the tarmac from Rhine-Main with a load of cargo, but two passengers in the back of a truck bound for depot overhaul were not listed on the manifest. Captain Victor Werner and *Fraulein* Ilse Braun landed at Andrews Air Force Base near Washington wearing wrinkled custodial uniforms, official stowaways without passports, orders, or tickets. They traveled under special restricted verbal orders. At Andrews they were rushed away by Secret Service agents before the plane continued on to final destination.

Vice President Lyndon Johnson worked alone in his office until a Marine escort showed them in. He had anticipated seeing Marlene Dietrich or someone who looked like her, and an army captain. Instead, the woman he had seen in Berlin was actually a German actress, her blue coveralls unflattering, her hair butchered, and she wore no makeup. She certainly wasn't Dietrich.

The man with her was a captain in the United States Army, according to his identification card. The Pentagon confirmed it, though he was similarly dressed, unshaven with glass cuts on his face, and shaggy. Nevertheless, Mayor Brandt had vouched for them and Johnson was keenly interested in their version of what had happened at the bridge. He had read reports of two incidents at the bridge within 24 hours—either could have led to a major international crisis. Colonel Powell had already briefed him on one version and the CIA gave quite a different version. He didn't know the truth, but he could see these two had been in the crossfire.

Johnson cut straight to the latest incident, which would likely make the evening news. Instead, Ilse began with a meandering tale of narrow escapes from *Stasi* and KGB agents that spanned central Europe. Her story included murder, mayhem, and espionage, and broke dozens of international laws. He found that interesting, but it was the shocking revelation about Soviet missiles in Cuba that propelled him to action. Werner confirmed everything. Johnson believed him even though the Pentagon and the CIA did not. "No one could dream up a story like that," he said.

Johnson phoned President Kennedy on the red phone behind him. "Mr. President, I suppose you've already been briefed on the recent incidents in Berlin?" Vic and Ilse heard only one side of the phone conversation. "Yes, sir.... They're right here in my office." He looked them over while he talked about them. "Yes, sir.... I do believe them." Then after a pause he added, "We'll be right there."

After disconnecting, he said, "My military aides found something in your size ma'am ... and a uniform for you, captain. Clean up some. You can use my private facility ma'am. Captain, my aide will show you where to change and get rid of that stubble. We're going to see the President."

When they reached the Oval Office, Evelyn Lincoln had already cleared the President's calendar for the day. Johnson led them straight in and told them to skip the preliminaries and get right to the Cuban missiles. Kennedy listened to that part of the story calmly but then asked Ilse to retell the entire affair from the beginning. He interrupted her with frequent questions and looked to Vic for verification.

"This is fascinating," he said at last. "I've tangled with Khrushchev and Castro, so I find your almost unbelievable story completely plausible. And your courage, both of you in getting past those murderers with this warning, is remarkable. The American people and West Germans too, would certainly join me in thanking you if they only could. But I doubt if this story can ever be made public, at least not for a long time. Maybe you can tell it to your grandchildren some day. No one else would believe it."

"What about those missiles, Mr. President?" asked Johnson. "What about the missiles?"

"Yes, Lyndon, we must deal with them immediately. Khrushchev is duplicitous but he won't get away with this. Let's get a U-2 up over Cuba right away; also have the Navy keep an eye on Russian shipping around Cuba. He pushed a button on his intercom. "Evelyn, set up a meeting with Bobby, Dean Rusk, and Bob McNamara now. Get the NSC and Pentagon here too. We have a crisis." He punched off. Then speaking to Johnson, he said, "I believe them, too, but I need technical evidence to corroborate this. I'll need to get some proof to Congress and the American people. That bastard won't get away with nuclear blackmail."

The President slammed his fist on the desktop. "Shit! The Pentagon needs to change our anti-missile defenses. They're oriented the wrong way." He punched the intercom again. "Call the Pentagon right now. I want to speak to the JCS Chairman."

"I'm afraid you're missing something else, sir," said Vic. All of them looked at him as if he had said something inappropriate. He continued, "Remember the first plan Ilse mentioned? It was a ground attack plan developed by Marshall Koniev to attack NATO. These must be connected. First, strike the United States with nuclear missiles, and in the confusion, straight to the coast with an armored corps."

During the silence that followed, there was a series of exchanged looks between Ilse and Vic, and between Kennedy and Johnson. "Why didn't anyone else see that?" said Kennedy at last. "I'll have to get NATO on alert as well as NORAD."

Within days, a U-2 spy plane snapped pictures of missiles being assembled in Cuba. The Navy and Air Force clamped a blockade around the island ninety miles off Florida's tip. NATO was on top alert. For thirteen days, Kennedy and Khrushchev stood toe to toe on the precipice of global war. Khrushchev finally blinked. Embarrassed and humiliated, he disassembled the missiles and removed them from Cuba; tanks in Eastern Europe remained steady in attack positions. Kennedy won that round, but it was not to be the last.

Moscow

Khrushchev, stung by his black eye from Cuba, was determined to do something about it. He ushered Fidel Castro into his spacious office in the Kremlin. "He finally showed some backbone," said Khrushchev. "Now he worries me more than ever. He's dangerous, how do they say it? ...a gunslinger?"

"...A loose cannon," said Castro. "He's popular with some people but he's made plenty of enemies, too." He blew smoke rings from his long cigar then jabbed it into sand in the bottom of an ash can. "There are those who want to see him out of the way and have made discrete inquiries about it. His election was a mistake and now he's cutting his own throat. His enemies are preparing for executive action."

"Rubski once thought we could do it. What do you think?"

"The machete cuts both ways. He tried to kill my brother and me. He's not impervious. I can easily reach him but I want protection."

"Do you have someone in mind to do this?"

"Of course," said Castro. "Some people have already put up the money and teams are prepared to move. We've selected two possible places. My choice is Miami; Dallas is the alternate."

"When?"

"Soon."

"How will it be done?"

"That's for professionals to decide. We don't want to know the details; we must only nod our approval. Doing it is easy but denying it is more difficult. We've developed a cover with inside help. We should wipe the slate clean at one time, repay all our debts and tie up all the loose ends."

"*Da.* I like that," said Khrushchev. "Let's clean up the mess Rubski made too. But cover your tracks well, comrade. They must not lead back here."

"We have a Judas Goat. He's in Havana now and will be in Moscow next week. Do you want to meet him?"

"*Nyet!* Does he know what he's involved in?"

"No, of course not. He's not so smart, but easily manipulated."

"And his name?"

"He works for the CIA. His name is Oswald."

91
Someday, Maybe....

The army selects officers for promotion by convening secret boards to review the records of those under consideration. Such a board met in Washington to consider eligible captains for promotion to major, but Captain Vic Werner's name was not among those selected. When his name was mysteriously added later to the top of the list, it was explained as a clerical error.

Actually, the chief of army personnel added his name at the behest of the President of the United States, Commander-in-Chief of the armed forces. That infuriated both the president of the promotion board and Colonel John Powell, who had recommended against it. This reversal had come hard for Powell, who had once viewed Vic as his own reflection, but it was fine with Jack Kennedy. He appointed Major Vic Werner as a military aide.

Presidential influence had preserved Vic's career so he stayed in the army he loved. Kennedy liked his panache and assigned him another difficult project. This one irritated the army's old soldiers even more, since it involved retooling the conventional army for unconventional warfare.

A new breed of soldiers, the Green Berets, impressed Kennedy as a way to handle the brushfire wars breaking out. Cold War struggles were not confined to Europe but had spread worldwide. Vic fully intended to become one of this new breed when he eventually escaped from Washington. He was too radical for the conventional army anyway.

Kennedy admired Vic's élan—good-looking All-American, smart, athletic, and not afraid to take risks—much like him.

But, he was also attracted to the enchanting Ilse Braun. "Why not Broadway?" he asked her. "You certainly have the voice, not to mention your acting ability, and you're entirely beautiful enough. One call to a supporter in New York is all it takes. He'll sign you for a musical."

"New York is too dreary," she argued, "too much like Berlin. I'm going to sunny California."

"But you'll be so far away from ...Vic."

Nevertheless, Kennedy pulled strings and her American citizenship papers miraculously appeared. Vic attended her swearing-in ceremony at the federal courthouse. Ilse proudly raised her right hand and swore the oath of allegiance to the United States of America.

"I dreamed of being an American like Dietrich," she told Vic afterwards, "but my happiness is still misplaced, lost somewhere over there, somewhere in Berlin. I can't seem to enjoy my new freedom."

Vic made reservations at The Four Seasons to celebrate her new status as an American citizen. Their good fortunes provided plenty to be thankful for, so he made reservations for dinner and an evening of dancing. He remembered the night at the Berlin Hilton after she sang for Johnson, and wanted to recapture it with candlelight, atmosphere, and *Dom Pérignon*.

He hadn't spent that much on wine in an entire year but he intended to enchant her. He tipped the *maître d'hôtel* a hundred dollars in advance to ensure the table, the mood, the service, every detail was unerringly perfect. This was the evening to roll the dice for the jackpot.

"Ilse," he began tentatively at dinner. He had rehearsed but words escaped him. She had already cast a shadow over their moment. "What you said earlier, about losing your happiness in Berlin, you meant Kurt didn't you?"

She didn't want to discuss it but she owed him the truth. "Yes," she said. "Kurt, of course, but not only him--Hilda, Ingrid, Karl, Ursula, they all suffered so much, and for what? I got everything I dreamed of so I should be the happiest person alive but I left so much of myself there...." She patted her hand over her heart. "It hurts, Vic. I have a hole here. I feel so responsible."

The waiter refilled their flutes with champagne then faded away as planned. Vic continued. "I want to fill that void, Ilse." He opened a small blue velvet box. The large diamond caught the reflection of the chandelier and sparkled.

"Oh Vic!" She covered her mouth and ran from the restaurant. When he caught up with her, she was sitting at the reflecting pool, dabbing her cheeks with a handkerchief. He sat beside her. "I'm sorry," she said. "It isn't your fault, Vic. I do love you—the only man I've ever loved. Please understand that much at least."

"Ilse," he said. "You must let go of the past. It's gone. We must start a new life."

She hooked a finger under a silver chain and pulled it from her bodice. Another diamond ring dangled there, even larger than Vic's.

"You ... you were engaged to Kurt?"

"No." she said. "Kurt bought it for Hilda. He asked me to keep it for him, for safekeeping. I took it with me to give to him in East Berlin. I was so naïve back then. There's no one now.... Everyone I love dies, Vic."

"Except me, Ilse—I'm still here, and I love you with all my heart. I want you to come with me to Houston and meet my family. They'll love you—they're Germans and good people. And I'm not going to die. I'll quit the army and stay with you in California. My career is shot to hell anyway. I'll get a real job doing something. We'll have children. You follow your dream and I'll follow you."

"Someday, Vic. Maybe...." Her words rang hollow. "Just don't give up on me, please."

92

Hollywood

Ilse rode the train alone to California. She wanted to see as much of her new country as possible, see it at eye level. She hated flying and hadn't learned to drive—that must be resolved when she reached Los Angeles. She wondered if it was true what everyone said about traffic there. The clacking rails and smell of the upholstery took her back—back in time and place to her other home in Berlin. The American landscape swept past unseeing eyes while her past and future gradually merged.

She was not a starry-eyed and starving entertainer looking for a big break in Hollywood. She already had her break—a big part in an upcoming movie—but it had come at a huge price. "How'll you live?" Vic asked her before she left. While he still wanted to dissuade her from going, he was genuinely concerned for her welfare. He knew he couldn't support her in Hollywood on his army pay. But money was the least of her concerns.

She had finally inquired at her bank about Kurt's Swiss accounts. At first she didn't believe what they told her. "There must be some mistake!" she exclaimed. "Did you copy these numbers correctly?" Kurt and Hilda's stash had grown to over two million dollars, heavily invested in technology and aerospace stocks. The banker suggested she hire a broker and she did. Her broker verified the figures again and recommended only a few changes in Kurt's portfolio, which now fell to her. She set up a cash annuity to support herself until she had income of her own. She fully expected to earn enough with her acting to support a decent lifestyle. The rest she left alone to grow untouched. She wondered if the money could somehow be used to fulfill Kurt's dream of a unified Germany.

The script for a movie lay open in her lap as the great American west passed before her eyes outside the train's window. She saw neither because her thoughts were elsewhere. The script was *An Afternoon in Paris*, and it was perfect for her. Kennedy had phoned Frank Sinatra and the script was delivered within days. There was no audition—a screen test was scheduled for as soon as she arrived.

Ilse settled into a small apartment in Pasadena. She loved the flowers there and remembered how Hilda had cherished them. When Hilda visited Kurt in Berlin, she always brought fresh ones to the apartment. "They remind me of when I was a little girl," Hilda had said. "They make me feel secure." Ilse hoped she had been buried near a garden when she died.

She reached out to the past in another way. She remembered the brave young woman who had sneaked across the barriers and showed Kurt how to cross, and she with him. Ursula had come to clean her apartment in Berlin several times to supplement her pay from the Hilton. They had mostly talked and worked together to clean—became close friends.

"Ursula loved freedom," she thought. "She risked everything for it. She would love the United States and I need her." One phone call to Willy Brandt in Berlin and another to arrange a ticket was all it took. Ursula did love California and easily cleaned the apartment in Pasadena, leaving plenty of time for them to talk and shop. Ilse needed few other friends.

But she learned to drive and bought an MG. When she was paid for her role in *An Afternoon in Paris* she traded up from the small apartment in Pasadena. "We're going to the sea," she told Ursula, and it was a seaside estate near Santa Barbara. She needed privacy now that she had been nominated for Best Supporting Actress and quickly landed another part as leading lady. She had already been to hell—this was surely heaven.

It was another beautiful day in Santa Barbara, but Ilse was not herself. Vic was coming for lunch on her terrace overlooking the magnificent Pacific Ocean and she was anxious, couldn't decide what to wear.

"Wear this one," suggested Ursula, her German accent still heavy. "*Die farbe*--It brings out the color in your hair."

"You know the color in my hair isn't natural, Ursula. I need to find something authentic, something real."

"*Herr* Werner is a real man. Why do you worry so much about seeing him again?"

"I'm not worried, damn it! I just want everything to be perfect. I need to ask Kurt about this new part and, and, everything."

"But, you know you can't do that. Why do you say such things? It frightens me." Ursula looked puzzled by her continuing references to a dead man. "And, this isn't a movie—it's only a lunch."

"I've decided." She held up the pale blue dress. She had worn one like it when she had breakfast with Vic the first time. She looked good in blue. "I'll wear this one. Will you touch it up, please, while I brush my hair?"

When Ursula left with the dress, she studied herself in the mirror. Her eyes drifted to the invitation, one corner slipped into the mirror frame: The Academy Awards, tomorrow evening. She couldn't go into Santa Barbara with Vic for lunch because her appearance would create a scene and she didn't want one of those. Thank goodness her evening dress for the awards had been already selected for her.

Ursula interrupted her digression. "Here's your dress, but you haven't done anything with your hair yet."

"I was distracted."

"Sit still. I'll brush it for you. But you must hurry; it's almost time for him."

A minute later, the doorbell chimed.

"Please stall him, Ursula." She took the brush. "Show him into the sitting room and offer him a drink. I'll be there presently."

The sitting room compelled one to stand. The magnificent high space was spanned from floor to lofty ceiling by a glass wall overlooking the Pacific. Waves struck the rocks with such force that white spray danced above the level of the window. Vic, standing mesmerized before the view, was prompted by some sensation to turn around. The force of a powerful sea was behind him, beauty and grace stood before him; he was captured and surrendered.

"Ilse."

"Vic. I can't believe you're really here." She had somehow crossed the room and held him in her arms. His lips were as warm as the sun though the air inside the mansion was cool.

"I can't believe it either. But I don't know which of you...."

"Vic," she interrupted. "Let's go outside. We'll have lunch on the veranda. The view is *wunderbar*."

"It is breathtaking."

"Sit here." She indicated a chair at a glass patio table facing the bluff. She sat across from him, with the sea at her back. "So I can look at you." Ursula had already set out placemats, silverware, and an iced bottle of champagne.

"So," Vic said. "Do you think you'll win?"

"An Oscar?" She smiled and shook her head. "I don't think so. I'm not well known and this film has no other nominations in any other categories so it isn't a favorite."

"But you were very good. I saw *An Afternoon in Paris* half a dozen times. Of course, the first time was at the White House with the President."

"I'm so sorry I missed seeing it with you, both of you."

"You were missed. President Kennedy frequently asks how you are. Who will you go with tomorrow night?"

"Thank you for missing me. I'm going with an actor. Our agents arranged it." She sensed Vic's disappointment not to be escorting her to her first nomination. "It's not a real date, Vic—just publicity. This is business."

"Well, whether you win or not, I think you're definitely the best actress."

"It's for supporting actress."

"I'm not talking about the Oscar."

"Oh." She looked at her empty glass, not remembering having tasted the champagne. "Would you pour, Vic?"

When he did, she only sipped. "Thank you. Now tell me what you're doing for our President."

"I'm just an errand boy, really. I was promoted to Major and the President dismissed all the charges against me, pardoned me—washed away my sins. But I can't go to Germany with him and I'll probably never be able to go to Russia, either."

"Who wants to?"

"That's my job, to travel with him. I carry the football—that's the briefcase with the release codes for nuclear war. I also monitor everything dealing with Germany, the U.S.S.R. or anywhere else in Eastern Europe."

"Where can you go?"

"I can only go to places in North America, South America, or Asia. Next up are Miami and Dallas."

"Oh."

"Ilse...."

"Yes?"

"I'm sorry. I just wanted to say your name. I can't help thinking about the woman I fell in love with. Sometimes your name just slips out ... like that."

"Vic, you know I loved you, too. I still do. Despite all that has happened to us. I'll always love you."

"I wondered if you still did," he said. "Things have changed so much. Sometimes I want us to go back to Berlin, where it all started."

"You can't go back. I certainly can't."

"I know. I want to go forward but I want to go with you. Ilse, I want you to marry me."

She had anticipated this—the cause of all her anxiety. She had hoped he wouldn't ask, today of all days. She took his hand and pulled him away from the table, toward the ledge. They stood before the enraged sea, an arm around the other's waist until she took him into her arms and held him tightly. She pressed her cheek against his. Her hand on his neck trembled and her tears wet both their faces.

"Is that a no?" he asked.

"Vic, there are just too many complications right now. I have too many ghosts, too many issues. I wouldn't make a good wife, especially an army wife, and my career is just taking off, thanks to the President's call to Mr. Sinatra." She stepped back. "How could I possibly get married now, Vic? I start a new shoot right after the Academy Awards."

"I always knew your success would get in our way. Don't misunderstand—I'm very happy for you. But now that you're a movie star and all...."

"It isn't that, Vic, not at all. I'm still just an insecure little girl. I know I'm pretending all of this—none of it is real ... is it?"

93

On Set at a Tragedy

"Okay, people. Let's take it from the top one more time. Take your places, everybody." Actors and camera operators shuffled to position for the twelfth take in a scene from *The Killers* starring Ronald Reagan as the villain. He wasn't in the scene, but Ilse Braun was. She had been thrilled to be cast with the great Reagan, perhaps overly agitated under the pressure of it. She had been congratulated too often for her Oscar win—sincere from some but resented among the seasoned actors. The director waved to her. "Ilse, come over here please. I want to have a word with you before we start again."

As soon as she reached him, she apologized. "I'm sorry I keep missing my cues today. My timing is off. These lines are confusing. I'll try to get it right this time."

He shoved his baseball cap back on his head. "Listen, honey. Do you know why the chicken crosses the road?"

"What?"

"Do you know why the chicken crosses the road?"

"I don't know! Why did you ask me that stupid question?"

"I just wanted to see if anyone was home." He grinned and her face turned red. "Do you have a favorite actress?"

"Yes."

"Yes? Well, who the hell is it?"

"Marlene Dietrich."

"Jeeze! Another Kraut—shoulda known. Well, let me tell you something. I saw the great Dietrich on set and you're not acting like her. Forget about your sorry-ass timing. Forget about the cues even. Hell, forget about me, the fucking director. Here, have some of this." He reached behind his back and pulled a silver flask from the back pocket of his jeans. He twisted the top off and took a drink, then passed it to her.

She glared back at him. Her eyes were red and her cheeks flushed but the line of her jaw crinkled. She snatched the flask from his hand, turned it up and drained it. Then she held it upside down to prove it was empty and handed it back to him.

He clapped his hands slowly. "That's my girl." He stuck the empty flask in his back jeans pocket. "Here's what I wanted to tell you. Take charge out there, honey. This is your picture. You're the lead actress. Forget about that supporting actress bull shit. I want you to take charge of this set. Take over the scene. The others will follow if you lead; they're a bunch of lemmings. You're either going to make this film a hit or a flop all by your lonesome. No one else here can do it, not me, not even Reagan. It's in your hands, baby. You go back out there and kick some ass. And remember, this is a *killer* movie. Be a bitch—be Marlene Dietrich."

"*Die Hauptrolle*—Why didn't you just say so?"

"Do you need a break before we start?"

"Hell no! Roll it."

The rest of the day went much better and she did lead like the talented star she was. Everything was perfect … until the phone call.

"Take ten, everybody," shouted the director. "Ilse, you have a call. Take it over there." He pointed off stage. "And please tell him…you know…."

She was as mad at the interruption as the director, especially when she was on track. "Hello?"

"Ilse, its Vic." It didn't sound like Vic and pandemonium in the background almost drowned out his voice.

"Vic, it's nice of you to call but I'm on a set, dear. I don't have time to talk now. I'm having trouble with my lines."

"Ilse, listen to me; I'm in Dallas." He seemed to choke, or was it a cough? "The President has been shot."

"What?"

"Jack Kennedy is dead!"

"No!" She said it so loud the director started in her direction.

"Regardless of what you may hear, he won't live. I was with him."

"No!" She screamed it this time.

"Ilse, listen carefully. Whatever you're doing now, leave it. Check into a hotel. Use another name. Don't stay there and don't go home. I'm positive Khrushchev was behind this. I'll send someone to you."

"No! Khrushchev? Vic…oh no! What have we done?"

The country shut down the day President Kennedy died. All over the streets of Los Angeles people gawked before television sets, businesses closed while people refused to leave wherever they were, just standing around in groups comforting one another, listening to the radio reports over and over. It was the same everywhere, and not only in the United States.

Disbelief blanketed Ilse, denial. She was in shock and could hardly remember what Vic had just told her. *Did he say he was there? He'd seen it? Did he say something about going to a hotel? Why? I have to get clothes first, then maybe. Ursula will be at home. I'll take her with me.*

She pushed the MG over the mountain roads so fast the whining engine cried out for her to slow down. She was still an inexperienced driver but she almost didn't care if she ran off the highway. The tires squealed in protest and the smell of burning rubber told her she had stopped too fast when she skidded into her driveway near Santa Barbara.

Ursula was hunched over on the front steps, crying—a box of Kleenex beside her and several wet ones crumpled on the steps. "The President is dead, Ilse. It was on television." Ursula followed her inside.

Ilse proceeded straight to the medicine cabinet and swallowed several Valium without water. Then she pulled a bottle of Chardonnay from the rack as she passed. She plopped on a chaise lounge on the terrace. Ursula followed. The sun was warm and she dropped her pink sweater and the silk scarf she wore in the convertible onto the grass.

Ursula settled on the lawn beside her, knees folded underneath. "*Schrecklich!*—It's horrible. What will we do, Ilse?"

"Open this." She handed the bottle to her housekeeper and only girlfriend. "And bring two glasses." Ursula had become her little sister, her new family. "No," she called. "Forget the glasses. Just open two bottles. We'll get stinking drunk tonight. That's what we'll do."

Ursula strained to lift Ilse to carry her to bed at one a.m. but she couldn't manage it. So she shook her hard but couldn't wake her either. The combined effects of the drugs and wine had done the job she intended. Ilse was out for the count, safe from old nightmares and protected against new ones knocking at her door. Ursula shivered in the coolness of the night breeze and staggered inside to find the navy blue blankets they often used outside. She kept them nearby to use on the terrace when Ilse couldn't sleep, which was all too often.

The phone had begun ringing after the first two bottles of wine and continued through the second two. Ilse insisted she ignore it. "I don't have anything to say to anyone, not tonight." But she fell asleep and the phone was still ringing.

Ursula covered her with both blankets and shook her head as she left her alone on the lounge chair. "*Lange schlafen, meine freund*—Sleep well, my friend." She stooped for Ilse's pink sweater as she passed it and slipped her arms inside against the ocean breeze. Flipping the terrace light off, she reentered the house to go to her own bed, but the insistent phone barked again. It startled her as she staggered past it.

She didn't want to listen to it ringing all night so she finally picked it up. "Hello?"

"Who is this?" It was a man's voice.

"It's Ursula. Who are you calling?"

"This is Mr. Sinatra. Is Ilse home?"

"Yes sir, but she's asleep."

"Good. Don't wake her. I just wanted her to know I'm sending someone to keep an eye on things tonight. So if you see someone outside don't be alarmed. Will you tell her in the morning?"

"Yes sir."

"Is the alarm system activated?"

"I don't remember. I'll check."

"Please do. Good night, Ursula."

As soon as the phone was seated, it rang again. She returned it to her ear, confused.

"Hello?"

"Ursula?"

"Yes sir."

"This is Vic. What hotel is Ilse in?"

"Hotel? She's asleep, *Herr* Werner. Here."

"What? There?"

"*Ja, Herr* Werner. She didn't go to a hotel."

"Damned Germans! I'm sorry, Ursula. I wasn't talking about you. I told her to go to a hotel tonight."

"She's already asleep, sir."

"Is she all right, Ursula?"

"Yes sir. She's ... she's fine."

"I'll arrange security for tomorrow morning. I can't get Secret Service for this but I know a retired Green Beret who lives near Los Angeles. He'll be there early."

"Mr. Sinatra is sending someone over. I think I see them outside."

"Sinatra sent someone? Okay. What do they look like?"

"I think there are two of them. One is sitting in the car in the driveway. The other is walking around outside."

"What are they wearing? What do they have with them?"

"Wait. One man just dropped down on the ground. The other one is getting out of the car. Wait. He dropped down too. Wait. I'm going to the window to see what they're doing. This is strange."

The phone clattered in his ear when she dropped it on the wooden table. Then he heard her leather sandals slapping the marble tiles as she walked away. Then he heard only tinkling glass, nothing else until the buzzing started.

94

Ilse Braun is Dead

The sun peeped over the mountains behind Ilse's estate and boldly proclaimed a new day, a day beyond all her yesterdays. Bright sunlight attacked her eyes and she squeezed her eyelids tightly against it. It started a drumbeat in her head that wouldn't stop. "*Mein Gott.* I slept outside again." She rubbed the back of her hand across her mouth. "California wine—this never happened in Germany." A cold shadow fell across her face, blocking the bright glare.

"Ursula? Is that you?" she asked. "I hope you made coffee." Her eyes were still shut and covered with her hands for good measure.

"Get up!" A gruff masculine voice startled her. "We're leaving right now." She shaded her eyes with her hands and tried to focus on it. The voice came from a face that appeared to be chiseled from rock. He was dressed all in black and wore a rolled stocking cap and leather gloves. He was over six feet tall and very muscular. Hair was buzzed close on the sides, but showing signs of gray that seemed out of place. She had seen heavy lifters at the gym and she knew he was one of those. He could have been a typecast assassin from the movie sets—his bearing commanded instant obedience.

"Who are you? Where's Ursula?" Her feet reached for the ground and she was aware of the crashing surf. She felt dizzy and her throat was as parched as the desert further east.

"We're leaving right now, ma'am. Major Werner sent me to get you."

"I'm not going anywhere." She stood up, but balanced against the patio table. "I want to see Ursula."

"No, ma'am—you don't want to see her."

"Yes, I do. She works for me and this is my home. I'm responsible for her ... I want some answers."

"Someone will explain it all later. My mission is to protect you and I intend to do it with or without your cooperation. Let's go."

"Go where?"

"To a safe place."

"I'm not going anywhere with you, not until I've seen Ursula."

"Then will you go peacefully?"

"Maybe ... yes."

"Come on then." He snatched her hand and pulled her toward the garage. Her toes hardly touched the ground as she ran to keep from being dragged behind his long strides.

"Slow down, damn it! My head is spinning."

He stopped as suddenly as he had started. They stood side-by-side before her garage door and he slipped her garage door opener from his pocket. He punched a button. The heavy door began a noisy upward roll.

She didn't remember parking her convertible in the garage, but there it was, facing out. She had never backed into a garage in her life and someone was slumped in the passenger side seat. She recognized the pink sweater—someone was wearing her pink designer sweater from Rodeo Drive. The door continued up and sunlight flooded the garage. She saw Ursula in her car. But, everything was wrong. Ursula's forehead was red—a hole dead center between her eyes, and blood had dried over her face. Her eyes were open in surprise and her mouth was still open, in mid-scream.

Ilse shrieked and fainted into the big man's arms.

She didn't know how long she was out but when she came to, she was bouncing unceremoniously in the trunk of a car. It was too dark to see anything, but the car advertised newness with that special smell, and the spare tire said she was not in the passenger seat. Expecting to find her hands tied, she thrust her fists upward. Her knuckles slammed against the trunk lid. When she discovered her hands were free, she screamed and pounded harder with both her fists.

The car braked suddenly, sliding on loose gravel. She braced herself against the tire and waited. The trunk lid popped open and the same expressionless face met her. She swung at it with a balled fist, but a massive hand swallowed hers. Then the other fist was captured the same way.

He stood before her completely without expression, holding one of her fists in each of his hands. "Miss Braun. I'm sorry to put you in the trunk but you were out of it. I was afraid you would wake up and attack me while I was driving."

"I want out of here right now."

"That'll be fine, as long as you don't swing at me or try to run away."

She looked around quickly finding she was in a mountainous forest with no idea where. She took a deep breath to calm her voice. "Was that Ursula in my car?"

"I'll explain while we drive. We must keep going."

"Where to?"

"Stop asking questions and get in the car now or back in the trunk."

"You killed Ursula."

"Just get in—pretty please, ma'am."

It was the worst ride of her life. All she learned on the drive was that a sniper had shot Ursula, the Green Beret Sergeant was called Stony, and he was taking her to his cabin in the Sierra Madres Mountains.

"I want to speak to Major Werner about this."

"Tomorrow."

Master Sergeant Stone was not very good company on a social scale. He spent his time checking security devices, chopping wood, cleaning firearms, sharpening his ax and Bowie knife, and generally making himself unavailable for comment. His log cabin was comfortable enough but it was so high in the mountains that Ilse never considered running away. He refused to answer any questions about what had happened the night before, saying only, "the major will explain when he arrives."

Magazines were the manly type—*Playboy, Field and Stream,* and *American Rifleman,* and all at least a month old. There was no television or radio, mail wasn't delivered up there, and she didn't bother to try to sleep. She couldn't anyway and she didn't want him to hear her crying in her sleep.

When Vic finally arrived in a large black sedan, another man came with him. They both wore dark business suits and she thought of the mafia.

"I wish you'd gone to a hotel like I asked," he began right off.

It did not begin well. She said, "Go to hell!"

It ended worse. "Let's take a walk," he said. "We need to talk." He walked outside, off the porch and into the woods. She lingered behind a moment with her arms crossed, just staring at his back. Then she reluctantly followed him at a distance.

When he stopped and turned she walked past him so her back was to him. "I want some answers, damn it," she said into the woods.

"The President was assassinated, goddamn it, and I'm convinced Khrushchev is behind it." The evident tension clasping his throat almost choked off his words. "The CIA, FBI, everybody is pointing fingers in other directions but I know the truth." He stepped around her and pointed into her face. "So do you!"

"I don't want to hear this, Vic." She turned half away and looked into the clouds. "I can't handle this."

"You must hear it." He moved to touch her but she sensed it and stepped away. "There were other things," he said. "Minor hits, as well as killing the President."

356

She swirled, prepared to strike. "Minor hits? Do you call Ursula a minor hit, you bastard?" She spun away, furious, and locked her arms around her shoulders to control their shaking.

"They were after you, Ilse." He waited for that to register. "They made a mistake. When she appeared at the window in your sweater, they just made a mistake. They didn't know you were sleeping on the terrace."

"Sleeping? Drunk!" she shouted into the sky. "This is my fault!" She slumped to her knees and Vic kneeled beside her. She cried into her hands and he handed her a handkerchief. "Ursula was killed," she sobbed, "because I was stinking drunk again."

A shout came from the house: "Is everything all right?" It was the other suit that had come with Vic.

Vic waved him away. She appeared to be trying to regain her composure so he waited. But he had to finish with this before he lost his nerve. "Sinatra sent two men to look after you that night. They were both killed, too. Each one shot with a single round to the head. Professionals did that."

"I didn't see any others, only poor Ursula."

"Stony and Sinatra's other guys took their bodies away before you woke up."

"Vic, that poor little girl escaped through that goddamned wall by herself," she choked. "And then she was killed in my home, my home—taking care of me, a stinking drunk!"

"It isn't your fault, Ilse," he said. He wanted to take her in his arms and tell her it would be all right, but he knew it wasn't true. "There was nothing you could do." He took a deep breath to continue.

She said, "I have to leave here, Vic. I need to arrange Ursula's funeral. I'm her only family. She left her dear mother in East Berlin to come with me. Poor Ursula! I lose everyone I love."

Vic hung his head. She wasn't looking at him so she didn't see on his face how much he was stung by her words, and how much he dreaded what he was about to say next. "We have to talk about that," he said. His voice was so low it was almost a whisper. "There won't be a funeral for Ursula."

She looked at him for the first time since he arrived. "What?"

"*Your* funeral is today," he said, forcing his eyes on hers. "*The Los Angeles Times* is reporting it; *Mirror* and local radio and television are carrying it. National news will pick it up tomorrow, but Kennedy will get most of the coverage. *Ilse Braun is dead.* Ursula will be buried in your place."

"What are you talking about?"

"There was a contract out on you," he said. "Khrushchev was behind it, and Castro set it up with international hit teams and inside help. It's payback for the missiles and the stuff at the bridge, you remember all that?"

"Wait a minute. What about the funeral?"

"Ilse, the media are reporting you were killed, not Ursula. The reports are that your housekeeper has gone back to Berlin. The contract has been completed so they won't be after you anymore."

"That's stupid!" Her voice shrilled. "I'm filming this week. I can't make movies if I'm pretending to be dead."

"You can't make any more movies, Ilse."

She burned on a short fuse at first—then exploded. "You did this!"

She slapped him, hard. Then she slapped him again. He stood his ground and took it, welcomed the sting on his face as far less than the pain in his heart. Tears streamed down his rugged face. She was too angry to cry any more, too completely sick.

"You took my career away? You bastard!" She was shaking in fury. "I don't even have a life without acting. I wish they *had* killed me!"

"Ilse...."

"Get out of here, damn it!" she shrieked. "Go away. I *never* want to see you again."

Vic turned and walked slowly away. He turned around when she collapsed in the woods but he didn't run back to her, not any more. Master Sergeant Stone and the United States Marshall from the witness protection program rushed to her side instead.

Ilse Braun was dead.

95

Vietnam

Sixty-millimeter mortars were as alien to the Montagnard tribesmen of Vietnam as the lands from whence they came. However, the lone foreigner crouched in their midst was accepted as one of them, a member of their tribe, a part of their land. He would help them, fight with them against the northerners who took away their young men, stole their crops, and forced their women to dig their bunkers. The Montagnards had accepted nothing about the war that had befallen them, nothing except the American officer who wore the Green Beret.

Major Vic Werner trained them to defend their villages, and from those willing to fight he recruited a mobile strike force feared by the Viet Cong. When they struck, they were vicious. Perhaps their intensity came from their mountain heritage, perhaps from the hard training and ingrained hatred of all Vietnamese northerners and southerners alike, or perhaps they sensed the unresolved bitterness of their leader.

He paid them well for doing what they would have done anyway. But he also armed them with rifles, ammunition, grenades, and now the 60-mm mortars with which to attack from afar. The concept was new to these tribesmen who preferred to look into the eyes of those they slaughtered. Those they captured alive they fed to their dogs, bit-by-bit, while they were still living—a finger, a toe, a penis, so the enemy could watch himself devoured by animals, one piece at a time. North Vietnamese were known to kill themselves rather than surrender to the bloodthirsty mountain men—Russian advisors too.

They listened intently while Vic spoke to them in their own dialect. He had learned it in Monterrey, California, at the language-training center and used it every day. Instead of trying to teach them to understand his language, he used theirs. These tribesmen sensed he was there to stay, not like the others who had come for a while only to return to their strange land so far away. He was there for the long haul. Vic Werner had nothing to return to.

When she kissed him on Ku'damm she had changed his life, and when she slapped him in the California mountains his life was changed again. He didn't accept how much he was altered at first, but eventually he realized he could never go back. Kennedy was dead, he was hated in the Pentagon, banned from Germany, could never get a visa for Russia. Ilse had dismissed him as so much garbage. "I never want to see you again," she had told him. It hurt still. While he was at Monterrey he stayed in contact with the United States Marshall who oversaw her transformation from Ilse Braun to Lili Brown.

Eventually, even the Marshall cut him off. "I can't report to you on any more of this Vic," he said. "This would ruin my career if they found out and they will find out. They always do. I'm moving her again and I don't want to see you around there." Vic knew that already so he finally stopped asking and tried to let her go. But he couldn't quite do that so he sent himself away instead, to Vietnam for the duration plus. No one cared much about him, as long as he stayed out of the way in a war no one wanted.

Further north in Hanoi, another officer orchestrated the re-supply of the northern fighters in the south. Russian ammunition arrived daily at the port of Haiphong, and Major Ivan Rubski inventoried it before turning it over for loading onto trucks. The trucks would carry the ammunition in convoys to Laos then south into Cambodia and eventually to be offloaded into supply dumps there. It would be portaged by bicycles and backpacks across the mountains to supply North Vietnamese Army soldiers and Viet Cong. Rubski was upset by reports that increasingly the shipments, after going that far, were intercepted by Montagnard tribesmen.

Rubski waged another war as well. He was responsible for receiving and arranging portage of drugs from various sources into South Vietnam to supply American troops. Rubski knew the war would not be won on the battlefields, but in the hash houses of Saigon and in street demonstrations in cities like San Francisco, USA. He used other connections to ensure the demonstrators had plenty in the United States, while he took personal cognizance of supplies to the American troops. While he was doing his duty in Asia, he made sure his share of profits made it into his personal account, preparing for the day when he would use it for his personal climb to power. After all, his father had left him nothing but the dacha on the Black Sea and all his old war medals.

96
San Francisco

The handwritten invitation from the Reagan's was completely unexpected. Lili Brown had never met Ron or Nancy, not really. She had begun filming the movie *Killers* with him, but in the first week Vic's call from Dallas had changed everything. *Rising Star Murdered*, the Los Angeles Times headlined. Her reported death meant a new leading lady for her part when she lost the one thing that had held her entire life together, acting. But that was another life. She had taken on other pursuits.

Ron and Nancy Reagan invite you for a weekend at Rancho del Cielo. Western attire. RSVP

She wondered why they would invite her to spend a weekend as their houseguest. Ilse Braun was out of the film industry and as far as anyone knew, she was dead. Lili Brown was an obscure philanthropist living in San Francisco and dedicating her life to supporting refugees from Eastern European countries and escapees from East Berlin. No one in California cared about them—they were communists.

The more she contemplated the astonishing invitation, the more she was intrigued by it. "At least it's something interesting," she said. She would absolutely go, but first she had shopping to do—boots, jeans, western shirts and a cowboy hat. "If they know about me, they know. If they don't know, I can still pull it off and have some fun. Just like old times."

The drive into Santa Barbara resurrected a flood of memories and regrets about what her life might have been. She pulled into a scenic overview along the Pacific Coast Highway and contemplated turning back. "Get over it," she told herself. "You accepted the invitation. You can do this. Face your fears." When she arrived at Rancho del Cielo, she was surprised to find them both waiting for her at the front door, smiling and waving. Sure enough, they were in cowboy garb. Reagan himself met her car in the driveway and carried her bags inside.

"We released the entire staff for the weekend," Nancy said. "Unless you want to cook, you'll have to tolerate mine."

"Come inside," he said. I split some logs this morning and I want to see how they burn. Have you been to Santa Barbara before, Lili?"

"Uh ... yes, I have."

When she was settled into her suite, she joined them in the den before a stone fireplace, where a fire blazed beneath a painting of El Alamein, Reagan's favorite horse. "Your home is lovely. Thank you for inviting me, but I'll confess I'm mystified why you did. You don't know me ... do you?"

"Lili, I know Hollywood as well as anyone," he said. "And, I know who you are. We both knew right away when we caught sight of you at the Palace of Fine Arts in San Francisco." Reagan smiled reassuringly. "I never bought that story about the shooting so I did some checking on my own. I buttoned-holed Sinatra in Palm Desert and he finally admitted it. I had to swear on my life to keep the secret, and if I know Sinatra I think he meant it." He laughed.

"Then you know why I can't make any television appearances. I love *Death Valley Days*, but I just can't do it, if that's what you want."

"No, no, that's not it at all. We really just wanted to get to know you. I never saw you on the set of *Killers;* the movie was a disappointment, as you know. Maybe you could have saved it for us, if.... It's a shame to have such a promising career end that way."

"I wish it were different, really I do, I loved acting so much, but sometimes we must accept change."

"Yes, we do," he said. "I'm considering a major change myself. That's another reason we invited you, to get your advice on my plans."

"I don't know," she said. "I'm not a very good one to give anyone advice."

"Well, I know you were close to Jack Kennedy," said Reagan. "And he was a good man with conservative ideals. I'm also a conservative and I'm upset over how California is being run, or run down I should say. What do you think?"

"Jack Kennedy helped me immensely, of course, but we really weren't very close. He was the President, and I was just ... well, me. But, if you're talking about politics, I don't want anything to do with that. I've had enough to last all my life. And I have my humanitarian work to consider. I must protect my identity, anyway, but, politics? No way! I'm sorry."

"Lili, I'm thinking about running for governor of California next year. Do you think I'd have a chance of winning?"

She contemplated the crackling fire. She didn't want to answer that but he had asked for her opinion and she owed him one. "Honestly ... no."

"Why not?" he asked, not at all put off by her answer.

"I hate to say it, but an actor as governor? It'll never happen. What are your qualifications? People don't even think of actors as real people."

"What would change that?"

She was on the spot, but she had to tell him something so she thought about it. "An old friend once told me that if you want something to happen, you must first envision it, believe in it with all your heart and then be willing to work every day of your life for your dream. It sounded so wise when he said it, but then he died young without ever realizing his dream. I can't even imagine how you could reach your goal. I'm sorry."

"Okay," he seemed to accept her answer. "That's fair enough. I respect your opinion and, frankly, others have tried to discourage me as well. But I can imagine it. I do see it happening and I'd like for you to see it, too, Lili. I believe if only a few very talented people with courage can visualize it, then we can bring it about. I want you to be one of those people."

"How is it possible? Can you be more specific? How can you possibly be elected governor of our largest state?"

"How strongly do you support President Johnson?"

"He helped me out of Germany and brought me to the United States. He introduced me to President Kennedy. In a way, he was one of those who saved my life. But close? ...I don't think so. I haven't spoken with him once since then."

"Well, I'm not asking you to go against him but I'm giving a speech to Republicans for Goldwater in a couple of weeks. Barry Goldwater doesn't have a chance to defeat Johnson anyway. But this speech gives me an opportunity to take center stage as a political figure for the first time. Someone will have to pick up where Barry leaves off after the election."

"What are you saying? You're already planning to run for President, aren't you?"

"No, no. Not now anyway. Let's just take one step at a time. I may find I hate politics as much as you say you do. But I'm willing to try at least."

"Okay," she said. "So you're giving a speech supporting Goldwater, but this is really to be your debut in the race for governor of California. But that isn't really it either, because you actually have your eye on the White House. What will you say in such an important speech?"

"Nancy thinks it should be about the environment, an important issue here in California." He spread his arms for emphasis, "Just look at this great country we live in." Then he said, "But I think our first priority should be reducing our heavy taxes—that's important here and will ring a bell all over the country. The government wastes too much of the taxpayer's money. Second, we must rebuild national defense to confront the Soviets. What do you think about those issues?"

"All of those are important," she agreed, all the while slowly shaking her head in disagreement. "But cutting taxes while spending more for the environment and defense seems not to make sense to me. You might still do both but you need a simple and unifying theme."

"Yes?" He waited.

"Big government is one—big brother." She got out of her seat and moved nearer the fire, warming to the subject. "The environment is certainly very important," she smiled at Nancy, "but you'll never get elected on that one. Unfortunately, Americans take their blessings for granted and you don't want to be taken for granted. Everyone wants clean air and water but very few will use their one vote, their only choice, on that."

She left the fireside for the window, looking out for carefully chosen words. "Defenses are absolutely necessary and taxes are unpopular with most people, but they're not topics that go straight to their hearts, feed their anger, or keep them awake at night. I wouldn't vote for you on those either. I just don't feel inspired."

"What would you vote for?"

"First, and this is important, first I want someone who takes charge, no matter what the issues are—someone to rise to the occasion and stand up for *me*. I want a strong and charismatic leader, someone who makes me believe he's as frustrated and angry as I am. I want someone who'll put it all on the line for what he believes, no matter the consequences. Everyone I know, all over the world, wants to strike back at evil empires, but we're small and powerless. But the President of the United States could do it for us. That's what my best friend tried to do—he stood up against overwhelming odds, and he risked everything for what he believed in. That's why I'll never forget him and why I keep working to advance his goals."

"How can a politician attack the government he represents and not look like a complete hypocrite?"

"That's the beauty of it," she said. "You're not a politician. That's precisely why you can do it. You can relate to people, show them you have common sense when it seems to be missing everywhere else, and say for them what they want to say themselves, only you can do it better—you can say it better than anyone I know. You could speak for me, for all Americans, people all over the world. You'll have to act like you're not an actor, just like I'm doing, but publicly. You can get that message across. Nobody delivers a line the way you do."

"That's certainly a new twist, all right."

"No," she said. "It's not a twist of something, rather a clear choice between opposites. Let the voters choose: Big government and great society on the one hand, or standing up against it and taking charge of our lives. If that's the choice, I know which one I'd take."

Reagan mulled it over. "A time to choose," he rolled the thought around, getting used to the idea, adopting it, making it his own.

"That sounds pretty good to me," he said.

He threw another log on the fire and poked it, making sparks rise in a miniature fireworks display. Nancy brought in desert and coffee. While she was serving, Reagan said, "Lili, I'll draft up some notes along the lines you mentioned tomorrow morning. Would you have time take a look at them before you leave?"

She had already raised her coffee cup, but she set it down again carefully before she answered.

"Tomorrow?" she asked. "I thought you were actually serious about this. If you are, let's start now."

Reagan and Lili worked late into the evening on draft after draft of the speech, tossing ideas out and scraping most of them on crumpled paper. The fire consumed the second best solutions, making room for better ones. By four a.m. they were too exhausted to continue and found themselves laughing at small jokes instead of working. He thanked her for her help. He held in his hand a fairly solid draft of the speech scrawled in pencil. "This looks pretty good," he said. "I hope we can work on another speech together soon."

"This isn't finished yet," she said. "Tomorrow we rehearse."

"I thought you were leaving tomorrow?"

"You asked for my help. When you don't want it anymore, please tell me because I don't want to waste my time. Otherwise we practice it, revise it, and practice it again. When it's perfect, then I'll leave."

97

"I need the Truth"

Reagan's speech drew raved reviews and launched his successful race for governor, which he won easily. Lili visited the ranch frequently during his campaign and gave generously of her time and money. She quietly helped plan and rehearse his speeches and develop political strategy in an unofficial capacity. She refused to attend large meetings or join his campaign staff, only working one-on-one with him behind the scenes and contributing a considerable sum to his campaign treasury. Sometimes she mailed or faxed ideas from San Francisco and sometimes she coached him on delivering speeches.

As time passed, she grew more confident that her changed identity was her new self. She gradually became more active with outside fundraising, tapping into her contacts in San Francisco's financial district through her charitable connections and considerable financial standing. Reagan won reelection for a second term as California's governor.

He phoned to thank her for her continued support. "Lili, it's time for you to take a more visible role. I need your help in Sacramento. Come up here with me and run my public affairs office. If you won't do that, just name any job. If we don't have one you like, I'll create one. I need you closer and we have to talk about the future."

"Ron, I helped you because I believed in you. I'm not at all interested in state politics for myself. Local issues would only distract me from my concerns overseas. I enjoyed helping you and I will continue, but that's enough."

"What's so important that you can't break away from it?"

"My major interest is still helping people escape the tyranny of big government—you do remember that promise don't you? Managing my trust fund keeps me busy, but it's a labor of love. I'm helping people get out of communist countries and East Berlin especially, and that's what I want to do more than all else. My work takes me to Hungary, Poland, and Czechoslovakia quite often. Someday, I may find other interests but this is quite enough for me now."

"I'm surprised you didn't mention Germany?"

"No. I haven't been back to Germany."

"Can I ask for your help again later?"

"I'd be disappointed if you didn't."

Lili opened mail at her San Francisco townhouse that doubled as her office. She used a part time secretary to help her with administrative duties, another East Berliner she helped escape from behind the iron curtain. "Erika, will you phone my broker, this statement of accounts isn't right."

When the broker was on the phone, she said, "I've been going over my account statements for the year James, and this just doesn't add up."

"I don't understand," he said. "You know stocks fluctuate with the markets."

"Of course, but I'm talking about the Helping Hands Fund. There are several deposits here I didn't make. Can you explain them?"

"Why, no," he stammered. "I thought you'd been making deposits and forgot to tell me. Are you sure you didn't?"

"I'm sure. Will you contact the Swiss Bank and inquire about it?"

"Certainly, I'll get back to you by tomorrow."

Lili had been using the money Kurt had left in the Swiss account, Kurt's and Hilda's New Life fund, to grease the skids for political prisoners in East Berlin caught trying to escape to the west. Unsuccessful escapees were kept in jail for at least three years, but Willy Brandt had put her in touch with a lawyer with a special contact in East Berlin. Together, they were able to pay off a certain unnamed high East German official to have some prisoners paroled and extradited into West Berlin.

All transactions were off the books, at least off official records, and the program received no government support on either side—all well below the radar, as Kurt had described his activities. Her only conditions were that all the people were those who attempted to escape—no criminals—and she talked to each one by phone when they were freed. That was how she found Erika, her valuable secretary.

"Lili, there's a call from West Berlin," said Erika.

"Thank you." She picked up the phone and spoke in German. *"Guten Tag!"* She said. "Welcome to freedom."

"Danke—thank you ma'am." Lili already knew he had been a laborer in one of the factories on Kantstrasse, across from Karl's old apartment. "Thank you for helping me."

"I'm honored to be able to," she said. "My friend would have wanted me to do this. Can I ask you a few questions?"

"Yes ma'am. Anything."

"I've been looking for my friend. His name is Kurt Meyer. Have you seen anyone by that name in jail, or anywhere else in East Germany."

He thought a few seconds before answering. "No, ma'am, I don't recall that name, but if I do I'll let New Life know about it."

"Thank you. What will you do now?"

"I'll get a job in West Germany. I'll leave Berlin and go to Stuttgart. I have family there."

"And did you leave any family in East Berlin?"

"Yes ma'am. My wife and daughter are still there."

"I'm so sorry. If we can help them, we will. Be sure to complete the forms with all the information before you go to Stuttgart so we can contact you later."

"Yes, ma'am. Thank you. I owe my freedom to you."

"You are welcome for my help, but you owe your freedom to your own courage and your efforts to escape."

When she disconnected Erika told her, "The banker is on the line again, Lili."

She switched lines and said, "That was fast James."

"Yes, Miss Brown. I thought this was important."

"Did you find out anything?"

"Yes, but it is confusing, I'm afraid. Do you have your statements for the past two years with you?"

"Yes."

"Look at the amounts of your withdrawals for New Life for the two years then look at the deposits."

"I see them, but what's your point."

"Well, we crunched the numbers in our computer and this is what we found. For instance, see the withdrawal for $50,000 in April of this year?"

"Yes."

"In June, see the deposit for $40,000?"

"Yes, that's one of those I'm talking about. I didn't make that deposit."

"Our computer crunched all of withdrawals and deposits, excluding capital gains and interest. For every withdrawal for New Life, there was a deposit for eighty per cent of the amount two months later. If you draw a line between them you'll see it."

"What does that mean?"

"Well, I don't know. I thought you might."

"I certainly do not. That's why I called you. Where did these deposits come from?"

"That's the most confusing part of it. They came from a bank in East Berlin. The money seems to be going in circles."

When Ronald Reagan launched his Presidential campaign in Sacramento, Lili stood behind him when he made the announcement. "I have to limit my time," she told him. "But I'll help you with speeches as much as I can."

"Can you work with me next week?"

"Only part of the week," she said. "I have something going on in Eastern Europe and I need to watch it closely. I may need to go there suddenly."

"I'm grateful for any help you can give. Someday, you'll give me as much time as you give those refugees."

"Well...."

From her townhouse office, Lili called her attorney in West Berlin, the one who helped broker bribes for parolees from East Berlin. "Sigmund, I've been interviewing these people coming out of East Berlin prisons for years and I'm making no headway in finding any useful information that I need."

"What can I do?"

"Can you pay your friend—that East Berlin lawyer, *Herr* Vogel—pay him some money to search files for me?"

"Still looking for Kurt Meyer?"

"Yes. He may be dead but I now have reason to hope he's still alive. If he is, he doesn't want to be found, and if he doesn't want me to find him, I won't just yet."

"Where does that leave us?

"Instead of looking for a live person, I want to confirm whether he's really dead. Have Vogel search through official death records, also go to all the cemeteries in East Berlin, and there is an old monastery somewhere near Halle, I'm not sure exactly, but have him find it and check it, too. His mother is buried near a vineyard at that monastery. Have him go there himself and talk to the monks. I need to know this—I can't rest until I know the truth. I'll meet his fee and any expenses."

369

"Are you sure you want to know the answer?"

"Look, I want Vogel to make a good search, but if he finds nothing, that will tell me something, too. I just need the truth about what is there."

98

Kansas City

The Republican Party's National Convention was as divisive as it had ever been. The incumbent, Gerald Ford, was the nation's first non-elected president and he committed the sin of pardoning Richard Nixon for his involvement in the Watergate scandal. Trust in government had reached an all-time low and the Republican Party was certain to pay for it at on Election Day.

Ronald Reagan's supporters clamored for a miracle in their rowdy Kansas City caucus. Reagan would address the convention, though the poll numbers showed the delegates would cast the vast majority of their votes for Ford—results were a foregone conclusion. Only a vicious attack, a low blow, or a bad slip by Ford would turn it around.

Reagan knew it was pointless. Hardcore party loyalists were unified against running an actor for President and his campaign treasure-chest was nearly empty. Even Lili had stopped throwing money at a lost cause.

His convention speech was considered one last opportunity to turn the momentum around and take the nomination away from Ford, but only a miracle would deliver that. The winner of the Republican primary would face Democrat Jimmy Carter in the run for the White House.

"Attack his intelligence," one supporter shouted to Reagan from the back of the caucus room. Another yelled, "Get tough if you want to win."

"No, hammer his character," someone else shouted.

"Blame him for pardoning Nixon. Hit him where it hurts most."

Reagan had heard enough and retired to his suite with only a few of his closest aides. "Please, would everyone just leave me alone to think about what I'll say?" His staff streamed out with heads down, already giving up.

"Lili, would you stay behind, please?" When the room had cleared, Reagan sat on a hotel-quality under-stuffed chair and she pulled another like it along side. "What should I do, Lili?"

She smiled at him. "You're not going to get the nomination, so you can just stop worrying about that," she said. "Don't do anything foolish. Think about the future, the long term. Since you're not going to be the party nominee for president, what will you do with the rest of your life?"

"I just wanted to make a difference," he said. "That's all. I've played people who made a difference in the movies but that was only acting. I wanted to make real changes in this country, in the world. I still want to be one of those people."

"Good," she said. You can do that."

"I can't do it by hanging around the ranch until I die of old age."

She held her breath a moment, deciding. "We have an hour before you speak. Do you want to work on your speech or can we just talk?"

"That's why I asked you to stay," he said. "For once, I'm at a loss for words."

"I want to tell you a story, so imagine a script about someone you don't know. You knew me before as Ilse Braun the actress and now as Lili Brown the activist. But, I'll tell you about someone you don't know, a little girl named Olga who lost her parents in a concentration camp then tried to fight the evil empire—she still does after all those years. She isn't motivated by ideology or politics, but by her friend and his family, just wanting to strike a blow for humanity. You'll have to promise not to repeat any of this but you may get some ideas about what to say, and what you want to do."

He listened.

When she had finished telling the story, he was deep in reflection. She left him there alone to consider what he would say and returned to San Francisco without waiting to hear his speech. She had important programs to manage that were making a real difference in the lives of some people.

Reagan spoke of the dangers of nuclear war and of a divided world. He rallied the delegates around the absolute need to protect freedom at all costs. The Kansas City Republican Convention was electrified by his speech—but still too late to steal the nomination. So he spent the next four years working at his ranch, writing columns and making speeches about those themes. In short, he spent his time preparing himself to be the next President of the United States.

99

Stunning News

Lili hadn't heard from Vic in years so when his letter arrived with the morning mail, she was stunned. The last time they spoke had been in the Sierra Madres Mountains. She had slapped him and truly meant it when she said, "I never want to see you again." She ripped the letter in half, unopened, and tossed it into the trashcan. Then she walked dazed out of her San Francisco townhouse.

The morning mist blew into her face and she walked fast along the piers near Fisherman's Wharf, compelling her mind to adjust to an abrupt reawakening, fleeing the unwanted intrusion. Her soul stirred with feelings long unattended. She walked with lengthy, quick strides all the way to Embarcadero before the sun broke through and she realized she had gone too far. She flagged a taxi to go home.

She avoided going into her study until after she had lunch, and with her salad she had two glasses of wine, double her new self-imposed allotment. Only then did she fish the torn letter from the trashcan. She opened it with trembling fingers, pressing the torn pieces together again.

Landstuhl

Dear Lili,

I really don't know where to begin. It probably doesn't matter, because I doubt if you'll ever read this letter anyway. I'm recovering in a hospital in Frankfurt before returning home, wherever that is. I've been out of the United States for so long I've lost track. But returning unexpectedly to Germany reminded me of you. I was compelled to write you again. I've never stopped missing you.

If you're still not interested in any of this, I won't be offended. I truly do understand how you feel. I'm writing this for my own therapy. I've been in Afghanistan with special operations forces fighting against the Russians. I was wounded, shot in the arm actually. I rode a camel to Kabul before making my way here. I managed to make it through six years in Vietnam, and other places I can't mention, before this indignity.

I volunteered for Vietnam right after that day, you know which one. I wasn't cut out for the infighting of Washington anyway. Real battlefields have actually kept me alive all these years. I frankly don't know what I'd have done without the wars. I've stayed overseas as much as possible, but I'm afraid the army will finally force me to retire since I don't have a snowball's chance in hell to make general. I have too many impolitic events in my background for that. I might be an embarrassment to someone. Anyway, I'm a soldier who's seen his last battle, and frankly, I don't know what I'll do with the rest of my life.

I'll admit I was heartbroken about the way we deserted the Vietnamese and turned our backs on our veterans. I probably complained publicly about that too much, too. I'm also sickened by the status quo here in Germany. After all we tried to do here the Wall still stands like a knife in our hearts.

I'm afraid of your reaction to what I'm about to say, but I must tell you, it's only fair. I've begun a manuscript about our experiences in Berlin, yours and mine, and Kurt's. I'm calling it fiction, since no one would ever believe it anyway. But, I'm staying as true to what happened as I possibly can. There are discrepancies in what I know about some of it. It needs your help to fill in some of the blanks. You may not even want to read it but it'll never be complete without you. I'll never be complete without you.

I'm sorry,

Vic

She brushed away a tear and locked his torn letter in her safe with other important papers.

"Congratulations, Mr. President." Lili spoke to Reagan on the phone at the White House from her home in San Francisco. "I saw your inauguration on television and it was inspiring. I'm so proud of you for staying true to your vision."

"It's our vision, Lili. You should have been here," said Reagan. "You deserved to share in this far more than others who were here."

"I'm sorry I missed it but I'm leaving for Poland tomorrow concerning Warsaw factory workers. I had to handle some pressing matters here before I go. You know how I feel about public appearances anyway."

"Poland is too dangerous for you," he said. "Why don't you come to Washington instead and handle my Eastern European desk at State, or work in the National Security Council? Better yet, run my communications office. I'll arrange it as soon as you say yes."

"You certainly are persistent," she said. "You don't owe me anything for my support, Mr. President."

"Ron," he said. "Just keep calling me Ron, Lili. Look, your commitment with your own time and money is a clear sign you want to help people, to change the world. I just want to give you an opportunity to do more."

"Someday perhaps, but until then I'll stay with the work I'm doing. I'm inspired by little people who stand up and refuse to be dominated."

"Will you come to Washington and brief me when you return from Poland? I'd like to have your analysis of Lech Walesa and the Solidarity movement—also that poet fellow, Havel, in Prague."

"Of course I will," she said. "And I have some views about the Soviet Union that might interest you, different from what you may have heard. Changes are underway there."

"Good," he said. "That's very good. I'm looking forward to talking with you again."

"Mr. President, there is someone who could help you. He's an army colonel, a very special person and he's leaving the army. I'll tell you about him when I get to the White House but you can never tell him I suggested him."

After Lili had spoken to President Reagan, Erika buzzed her. "Sigmund is on the phone from West Berlin."

She grabbed it. "Do you have any news, Sigmund?"

"Yes and no," he said. "I paid Vogel to run your investigation into Meyer's death. He went through all the public files for death certificates but they are very incomplete. There was a fire in 1965 that destroyed many of the earlier records."

"I see."

"And he visited every graveyard in East Berlin to review the records and headstones of those buried there, even the old Jewish cemetery. He was very thorough but I'm afraid he found nothing there of interest to you."

"Oh."

"But he finally found that old monastery. It's supposed to be closed—made illegal by the government years ago—but this one is an exception, tucked away in a remote hilly vineyard. Vogel said the monks have been making payments through the church to someone highly placed in East Berlin for years. The money is laundered through a mysterious *Stasi* official, unnamed of course. This is very unofficial, but Vogel says the monks are running an operation much like yours, only with money they make from selling the untaxed wine."

"Oh. That is very interesting."

"There's more. He found four Meyer graves in the vineyard. Ingrid, Inga, Karl and Kurt—those were the names on them."

She sighed and after a minute said, "I see. Is that all?"

"No, that isn't all. Vogel talked to one of the monks over several bottles of their wine. It was too late to get back to Berlin that night so he stayed in the monastery—can you imagine a lawless lawyer in a church drinking wine with monks? Well, anyway, after the second or third bottle, the old monk admitted he had been a close friend of Karl Meyer. He said the old man Meyer was a little crazy and lost his mind from time to time—killed in a shootout with Russians on *Unter den Linden*."

"That sounds right."

"Well, Vogel asked him when Kurt was buried there, since that was his main purpose. Know what he said?"

"That's the whole point. What was the year?"

"Never!"

"What do you mean, never?"

"He never was buried. The monk said some guys in dark suits came out there and paid them to dig a grave—they tossed a sack of potatoes in it and filled it back up. Then they paid them to put a cross up, just like the others, one that said Kurt Meyer on it. It's an empty hole, unless you count the potatoes."

"Why?"

100

Revolutionary

"This is nice," said President Reagan, sitting in the rose garden behind the white house, "but I miss my ranch already." He had removed his suit jacket and rolled his sleeves up two turns above his wrists. "I get too cooped up in there. I need fresh air." The President had annoyed his office staff by moving his private meeting with Lili Brown outside and beyond earshot. Most of his staff was suspicious of his unofficial kitchen-cabinet advisor. They sat in the shade of a tree well away from eavesdroppers and shared iced tea, jellybeans, sunshine, and roses.

"It is a lovely day," she said. "Washington is actually beautiful this time of year. I love the cherry blossoms."

"Yes it is," he said. "I can arrange for you to live here."

She smiled. "Not yet, Ron. I can't give up my quest right now."

"Fine but tell me, how am I doing, Lili?" he asked. "Am I still on message, hitting my cues, my timing still good? What so you think, coach?"

"You're saying all the right things, Mr. President," she said. "People are starting to believe what you say about leaving communism on an ash heap. Even East Europeans hear it and they're encouraged, too. But...."

"But what?"

"But where's the action? I don't see anything happening to support the rhetoric."

"State is exploring some ideas. What you told us about Poland and Solidarity was useful. I'd like you to talk to my NSC staff while you're here, they need to hear it." He squeezed a lemon into his tea and stirred the ice around a few times. "Changing the world isn't all that easy, you know? Even God needed seven days."

"All you need to do is create the opportunity—the world will change itself. I think people are ready for a revolution."

"Revolution? That's a strong notion. I suppose you know where such a revolution might start?"

"The seeds could be sown in Vienna at the arms control negotiations. All the possibilities come together there. Vienna is the only place where east and west converge with all the opportunities on the table. Anything can happen there."

"Those negotiations have never accomplished much. They're just never-ending dialogue, all hot air. Actually I think that is what everyone wants, just a place to yakkity-yak. I suppose talk is something but you said action was needed. What are you getting at Lili?"

"Resistance to socialism is increasing already. Budapest has always been defiant, but now the same ideas are gaining strength in Warsaw and Prague—even in East Germany people are talking openly about change. There's been a seismic shift that is almost unnoticed so far. Only two people can make these changes real."

"Two people? Who?"

"You and Gorbachev," she said. "Few really understand what he's saying and doing. I'm not sure even he knows the power he's unleashed. He's taking a very great risk by openly stating such radical ideas. Hardliners in Russia are determined to stop him because they feel threatened by changes. I believe if you shake the tree hard, fruit will fall. It might be Gorbachev who falls but it might even be communism. It's a big gamble but well worth it ... in my opinion of course."

"Do you really think just two people can change all that bad history, all that hostility?"

"No. You'll need lots of help. But you already have more than you realize and I'm not talking about government bureaucrats. My friend once said the people at the top can't see us, can't even admit we exist, but those who will make this happen are the little people, the unidentified. They'll remain invisible until the right moment but they'll step up when the time is right. Most are independent of one another and might not even know the others exist, they're just doing the right thing, what they are driven to do by some unseen force, a thirst for freedom. We just need someone to make it all conceivable, a unifying ideal. Mr. President, we're very busy down here below the radar. We need your help from here."

"You see yourself as one of these little people, don't you? Just what are you doing, Lili? Nothing illegal, I hope."

"You really don't want to know the details. But I'm just getting people out of East Berlin and other cities, people risking their lives for freedom. You know, giving up the acting career I wanted more than anything in the world was the best thing that ever happened to me. Being forced to change made me follow my heart instead of the ghosts in my head."

"I see, but how can I spark this revolutionary fire you spoke of?"

"Well, there is no one clear solution but I mentioned Vienna as one way to light a fire. Gorbachev called for all nuclear weapons to be removed from Europe. Perhaps it was a bluff or maybe not, but no one took him seriously except pacifists and college students. Call his hand. Publicly dare him to pull completely out of Europe. They need to do that anyway because they can't afford the arms race anymore. Do it on a grand stage so it gets the world's attention. He's opened the door—walk through."

"Well, I guess I have nothing to lose by making another speech. I do that pretty well."

"You have nothing to lose and everything to gain. But keep in mind, Gorbachev can't just pull out of Europe unilaterally. He needs political cover; he must ensure the security of the Soviet Union or it will backfire on him and everything will just stall again, as it always has. This must be a mutual arrangement so you'll have to put some chips on the table, too. And you'll have to force reluctant NATO nations to the table."

"You're talking about pulling some of our troops out of Europe? That's a very radical idea in the midst of the cold war."

"Yes, but who knows, we might be seeing an end to the cold war. And you'll take some heat for even suggesting it. But you know what? It has to happen sooner or later—most of old Europe doesn't even realize the Marshall Plan is over. You'll have to push them to get off their fat butts and put everything on the table in Vienna—everything—not just nuclear weapons but conventional forces—tanks, artillery, troops, everything. And there can be no backsliding when they realize it might actually succeed this time. Many will try to make it fail because it's unnatural to disarm, bad for business, power is threatened. If you want anything to happen in Vienna, you'll have to drop a bombshell there. Shake things up. Unless ... unless you want to be the President that just talked tough, like in the movies."

He cleared his throat. "Well, Lili, you certainly come right to the point, don't you?"

"That's why you need me. You can't fire me but you don't have to listen to me, either. You said once you wanted to make a difference. I might be willing to do my part but only if you're serious about that."

He laughed. "No, I can't fire you—you never accepted my offer of a job. Do I detect your resistance might be softening?"

"I'm not sure about that," she said. "But I do see a different Europe emerging. World War II has been over for forty years and we're still living within lines drawn by Stalin, Churchill, and Truman. The future is in front of us—we need someone to show it to us."

"My offer of any job is still open. Help me with this, Lili. State and Defense will drag their heels all the way. I need someone to ram this through. Let's get started, you and I."

"I would only be buried inside the government—defanged. But do you remember that army officer I mentioned before, the one who was forced to retire?"

"Yes," he said. "I called the Army Chief of Staff and he told me Colonel Werner is a recluse in a mountain cabin. He's writing a book or something. He doesn't even have a phone up there. He said Werner would be a serious problem for the army. Apparently he's some kind of troublemaker."

"Remember Kansas City, Mr. President? I told you about a man with me in Berlin, a man with incredible talents and courage. If you want to shake up Vienna," she said. "You'll need a serious troublemaker. Vic Werner is that man. I don't want to tell you how to do your business but if you're serious you'll need him or someone just like him. Just don't mention me, please."

101

New *Stasi* Headquarters

Mischa Fox had moved from his old headquarters to a new and improved one but he hadn't given up his bad habits. He lit another Marlboro from the glowing tip of a stub and crushed out the butt—third in an unbroken chain. He had summoned his second deputy, Heinz Claus, and waited for him to arrive for another fiery argument. Heinz was always difficult, but this time would be worse than usual, if that was possible. An old acquaintance of Heinz's had fallen from power and Fox could well gauge the reaction to his having pushed him over the precipice. "I regret it, too," Fox had told Emmi earlier that morning, "but this is a difficult business. There will always be casualties."

Fox heard the rubber wheels humming along the newly tiled halls aimed straight for his door. He sucked in more smoke, driving another nail in his own coffin.

The door slammed open and careened off the doorstop. The wheel chair surged through, powered by arms strong from years of using it. An elbow blocked the door ricocheting off the stopper. *"Du bist wohl verrückt!* You crazy son-of-a-bitch!" The graying-blond man, sixtyish years old, was strong above the waist, but his pants legs were almost empty. His lifeless feet were strapped to the stirrups to prevent them from falling off the chair during such wild rides—his face was red with anger.

"Calm down, Heinz." Fox stood defensively behind his desk. "These things happen." Fox crushed his half-finished cigarette and absently shook another from the pack.

"These things?" He stopped the chair inches from Fox's toes. "These things are people's live, you idiot!"

"Lower your voice," Fox said. "I won't have the staff hearing you raise your voice to me." He flipped his lighter and lit the cigarette—more smoke billowed into air already thick with it. Another one burned untouched in the ashtray. He smoothed his new English-tailored suit.

Heinz lowered his voice. "I should have stayed on the other side. You people are your own worst enemies. Dumb!"

"I didn't know the man we put in Willy Brandt's staff would be caught. I didn't think Brandt would resign as chancellor. How could I possibly have known that?"

"Brandt was working for Germany. *Ostpolitik* was a good idea. Sometimes you must trust people, Fox, even your enemies. It was stupid to put an agent there. You must assume they'll be caught. They usually are."

"Don't you of all people lecture me about trusting my enemy." He snuffed out the tobacco. "Can we change the subject now?"

"It's always the same old subjects with you—sex for secrets, money for secrets, power for secrets, kill for secrets. Do you even know any other subjects?"

"How about negotiate for secrets?"

"That's the worst one I've heard yet."

"You're a grumpy old man, Heinz. Hear me out."

He waited with his jaw clinched.

"Those arms control negotiations in Vienna have been going on for a long time, but going nowhere."

"Of course not," he said. "Our illustrious leaders don't want them to go anywhere. What's new?"

"I want you to brief the Warsaw Pact delegates who go there—not just the Germans, all of them. This has already been cleared with Moscow. We can exploit them by gathering more information about NATO while building a better database for ourselves. Eventually, we can use it to sway opinions our way."

"More propaganda? Sway whose opinion? Nobody believes any of that anymore."

"Soviet opinion, the Western press, NATO, everyone's opinion can be turned. Don't be so hardheaded. We can convince the world that we really want change and it's the West that isn't moving."

"Fox, you really don't want me to get involved in that kind of thing. Surely you know that."

"Why not?"

Heinz rubbed his finger along his eyebrow while he thought about it.

"Because I really do want change."

102
Tear Down This Wall!

Reagan had phoned Lili at her home in San Francisco in early June. "I'm going to Berlin, Lili. I want you to come along. I need some of your Irish charm.

"I'm not Irish, Mr. President, and I'm not very lucky," she said.

He laughed. "I know you're not Irish. But you are lucky," he said. "And it's time for you to see Berlin again."

"I go to Europe often," she said, "but I've never been back to Berlin in all these years. Maybe it is time to go, even Dietrich went home again."

"I want to discuss some things with you on the trip, official business. Your country needs you and I need you. This is your President asking, so you can't keep saying 'no' forever."

They talked about many things on Air Force One, but Reagan eventually got around to asking her to accept an appointment as his a special envoy for East European Affairs. She could have the title of Ambassador and could set up shop anywhere in Europe.

Lili still hesitated, "I appreciate your confidence in me but I'm not a diplomat, and I never, ever, wanted to be in politics."

"Don't decide just yet, Lili. I know this is a lot to ask. Just don't reject it. Think it over while we're there and make your decision afterwards."

She appeared outwardly composed on the trip over but she needed all her neglected acting skills to conceal her nervousness. But beneath her buried fears she was becoming excited about finally going home. When Air Force One's landing at Templehof was announced she realized just how much she was still connected with Berlin, the city of her past. As they passed low, she strained to find her old apartment building without success, but she realized in her heart she had never really left Berlin at all.

It was a very warm summer day in mid-June when Lili took her place in a folding chair facing the splendid *Brandenburger Tor*. Two rows of Doric columns were crowned by the *Quadriga*, the copper statue of winged victory in her four-horse chariot. Lili closed her eyes and her thoughts streamed through the grand entrance used by a triumphant Napoleon many years before. She began another journey through that gate, over the Wall and beyond...

383

...A journey to an ancient church with a rebellious priest and a private army of monks, an old one-legged man who drank the church wine, and a loving sister who died protecting her brother's secret. The old man himself had died just beyond that gate, just across the avenue from where she sat—she could almost see where he lay in a pool of blood. She re-lived heart-stopping pursuits in a '57 Chevy, racing through subway tunnels, crawling through sewers, leading the head of Stasi into a confessional booth, and a Russian general trying to kill her.

Lili remembered a man who gave up everything—his fortune, his fiancée, his future, and his life, trying to restore the unity of his country. Kurt steadfastly refused to accept the wall that still stood before her. She saw an old Nazi waving his gold handled cane at her and telling her to undress, and how she washed his blood from Kurt's hands. She remembered singing Dietrich's love songs before adoring fans, having coffee with the mayor of Berlin, and Hilda crying for Kurt to save her before she ran out of time.

She remembered a handsome young officer willing to give up his career, risk prison, break every law ever written, and disobey orders, all just because she asked him to help. She remembered wearing his uniform to cross the border, and what had happened in the front seat of the car. Her pulse quickened. She saw him again through misty eyes and realized she still loved him, she always had. The melody from Stand By Me throbbed in her temples. Melancholy for what might have been swept over her as the past paraded by...

Reagan patted her hand, interrupting her thoughts with his classic smile. "Wish me luck, Lili. This one's for you." He walked confidently to the lectern through delirious cheers of Berliners.

He smiled to Nancy and made eye contact with Lili. He drew himself erect and looked out over an expectant crowd, collectively holding their breath.

The famous gate, so familiar to her, framed him now. He was starring in his biggest role and on the grandest stage in the world. He began in a strong voice. "General Secretary Gorbachev, if you seek peace, if you seek prosperity for the Soviet Union and Eastern Europe, if you seek liberalization—Come here, to this gate!"

His words pounded in her ears, new words but a familiar theme. She had told him, "Find the largest stage in the world and challenge him." Reagan looked fiercely determined, sincerely himself yet reflecting exactly her very own thoughts in stronger words. Her life story was wrapped in everything he said.

He continued. "Mr. Gorbachev, open this gate!"

Cheers drowned him out before he finished. Reagan, the master of the moment, waited for that perfect instant between suspense and expectation to deliver his next line.

Then, when the crowd held its breath, he said, "Mr. Gorbachev, tear down this wall!"

They cheered, surged, and appeared ready to tear down the wall themselves. She smiled through tears of happiness streaming down her cheeks. She dabbed at them with her handkerchief and she knew. She knew exactly what she had to do.

When the speech was over, only those waiting for such defining moments in their lives were left on the streets, their thrill of anticipation replaced by bewilderment about what came next. She, on the other hand, understood her purpose and place exactly. Lili knew what came next.

"Lili," asked Reagan after all the formalities. "Would you ride with me in the limousine to the plane? I want your critique of my speech."

"I don't want to go the airport," she said. "I might change my mind about staying."

"So you'll accept my offer?"

"I've decided to stay, even if you withdraw your offer."

Lili remained in Berlin, determined to be an eyewitness as the results of their sacrifices so many years before, sacrifices lost in obscurity and secrecy, finally unfolded.

But she did not stay just to watch, she stayed to make sure it happened.

103

Pack Bags

Inside the new *Stasi* headquarters, Heinz Claus had been summoned again to Mischa Fox's office. He turned his wheel chair sideways to reach the door handle and rolled in. "What is it?"

"Don't you ever knock?" asked Fox brusquely.

General Heinrich Ebert sat stiffly at the conference table across from Fox. "Claus," Ebert said, acknowledging the presence of the man he disliked intensely. Then he averted his eyes from the wheel chair.

The feeling was obviously mutual. Claus ignored Ebert altogether and asked Fox, "Why'd you call me over here?"

"I'll get right to the point. You're going to Vienna this time—no more excuses."

"That's a big mistake," he said turning his chair back to the door. "I have nothing to contribute there."

"Wait for me to finish!" said Fox. "Reagan is tossing out radical ideas for the new round of negotiations and I think they're serious. They're even talking about reducing troops all across Europe. We need to find out what they're really after and keep the lid on it. We can't let this get out of control."

"We should take the lid off and let it go wherever it will. You know my feelings about all this already."

"I know, I know. That's why Ebert is going too. His job is to discipline delegates who have been getting too enthusiastic. He'll be working with a KGB representative, General Ivan Rubski. You remember his father. Rubski and Ebert will keep people in line, including you."

"Oh yes, I remember Nikoli Rubski. He put me in this chair. I'll kill his bastard son!"

"Heinz, Ivan had nothing to do with what happened to you, so forget about that. Besides, your father killed his father. Your job is to find out what NATO really wants out of all these troop and armament reductions—nothing more."

"Fox, I don't want to go to Vienna," he said. My home is here in Berlin. I don't travel well in this contraption. I absolutely will not fly."

"I had a van specially fitted for you. It has a lift on the side, special seat and a toilet. Electronics, communications, and photographic equipment are already installed. I had it modified at the plant in Halle, just for you."

"I'm thrilled," he said, sopping with sarcasm.

"Work with me on this, Heinz. This might prove very interesting for you."
"I'll go if it's an order, but I have things to do before I go." He wheeled
about and left, slamming the door behind him.

Fox and Ebert stared at the door after it slammed. "I wish you wouldn't
send him," said Ebert. "He's trouble and you know how I feel about him."
"You're a grown man now, Ebert," said Fox. "Get over it and do your job."
"There'll be trouble between Claus and Rubski. You know their history."
"Perhaps, but I need to get Heinz out of Berlin for other reasons. After
Reagan's speech there were some personnel changes and I can't take a chance on
having him here right now," said Fox. "Just trust me on this. And try to get along
professionally—you don't have to like each other. While you're there, Ebert, relax a
little, take in some opera and concerts. You're wound up too tight. Vienna is the city
of music and you need some refinement."

Heinz Claus closed the door to his office, picked up the phone and dialed
a local lawyer. "Vogel, meet me at the Café Gazebo. I need to talk to you."
When Claus arrived at the café, he wheeled to a back booth near the water
closet. He parked beside the seat where a portion had been cut out of the booth to
accommodate his chair. He had been a frequent visitor there over the years. While he
waited for the lawyer, he watched the cuckoo jump out of the clock and dance
around silently. The sound box had been broken for several years. He ordered a
pilsner and waited.
Vogel entered the front door and slid into the seat across from him. "What
is it?" he asked.
"I'm being sent to Vienna."
"That will complicate our work."
"I know, but I don't want it to stop. I want New Life to continue as long as
your contact in the west keeps sending money. Deposit it into my account and I can
make the transfers from Vienna. I've already signed prison release documents and
exit papers in advance, but I want you to call me before releasing anyone. You know
the conditions—only attempted escapees, no real criminals. I want to stay informed."
"Fine. I'll still need my usual twenty per cent to cover expenses."
"Of course. No problem—more if you need it."
"It's enough for a good cause."
"Here are the signed release documents and exit permits. Keep these
protected." He pushed a folder of official papers across the table.
"Naturally."
"Well, I need to go. I have other things to do before I leave."
Vogel cleared his throat. "Before you go, there's something you should
know."
Heinz drained his pilsner and waited. "Yes."
"Our contact in the west has been looking for a man named Kurt Meyer."

"Oh?"

"Yes. They paid me to search death files, cemetery records, and even investigate a monastery way out in the wine country."

"And?"

"I found the grave of Kurt Meyer there..."

"But?"

"But he isn't in it."

"I know. What did you report?"

"That his grave is empty."

"Just keep New Life alive. I don't want that program buried in Meyer's grave."

104

Brasstown Bald, Georgia

Vic Werner, a mountain recluse, watched through field glasses as an army sedan spun tires over a steep graveled incline. The sedan was navigating an abrupt mountain trail to his cabin near Brasstown Bald. He waited for the hard-road vehicle to stop in front of his new hideaway home before he clicked on the safety of his 30-30 deer rifle.

An officer left the military sedan steaming in the driveway beside Vic's four-wheel drive Jeep. The hardtop road car was overheated and the driver opened the hood—a cloud of steam rose over the engine block. The driver fanned it with a manila folder.

"Better add water when it cools off," Vic said. "There's some over there." He pointed to a stream cascading over the rim of a large rock. A bucket rested nearby.

White clouds drifted high over the scenic Blue Ridge Mountains in the distance spanning Alabama, Georgia, North Carolina, and Tennessee. Vic watched them with a feeling that his new life was somehow threatened by this army invasion of his privacy. He leaned the rifle against the log wall as a young army major climbed the steps wearing a dress green uniform. The officer eyed the rifle and started explaining his intrusion before he got to the porch.

Vic opened the screened door and went inside. The major followed him in. A log fire blazed beside a table holding an electric typewriter, powered by the same generator that supplied light. Reams of used and unused paper were stacked or crumpled nearby.

The major was saying something about going to the Pentagon. "I don't even have a suit," Vic told him. "I'm finished with the army, retired, and my uniforms are stored in a warehouse down in Atlanta somewhere." Faded blue jeans and wrinkled flannel shirts were the only civilian wardrobe he needed in his mountain retreat. "What's this all about?"

"I don't know, sir. The chief of personnel sent me out here to bring you to the Pentagon." "You didn't do anything to get a court martial did you sir?"

"I've done plenty to warrant a court martial, but all that has already been pardoned by President Kennedy."

"That was a long time ago, sir."

"Not as long as you think, young man."

It was too late to start back that day so Vic had the major and his driver stay overnight in sleeping bags until they left at four the next morning. Vic had never spent much time in the Pentagon but had been officially assigned there when he was a military aide to Kennedy.

He always felt out of place in the five-sided puzzle palace and only went for mandatory roll calls and inspections. He wasn't happy to be taking a ten-hour car ride to a place he never liked, but the major had carried official orders and as long as he was a military retiree he was still subject to orders. He did relish the idea of going into the land of suits wearing his mountain clothes—a statement of disdain for that side of the army. He was a field soldier after all, but he was intrigued to learn what would make the army want to see him again.

He thought about the time Fox held a gun on him just before he jumped from the bridge—he had been reliving much from those days as he worked on the book. The sedan finally stopped at the River entrance of the Pentagon and the young officer held the door open for him.

The major led him through security checkpoints and long corridors to the E-Ring where the service chiefs held court. "Retired Colonel Victor Werner reporting, sir." The Chief of Staff of the Army didn't return his salute or acknowledge his presence for several minutes. When he did, displeasure registered on his face, personal contempt as their mutual dislike was deep-seated.

"I thought you would at least dress appropriately to come to the United States Department of Defense, Werner." The four-star general had once been under Vic's command in Vietnam. The general had been a major then and worked for Vic as a subordinate when Vic was a lieutenant colonel. Now Vic's subaltern wore four stars and commanded the entire army while Vic had been stymied as a colonel and forced to retire. He hadn't liked the man back then and he didn't like him any better now, but that officer had been politically connected and was promoted while Vic was dispatched to the far reaches of the earth to fight wars no one else wanted. Their distrust was mutual and that was why having been ordered to report to him was so intriguing.

"I'm retired," Vic said. "All that other crap is behind me. I only have happy thoughts now. I'm a civilian in case you haven't noticed from my clothes and beard."

"Not anymore," the general said. "You've just been recalled out of retirement, back on active duty."

"I don't want to be un-retired. I like sleeping late."

"Personally, I don't care what you like Werner. You're back under orders as of today."

"Why? Who do I report to ... sir?"

"Officially, you'll report to the Deputy Chief of Staff for Intelligence. But you'll be on detached duty."

"I don't want to go back to Afghanistan. I was almost killed there and the army couldn't get me out—had to find my own camel. I don't want to go back there."

"Austria."

"Austria? That's a neutral country. We don't have a special operations program there."

"You're the military representative to the arms control negotiations in Vienna."

"I oppose gun control of any kind," he said. "With all due respect, I'm not a negotiator, sir. I kick down doors and break things, kill bad guys, create chaos and all that shit."

"That's precisely what he wants you to do."

"Who?"

"The Commander-in-Chief, the President of the United States."

"There's some mistake. You got the wrong name."

"It's a mistake all right and I've already told him that. But we both follow orders. That major is detailed to you while you're in Washington. Have him run you up to Fort Meyer and get yourself a military haircut and a shave, take a bath, and get some uniforms and civilian suits. You'll need both."

"Yes sir."

"You'll get hundreds of briefings this week from state, defense, CIA, NSA, and everyone else. You'll leave for Vienna next week. If you need something, tell that major. Don't bother me."

"Yes sir."

"And, Werner, when you come back to the Pentagon tomorrow," said the general, frowning. "Wear a uniform with brigadier general stars."

"What ... sir? Excuse me?"

"Don't expect me to pin stars on you in a fancy ceremony—just do it yourself. You'll never be a real general."

"What's my mission?"

"I don't have any idea, don't care either. The President said you'd know what to do when you got there."

Vienna

Bright sunlight streamed into General Vic Werner's window in Vienna, suggesting a better day. He sat ramrod straight while he painstakingly signed his name to a letter before he changed his mind and discarded it. The floor was littered with failed, crumpled earlier attempts. He aligned his pen next to a draft manuscript at the corner of his desk and read over the note one last time:

The Honorable Ms. Lili Brown
Leberstrasse 65
Berlin-Shöneberg
The Federal Republic of Germany

Dear Lili,

As I addressed this note, I realize how thrilled you must be to live in Dietrich's former home. I never dreamed you would return to Berlin under any circumstances, much less these.

Finally, the manuscript is completed, and I will send it to you next week. I wanted to warn you it was coming. I hope you will read it carefully and that revisiting our experiences will not be too painful for you.

Tonight I am attending the American musical "Cats" at the Vienna Renaissance Theater. The Burgermeister's box was available and I was lucky enough to get it. I only wish you could be there, too, either sitting with me or on stage singing "Memories."

Memories have overwhelmed me these past weeks, particularly with recent events in Berlin. I was proud of your courage in going back to the wall and surprised to learn of your recent appointment. As always, the unexpected is typical with you. Frankly, I was even more surprised to find myself in Vienna in a most unlikely assignment for me.

Now that we are practically neighbors, perhaps we could meet again in Berlin one day. You may recall a certain café off Kurfürstendamm that is familiar to both of us.
Sincerely,
Vic

Finally satisfied, he folded the note, sharpened the creases with his pen and slipped it into an envelope. He placed it at the edge of his desk with several official letters and glanced at his watch. He was expected at the American Embassy to greet guests to celebrate American Independence Day.

Lieutenant Jones opened his door on the first chime of a large grandfather clock standing sentry in the hall. "It's time, sir," he said, holding the general's tunic out to him. Seven colorful rows of combat ribbons cut straight across over the left pocket, and a single silver star sparkled on each epaulet.

"Will the mail go out on time, Lieutenant?" He glanced in the direction of his outbound correspondence.

"Yes, sir," The lieutenant snapped. "Austria's just like Germany. The mail and trains are always on time. Some things never change, sir."

The general slid into the back seat of the sedan, smoothing the wrinkles from his uniform.

"We should be there in fifteen minutes, sir."

The ride from his rented villa in the Vienna Woods to the embassy was usually uneventful. He watched the landscape slip by the window. "What was that last thing you said a moment ago, Lieutenant Jones?"

The aide-de-camp thought a moment. "I think I said, 'some things never change,' sir."

"Ah, yes," he sighed, "some things never change...." Vic closed his eyes and leaned against the headrest behind him and he was there again, back in Berlin years before. It was December 1961 and a chill somehow penetrated the July heat...

...snowflakes swirled high above Kurfürstendamm, the promise of adventure hung heavy in the air. Anything could happen in Berlin. I turned the collar of my overcoat against the wind and hurried from my Mustang to the Hilton. Under my coat the fully loaded service .45 felt heavy. I hesitated at the entrance to admire a glossy photograph of Ilse in a man's suit and fedora. She sang to me—I still hear her singing those love songs.

The piano bar was packed, as it was every night when she did Dietrich. She was already on stage when I entered. She saw me and smiled, but every man there smiled back. We were all in love with a dream. I sat on a barstool and watched her in the bar mirror. I ordered whiskey, straight up, something strong.

I looked up as the bartender set the drink on the bar and I spotted Kurt come in. He looked more eastern than western in a black turtleneck, navy jacket and billed sailor's cap. He swept his blond hair back out of his eyes, and looked over every face in the room. She winked at him and that hurt. He leaned against the bar and ordered Schnapps and a Lager. The bartender brought his drinks with a word of warning on the paper napkin. Kurt looked around the room, downed the shot, crushed the napkin, and rubbed his finger over his eyebrow in that nervous way I'd seen before.

Ilse had captured everyone's attention except for the big man watching from across the room. I recognized the ugly Russian as General Nikoli Rubski. His burn blazed red, indicating he was mad as hell. I was glad he hadn't recognized me.

Kurt tossed the napkin on the bar and walked toward the laundry room and changed into a waiter's jacket and glasses. He was a spy but he had gall. No wonder they called him Chameleon, but his change didn't fool me and I knew it hadn't fooled Rubski, either.

Kurt stationed himself near an exit and held the tray as if collecting glasses. I was almost lost in Ilse's song again when his tray rattled. An obvious Stasi agent whispered to Kurt and I could see his pistol. Ilse saw it, too. She stopped singing Lili Marlene in the middle of a verse. Everyone gawked until she screamed at the top of her lungs. "Fire!" Hundreds of people rushed the doors in pandemonium, women screamed, men shouted. The bartender hit the fire alarm. It was total chaos.

Kurt punched the goon and got away from him. I lost him and dashed into the street. A black sedan flew past, spraying slush all over my suit, and I followed it. Kurt crashed through an emergency exit, right into Rubski's balled fist. I saw blood from Kurt's broken nose dripping down into the white snow. Rubski said, "You will come with me. Komrade Khrushchev has a few questions."

I shouted, "Hey, Rubski ... hold it!" I ran as fast as I could in the snow to stop him, but he shoved Kurt into his Mercedes and sped away. The snow tires dug in, flinging slush and gravel in my face. I watched them speeding away until she caught up with me. That's when the race for our lives began.

..."General Werner, we're here." Lieutenant Jones broke through his daydream. "We're at the Embassy for the reception."

"Right, Lieutenant. I'm ready to go!"

105

Moscow

"Chairman Gorbachev!" President Reagan appeared self-confident at his first summit in Moscow. It was quite a different meeting from the earlier summit between Kennedy and Khrushchev in Vienna. A small entourage accompanied Reagan when he extended his hand to his cold war adversary. This was the first face-to-face meeting of the two leaders who could change the world by ending the military standoff in Europe. Reagan's cheerful demeanor was in contrast to the solemn Russian officials standing rigidly behind Gorbachev.

"I'd like to introduce someone," Reagan said. "This is Ambassador Lili Brown." She shook Gorbachev's hand, smiled at him and he smiled in return. She noticed his birthmark and thought of Rubski's scar. She had steeled herself against Russians with scars and the damage they could do, even with her hand in Gorbachev's, she thought of Rubski's burned skin under her nails and shivered. She hoped for a better result this time.

"I hope the weather is not too cold for you," said Gorbachev.

She shook her head no, not trusting her voice at that moment.

Reagan said, "Lili is a very good friend and my special envoy for Eastern Europe. She has long been active in refugee concerns and now serves as my special envoy in Berlin. You may contact her directly any time you wish."

Gorbachev nodded. "Ms. Brown, I hope we can work together on important issues, perhaps when I go to Berlin next year."

"That would be my privilege, Mr. Gorbachev."

Reagan had summoned her to Moscow specifically to meet Gorbachev since she had pegged him the wild card that made dramatic change possible though she had never met him. How such change was possible was still unclear. After the formal welcome, Reagan withdrew to a secure conference room in the American Embassy for private discussions with staff. He spoke to Lili first. "I'm pleased you accepted this appointment, Lili. I wish you had a larger staff but I ruffled feathers at State just to get you there. Are you all right?"

"I'm perfectly fine, Mr. President. Emily is my strong right arm to help me with State and most everything else." Emily Bronson was her political assistant, a professional Foreign Service officer selected by State. "I need only a secretary and driver beyond Emily and I've hired my own. There are many who help me in other ways."

Then Reagan unsettled her with a direct question. "Have you been in touch with General Werner in Vienna, yet?"

"Yes ... well, no," she stammered. "Actually he sent a letter and I owe an answer to that."

"You haven't talked with him? He's there only because you wanted it, Lili. The Army Chief was not pleased to return him to active duty."

"I hope I didn't cause too many problems."

"Its fine, but we need to get things moving like you said."

"What should I do?" she asked.

"The only way the hardliners will face change is through confrontation. I want you to stir things up, Lili," said Reagan. "That was our agreement, remember? That was why we re-called Werner. You once complained to me about the lack of action. Now I'm asking you the same question. Where's the action?"

On the other side of Moscow in a dirty industrial zone near the rail tracks, men entered a warehouse in small groups under the cover of darkness. Some walked, others came in government sedans. They were a select group of thirty government, military, KGB, and business leaders within the Soviet Union, a shadow government intent on overthrowing Gorbachev and reestablishing a dictatorship.

Roll call was taken. The chairman of the group, Leonid Agromovich, opened with a financial report. "*Komrades*, I must report that our financial condition is *not* good. We are short necessary funds in our operating budget, but I believe it's still sufficient for our immediate requirements. Once we're in control of the government, we will have all the assets of the state at our disposal."

A man raised his hand in the second row and waved to attract his attention. "*Da, Komrade.*"

"Will we continue the black market in Afghan opium to add to our revenue this year?"

"*Da!* We must continue all financial efforts even after our takeover. We will have unforeseen expenses. We need even more innovative methods to support our needs."

The unnamed organization's objective was clear—a *coup d'état* to oust Mikhail Gorbachev. His new policies of *glasnost* and *perestroika* threatened the old ones of traditionalists like Stalin, Khrushchev, and Brezhnev. Gorbachev and his new ideas were dangerous to them because they meant certain change—he must be removed before the country was irrevocably altered.

Another speaker stood and interrupted the discussion. "When will we make our move?" The question came from General Ivan Rubski, son of General Nikoli Rubski—Rasputin—who had died in a terrorist attack in Berlin. The younger Rubski was known as an irritable and demanding plotter who chaffed at not having the shadow chairmanship himself. But by virtue of his position on the revolutionary committee, Rubski would move up to command the entire Soviet army after the coup. He was ready.

"That hasn't been decided," said Agromovich. "But we must move when Gorbachev is out of the country on one of his pandering trips to the west. The government will be in our hands as soon as our take-over is revealed. He can seek asylum somewhere else. This will be a bloodless coup."

"I strongly disagree, *Komrade!*" Rubski shouted. "We must set a date now so I can make concrete plans. That's the only way to assure success. We're just drifting and getting nowhere. Given enough time, Khrushchev will find out and we will all face a firing squad together – that will not be bloodless."

"Thank you for your views, General. I'll consider your suggestions and in a few months we can discuss them in a special committee."

"That's doing nothing! We must plan now. We should move at the fortieth anniversary of East Germany. We know he's going to Berlin for that and we'll have the resources to do it and the time to plan it in detail. And we must give this movement a name. I propose the 'October 7 Revolution!' That's more than a name—it's also a mission and a timetable for action. Then we can take measures to set a take-over in motion."

"I believe it would be best just to keep him out of Moscow," said Agromovich. "We can simply make an announcement while he's in East Berlin, a press release and a bloodless coup."

"A bloodless coup?" shouted Rubski. "A bloodless coup? There is no such thing! Our blood will cover red square! The only way to rid us of this poisonous snake," he growled, "Is to cut off the head!"

106
West Berlin

Dear Vic,

Your note arrived several weeks ago and I'm sure you are wondering why I haven't replied sooner. I'm still trying to separate everything that has happened to us from how I feel about it. I'm not making this very clear but I know you understand my meaning. I wonder why I can't just pick up the phone and talk to you but I'm sure it's too soon, or too late, for that.

I wanted you to know the manuscript arrived last week but I have not been able to bring myself to open it yet. I think I will have to escape from the city with it for a few days so I can come to grips with all this and still give you my heartfelt opinion. But I don't know how you can write the finish before you know how it ends.

Congratulations on your promotion and your assignment in Vienna. The President expects big things from you there, he told me as much in Moscow. I'm proud of having known you, and I want you to know that I'm dealing with my life as it is.

The assignment I was given here is daunting. I wonder if I can do it without your help. Yet, even the thought of asking you to help me again frightens me.

I'll be in touch soon. Perhaps one day we really can meet again on Ku'damm.

Yours very truly,

Lili

She looked beyond the windowpane to the pedestrians on the sidewalk, but she didn't see them. Instead, she saw her home in Santa Barbara, California ... *it was the day after President Kennedy was shot and she awoke with a terrible headache....*

A slight drizzle had begun outside but she hadn't noticed the umbrellas popping up on Leberstrasse. The door opened behind her but she didn't hear it either. A voice somewhere in the room behind her beckoned her back to Berlin.

Emily cleared her throat and tried again. "Madam Ambassador, it's time to go now." The Secretary of State had assigned Emily Bronson as political assistant to Reagan's Ambassador-at-large to keep a political novice from getting the country into a shooting war.

Lili turned, puzzled, facing her aide and needing a moment to return from distant memories.

"It's time to go," Emily glanced at the grandfather clock. "The mayor is ready to receive you."

"Thank you, Emily. Just give me a moment, please. I'll be right out. Do you have the gift, the candy dish with the Presidential Seal?"

"Yes ma'am. I had it wrapped in navy blue paper with a white ribbon. And the card is as you requested."

"Wonderful, I'll meet you at the sedan in a moment."

For Lili the time had flown forward yet time seemed to be starting all over like a movie rewinding, playing in reverse at fast speed. She had been too busy to contemplate it before but long buried memories were randomly surfacing, coming back from the grave. This was her first official call on the Mayor of Berlin. The Mayor of Berlin...

...Mayor of Berlin Willy Brant had spoken on the phone to Lyndon Johnson after the fiasco at Freedom Bridge. It had all been a blur until she and Vic found themselves in the Oval Office across from President Kennedy. His call to Frank Sinatra, her part in An Afternoon in Paris, the Oscar, she couldn't believe her own life. Had all of that happened just to make this possible? It hardly seemed likely. But nothing made sense any more, it never had really. It was a fantasy too unbelievable to be true, especially that horrible call from Vic that had changed her life....

"Is something wrong, Madam Ambassador?" Emily Bronson walked between her and the window, inserting herself into her frame of reference. Water puddled around Emily's feet, dripping from her raincoat onto the hardwood floor.

"You seem distracted today. Shall I phone the mayor's office and reschedule the meeting?"

"No." She managed a faint smile. "I'm fine. I was only reminiscing. Do I need my umbrella?"

"I have one for you."

"Thank you, Emily. I don't know what I'd do without you." As she passed her desk, she rested one hand on the unopened manuscript, dragging her fingertips over it as she walked by.

"Emily I'm so excited! Willy Brandt has been my good friend for years, as mayor, as chancellor, as an advisor for New Life—I can't wait to see him again."

"But Willy Brandt is out of politics now," said Emily. "Remember?"

"Of course, I know that," she smiled weakly. "I'm just thinking back too much. I can't wait to see the new mayor. I want you to come in with me. I haven't been in that office in … in a very long time."

107

Vienna

The official office of the United States Delegation for the Negotiations on Force Reductions in Europe was sited in an inconspicuous residence in the suburbs of Vienna. The city had been the neutral site for NATO and the Warsaw Pact nations to argue about nuclear reductions for years, without notable progress.

Now they were preparing to argue about reducing conventional forces—tanks, artillery, infantry, and logistics— all over Europe for the first time. Skeptics flourished. Many wanted to ensure there would be only more talk and no action. General Vic Werner was not among those.

He sat quietly in the secluded conference room at the right hand of Ambassador George Wainwright, the senior United States representative to the negotiations. Privately he wondered why Lili had written that President Reagan expected big things of him. No one had yet given him a mission—just go to Vienna. He had never met Reagan but recalled what the Army Chief of Staff had said: "You'll know what to do." What did that mean?

The military representative was charged with advising the Ambassador about military ideas developed at NATO for negotiations with the enemy. The goal was to make balanced force reductions so every nation's security was protected during the drawdown.

In his last weekly report to the Deputy Chief of Staff for Intelligence, Vic had ended with, "Why don't you bring me home? I'm useless here."

Ambassador Wainwright had called an urgent meeting of the delegation about a change demanded by Reagan prior to the first plenary session at the Hofburg Palace. The first task for all twenty-three nations was to name the new talks. All had been in agreement until Reagan threw a monkey wrench into the gears.

NATO had agreed to call this "the negotiations on Conventional Armed Forces in Europe," CAFÉ for short. It seemed to fit since more time was spent in Vienna coffee houses than anywhere else. The communists would argue against any name, but finally agree in the end. Agreement had already been arranged in café meetings beforehand. Everyone was happy until now.

Wainwright had received a midnight call from the White House staff demanding the name be changed. His orders were, "Anything but CAFÉ." Vic knew the origins of that dissent—it came from the woman of many surprises. He wondered how she had gained so much influence with this president.

Lili had sent Reagan a secret back-channel telex and Vic was blind-copied on it. "The name CAFÉ represents a continuation of nothing but coffee claques," she wrote. "If you want action in Vienna, we must prevent that from the very inception. This is a signal you mean business." Her straightforward language surprised him—sounded like the fearless Ilse he had once known but he doubted even Wonder Woman could save this.

"Goddamn it," stammered Wainwright. "Doesn't the president of the whole fucking United States have anything better to do than fiddle with a name for this useless blabbering?"

Vic recognized his cue. He had been trained that once orders were issued, you saluted and obeyed. He began diplomatically with the Ambassador. "This is a great opportunity for you, Ambassador," he said. "You can prove from day one that we mean business. This puts you in the spotlight."

"This is not the spotlight I want to be in, general." Wainwright simmered. "This is embarrassing. I voted for that name just last night and State agreed. Now I have to beg our allies to change. They'll think I renege on agreements."

"Not at all," said Vic tactfully. "It shows you're flexible, dynamic, and willing to make dramatic changes. They'll see you as the one who sets the pace around here and dares them to keep up. Challenge them to take chances!"

Wainwright sulked, shaking his head, wringing his hands. "I prefer to be systematic and cautious."

Diplomacy wasn't working. Vic waved the others from the room. When they were gone, he spoke in military terms.

"The purpose of this whole exercise, Mr. Ambassador, is to get the goddamned armored corps the hell out of Europe, not to just fiddle-fuck around here for another forty years. Get with the program, George! The President didn't send either of us here to suck our thumbs."

Wainwright's back stiffened and his face turned red. "I know I have to do it, General, but I don't have to like it. You had better back me up on this."

"I'll do more than back you up. I'll take the point. I'll call every NATO military rep tonight and tell them to get behind it or we'll pull our divisions out of Europe and let the Russians have it."

"They'll never believe that."

"Probably not … but they'll hear it clearly, and when an American general says it they'll sure read about it in Paris."

"And in Washington," said Wainwright.

"Yeah! That's what I mean."

The Imperial Castle of the Hofburg dynasty spreads over forty-eight acres of the inner city of Vienna. Formerly the Hofburg anchored all of Europe. For more than six centuries it was the seat of the ruler of Austria, and for two and a half centuries the seat of the German Emperor. The President of Austria still worked in rooms once used by Maria Theresa. The Vienna Boys Choir sings there, the crown jewels are stored there, and the nations of Europe seek peace and security in the great halls.

The East German delegation arrived for the first meeting and General Heinrich Ebert accompanied the ambassador as his military advisor. Heinz Claus found his way alone in his special van with wheelchair access, also equipped with special photographic equipment operated by a *Stasi* driver. Special parking next to the entrance afforded a perfect view of Prince Eugene on his rearing marble steed, and close ups shots of anyone going inside.

"Get a picture of everybody," said Claus. "Send everything to Fox."

He wheeled his chair onto an elevator crowded with delegates on their way to the top floor. Many arrived early to meet old acquaintances from former talks, which had lasted years and accomplished nothing. The coffee shop outside the meeting room was filled with a dozen languages and the aroma of espresso, Turkish coffee, and *Sacher* torts. Claus rolled to one corner, pretended to read a newspaper but quietly watched the interactions of allies and enemies.

The Americans pushed straight through the coffee shop in one group, anxious to go to work. Vic marched with Ambassador Wainwright, wearing a tailored navy blue suit, starched white shirt, and silk tie. Despite his fine civilian clothes everything about him read soldier.

Claus studied Vic's matured face and graying hair and saw someone familiar. He considered the possibilities. He noticed Vic had some difficulty holding his pen and remembered that the officer he knew had been wounded in Afghanistan. He realized Fox might have been right, these dull talks could prove interesting.

The Soviet delegation entered with as much bravado as the Americans. Brigadier General Ivan Rubski led the pack, looking out of place in his ill-fitting woolen suit and narrow tie. He secured a corner of the conference room and drew the communist bloc delegates around him with their military advisors.

Claus listened in with an ear attuned to Russian.

"We have information the Americans will try to change the name again. We'll protest vehemently. Poland, you'll argue that agreements should not be changed at the last minute and this is only an attempt to stall. Hungary, you'll ask how we can negotiate in good faith if their side is unclear why we're even here. Bulgaria, you..."

He instructed every delegation then concluded, "The Soviet delegation will finally resolve the problem by accepting the change from CAFÉ to CFE, provided the actual name remains unchanged. We'll say this is only so the United States won't lose face. They'll owe us one. Do exactly as I've instructed. That is all."

The first session was called to order and went exactly as planned. The acronym CAFÉ was changed to CFE and the press took photographs. The press release announced the first meeting had been successful and everyone smiled.

Even General Ivan Rubski smiled—he had thoroughly studied the dossier on Werner and knew he had somehow been involved in his father's death. He pondered those possibilities.

108
Europe Waits

Line by line, word by boring word, the Vienna convention slowly approached a broad framework for the incremental reductions of troops, tanks, aircraft and ammunition from central Europe. The devil was in the details but once those were agreed the changes in the military concentrations in Europe were more likely than at any time since the end of World War II.

The possibility for demilitarizing Europe created a heady atmosphere in Vienna and all over the world. The winds of change, however, blew first over Berlin as it always did.

While diplomats debated high profile solutions, lesser-known people made large cracks in the walls dividing Europe. New Life, a band of monks, and a special refugee trust in San Francisco aided people fleeing tyranny. But people still died trying to cross artificial boundaries. The banks of the Spree and Havel Rivers were spotted with white crosses, the Berlin Wall was painted with eulogies, and flowers were laid where people still died seeking freedom.

But hope for change replaced desperation—guards with shoot-to-kill orders sometimes looked the other way.

Ronald Reagan returned to California leaving George Bush to complete his agenda. Bush reaffirmed Lili's appointment at the insistence of Reagan and over the continued protests of State. "She'll stay there until she's ready to leave, George. You might as well keep her on our side."

Mikhail Gorbachev continued to rattle the Soviet meritocracy with his radical ideas that stirred faint hopes in the vast empire. The idea that freedom might be possible captured the imaginations of the Solidarity Movement in Poland, the Velvet Revolution in Czechoslovakia, and the never-ending resistance in Hungary.

Refugees pushed barriers, opposed restraints, and weakened alliances and the Soviet Republics grew restless. All of this was on display in a microcosm at the Hofburg Palace—reports to capitals grew more urgent. Such changes were a direct threat to those determined to stop it. Chief among those was the son of Rasputin, Ivan Rubski.

The second anniversary session of the negotiations was scheduled to begin. The chairman held his gavel in the air just as the Warsaw Pact delegates gathered for their instructions from Rubski. He laid the gavel back on the table.

"Today, Bulgaria will accuse NATO of stalling. Demand they accept our security framework and warn the negotiations are in danger of collapsing."

The Bulgarian delegate had criticized Soviet inflexibility for weeks. "That's wrong," he argued. "Our framework is weak and skewed against NATO. Withdrawals must be balanced, not one-sided. They can't possibly accept our terms so we must either agree to theirs or develop a better one."

Rubski stamped his foot, furious. "Either you'll do this my way or I'll replace you with someone who will!"

"Go ahead and replace us all—nothing will change."

"Enough of this," he fumed. "Hungary, blame the United States for the lack of agreement on armored infantry vehicles."

"I'll do it one more time," he said, "but when will we suggest a better plan? Ours isn't fair or balanced. It makes no sense—frankly I don't even understand it."

"What's wrong with you people?" Rubski exploded. "We'll lose everything if we continue this way. I'm calling a meeting, tonight." He checked his watch. "All political and military representatives are required at eight o'clock. No exceptions!"

Vic watched Rubski's agitation with amusement. He remembered shooting his father, Nikoli Rubski, and thought about putting a bullet through this one. He also noticed the ever-present East German delegate in the wheel chair—he never attended Rubski's meetings. Instead, he huddled in privately whispered conversations with West Germans, crossing battle lines. Vic knew he was a *Stasi* agent, he had certainly seen enough of those, and was curious why a West German ambassador and an Eastern *Stasi* agent were so friendly.

Vic was bored by endless debate over vague concepts and had missed a glacial change that had already begun. The seemingly futile talks had become a quiet battleground of resistance—he understood that well enough since unconventional warfare was his specialty.

He finally realized why he was in Vienna. "The President said you'd know what to do," the army chief had told him. He considered what he had just seen. Rubski was facing a revolt among his followers while East and West Germans were openly consorting. Germany was actually coming together while the Soviet Union was disintegrating—the walls had begun to crumble before his eyes and he had nearly missed seeing the cracks.

Vic studied the disabled *Stasi* agent behind the two German delegations. He also seemed to be enjoying Rubski's problems and even had the air of a conspirator. Vic wondered why he had missed this too—the man looked vaguely familiar but he dismissed that as impossible. He closed his eyes and summoned a vision of

Kurt lying face down in blood. Then their eyes met and the crippled man rubbed his forefinger over his eyebrow.

Vic moved to stand but the gavel banged the meeting to order. Claus wheeled hurriedly from the conference room but Vic was pinned to the table beside the Ambassador.

Vic rushed to his office as soon as the meeting ended. He believed the crippled German might well be Kurt and he was angry with himself for not realizing it sooner. He wondered what Lili would do if she knew he was alive—a *Stasi* agent.

He slammed his door and pulled the encrypted phone from a locked cabinet then connected to the CIA station in Berlin.

"This is General Werner in Vienna," he said. "There's an East German here I need identified. He's in a wheel chair and I'm faxing a copy of a file photo to help you. I believe he's *Stasi* but I want to know everything you have on him."

"Yes sir. I'll look into it and get back to you. What's his name?"

"His name is Heinz Claus. Ever heard of him?"

"No. But I'll check and get back to you with what we might have on him tomorrow."

"Can't you do it sooner?"

"I don't think so sir, but I'll do what I can."

"When you have it, get a message to me. I don't care what time it is. I'm very interested in his biography from the early sixties."

109
Remember Your Real Friends

The mandatory meeting Rubski called at the Soviet Embassy started late and he hated waiting. Ebert arrived early and Claus was on time. The other delegates drifted in until half past eight. Rubski rapped his knuckles against the table. "All except the Soviets and East Germans were late. I called this meeting at eight and I expect all of you to be on time. Your conduct in plenary meetings has been disrespectful and I will not tolerate that. From now on, I insist on strict adherence to my instructions and no more discussion about it. Understood?"

Claus saw an opportunity to irritate Rubski further and used it. "But, *komrade!*" he said. "Chairman Gorbachev encouraged us to speak our minds, even to criticize our government. Are you rescinding his policy?"

"Shut up, Claus!" Rubski's face tightened. "I warned Fox not to send you here. You're a troublemaker; you always have been. I know all about your past...." He cut himself off abruptly. "I alone answer to Moscow for what happens here. My orders will be obeyed. You are all dismissed!"

All rushed for the doors except Ebert who remained in whispered conversation with Rubski. Claus waited for the aisle to clear to make way for his wheelchair. Rubski shouted, "You stay, Claus!" He wheeled about to face the music.

"Claus, you'll leave Vienna tomorrow. I've seen you encouraging this dissent. You're an instigator and I'll refer charges for your conduct here."

"I don't answer to you," He said calmly, "but I'll be happy to leave. Fox knew I didn't want to come but he sent me anyway. But I'll only leave when he recalls me to Berlin, not you."

"I'll see to it," said Rubski. "In the meantime, you will attend no more meetings."

"I also was against your coming," added Ebert. "I'll support *Komrade* Rubski's complaint. I warned Fox not to bring you into *Stasi* from the beginning. That was the biggest mistake he ever made."

"You warned him against letting me live," said Claus. "I owe you nothing." He spit on the floor.

"Get out!" yelled Rubski. "I don't want to ever see you again at the Hofburg. Get out now!"

As soon as Claus reached his van, he patched a radio call to Fox. He wanted Fox to hear the news from him first, knowing Ebert and Rubski would craft their words carefully before sending written cables that would not be seen until the following morning. Since Vic had recognized him he should leave anyway. He wanted to check in with New Life in Berlin and continue his personal operation of getting more political prisoners safely out of East Germany.

His call went through. "Fox, this is Claus. I told you there'd be trouble if you sent me here."

"I expected as much," he sighed. "Tell me about it."

"Rubski flew into a rage when the delegates protested his asinine policies. He called a meeting to berate us all and got so angry with me he almost exposed my past. After the meeting, he ordered me out of Vienna. I'll be glad to leave but only if you tell me. Ebert supports Rubski on this."

"Ebert is an idiot," said Fox. "I chose you because you have a spine—even broken yours is stronger than Ebert's. But Claus, you have been a pain in my ass since that first night we met in church!"

"You knew that before you hauled me off the bridge," said Heinz. "I won't apologize to you or to them."

Fox was calm, almost reflective. "I thought I could change you. I guess I was wrong."

Claus considered that a moment. "You did change me some, Fox. I better understand you now but I still don't often agree with you. There's another problem here you need to know about. Werner finally recognized me. That's another reason for me to leave. Shall I come back to Berlin?" His question was met only with silence. "Fox? Did you hear me? Do you want me to leave now?"

"I'm leaving that to you."

"Me?" He asked. "We don't operate that way, Fox. This is your organization—you're the boss or did you forget?"

"I knew there would be problems with Ebert and Rubski before I sent you and I don't really care about Werner anymore," he said. "But I wanted to see just how far those arms talks would go. I never thought any of it would go this far. Claus, we can never go back to the way things were, can we?"

"Is that so bad?"

"I don't know," he said. "But I'm a little worried."

"Well, what do you want me to do, Fox?"

"Listen, Claus. I hauled you off the bridge because you have talent and determination, maybe even a view of the future that I couldn't see. I wanted to see it too, but I never thought your vision for Germany was possible. Maybe you were right. I wanted you on my side just in case you were. I'm turning you lose, but if you get in trouble I won't rescue you again."

"You're firing me?"

"No," he said. "I'm making you a free agent again, the way you've always wanted it. Don't ask me for directions because I can't tell you what to do anymore. Do what you need to do—do what's right."

"Fox, be careful what you say. This could place you in jeopardy."

"I've considered that," he said. "When that day comes, and I believe now it will come, just remember who saved your ass and protected you when no one else would. Remember who set you free. Remember your real friends."

Ivan Rubski slammed the door and threw his pen at it, leaving a blue tic where the point struck. He re-read Fox's reply to his telex. "Your position regarding Claus is quite clear but you must not allow personal animosities to hinder our important mission." He read it aloud to Ebert. "I must remind you that the identity and backgrounds of present and former *Stasi* operatives remain classified at the highest levels."

Ebert had received essentially the same reply with one addition: "Divulging information about former *Stasi* agents is a serious infraction of State security. Of course, I don't need to tell you that and I know you'll emphasize that to your Soviet colleague."

Rubski recovered his pen and ran the bent point over a scrap of paper. It no longer marked so he tossed it with the trash. "We can't allow that collaborator to get in our way," he said. "We must handle the situation here."

"What are you thinking?" asked Ebert.

"If Fox will not support us, we must take matters into our own hands, and soon."

"Are you saying to kill Claus?"

"Isn't that obvious?"

"But that isn't easy in Vienna. We should get him back to Berlin where we have more assets."

"No!" said Rubski. "He'll have Fox's protection in Berlin. It must be here. I'd gladly do it myself but I have a bigger obligation in Berlin. That's another reason Claus cannot be allowed to return there."

"He irritates Fox," said Ebert. "I'm not so sure he'd protect him again. Claus is his biggest personal failure. He might actually welcome his disappearance."

"This is too important," said Rubski. "Get rid of him now, Ebert. That's your job. Do it!"

"Me? How?"

"Keep it simple." Rubski frowned and began pacing. "Just go to his house and kill him. Dump his body in the woods or the Danube. I don't care. How hard is that? He's a cripple!"

"I have a better idea," said Ebert. "I'll kill him in his house and blame the Neo-Nazis. I'll leak his background as a spy and his murder of the old Nazi, Abel. He even had a Jewish girlfriend. There's plenty of motive for the neo-Nazis."

"Good!" Rubski smiled again, baring his yellow teeth. "Then it should be easy to cover up. Even Fox won't know."

"But don't take Claus for granted," said Ebert. "He was once known as Chameleon. He's tricky and he won't give up easily."

"Use butcher knives and spray paint to make it look authentic," said Rubski. "And Ebert," he said. "You must do it on the evening of October 6th."

"Why? Aren't you coming with me?"

"I can't, as I said. I have a much bigger mission in Berlin. You can handle the chameleon—just a little lame lizard now." Rubski mimicked aiming a rifle. "I must kill a big bear, a very big one." Rubski explained the entire plan for killing Khrushchev and taking over the Soviet government.

110

Man with No Legs

Vic had been anticipating the CIA analyst from the Berlin Field Station to return answers about his crippled suspect, Heinz Claus a.k.a. Kurt Meyer. When the secure phone first buzzed, he grabbed for it. "General, we've been through our files on this Claus character and he's pretty much a mystery. We call Mischa Fox 'the man with no face' because we've never figured out what he looks like. Well, we call Claus the 'man with no legs' because we don't know where he came from or how he got there."

"But he has legs," said Werner. "He's paralyzed."

"It's a joke sir!"

"This isn't a joke, goddamn it!" His frustration rose and his voice with it. "The man can't walk and I want to know why."

"Why he can't walk? We don't have anything about that in our files either."

"Find out!" Vic was shouting but backed off. "This is the CIA I'm talking to, isn't it? Ask around, pay somebody, get off your fat ass and go ask him, damn it. I want to know."

"Yes, sir," the analyst stammered. "Uh, we're sure he's one of Fox's top guys and he's in Vienna to gather information about NATO's positions on the negotiations, we've figured that much out, but it's not so clear why Fox would send such a high deputy unless he just wanted him out of Berlin. Claus has the reputation of being a renegade and making trouble."

"Did you find out about the years 1961-1963?"

"He was completely unknown until 1965. That was our first report of a man in a wheel chair at *Stasi*. His name doesn't pan out in public records but those may have been changed—they often do with agents."

"Would you keep checking, please?" He asked politely. "I really need to know."

"Yes sir. Why the sudden interest?"

"He reminds me of someone, someone I ran into back then, but his face is different and the man I knew wasn't crippled. I think something happened to him around that time that may have injured him severely—even possible reconstructive surgery. I may contact him myself but I'd like to know as much as possible before I do."

"Sounds like a long shot but if you find out anything would you let me know, sir? So I can update our files."

"Yeah, sure thing." Vic's had already switched mental gears to another issue from the negotiating chamber. "What do you know about refugees trying to get out of East Germany? That's a hot subject on the margins here. I overheard this crippled guy talking to the West Germans about finding a way to get through the fence. Austrians and Hungarians may be involved, too. What's your take on that? Are they unofficially cooperating?"

"All we know is a bunch of East Germans are heading for the Austrian and Hungarian borders. They started small but their numbers are increasing fast."

"Is Ambassador Brown aware of this?"

"Oh, yeah!" he said. "That woman knows everything. She's a total pain in my butt. She's in here bothering me for details almost every day. Or else, she waltzes in with something we didn't know—like we should have known already. She has more sources than we do. Sometimes I think she's over there stirring up this refugee fuss all by herself."

"Surely you're joking?"

"No sir," he said. "Ambassador Brown thinks she's Saint Christopher or somebody. She travels in Eastern Europe more than Gorbachev. She has more visas then the Pope. She's a good looker but she's a handful."

"Now that's interesting," said Vic. "Keep checking on Kurt ... uh, Claus for me. And if you find out anything, page me anytime." Then he added, "And listen, if Ms. Brown comes to Vienna, tell me that even faster."

"I'll send up a red star cluster. She's more than I can handle."

"I know," he said. "I know that all too well."

111
Special Delivery

Emily Bronson was preparing to go home after yet another long and stressful day with Ambassador Brown at their offices in Berlin. Lili was tireless in her involvement with the recent flow of refugees from across the iron curtain. She multi-tasked every waking minute—phoning, talking with refugees and diplomats, coordinating plans outside the normal realm of a government representative, traveling to make personal contacts with persons unnamed. She called the White House and CIA; she called Pope John-Paul. She had even called the President of Austria to request he open the border and permit more to cross—all with no guidance or approval from State.

Emily worried about her boss's overstepping but was reluctant to do anything about it.

"I'm going to work at home for a few hours," Emily called upstairs. The Soviet Ambassador to East Germany was coming to their office for a meeting on an unspecified topic the next morning. "I'll bring some talking points for the Soviet's visit when I come in tomorrow," she added over her shoulder as she quickly closed the door in case her boss remembered some last minute detail.

But Lili's thoughts were absorbed with something entirely different.

Her private residence at 16 Leberstrasse was on the second floor, above the official offices. The offices were limited but she didn't need much—just space to plan, receive and send messages, book travel, and accept the occasional visitor like the Soviet Ambassador. She didn't need much living space either since she lived alone. She answered to no one—that fact riled the Secretary of State and national security officials. She was her own taskmaster. The State Department occasionally tried control her but learned she would phone President Bush immediately.

"I'm doing this because Ron asked me to. Tell them to leave me alone or I'll quit."

"But Lili, State coordinates foreign policy."

"You said I would remain free to act as your Ambassador-at-large. I resign. I'll do this my own way. I don't need the State Department or their puny checks."

"I'll call them, Lili," he conceded. "Just stay. Please?"

Lili stepped from a hot bubble bath and dried condensation from the mirror. Water puddled on the tiled floor, cool against her bare feet but slippery. She stood before the mirror, stopped drying, and lowered the towel to catch her full reflection. She examined her body, turned slowly and checked from another angle. Finally, she picked up a dry towel and wrapped it around, holding it securely under her arms.

She examined the image in the mirror and wondered about the person beyond the flat reflection. *What have you done with your life, Lili?*

She wrapped another towel around her hair and while her hand was up she caught the numbers tattooed on her wrist, no wristwatch covered them now. She scratched the uneven black numbers under her skin with a fingernail. *What happened to little Olga? For this, she was spared?*

She studied that familiar face—changed over the years. *What happened to your life, Ilse? Why were you saved at Freedom Bridge? Who are you?*

October's chill touched her, seeping around door facings and windowsills. After the warming bath, she lit a wood fire to barricade against the frosty invasion.

She opened a bottle of Riesling to accompany Mozart while studying refugee reports from East Germany. *Vic's in Vienna—Mozart's city—wonder what he's doing?* She was guilty of being unresponsive to his entreaties so she concentrated instead on refugees and whether to raise that with the Soviet emissary. The purpose of his meeting was unspecified—Emily said his staff was vague. *I'll wait until he gets here to decide—play it by ear—'by the seat of my pants,' as Vic says. What was it he said about...?*

The doorbell chimed at the main entrance on the first floor—the official offices. She only answered that door when one of her reporters, that CIA captain called them her spies, was expected after hours. She was still wrapped in heavy towels so she peered down from an upper window onto the front stoop.

A young man ran away and jumped into a beat-up van. He flooded it with his rushed attempt to start it but he got it going on the second try and sputtered away. She thought of Vic in his Chevy. *He was proud of that car yet he pounded it in with a hammer. That must have broken his heart—as I did.*

She found slippers and a robe to investigate the doorbell—towel still covering her damp hair. She started down the squeaking stairs. *Maybe he left a message?*

Sometimes her refugee reporters left written missives at her doorsteps after hours—new intelligence or thank you notes. New Life benefactors volunteered to keep vital information flowing across international borders. East German monks even sent their escapees to her with missives. An informal, unofficial network—an underground express, a midnight train—had come together, connecting Lili with hundreds, perhaps thousands, of 'little people.'

She hired more temporary staff and opened a second New Life office with personal funds—Kurt's funds—to meet with refugees and handle increasing interviews and resettlements. She read all reports carefully before turning them over to that CIA captain—he reminded her of a young El Supremo shouting through Mayor Brandt's car window.

Emily usually collected the messages with the morning mail but this man had rung the bell before running. *Maybe the East Germans got out through Austria. That would be worth the trip downstairs.*

She touched the switch for the lower-level lights but decided against that and moved downstairs in the obscurity of darkness. She moved drapes to look out but imagined Ursula at her window in Santa Barbara—closed them and drew her robe tighter.

She started back up the stairs but stopped. *Damn! I've come this far—I'll look—face my fears.*

She snapped open three deadbolts and unhooked a chain to crack the door to see outside. A large flat package wrapped in brown paper and tied with string leaned against the wall on the stoop. She closed the door quickly. It couldn't be a bomb—shaped wrong and too thin. *A goodwill gesture from the Soviet Ambassador before his visit?* She re-opened the door and glanced about, dragged the package inside then triple-bolted and chained the door.

She ripped the brown paper away. Inside was a narrow plywood box, tacked shut and sealed. It smelled musty. She went to the kitchen and found a butcher knife, wedged the sturdy blade between the seams, gnawing at the wood. She attacked the cracks until inch-by-inch the edges loosened enough to get a finger in. Rusty nails groaned at being disturbed after a long sleep.

Content of the wood crate was wrapped in a cloth. She stepped back and found a note from the outer wrapping had fallen on the floor. It was addressed to the Honorable United States Ambassador, Lili Brown. *Ah! It must be from the Soviets.* She pulled the note from the envelope and sat on a chair near a lamp to read.

The note was as shocking as what she found in the package.

Sixteen Leberstrasse in West Berlin had once been Marlene Dietrich's apartment but Lili had made it her office and transformed one room into a "Dietrich Room." There she preserved some of the movie star's early history and Lili found peace there that often eluded her elsewhere. She decorated the room with period antiques and artifacts from the actress's career. This favored room served as the official greeting area for visitors and offered interesting conversation pieces for unexciting visitors.

Emily usually orchestrated the main offices, operated the communications center, and handled routine matters while Lili lived upstairs and traveled frequently to humanitarian hot spots. Emily arrived early that morning to go over notes she had prepared overnight for the Soviet ambassador's visit.

"Ambassador Brown, I have some notes for Chernenko."

"Emily, would you please call me Lili?"

"Yes ma'am."

"Are we friends, Emily?"

"Yes ma'am."

"Then stop saying 'ma'am' and call me Lili, damn it!"

"Yes. Okay … Lili."

Lili took Emily's hand and led her into the Dietrich Room. "I want to show you something that came last night." They stood together before the fireplace. The painting, *Angel of Peace,* that had hung there was gone, replaced by a framed black and white poster. It was Marlene Dietrich in her first movie filmed in Berlin, *Der Blaue Engel.*

"Oh!" said Emily. "The Blue Angel—a lovely addition to your collection. And it's signed, too." She squinted to read it. "It's … it's signed to ... Ilse. Is it an original?"

"It isn't an addition to my collection, Emily. This *was* my entire collection, the very first and only piece I owned."

"It's remarkable," she said. "But I've never seen this one before. And who's Ilse?"

"Emily if my dream for Germany ever comes true I'll be leaving politics for good. I think you have a promising career ahead of you and I've recommended you for promotion. My post will certainly be eliminated as soon as I resign since it was only created to appease me. There are some other important positions in the Foreign Service. Think about what you want to do after I leave and tell me soon."

"Thank you ... Lili."

"I'm telling you this now because I need a friend, someone to talk with personally, not professionally. I want you to think of me as Lili and be my friend—I don't have many."

"That's just not...."

"Humor me. Can we talk about something personal?"

"Yes, of course."

417

"What do you know about me, Emily?"

"Well, I know you're a presidential appointee and there's resentment at State about political appointments—yours especially. Did you know they put me here to keep an eye on you?"

"Of course I knew it," she said. "And you've done a wonderful job of maintaining your loyalty to them and to me. Thank you for telling me though."

"I think you've won me over to your side," she said. "Most appointees buy their appointments with campaign contributions. I don't know how you got yours, and frankly I don't care. But sometimes you act more like a soldier than a diplomat. I guess that's my way of saying I respect you and I do want to be your friend."

Lili laughed and led her to a sofa. "Thank you for keeping me out of trouble with State, Emily. I know you must be afraid I'll spoil your career with my crazy antics. I'm not a diplomat, but I'm certainly not a soldier. I'm afraid of guns. I'm really an actress guilty of impersonating a diplomat. Someday I'll explain all that, but right now I want you to see the note that came with my poster."

"The poster was yours? Who's Ilse?"

"I haven't seen it for many, many years," she said. "I never expected to see it again but it was returned unexpectedly last evening with this note." She handed the envelope over to Emily, who first examined the handwriting.

"It appears to have been written by a German," she said.

"Yes, it was. Read it."

Emily opened the note and read aloud, "*Liebe Botschafter Braun*—Dear Ambassador Braun, I apologize for the delay in returning your property but I forgot about it until recently. I hope we can meet again but it's still too soon. *Willkommen bei Berlin*—Welcome back to Berlin." She read it again and looked up. "This is very unusual, and he used the German spelling for Brown—that's incorrect. Who sent it? And how'd he get your poster?"

"I left here many years ago in great haste to leave and never had an opportunity to recover it. This was my pride and joy then. Dietrich, herself signed it for me."

"But it says to Ilse?"

"Emily, only three people besides me knew about this poster. One was Dietrich and I'm sure she forgot about me before the ink dried. Another is presumed dead. The third is an American in Vienna and he wears his feelings on his sleeve."

"Then...?"

"Then I think a fourth person I met only twice removed it from my apartment after I left. I'm sure that's who returned it."

"Who?"

"Mischa Fox."

Emily jumped when the doorbell chimed and dropped the note on the table.

"Oh no!" she said. "That's Chernenko and we didn't go over my notes."

Lili laughed. "Don't worry. We'll improvise. He asked for the meeting so let's hear what he has to say." Emily started for the door.

Lili stopped her. "Let me get it."

Chernenko was standing behind his aide when Lili pulled the door open, clearly expecting staff to appear first. "I'm Lili Brown. Welcome to my home." The aide glanced to his boss who was equally confused. "Come in out of the cold."

Emily and Lili both helped with their overcoats. "You see Ambassador, I have a very small staff," she explained. "Emily and I handle everything here." Chernenko had never met such an Ambassador and looked confused. But officials higher than him required this meeting and he was anxious to finish it.

The Soviets waited awkwardly until the ladies served tea. No one really wanted tea but that was protocol for an official meeting. With pleasantries out of the way, Chernenko recited his memorized speech. "Madam Brown, it is my distinct privilege, as Soviet Ambassador to the German Democratic Republic, to invite you to East Berlin as a personal guest of General Secretary Mikhail Gorbachev on October 7th. The occasion is a military parade in celebration of the 40th anniversary of the Deutsche Democratic Republic. The chairman would be honored if you would share his viewing box."

He passed a typed invitation to her and leaned back, awaiting her reply.

Lili laid it aside without reading it. "Ambassador Chernenko, would you please explain why your country prevents those same Germans you ask me to celebrate from traveling freely about in their own country?"

Her question was unexpected and he was unprepared without instructions. Color flushed his cheeks and he crunched the arm of his chair until his knuckles turned white. His aide whispered into his ear. Chernenko finally sputtered, "The Union of Soviet Socialist Republics has no legal authority over East German internal affairs. You must ask them that question."

"But you are the occupying power."

"Please send your question via diplomatic pouch so my staff can provide an official answer."

"Did you know there are now 750,000 East Germans with applications to leave East Germany still pending?"

"Please, an official communiqué."

"Thank you, Mr. Ambassador," she said. "And please inform Mr. Gorbachev that I humbly accept his most generous invitation." Chernenko stood, relieved, but she added an afterthought, "Oh! Will I be permitted to enter through Brandenburg Gate?"

"The gate is closed, madam. All guests must enter through Checkpoint Charlie."

"I'm disappointed," she said, "but I'll come anyway. "Please remind Mr. Gorbachev that President Reagan implored him to open that gate. When will he do it?"

Chernenko stood quickly and snatched his overcoat from the cloak rack. Lili remained seated as he hastened his retreat to the exit. Emily moved to escort them out but Lili held her back. Chernenko tossed his overcoat over his arm and rushed into the cold without donning coat, hat, or scarf in his haste to withdraw.

Emily was shaken. "You insulted him."

"Yes," she said. "I did get his attention didn't I?"

112

Welcome Home, Friend

Vic was exasperated the Berlin field station could not compile a useful dossier on Heinz Claus. He was sure he was actually Kurt but several contradictions troubled him. Kurt had hated the *Stasi*, killed a top agent, and defied Mischa Fox. If he had somehow survived the shoot out on the bridge—he would have faced a firing squad. Rubski had killed his family and he hated Russians, Rubski especially—the Kurt he knew would never work with his son. His instincts insisted the man was Kurt but the premise was illogical. Yet the man seemed to enjoy Rubski's problems at the Hofburg, was clearly involved in private east-west conspiracies on refugees—he always advocated reunification of Germany. Finally, that rubbing of his eyebrow was unmistakable—no one else did that.

Lili had believed Kurt was dead all those years—finding him alive and working with former enemies contradicted everything Kurt Meyer meant to her. If he actually worked for Fox while she still pursued his dreams—that was a nightmare, both lives wasted. Vic's head ached from trying to sort it out. If the CIA didn't know the facts he would find out himself. Lili deserved to know—he deserved to know.

Vic phoned a friend, the Czech military advisor. "Ludwig, this is Vic."

"Hello, Vic. Thank you for lunch last week," he said. "I want to reciprocate. We'll drink some more *Budvar*."

"Sounds great," he said. "Just let me know when and where. I have some questions about ammunition classifications to discuss with you."

"Fine, let's make it next Wednesday. Say, at 2:00? Café Landsmann?"

"Good, I'll make a note," he said scribbling it into his planner. "Can I ask you about one of your colleagues from East Germany?"

"Of course. General Ebert?"

"No," said Vic. "The man in the wheelchair, Heinz Claus."

"Oh that one!" The Czech sounded surprised. "What do you wish to know? I don't really know him very well."

"I know who he works for—that's obvious. I wanted to speak with him about a mutual friend but he wasn't at the session today. How can I contact him?"

"He doesn't socialize," said the Czech. "Stays to himself—he's a bitter man and bristles if anyone gets close. Be careful of that one. But I have seen his van parked in the country at a small farmhouse. I've heard he stays there."

"Where is it?"

"I don't have an address, but I can give you precise directions," he said. "Look for his van. It's in the Vienna Woods, about ten kilometers from your villa. Take down these directions."

Vic followed the directions and easily located the cottage in the Vienna Woods—a Bavarian-style cottage crowned by a peaked roof and painted pale yellow. It was partly concealed, well back on a shady lane. A rickety barn stood behind it, the only evidence it was once a real farm. Wilderness encroached on the cottage over the years, giving it the appearance of a hunting cabin. But window boxes filled with colorful and fragrant flowers indicated a woman's influence. Other than the flowers it was a masculine home—judging by the wooden ramp, equipped for a wheel chair. Vic remembered Ilse saying flowers of Pasadena reminded her of Hilda. This window garden was a well tended memorial.

Heavy shades were drawn over the windows to discourage snooping. Vic cruised past once in his car then backed into a concealed logging trail to park. He crossed through the woods to the back of the house first. He wanted to scout before confronting a ghost. Dense woods were dark already and small animals rustled leaves and brush near the trail. He circled through the trees and underbrush to reach the old barn and pushed the door open. The van with a wheelchair lift he had seen at the Hofburg was parked inside—backed in for a quick departure but all doors locked. Vic's shoes crunched over the gravel driveway as he crept through the darkness. Only faint starlight filtered through a canopy of trees.

He decided to keep it simple—knock on the door and confront Kurt. He walked slowly, hands extended to protect his eyes from low branches. He stumbled and sprawled over something in the path.

He felt for the unexpected obstacle, expecting to find a fallen limb. But he touched clothing—warm, wet, and he smelled fresh blood. Vietnam jungles flashed in his mind's eye. He touched legs but they were whole. He felt for the man's face—his throat was cut, gaping open, eyes wide and blood everywhere. Vic wiped his hands on the dead man's shirt and crawled away from the corpse. Heinz might be dead—he had recently believed his alter-ego was dead already.

Vic heard a loud crash at the front of the cabin. Angry German curses filled the cabin. Vic crouched beneath a windowsill at a half-inch crack of one shade. Ebert stood in black coveralls, a utility bag slung over one shoulder. He brandished a bloody knife, crossing the room to the crippled man in his wheelchair. Ebert kicked, toppling the chair. Kurt crabbed backwards on massive arms, retreating from the slashing knife. Vic ran for the open door, unarmed.

Kurt growled at Ebert, "You goddamned Russian-lover."

Ebert kicked the empty wheelchair aside. "You're a dead man, Meyer." The blade sliced inches from Kurt's face. He shoved backwards again, dragging dead legs as dead weight. Then he faced his attacker from the floor.

Ebert kicked at his kidneys. "The charade is over, Chameleon. Tonight you'll be exposed as the traitor you are."

Kurt grunted, "You're too incompetent to kill me, Ebert."

"Fox can't protect you anymore." Ebert dumped his bag on the table. Paint cans and butcher knives fell out and clattered.

"Where's Rubski?" demanded Kurt. "I thought a man would come for me."

"He had more important business than you. He went to Berlin to kill Gorbachev. Two traitors will die this week."

"I see you brought paint—Hitler was a painter, too."

"Funny," said Ebert.

"You might kill me," said Kurt, "and Rubski might even kill Gorbachev, but you can't stop this. The world will soon forget men like you."

"Not quite." Ebert edged closer, shifting his knife for a better grip. "The October Seven Revolution will save Russia. Nothing can save you. Say your prayers, Meyer."

Vic stepped through the broken doorframe behind him. "Ebert!"

He swirled. "Werner! This is perfect! Fox should have finished you at the bridge, too." He snatched an automatic pistol from his belt, pointed at Vic and fired wildly, missed.

He barely got off a second wild shot. A strong hand snatched his feet from under him and the bullet flew high. Ebert and the pistol hit the floor together.

Ebert squirmed and swung the knife at Kurt again. Kurt blocked it with a forearm. He dragged Ebert kicking into a bear hug. Hard fingers crushed Ebert's larynx then twisted his neck until it snapped. Ebert's foot kicked once and it was over.

Vic got up off the floor. "Kurt, is that you?"

"Yes," he said. "It's me."

"What was this all about?"

"Help me into my chair, please."

"We need to talk," Vic said as he turned the chair upright and lifted Kurt by his armpits.

423

"We can talk on the way to Berlin," said Kurt.

"Berlin? We can't just go to Berlin."

"Did you hear Ebert?"

"Not much. What was he talking about?"

"He said there's a coup to kill Gorbachev on October 7th, that's tomorrow. Rubski and Gorbachev are both in Berlin."

Vic looked at the Kurt. "Just call Fox," he said.

"I can't. He cut me loose and told me not to call him. I don't know what he'd do anyway. He may even be part of this for all I know. I never fully trusted him."

"I'll get your van," said Vic. "Where are the keys?"

"Where's my driver."

"He's dead."

"Damn, another life wasted."

"Let's go. We can talk on the way."

"Can you drive?" asked Kurt.

"I guess you never rode with me," said Vic. "You're in for an experience."

Kurt tossed Ebert's pistol. "Don't forget this."

Vic caught it with his left hand. "Let's go," he said. "I've missed Berlin."

"Welcome home, friend!"

113

Insurmountable Odds

General Ivan Rubski braced stiffly behind the driver of the black Mercedes, a newer model of the car his father had enjoyed—strange how Nikoli Rubski had hated everything German except their exquisite motorcars. The driver parked in the shadows near the sprawling warehouse district and the general used night vision goggles stolen from the US Army in Berlin to observe one particular building. The Soviet army, soon to be his army, would use that large building as one of those to marshal equipment before the big military parade to celebrate the upcoming 40th anniversary of the East German Republic.

Rubski watched two familiar Russian soldiers approach the building, one scouting the perimeter as the other checked inside. Rubski had waited an hour for them but he sat tight to keep watch for another quarter-hour to verify they weren't followed. He had personally recruited both soldiers and trusted them with this dangerous mission, but he would take no chances with a bloody *coupe d'état*.

Finally, he walked quietly into the warehouse and over solid concrete flooring. The space was crammed with military hardware aligned in rows in march-order for tomorrow's procession. He searched for one particular missile carrier in the center of the line. When he found it he opened the door and checked inside the cab with a penlight, then in the bed of the truck under the tarp. Satisfied, he moved toward an office near the rear of the building. As Rubski stepped into the dark office he froze—the sinister click of a safety snapped into firing position.

A deep voice challenged him. "October!"

"Seven!" Rubski supplied the necessary password. "I'm glad you're cautious Gorky," he said, "but turn on a light so I can see."

Gorky flipped on an overhead light, a single bulb hanging from the high ceiling of the bare office. "General, we await your orders." The second soldier, his rifle also ready, snapped to attention.

"The mission is on, men. The council finally agreed to my plan. The idiot Khrushchev is handing the motherland over to the capitalists' pigs and he must be stopped. We must protect the Soviet Union—no man is more important than that."

"What are our orders, General?"

"Gorbachev will view the parade from a reviewing stand in the center of *Unter den Linden*," Rubski began. "Gorky, there is a missile truck out there on the

floor, number G17782, already rigged with high explosives, the
Czechoslovakian type. In addition, fuel has been added to the missile in the
launcher, doubling the power of the blast. A remote control is already installed
for me to control the vehicle and detonation once it gets within range. You'll
drive the truck in the parade and jump out on my command before it reaches the
reviewing stand. You'll be met by Kominski, who will take you to the *Komische
Oper*. There are two switches under the steering column—one to activate remote
steering and the other to switch on the explosive device. I'll show you exactly
how to activate them, so you can switch them on before you jump out. Keep
your radio on, the one I gave you. I'll steer the truck myself by remote control
and detonate the explosives."

"*Da* General."

"Kominski will have a car and documents to take you to Bratislava. We'll return
to Moscow as heroes. The October Seven Revolution will change the course of
history."

For Vic and Kurt, the drive from Vienna to Berlin was over 700 kilometers
and took all night even with Vic driving at breakneck speeds. The van nearly
flipped several times when he swerved to avoid treacherous potholes. Traffic
backed up as they approached international borders but Kurt's *Stasi* credentials
gained quick clearances. Vic pushed the van as fast as it could go but it could
never match the speed and maneuverability of the old '57 Chevy. They caught
up on history as they rode.

"I still can't believe you're still alive," Vic said. "I saw you die on Freedom
Bridge and we've believed you were dead all these years."

"I almost died, nearly bled to death. Fox saved my life by getting me to his
personal doctor quickly but no one could repair the spinal damage. The bullet
through my chest severed my spine. And Rubski had rearranged my face so
badly I needed plastic surgery. Fox didn't ask me how I wanted to look—we
weren't on speaking terms then. That's how I got this face."

"Fox was your enemy. Why'd you join forces with him?"

"I just wanted to die at first, but I didn't and Fox didn't kill me. Then I wanted
to leave East Berlin but Fox allowed me to move Ingrid and my father's bodies
to the cemetery at the monastery where my mother was buried, near our family
home before the war. My family was at rest and I could no longer leave. I
wanted to search for Hilda's remains … and our baby, but…. When she died
there was nothing left for me, all my dreams were wrecked. I was depressed,
suicidal, for over a year. What's a crippled crazy spy worth? Well … Fox
thought I was worth something."

426

"How about Lili ... Ilse, I mean? How could you not tell her you were alive? You were her only attachment to reality."

"I regret breaking my promises to her but I couldn't do it. When I recovered enough to realize how it might affect her, I was this way," he said, slapping his withered legs. "In a way I died and came back as a different person, cut off from everyone I loved and everything I had believed in. Besides, Ilse was your responsibility by then. She loved you—why didn't you marry her?"

"God knows I wanted to, but first it was her career, then Kennedy and the Cubans, then Ursula. Then we fought about all that. Do you know any of this?"

"I know most of it," said Kurt. "I found out some of it on my own and Fox filled in the rest. His international network is quite remarkable."

"You should have reached out to her in some way," said Vic. "She never got over losing you. She thinks you died on the bridge and holds me responsible for leaving you there."

"She knows I'm alive—nothing else except that I'm alive. And I know what happened on the bridge," Kurt said. "Fox told me how you threw her over to save her then jumped yourself to pull her from the river. You made the right choice and Fox was impressed by your courage. She's beautiful, brilliant, and totally screwed up. I was afraid to contact her, even when she came to Berlin. I'm sure Fox sent me away just to put some distance between us and he was right to do it. I knew she'd think I sold out and would be disappointed. I didn't want to disillusion her or complicate her life anymore."

"It is odd how all this worked out with you and me both in Vienna and Ilse in Berlin," said Vic. "That's a remarkable, almost unbelievable, coincidence."

"It isn't a coincidence," said Kurt. "She set it up. She knows I'm somewhere near and she arranged for you to be here."

"You are crazy!" said Vic. "That's impossible."

"Listen for a minute—she didn't exactly plan it that way but she found an opportunity when Reagan went to the wall. He always wanted her to work for him but she never would, not until then. She finally saw the chance for what she wanted and improvised. She was always good at that."

"If you never contacted her how could she possibly know you were alive?" asked Vic.

"She unknowingly hired my own lawyer to investigate my death and discovered I wasn't buried in the grave marked for me. She almost certainly guessed I was re-circulating refugee funds, too. We're working on the opposite ends of the same refugee network—New Life. She's a smart lady."

"This is hard to follow."

427

"I've already explained how Fox was worried about me being in Berlin with her across the wall. He sent me to Vienna because she was in Berlin, so her presence unwittingly caused that. Fox wanted to get me out of the way and Vienna was a place to dump me and still keep a string on me."

"That's a stretch but let's say it's true about you and her," said Vic. "But my being in Vienna is still a mystery—I never could figure that. She barely acknowledged my existence, said she never wanted to see me again, and won't answer my letters. She hates me."

"She had everything to do with you. You were called out of retirement for this," said Kurt. "She convinced Reagan to do it."

"I don't believe that."

"It's true. Our best sources are in Washington."

"I don't believe any of this."

"That's your problem," said Kurt. "Let's talk about what we'll do in Berlin."

Vic and Kurt had never quite trusted each other when they had been forced by Ilse to work together years before. Now they were older, wiser, on opposite sides but connected by a common aim. They discussed courses of action in Berlin but their options were limited. They functioned only on adrenalin. Every time Vic looked at Kurt, he remembered how Ilse had flung herself into the gunfire on the bridge to save him, and how Fox held a gun on him while he held Ilse in his arms.

After they rode in silence for a time, Vic asked, "Why did Fox let me save Ilse on that bridge?"

"I'm not completely sure about that even now, but Fox has never let her go—he was fascinated by her from her singing Dietrich to her courage in facing him and Rubski. He followed everything she did after that," said Kurt. "He considered her a very unusual woman—a star in his universe, one of his few unconquered people. We even watched her movie together several times. When the first reports came in that she was killed, he was as devastated as me. I think he was infatuated with her because she was unattainable."

"And Rubski?" asked Vic. "Did Fox betray him?"

"I think he realized on the bridge how alone he was. I believe he saw his future with Germany, not Russia. He placed a heavy bet by allowing you to escape with her and letting me to live. He still hopes to survive when his two worlds collide."

"How?"

"I have no idea—unless he believes he has made a few friends. But I still don't trust him and I've known him for thirty years after he saved my life."

The odds of stopping Rubski were almost insurmountable. They could only presume how he might implement his plan but they knew Gorbachev was the target and they assumed it would occur when he was exposed during the parade. Fox's role and his loyalties were still questionable so they were alone in stopping Rubski's plot.

Kurt was confined to the van by his disability but it was filled with communications equipment. As they approached the city he donned earphones and turned dials for radio intercepts. "They must communicate," he said. "Maybe I'll pick up something useful." Vic would move on foot and stay in contact with Kurt by handheld radio. That was their only plan.

Unter din Linden was already closed to traffic so they parked on a closed side street using Kurt's *Stasi* parking pass. From the van Kurt would keep the reviewing stand under observation as well as the corner where the parade would turn to pass in review. Vic found one of the driver's uniforms in the van and squeezed into it. It was a tight fit. He shoved Ebert's pistol under the tunic, picked up a mobile short-range radio and stepped into East Berlin. He walked along the main avenue away from Brandenburg Gate and tested the radio. "How do I look?"

"Too old for a corporal."

Kurt scanned a number of frequencies within range but picked up only signals concerning ceremonial preparations. Vic patrolled *Unter den Linden* and numerous side streets looking into windows and doorways, anywhere Rubski might lurk. They needed a lead quickly—time was running out.

114

Parade of Misfits

The elaborate celebration involved a typical communist-bloc military parade staged for East Germany's fortieth anniversary, with numerous official and public events afterwards. Lili prepared to arrive in East Berlin early, hoping to speak with Gorbachev after the hard questions posed to his ambassador. She had anticipated Gorbachev would receive a critical report from his envoy.

She chose a conservative navy blue suit with a miniature American flag pinned to the lapel, white gloves and hat, and a red scarf to complete the national colors of her adopted country. She knew she would stand out among the conservatively dressed Eastern diplomats. Emily had sent a telex informing the State Department of the high-profile invitation. The reply came immediately: "Don't accept until we consider the ramifications of a public appearance with Gorbachev under these conditions."

"I've already accepted and I'm going," said Lili. "If they don't like it, they can fire me."

"What should I say?" asked Emily.

"Tell them exactly what I said, Emily. Don't change a single word."

Kurt concentrated on radio intercepts in scanning for Rubski and hit on the control net at Checkpoint Charlie. "Eagle One has cleared." A few minutes later he heard, "Lion One has cleared." Eagle and Lion were codenames for primary United States and British visitors as they crossed into East Berlin at Checkpoint Charlie—no mention of the French. "Maverick just passed through." He wondered who that might be and scanned his binoculars around the reviewing stand. Official guests emerged from diplomatically-licensed sedans near the reception area before being routed to a designated parking zone to stand by until the parade ended.

Kurt was stunned by what he saw. There was Lili—Ilse—magnified larger than life in the field glasses. Her presence, so close and in living color, was remarkable. He had followed her career closely, seen her award-winning performance with Fox, a replay of the academy award ceremony, and kept several snapshots of her taken by Fox's operatives. He was proud of his role in advancing her initial acting career at the *Berliner Ensemble* but knew he could not have taken her this far. He had only realized her acting was an escape from reality after he discovered her secrets about *Dachau*.

She was beautiful and confident in maturity—more stunning than her pictures. She had clearly left the stage of her imagination and become a veritable gift to humanity, to America, and to illusive German unity. Kurt pushed the talk button on the short-range radio connecting him with Vic.

"She's here."

"What? Say that again," said Vic.

"Ilse—she's on the reviewing stand."

"Ilse? With Gorbachev?"

"Yes, she's very near where he'll sit."

"Oh, hell!" said Vic. "We have to do something."

Kurt refocused the glasses for a wider view. She was positioned directly behind Gorbachev's reserved seat, though he had not yet arrived. Directly behind her sat Mischa Fox, scribbling a note. He handed it to his assistant, who handed it to an aide, who handed it to Lili.

Lili was slightly nervous at the notion of being back in East Germany, especially East Berlin. Proximity carried memories affixed to strong feelings.

She remembered when she had crawled through wire with Kurt following Ursula's trail. Her worse nightmare had come to life at the Gazebo Café, not far from where she now sat. Kurt would never discuss what he had done to her tormentor. Kurt risked everything for principles he considered sacred. She remembered how Vic had gone with her to find Kurt only because he loved her. He had sacrificed everything yet she had scorned him, blinded by....

A young officer approached her, interrupting her memories. He extended a note and she accepted it in her gloved hand. She noticed how serious the young man looked, old before his time, how old they all had become. She smiled at him anyway and saw he almost smiled in return. She couldn't open the note through her gloves so she rummaged in her purse for a nail file. Before she got the note opened the official delegation arrived to embarrassing fanfare. Gorbachev climbed the steps with exuberance, two at a time, smiling in all directions, waving. When he found his seat, he turned as if he knew she would be there. Lili knew everything had been planned with media photographs in mind—propaganda that had put State in a quandary. She didn't care.

"Ambassador Brown," he said. "I'm delighted you accepted my invitation."

"Thank you for remembering me," she said. "I'm honored."

431

"How could I forget you?" he asked. "And Ambassador Chernenko was very impressed with your forthright questions. He'll never forget you either."

Gorbachev was smiling and she smiled with him. "I assumed he would report to you."

"He certainly did and I've given your entreaty some thought. You'll be happy to know that I won't oppose East Germans allowing refugees into Hungary and Austria or relaxing their travel restrictions."

"You'll allow it?"

"Lili, sovereign nations do as they wish," he said. "People should be able to travel freely. Of course, it's an East German decision but I won't stop it. In fact, I strongly encouraged them to give it favorable consideration."

"Thank you Mr. Chairman," she said. "Thank you so very much, but you do realize this may have wider consequences?"

"Of course," he said. "Perhaps we can discuss those consequences later. I must start the parade now or we'll be here for the rest of our lives." Gorbachev raised his hand as the signal to begin the parade. Guests scurried back to their seats. Lili was not very interested in military hardware so she turned back to the unopened note. She slipped a nail file inside the envelope and slit it. She had seen the distinctive writing before.

I hope you received the package in good condition. Warm regards. M.F.

She turned and checked every face in the box, but without hearing his voice, she didn't recognize the older Mischa Fox.

Ivan Rubski was positioned exactly where he wanted to be, atop the warehouse for the *Museum für Deutsche Geschichte*-German History Museum. He had an excellent view of where the stream of parade vehicles would turn onto the avenue *Unter den Linden* in front of Brandenburg Gate, originally named Peace Gate. He opened his map and double-checked route and sequence. The parade would pass Embassy Row—all eyes looking west while he controlled their destiny from the east.

Nearby was the *Zeughaus*—the arsenal. From there one could see the 19th century statues of the heroes of Germany's wars against Napoleon. The changing of the guard at the *Neue Wache*—New Guard House--would have special meaning this day—October 7th would be the day for changing the guard of Mother Russia. Rubski was prepared to take drastic action to return a military dictatorship to Russia, restore the iron hand of Stalin and Khrushchev. His father

432

would have approved this rendezvous with fate—history would be written near where his father was killed by the crazy German, Kurt Meyer's father.

He checked his watch. "Meyer should be dead by now."

Crowds gathered along the parade route, people seeking any diversion from their daily futility, as the parade began. After Gorbachev raised his hand, Rubski listened to the rumbling of heavy military vehicles starting their engines in their assembly areas. He missed the Afghanistan assembly area where mighty Russian tanks prepared to seize Kabul, too fast for anyone to stop them. That was the Russian army he was proud of, the one to have again. Rubski keyed his small radio.

"Are you in position?"

"*Da*, General. Everything is ready."

On the street, Vic also heard vehicles start up their engines and also remembered Afghanistan. He thought about stinger missiles knocking Hind helicopters out of the sky in balls of fire. The pain in his right arm was a frequent reminder of days best forgotten.

On his way to the museum warehouse, Rubski had rushed past an older East German soldier talking in German on a hand held radio, the type used by *Stasi*. That was unusual but he had no time to investigate then—this day was reserved for more important matters. He opened the front door with a key provided by the movement's director of logistics and locked it behind him. From the roof, he had perfect sight of the reviewing stand on a shady island in the center of the avenue. He would see the missile carrier as soon it rounded the corner and could easily steer the vehicle bomb to its target with the radio-controlled device. The New Russia was moments away.

While Vic was on the radio with Kurt he had caught sight of a Russian general rush past, entering a locked building. He was distracted by Kurt's report of Ilse's presence and got only a glimpse. On second reflection he was sure it had been Rubski and called Kurt. "I think I saw him enter the storehouse for the history museum."

"What do you need?"

"Warn Fox. I don't think I can reach him in time. They're all in danger."

"I'll try."

Kurt keyed his radio for *Stasi* Headquarters. "This is Deputy Director Heinz Claus. I must speak to Fox right now. This is an operational emergency."

"We can't reach him, *Herr* Deputy. The parade has already begun."

"I can see him in the reviewing stand. Can't you get a message to him?"

"Only after the parade. His driver is in the parking area with all the others. He has no radio with him and the street is closed."

"*Scheisse*! That'll be too late." He disconnected.

His connection with Vic's handheld squawked again. "I'm there but the door is locked from the inside. Is there another way?"

"You'll have to solve it yourself. I must go now."

"Where are you going?"

"Use your initiative, as I am."

Kurt dropped the radio into a pocket and rolled his chair onto the mechanical lift. He slid the van's door open and faced bright sunlight on an otherwise dismal day.

Vic checked the building for a way inside but found only locked windows. He broke one with his elbow, unlatched it from inside and climbed through. He heard footsteps and voices on the roof and followed them up.

Rubski was using his radio and speaking in Russian.

"I see it," he was saying to someone. "Straighten it out and drop back. You're following too close to the truck in front. I need room to maneuver."

Vic ran up the steps and aimed Ebert's pistol at Rubski. "Drop that!"

"Werner!" He swung his own pistol around and fired first.

The shot slammed Vic backwards. He tumbled into the stairwell and kept going. At the bottom he fought nausea as a wave of pain burst up from his thigh. He fought for consciousness. He looked for the pistol and saw it on a lower level—a mile in his condition. He couldn't reach it and had no time to crawl. He tried to stand on one leg and fell back. He ripped off a shirtsleeve and cinched it tight over his thigh. He tried to stand again but fell back. He almost passed out, fought for clarity. He assessed—a bullet in his thigh, an ankle broken in the fall, bruises. He looked around for a prop. Wooden boxes stacked nearby might yield something useful.

One box for un-displayed museum artifacts was long and narrow. The lid could serve as a crutch or weapon. He lifted it. Inside was something better, an ancient Prussian saber in a tarnished scabbard. He pushed himself up using the sheathed saber as a walking cane. He started up, heard Rubski on the radio.

"Activate the switches under the steering column now."

The radio crackled and he heard, "*Da*. It's done."

"Get out. Jump!" Rubski dropped the walkie-talkie, taking the toggle in both hands. He was focused on his target. Vic saw what Rubski was watching. A truck driver jumped from his truck fifty meters from the reviewing stand.

Kurt frantically rolled his chair behind the spectators lining the street, looking for an opening. He found a space cordoned with yellow police tape directly across from the reviewing stand. Uniformed police kept that area clear for security reasons, a standard procedure. He flashed his *Stasi* identification. "You can watch from there, sir," a policeman told him. "We know who you are."

The rolling procession of military vehicles on the avenue separated him from the reviewing stand, but he could easily see Gorbachev, Fox, and Ilse all close together. They were vulnerable to anything—he didn't know the nature of the threat. He had to warn them. He gripped the wheels tightly and eased over the curb, leaning well back to keep his balance. He hit hard, bounced, but stayed upright. Policemen shouted, "Stop, sir! You can't go out there."

He timed his run through a small gap in the trucks. He had to move fast—if they reached him first he would be dragged back to the curb. He pushed hard between the trucks. The rumble from his left was coming fast. He turned and faced the front bumper of a missile-carrier only twenty meters away.

Vic shouted, "Drop it Rubski!"

Rubski held the toggle steady and grabbed for his pistol.

Vic swung the saber and the scabbard slid off, blade glistening. He lunged as the Russian fired. The first missed. He fired again. The bullet burned through Vic's side. He pushed with his good leg, drove hard, and thrust forward his full length. He drove the Prussian saber through Rubksi's soft middle and pinned him kicking to the tar roof. Vic swept the pistol away and grabbed the device, crude radio-controlled electronics with a simple toggle on a black box with antenna. The bomb had to be inside the truck the driver fled. He saw the red button blinking and the truck bearing down on Kurt's overturned wheelchair. He shoved the toggle full to his right and watched the truck veer sharply left. It barely missed Kurt and swerved into Embassy Row. Vic drew a deep breath and touched the red flashing button with a trembling finger. The light went off.

The truck crushed Kurt's wheelchair but missed him by inches as he rolled away. Brakes squalled along the parade route where vehicles rear-ended one another with crunching noises. Equipment piled up in a tangle of wrecks and enraged officers. The uncontrolled missile carrier broke through the iron fence surrounding the Soviet Embassy and stopped at the front door. Guards surrounded it immediately.

Police surrounded Kurt sprawled beside his crushed wheelchair. A protective police cordon had surrounded the reviewing stand as soon as the chair was spotted in the road. Lili saw a distinguished-looking man in western clothes walk from behind her to the wheelchair that stopped the parade. He stood over the cripple shaking his head, hands on hips. "Will you never have enough of these dramatics?" Lili recognized his voice.

Gorbachev was hustled off from the platform by security but he spoke to her as he passed. "There was a coup attempt but don't worry. I'll keep my promise." Then he was gone.

115

Ode to Joy

Austrian and Hungarian borders were soon opened for eastern refugees to cross the iron curtain and East Germany lifted travel restrictions to West Germany. When asked about stopping it, Gorbachev refused to comment—many believed he was behind it. Once the impenetrable wall was cracked, it was doomed to fall.

On November 9th, the wall was opened officially and the Brandenburg Gate on December 22nd. People on both sides battered the reinforced concrete with sledgehammers and Ambassador Lili Brown was there almost every day, watching and picking up chips of the wall to slip into her handbag. She didn't know why she did it—just couldn't stop. One day she even borrowed a sledgehammer to pound the damned thing until her arms so ached she could no longer lift it. It was the happiest she had been in a long time. Leonard Bernstein traveled to Berlin to direct the Berlin Philharmonic in *Ode to Joy,* a special tribute to the collapse of the Berlin Wall at the hands of those it had divided far too long.

Lili Brown submitted her resignation explaining her job was finished. But she said she intended to remain in Berlin for an unspecified period to keep a date with old friends. She recommended Emily for promotion and for an important assignment. Emily was appointed Deputy Chief of the United States Mission to NATO to oversee the integration of former Warsaw Pact nations into the alliance. The curtain had fallen on Lili Brown's last act.

Ilse Braun, however, sat at a certain sidewalk café on Ku'damm all alone on Christmas Day. She sipped white wine and nervously twisted a strand of hair as she waited, looking at her watch then over her shoulder. She waited anxiously and sat on her hand to stop it from twisting the loose curl. She wore jeans this day, which attracted more than a few admiring looks, and a cashmere sweater under a leather jacket. She had left her New York Yankees cap at home. She was embarrassed—an aging twenty-five year old girl—wondering if she could still act that part or if acting was finally over.

Then she saw something that stirred her as it had so long ago. She remembered her part well. She didn't need to rehearse—her whole life a rehearsal for the big show. A vaguely familiar man approached, older than she remembered, but still quite handsome. He moved slowly, limping with one leg in a cast. And he pushed another even older man in a new wheelchair. *God, they look good to me!*

Anything can happen on Kurfürstendamm and often does. Reunification had very special meaning that day in the cold sunlight of a busy sidewalk, but one reunion wasn't really so different from thousands of others. They were occurring all over Germany. Shouts and tears along the bustling avenue were the true ode to joy. The events of recent days gave significance to all the previous days of their lives. Their reunion, their Berlin connection, was slightly more special than most.

"I've kept this all these years," she finally told Kurt after two hours of tears and talking. "I carried it with me to find you, but after the bridge I couldn't part with it." She removed the silver chain from her neck, unfastened the diamond ring, kissed it, and handed it to him. "Finally, I can return it to you."

"Hilda never saw it," he said sadly. His eyes clouded over, but he held his emotions in check on this final mission of his life.

"I want to be alone for a while," he said. "You know where you can find me." He turned his chair to leave, but stopped and rolled back.

Kurt handed the ring to Vic. "See if you can find the proper place for this."

THE END

About the Author

Richard Taylor is a product of the Cold War, having served two years in Vietnam and over six years in Europe.

From the army's operations and plans staff in Heidelberg he was first acquainted with the real threat of Soviet invasion. On NATO's International Military Staff, he was involved in plans and policies for nuclear war, conventional arms control negotiations, and confidence and security-building measures in Brussels and Vienna.

He considers himself one of the multitudes of "little people" who chipped at the Berlin Wall dividing people and nations for thirty years.

Taylor has published an account of his years in Vietnam in ***Prodigals: A Vietnam Story*** and a history of American veterans in his book ***Homeward Bound: American Veterans Return from War***. He also served as an advisor in Iraq for two years and has published on Amazon a heartfelt story of two American soldiers in ***The Raptor and the Mourning Dove***.

He lives in Atlanta with his wife. Their children are grown.

Made in the USA
Charleston, SC
20 March 2012